THE SILVER STAG

A. L. JAMBOR

AUTHOR'S NOTE

This is a work of fiction. Names, characters, places, and scenes are either the product of the author's imagination or are used fictitiously, and any resemblance to actual persons, living or dead, business establishments, events or locales is entirely unintentional.

Book Cover by Amy Jambor

Photo Credits:

depositphotos.com/interactimages

depositphotos.com/Mr.Prof

depositphotos.com/redrockerz99

depositphotos.com/GeraKTV

© Can Stock Photo / anton_novik

* * *

This book is dedicated to my husband, Hans, who is my love story.

Contents

A Short History of Dorley, England

The sordid history of Dorley, a small village nestled in the heart of East Anglia, is not well known, for it was buried by the Huxley family shortly after they were awarded the land and sought to disassociate it from its former master.

Dorley, a pleasant, green land, was invaded by a Germanic tribe after the Romans left Britannia during the fifth century. The peasants, faced with the prospect of death or slavery, chose to assimilate their two cultures, and the settlement remained. A scholar named Jonah christened the settlement Dorley, which in Hebrew means home.

Six hundred years later, the peasants who dwelt in Dorley were simple folk who believed in the Christian God, but there were still those who sought the help of a healer whose practices included those commonly associated with witchcraft. They lived in huts, raised sheep, and did their best to survive the harsh conditions of life in eleventh-century England.

After Halley's Comet traversed the sky in 1066 foretelling the Norman conquest of England, the Normans built castles and William the Conqueror gave land to the men who had fought for him. These men were charged with keeping the peace and providing knights to fight for the king.

One such man was Symond, the tall, red-haired son of a nobleman whose warrior skills matched those of the relentless Scandinavian invaders. He fought well and accumulated wealth by means that still remain a mystery. Besides providing knights for the crown, Symond had a private guard for his personal protection, miscreants of low character eager to do his bidding.

Only a handful of men knew of Symond's proclivities, and they shuddered when they learned that he had been given land in East Anglia near a village where men raised virtuous daughters. These men tried to dissuade the monarch from granting this fair land to Symond, but despite their petitions, the king, who recalled Symond's valor during battle, believed that by rewarding him with an earldom, Symond would be forced to quell his darker nature.

William's hope that Symond would become a better man following the ceremony to confer his new title was misguided. Instead, once he was in charge, Symond was free to practice a pagan religion that had once believed in blood sacrifice as a means to gain eternal, physical life. While most practitioners had evolved and abandoned the ritual, Symond held that those who had eschewed it had done so because it didn't bring them everlasting life, which he believed would only manifest when the annual, sacrificial offering was but a few days old – and the issue of his own loins.

Shortly after his tent was raised on the land near Dorley, Symond ordered that a marble altar be built in the woods that lay between his land and the village. Marble from Sicily was brought to Dorley, and craftsmen hired from Greece recreated an altar Symond had seen in a Grecian temple. When it was done, Symond called his most faithful guards to his tent.

At the height of the full moon, the soldiers were to go to the village, find an adolescent girl, and bring her to Symond. After the guards entered the town, the daughters were taken from their homes. One was chosen and taken back to Symond's tent. Once the villagers were aware of what was happening to the girls taken to Symond, many tried to run, but the guards were quick to find them and bring them back. Some fathers stood up to the guards and were cut down. Others remained mute as their daughters were chosen for sacrifice.

The lass would be taken to a tent surrounded by guards, and then Symond would come to her after a ceremonial bath. The frightened girl would often try to escape only to be thwarted by the guards, and since Symond was a large man, he easily overpowered the lass and would implant his seed in her womb for several nights until the girl was found to be with child. She would then live out her days in a guarded tent until she gave birth.

After delivering her child, the girl's throat would be slit, and her blood collected as a separate offering to the blood-thirsty, nameless deity Symond worshiped. Symond would carry the infant to the center of the forest, lay it on the altar, and hold a dagger above it while chanting a prayer. The words would intoxicate Symond, and as he plunged the blade into the infant's heart, he was unaware of its cries. One of his guards would collect the babe's blood, and Symond would drink, believing the sensations flowing through him were changing his human body into an immortal vessel.

When they were not looking for potential victims, Symond's soldiers would terrorize the villagers and use the women both married and single, for their own unholy pleasures. The babes that resulted from their couplings were stigmatized for their bastardy unless the father chose to raise the male offspring.

During his reign, Symond built a stone keep. It was built near the pond, which fed the moat surrounding it. Its great hall had a table to seat fifty men, and the kitchen was in use 'round the clock. Each corner of the courtyard had a tower, and after it was completed, the girls would stay in the tower far from Symond's bedchamber to muffle the sound of their plaintive cries, and he would visit them only when he needed to release his seed.

Prologue

Ainslee watched her granddaughter writhe in pain. Karli's belly had grown too large, and Ainslee understood that if this labor continued, she would have to cut the babes from their mother's womb, as she had cut Karli from her mother's womb. Lesa had died, and Ainslee feared that her granddaughter would, too.

Ainslee still practiced the ancient, pagan religions, but occasionally, she would call upon the god of the Christian pilgrims who came to the village to proselytize. She dearly loved her granddaughter, and prayed for her safe deliverance. When the last word left her lips, Karli screamed, and her heart stopped beating.

Ainslee went to the girl's side and put her hand on Karli's chest.

"NO!" she cried.

She had readied her blade and kept it by her side while Karli labored; now she held it above Karli's belly and cut a line from beneath her breast to her hip. Two babes lay inside Karli's womb, and Ainslee gasped when she saw how tightly they held each other's hands.

Gebhard, Ainslee's thirteen-year-old grandson, had been banished from the hut while Karli labored. He lay on his back near the fire when he saw a streak of light across the sky and heard the cry of a newborn babe. Gebhard cried out and shuddered at its meaning, for that child would forever be marked as

1

one born under a portentous star. Then Gebhard heard the cry of another babe, got up, and went inside the hut where he saw his grandmother cradling one infant while the other lay on his dead mother's belly.

"Get a cloth from the bundle and wrap him," Ainslee said.

Gebhard obeyed his grandmother and wrapped the boy. He held him while keeping his eyes on Ainslee and away from Karli, but Ainslee stared at Karli's face so she wouldn't forget her fair granddaughter's beauty.

"She was cursed with beauty," Ainslee said. "They would have left her alone if she be plain."

"There was a star," Gebhard said. Ainslee eyed Gebhard. "It was bright and had a tail."

Ainslee bit her lip.

"And ye saw this star with thy own eyes?"

"Aye. I shouted when I saw it."

Ainslee nodded.

"I heard ye."

"What does it mean?"

Ainslee looked at the boy in Gebhard's arms as fear rose in her heart.

"I don't know what it means."

Gebhard heard the quiver in his grandmother's voice and trembled.

"Maybe it's a good omen," he said.

"Aye. We shall believe that for their sakes."

Gebhard glanced at his dead sister.

"She must be buried."

"Go to Joslin and tell her the babes are born. We will need her milk."

Gebhard lay the babe down at the end of Karli's cot and ran to fetch Joslin. Her babe had caught a fever and died a week before. Ainslee held herself against the gratitude that rose in her heart over the death of an infant, but it wouldn't go for it meant life to these.

The babe in her arms moved, and Ainslee kissed her forehead.

"We must name thee well," she said. She looked at the boy. She thought of the star and what it might mean for good or evil. She had to give them names that would protect them from fear.

"Ye shall be Greyson," Ainslee said. "A protector."

She looked at the babe in her arms.

"And ye shall be Rotrude for ye must be powerful so that ye might live a long life and bear children with ease."

Ainslee placed Rotrude beside her brother and stepped back. A sense of calm washed over her as if the spirits were pleased, but she wept for she understood that these children were special, chosen above others to lead, or save, or sacrifice their own lives so that others might live. She hoped their names would shield them from the worst that life had to give, and then she put her hands on their foreheads and prayed as she'd seen the Christian pilgrims pray, hoping to impart the wisdom she had gained during her thirty-eight years on Earth.

* * *

1086

ROTRUDE BROUGHT THE WOOD INTO THE COTTAGE AND SET IT beside the fireplace. Greyson had returned from the village. She sensed his arrival and went to the cottage door, where she saw her brother's forlorn face.

"So, it's true," she said.

"He's taken Anja."

Rotrude fisted her hands.

"We have to stop him, Greyson."

Greyson eyed his sister. Rotrude's sense of justice often outweighed her good intentions, leading her to take actions that endangered her own life. Greyson had seen the lord's guards and read their hearts. They were loyal to their lord and would end Rotrude's life without blinking an eye.

"Are ye listening to me?" she asked. "We have to do something to protect those girls."

"And what shall we do, Rotrude?"

"We have to eliminate the threat against them."

Greyson cringed when the words left her mouth.

"Don't ye remember what Ainslee taught us?" Greyson asked.

"I remember her words, but I'm not bound by her rules any longer."

3

"Those rules cannot be ignored. She warned us about taking the life of another. She said it would bring death to our door." He went to her and put his hands on her shoulders. "Rotrude, please hear me. If we don't live by those rules, we will suffer the consequences."

She shrugged his hands off her shoulders, thrust out her chin, and folded her arms over her chest.

"We aren't permitted to end his life with magic," Greyson said.

Rotrude clenched her teeth.

"He's hurting children," Rotrude said. "He's killing babies!"

"We must find another way to end this."

"If ye insist that we can't use magic to end his life, then we must use it to protect the girls. Ye could put a hedge of protection around the village."

"The farmers must take their sheep to pasture. The hedge is impenetrable."

Greyson looked at his twin and saw her frustration. Rotrude was a lovely young woman with dark blond hair and blue eyes. She wore her hair in a thick plait that hung over her right shoulder. Her clothes were those of a peasant with embroidered touches on the tunic.

"We can take them to another village," Rotrude said.

"Do ye think they will leave their families?"

"We must persuade them," Rotrude said.

"And if they refuse to be persuaded?"

"Dear Lord, Greyson. The time ye are wasting with thy endless questions."

Rotrude looked at her tall brother. He had the same long, dark blond hair and blue eyes. Since he began growing a beard, he kept it trimmed. He wore a long tunic over his pants.

"We have to stop him, Greyson."

Greyson sat at the table. He ran his finger over a slender cut in the wood, evidence of Rotrude's wrath, a place she had stuck a knife during an argument with Greyson. He often thought her passion would be her undoing, and now he feared that things had reached a point where words would be insufficient to stop her from acting on those desires.

Ainslee had been clear about the rules and would remind Greyson every day that the most important rule was that life, anyone's life, was sacrosanct. Taking another's life would bring dire consequences: justice meted out by an unseen force in the universe. It might come today, or hundreds of years from now, but it would come, and the perpetrator would suffer.

Rotrude came to the table and sat across from him. She saw him touching the cut in the wood.

"I keep thinking of something Ainslee told me," Greyson said. "She named me Greyson because it meant protector and that I was to protect those who could not protect themselves. She said this is why I was given these powers."

"The star gave ye those powers," Rotrude said. "As it gave me mine."

"Perhaps that's why ye are so passionate," Greyson said. "Because ye feel other's pain."

"Perhaps." She exhaled sharply. "But we still have to find a way to protect those girls."

Greyson smiled. "What ye said before, about taking the girls away, it is a good idea, but Symond's reach is long. In time, he would find those girls."

"We can take them across the water to Normandy."

"Ye would have them dwell in the house of the enemy?" Greyson said.

Anger flashed in her eyes, and she slapped the table with her hand.

"Ye are always finding fault with my ideas."

"And ye are always finding fault with my honesty." He leaned forward and looked her in the eye. "It is a good idea, Rotrude, but we must hide them where no man can find them."

"No such place exists in this world," Rotrude said.

Greyson's eyebrows rose.

"Ye are right. There is no such place in *this* world."

"So, we are again at an impasse," Rotrude said.

Greyson sat back and clasped his hands over his belly.

"Rotrude, when I was young, I often had visions of a beautiful place with rolling green hills and sunshine." He sat back. "My spirit was peaceful, and I thought I was in heaven."

"Heaven," Rotrude said. She scoffed.

"But what if I had those visions for a reason? What if I am supposed to create this place?"

Rotrude straightened her back.

"I have seen ye fix broken tools, but never anything larger than this cottage. I doubt thy powers would create such a place."

"I've never tried!" he cried. His eyes glowed with excitement, and he leaned toward her. "I have to try." He grinned and closed his eyes. "I can see it so clearly. A village, and at its center, a building made of stone where we can meet for a communal meal every evening at sundown. It will be a place where the broken can find rest."

For a moment, Rotrude found herself caught up in his dream, but unlike her idealist brother, Rotrude's doubt would always intercede.

"Do ye really think ye can create such a place?" Rotrude asked.

Greyson opened his eyes and looked into his sister's skeptical eyes.

"I won't know until I try."

"Then go. Get up and start working.

Greyson smiled as he stood.

"And while I'm conjuring this new world, I would ask that ye abandon any ideas regarding the death of this lord."

"This I cannot promise," Rotrude said. "But I won't act on them until after ye show me heaven."

Greyson wandered into the woods and contemplated the trees. He spied the old shelter Rotrude had built for herself to avoid Symond's selection. As a girl, she watched the moon and would go to the woods where she'd built the shelter with tree branches and pine boughs. Her psychic senses told her when the soldiers were gone so she could return home. She tried taking others with her, but the girls would cling to their mothers and refuse to go with the "witch."

When Ainslee died, Greyson and Rotrude were twelve, and the townspeople told them to leave the village. They had seen Greyson conjure, and believed that Rotrude read their minds. Still, Ainslee had instilled in them a sense of responsibility for their neighbors, and while Greyson had a forgiving nature, a resentful Rotrude would still prepare remedies when they came to the cottage asking for help with a sick child.

Greyson's magical skills had come to fruition when he was six. Ainslee had given him a bowl of beans, his least favorite food, and he wished the beans would turn into grapes. When they did, Ainslee gasped, and then took him to a crone who taught him how to use and control his powers. He often envisioned things he had never seen with his eyes before. Greyson had conjured many things since then, but at twenty, he had not yet stretched himself to build anything larger than the cottage he and Rotrude moved to when the villagers drove them out.

Greyson studied the leaves, the stones, and the dirt beneath his feet. His conjuring came from images in his mind, but in order to keep the girls out of the lord's reach, they would have to go to some unknown place where no one had gone before. It couldn't appear on any map or have access by water or land. In order for them to be truly safe, they would have to be taken to some other *world*.

Greyson looked at the sky. The moon shown at night, but it was the only other world he had ever seen. Heavenly bodies were bright but small, too small to live on. No, Greyson wanted his world to be just like the one he lived in now. A replica of this world, only better, kinder and more loving. A place where the battered and bruised would find peace.

As he imagined this new world, he felt a mighty wind lifting him off the ground. He closed his eyes in fear, but when the wind stopped, he opened them and saw that he was standing in a lush valley with rolling green hills and sunshine. A few feet away, a large stag with an eight-point rack stood, its head held high. Greyson was struck by his beauty and grace. The stag looked into Greyson's eyes, nodded its head, and then ran to the forest a mile away.

"This is heaven," Greyson said.

Greyson wandered across the land, stopping only to touch the leaves or feel the bark of a tree. The air was sweet, and the temperature sublime. He recalled his vision of the stone building and closed his eyes. When he opened them, a circular building stood before him.

The wooden entrance doors were elaborately carved and embedded with gold swirls. The windows were colorful and shone with a light from within. He went inside and found a long, rectangular table with many chairs on each side. It was just as he had seen it in his vision.

Greyson returned to the spot where he had landed when the wind stilled. He imagined himself at Rotrude's table, and the wind returned to carry him home. While this might work for him, he wasn't sure how he would transport those whom he intended to save.

When he walked inside the cottage, he saw Rotrude melting copper to create one of her pendants, and she smiled when he entered.

"So, have ye created a safe harbor?" she asked.

"Aye, and it's just as it was in my vision."

"Ye will have to show it to me."

"I don't know how to show it to ye," Greyson said. "I get there through my imagination."

"Then how are we to transport the girls?"

"That is a mystery yet to be solved."

Rotrude eyed her twin and shook her head.

"So, tell me about thy paradise."

She poured the melted copper into a mold, and suddenly Greyson remembered the stag's magnificent head. He imagined it as one of Rotrude's molds, and it appeared on the table. She saw it, picked it up, and examined it.

"He's very handsome," she said.

"He greeted me when I arrived in heaven."

Greyson recalled the stag and how it nodded its head, but in this vision, the stag didn't run away. He stood still while sunlight bathed him in silver.

"Do ye have silver?" Greyson asked. Rotrude touched the large silver pendant she was wearing. "Can ye melt it down?"

"Why don't ye just imagine a silver pendant?" Rotrude asked.

"I think ye are meant to make it," Greyson said.

She took off the pendant, melted it, and then poured the liquified silver into the mold.

"That was my favorite pendant," she said. She eyed Greyson. "Ye know ye cannot call it heaven."

"Whyever not?" Greyson asked.

"Because to these girls, heaven means death. We must call it something else."

Greyson sat and recalled the way he felt as he basked in the glory of the new land he'd created. He remembered how the forest met the sky. It was a haven for the lost, and he smiled.

"Havenwood," he said.

"That is a fair name," Rotrude said. "So, why have I sacrificed my pendant?"

"I'm not sure," Greyson said, and then he envisioned the silver stag broken down the middle. "We have to break it down the middle."

"Ye want me to break it in half?" Rotrude asked.

"Yes." He saw the two halves being worn as pendants, one around his neck, and one around Rotrude's. Greyson's eyes lit up. "Old Hannah taught me a Greek myth about Charon, a ferryman who took people across the river Styx to Hades. Ye had to pay him a coin, which was placed in the dead person's mouth when they were buried. I think that pendant will be the coin we use to transport them to Havenwood."

Now, Rotrude's eyes lit up as she understood what he was saying. She took two copper pendants out of a small wooden box and removed their leather cords.

"How will the pendants work?" she asked.

Greyson thought about the two halves.

"We must press the edges together to reform the stag's head. That will bring the wind."

"What wind?" Rotrude asked.

"The wind that transported me to Havenwood."

Rotrude tested the silver. It was cooling fast, so she used an awl to poke two holes at the top before using a small chisel to create two halves.

After she took the coin out of the mold, Rotrude used the chisel and a wooden mallet to split the coin in two. She used the awl to smooth the holes at the top of each half and threaded the leather cords in each piece before handing them to Greyson.

"Smooth the edges," Rotrude said. "I believe that will enchant them."

Greyson lifted one half, ran his forefinger over the rough edge, and then repeated the procedure with the other half. He held the halves near each other. Sparks flew and the halves were drawn to each other, which caused Rotrude to smiled broadly.

"Shall we try them?" she asked.

Greyson picked up one half and put it around his neck. Rotrude put on the other half, and then she pressed the sides together to make the stag whole. A mighty wind blew, and she grabbed Greyson's arms. A few seconds later, they found themselves in a lush, green valley.

"Welcome to Havenwood," Greyson said.

* * *

SYMOND'S GUARDS WERE THE FIRST TO NOTICE THE ABSENCE OF adolescent girls when they went to the village. The farmers complained that their daughters were missing, and it was Symond's duty to find them. Symond disagreed and held the farmers responsible for interfering with his ritual. He had them hanged, and their wives were given to the guards.

Greyson grieved for the farmers, and he decided that in the future, they would only take those girls who came to Rotrude asking for help. Rotrude reluctantly agreed.

Symond had his guards visit other villages to steal their daughters, and the rituals continued. Rotrude, unable to save the girls unless they came to her, made a decision to disregard the rules and sent a letter to the king accusing Symond of practicing witchcraft. It was a dangerous ploy since she herself had been accused, but if it would stop the blood-letting, she was willing to burn.

Instead of a pyre, she received a response in the form of a noble named Edmund Huxley, who was sent to Dorley by the crown. A noble by birth, Lord Huxley was greeted with a feast at Symond's table, but he found Symond to be impenetrable. He was unable to catch the earl in a lie and knew he would have to find another way to expose Symond's witchery.

When Symond retired for the night, Huxley called his guards and told them to offer wine to Symond's men so as to intoxicate them. As the wine loosened their tongues, Symond's guards talked about the sacrifices. The next day, Huxley's men showed Edmund the bloodstained altar in the forest. Symond's pagan practices were confirmed, and Edmund went directly to the king.

An investigation revealed that over the course of twenty-five years, infants had been slaughtered in Symond's twisted fantasy of eternal life. The king ordered Symond's execution. As a reward for his swift discovery of Symond's evil rituals, the land was given to the Huxleys, and then divided between Edmund and his younger brother, Bruce.

Edmund, whose personality pleased the king, also received a hereditary peerage and the keep. Bruce was given the land that bordered the sea where he built a trading port. Of the two, Bruce amassed a greater fortune, while Edmund prospered by building a highway from Mercia to Kent. It lured tradesmen and merchants alike. Its modest success gave Edmund the income he needed to support his keep and to wed the daughter of a wealthy baron.

Over the years, the village grew, allowing Lord Edmund Huxley to maintain his keep. He also obtained permission from the king to call himself the first Earl of Dorley and thereby changed history. It was as if Symond had never existed.

The keep survived for hundreds of years, but at the dawning of the eighteenth century, the village began to decline. The demands on the Huxley fortune brought with it a family tradition that lasted well into the twentieth century.

Huxley men found that their charm and good looks would serve them better than the farms in the village. They were always able to find wealthy men with eager daughters whose dowries were more than sufficient to maintain their lifestyles. They didn't, however, use this money to maintain the keep, which began falling into ruin during the reign of Henry the Eighth. Two hundred years later, it was a crumbling relic of its ignoble past.

But as with other Huxley men, Lord Beau Huxley found a bride who brought a dowry that paid for a large manor house to be built early in the nineteenth century. It hid the keep's ruins, and a garden complete with newly planted oak trees at the back of the house concealed the keep from those inside the house.

At the dawning of the twentieth century, the manor house was in dire need of restoration. Its last makeover came through Lord Reginald Huxley's marriage to Eliza Stafford, whose father owned several cinemas throughout England. He had gladly endowed his daughter with a healthy dowry, for she would be heretofore known as Lady Eliza Huxley. Fortunately, not only were they a suitable match but they also shared a great affection for each other.

And in the woods, hidden from the world, a healer lived in a small cottage. Her longevity surprised her, for it was an unexpected gift that allowed her to continue her work. She saved people who were in dire need by taking them to another world.

The healer had learned how to conceal her cottage from those who sought her without an invitation, so she lived in peace. She attended the annual festival in Dorley, where she sold her pendants and other charms, and this is where she found those who desperately needed her services. It was a good life, and she was content.

But the healer had broken the rules that governed her kind and caused the death of a human being. So many years had passed, and the human being who died was so utterly despicable that she grew to believe she had done the right thing after all. She'd forgotten what her grandmother taught her, that the consequences will visit you, maybe today, maybe hundreds of years from now, but they will come, even to one who ended the terrible reign of Symond the Butcher of Dorley.

Margaret Huxley

Chapter One

1939

MARGARET OPENED HER EYES AND SAW THE SUNLIGHT STREAMING through her window. She jumped out of bed and went to her mother's bedroom two doors away. She pushed the door open and saw that her mother was still in bed with a breakfast tray on her lap. Margaret ran to the bed, leaned against it, and put her hands under her chin.

"Margaret," Lady Eliza Huxley said.

"Mummy, can I have my present now?"

Eliza smiled. "What time is it?"

"The sun is up."

Eliza looked into her daughter's deep, brown eyes. She put one of Margaret's brown plaits behind the girl's shoulder.

"It's too early, Margaret. You know I can't give it to you until your father comes home."

"But you said you had something else for me," Margaret said.

Eliza's brows drew together, and then she smiled.

"Yes. I do have something else for you."

Eliza put the tray aside and opened the drawer in her nightstand. She pulled out a flat, wrapped package and handed it to Margaret. Margaret's eyes lit up as she tore open the wrapping and saw that it was a clothbound journal. She had seen one in London and had asked if she might have one, but her mother had told her no.

"This is why you wouldn't buy it that day," Margaret said.

Eliza nodded. "I didn't know what to say when you asked for it."

Margaret put her arms around Eliza's neck and squeezed.

"Thank you, Mummy."

"You're welcome, sweet girl."

Margaret returned to her room and put the journal on her dressing table. She pulled her nightdress over her head and threw it on the floor. Margaret eschewed the assistance of her nanny turned personal maid, a Miss Tinsdale, and preferred to choose what she wore. Margaret went to her armoire, looked through her dresses, and then saw the frock Eliza had bought for her when they were in London.

When Margaret spied the pink pinafore with the white blouse patterned in pink and yellow rosebuds in Harrod's, she screamed with glee, but Eliza said she thought the dress was a bit young for Margaret, who would be celebrating her twelfth birthday. But Margaret loved the outfit, and Eliza yielded to her daughter's wishes. Margaret's father was due back from his trip to America, and she wanted to look her best when he arrived. She would wear it for her birthday dinner. Now, though, Margaret took an old dress from the rack, one that would allow her to play outside with no thought of keeping it clean.

Margaret liked taking care of herself and enjoyed feeling independent. She wanted to know everything, and her curious mind often vexed her mother, who was content to be an ornament on her husband's arm. Eliza enjoyed dressing in fine silks and satins, furs, and jewelry fit for a queen. She always knew what was proper and would try to subdue Margaret's natural enthusiasm. Still, she loved Margaret's free spirit, and she would give her daughter free rein whenever Lord Huxley was out of town.

When Margaret was dressed, she returned to her mother's bedroom. Eliza was seated at her dressing table, so Margaret sat on the bed and watched her mother apply her makeup. She cocked her head as she watched Eliza pat her nose with a powder puff.

"Why do you wear makeup?" she asked.

"Because I want to look my best," Eliza said.

"But you look beautiful."

Eliza smiled. "Thank you, my dear."

"But you *do* look beautiful. You don't need makeup."

"Perhaps not, but your father prefers that I add a touch of color. He thinks I'm too pale."

Margaret slipped off the bed, went to her mother's side, and looked in the mirror.

"Am I too pale?"

Eliza smiled. "Not at all. You have nice, rosy cheeks."

"But you have blue eyes."

"You have lovely eyes, Margaret."

"They're brown, like a cow's eyes."

Eliza glanced at Margaret.

"Brown eyes are warm. They speak of a kind heart."

She put her arm around Margaret's waist and pulled her close.

"I wish I had eyes like you," Margaret said.

"Well, maybe your children will have blue eyes."

"Do you think I'll have children?"

"Of course, you'll have children."

"I don't know if I shall be a good mother."

"Whyever not?" Eliza asked.

"Because I could never be as good as you are."

Eliza sighed. "You're very sweet, dear." She squeezed Margaret. "Now run along, and I'll join you for breakfast."

Margaret liked to talk, and her endless conversations were tiresome as they always included a litany of things that she didn't like about herself. If Eliza permitted Margaret to continue, she would be refuting those opinions forever. Eliza was saddened by Margaret's insecurities, but since she had never felt unattractive or unworthy, Eliza found it difficult to empathize with her lovely daughter.

Eliza would often try to cajole Margaret with platitudes that meant little to the girl, things her own mother had taught her, and it would placate the child for a few days. Then, Lord Huxley would return from London. At first, he would praise his daughter, and Margaret would bask in his attention, but those moments passed swiftly, and soon, Margaret would be sulking in her room to avoid his disparaging remarks about her looks.

"She's rather plain," he said one evening at dinner.

"I think she's lovely," Eliza said.

"She slouches a bit, too."

"She's just a child."

"She's nearly thirteen. Didn't they teach her anything at that school?"

Margaret had listened at the entrance to the dining hall as her parents argued over their daughter's physicality and deportment. Miss Tinsdale stood a few feet behind her and allowed Margaret to hear what her father was saying. He confirmed everything Margaret believed about herself, and she began to weep.

That morning, an hour passed before Eliza came to the breakfast table, but Margaret had read the newspaper while waiting for her to arrive. The girl had a gloomy look on her face.

"What's wrong?" Eliza asked.

"I don't like their chancellor," Margaret said.

"Oh, you're reading about Germany again. I don't care for Herr Hitler either."

"I saw him in a newsreel, and it gave me goosebumps."

"Some find him charismatic, though, at least those who agree with his rather crude ideas."

"I don't like him," Margaret said. "I think he looks like Symond."

Eliza narrowed her eyes.

"Symond?"

"He was the first lord to live in the keep. He sacrificed babies and drank their blood so he could be immortal."

"Where on Earth did you hear that?"

"I read it at the library."

"Our library?" Eliza asked.

"No, the library in town. The librarian helped me find it."

"Well, I shall have to speak to that librarian. I don't think such things are appropriate for a young girl to read."

"It's part of our history. He was replaced by Edmund Huxley, who was then named the first Earl of Dorley."

"Ah, yes, I've seen Edmund's portrait."

Margaret's eyes widened.

"Where?"

"I think it was in one of the bedrooms before we started

17

renovating the house." Eliza pursed her lips. "I think they put it in the attic."

Margaret twisted her mouth.

"I haven't seen any portraits up there."

"Well, then, perhaps it was donated to the museum."

The butler served their breakfast, and the ladies ate in silence. When she was done, Margaret looked up at Eliza in earnest.

"Father said he won't let me marry a poor man even if I love him."

"He's correct. You have a title, Margaret, and a duty to marry well."

"And that means marrying someone I don't love?"

"If necessary."

"Do you love Daddy?"

Eliza pursed her mouth before answering.

"I appreciate your father's finer qualities."

"But do you love him?"

"I love being his wife. Now, stop asking questions and go see if the mail's arrived."

Margaret twisted her mouth as she slid off her chair. She went to the table in the foyer, retrieved the mail, and brought it to her mother.

"Oh, good. I've been expecting something. Let's hope it came today." Eliza glanced at Margaret. "Why don't you go outside for a while?"

"What were you expecting?"

"It's none of your business, young lady. Now scoot."

Margaret left her mother and wandered out the front door. She walked through the garden and over the field that lay between the garden and the old moat around the keep. Margaret stepped into the soggy ground, and her shoe sank into the mud. She lifted her foot, and the suction nearly took her shoe off. By the time she made it to the other side of the moat, the thick layer of mud on her feet left a trail behind her.

The keep Symond built was nothing more than a pile of stones with one tower and one wall from the great hall still intact. The windows had lost their glass panes, and the ghastly decrepitude of the place sent a shiver up Margaret's spine, but she walked across the floor of the great hall and gazed at the massive fireplace that still held iron rods for cooking pots. She noticed a loose stone at the base of the fireplace and pulled it out, hoping to find an ancient note on parchment hidden behind it. Alas, there was nothing there, so Margaret replaced it before returning to the moat. This time, she chose a drier path, but it did little to improve the state of her shoes.

Margaret went to the end of the driveway and looked down the road that led to the town of Dorley. She was tempted to walk to town, but the sky threatened rain, so she went home. Margaret climbed the stairs to her room, took off her dirty shoes, collected her new journal, and took it to the attic.

The manor house wasn't like the large manor houses one saw in Hollywood movies. It was small in comparison with only six bedrooms and six baths. The first floor had a sitting room and a drawing room separated by a large foyer. The dining hall was behind the drawing room and the study behind the sitting room. A large kitchen occupied the rear of the house, and it contained a second staircase to the upper floors. There was one bathroom on the first floor off the main hallway behind the coat closet.

The six bedrooms on the second floor were off the main hallway. Three were occupied by the family – Lord Reginald Huxley, Eliza, and Margaret, and three were guest rooms at the end of the hallway separated from the family bedrooms by a bathroom and the door to the attic. The family bedrooms had their own baths while only one of the guest rooms shared this amenity.

Margaret had created a sanctuary in the attic. A window facing the front of the manor house had the original glass panes, which had been added sometime in the eighteenth century. The glass was not clear, but it still allowed one to see cars coming up the driveway.

Margaret had used the broken, discarded furniture that littered the space to fashion a cozy den. A divan covered in Oriental brocade was under the window. Its back had been slashed, and white cushion filling hung from the tear. A small table missing a drawer sat between it and a legless comfy chair. On the table was an oil lamp with no chimney, a box of matches, and a mason jar filled with pencils.

Bookcases that had been replaced by newer models lined the walls. As her father bought new books for his library, the cast-offs were brought up there, and Margaret had read them all. Her favorites were the tales of knights and damsels, jousting matches, and wizards whose spells worked for good and not evil.

With her new journal in hand, Margaret tucked into the comfy chair and took a pencil from the mason jar. She lifted the cover and stared at the inscription on the first page.

"To my darling Margaret from your loving Mummy. Happy 12th Birthday, sweetheart. May, 1939."

Chapter Two

Margaret was contemplating the next sentence in her story when she heard her father's Daimler coming up the driveway. She went to the window and looked down at the top of the Daimler and then ran down the attic steps. Miss Tinsdale was standing at the top of the main staircase, eyeing her charge suspiciously as she was wont to do. Margaret slowed her pace when she heard Eliza call to her from her bedroom.

"No running down the stairs, Margaret!"

Margaret looked up at Miss Tinsdale and thrust out her chin before taking her first step down. She quickened her pace in defiance of her mother's warning and was there to greet her father as he entered the open door. Lord Reginald handed his coat and briefcase to the butler before kneeling to embrace Margaret. She wrapped her arms around his neck and squeezed.

"I've missed you, Daddy," she said.

"I've missed you, too, princess."

Margaret pulled away.

"Now, you know I'm not a princess," she said in a serious tone.

"You are *my* princess."

Margaret blushed, and then took her father's hand. She led him up the stairs to her mother's bedroom and then stood at the door to watch them embrace. They planted a kiss on each other's cheeks, and then Eliza brushed something off his shoulder.

"I wasn't expecting you before dinner," she said.

"I phoned ahead and had Bryan drive up to London."

"But no one told me."

"I don't have to consult you on my travel arrangements, Eliza."

There it was, the edge in his voice that served as a warning not to take the subject further.

"Of course not," Eliza said. "So, how was your trip?"

"Uneventful. We've put off the vote until next week."

"So, you'll be going back."

"First thing Monday morning. Bryan will drive me to London, and he'll stay until I'm ready to return."

The frown on Eliza's face went unnoticed by Lord Huxley as he took off his tie.

"I must dress for dinner," he said. He looked at his wife's dress. "Is that what you're wearing?"

Red patches appeared on her cheeks.

"No, of course not. I was about to call Martha when you came in."

"Good. I've invited the Comstocks to join us this evening. I hope we're serving something decent this time."

Eliza swallowed hard and then smiled.

"I knew you were coming home, Reg, so I asked Edith to prepare lamb."

"Right, well, that should do. And I want you to choose the wine. Don't leave it to Finley. He's a decent butler, but he knows nothing about wine."

Reginald left her and Eliza sat at her dressing table. Margaret watched her mother wipe a tear from her eye. Martha walked past Margaret and stood near Eliza, awaiting her orders.

"The blue dinner gown," Eliza said.

"Yes, milady."

As Martha went to the armoire, Margaret went to Eliza and stood by the dressing table. She smiled as she watched her mother touching up her makeup.

"I'm going to wear my new dress tonight," Margaret said.

Eliza stopped with her hand in midair and looked at the mirror.

"Oh, Margaret. I'm sorry, dear, but we're having guests for dinner and we won't be able to celebrate your birthday."

Margaret's face fell.

"But you promised…"

"I know, darling, but I didn't know your father had invited guests." Eliza turned to face Margaret. "Why don't we go to London and have lunch at the Savoy. You can wear your new dress, and we can have tea just like the King and Queen."

Margaret pouted, and then nodded. Eliza embraced her and kissed the top of her head.

"Thank you for being so understanding."

Martha laid the blue gown on the bed, and then Eliza put her hand on Margaret's shoulder.

"You should go now and eat your supper, Margaret," Eliza said.

"Yes, Mummy."

"And Martha, please go and tell Edith that Mr. and Mrs. Comstock are expected for dinner."

"Yea, milady."

Margaret walked to the door and looked back once before heading to the kitchen. Her parents were expecting guests, which meant that Margaret would eat her supper in the kitchen. She followed Martha down the back stairs to the kitchen and watched her tell Edith to set two more places at the table. Truth be told, Margaret preferred eating in the kitchen rather than with a group of adults whose conversation consisted of society gossip, the threat of war, and Parliament. Also, when Margaret ate alone, she didn't have to follow the rules imposed by her father. She could eat quickly and return to the attic far away from the adult world.

Her father's invitation to the Comstocks might have put an end to her special birthday dinner, but when she sat at the kitchen table, Margaret saw that Edith had placed her birthday cake at the center. It was white with pink roses. Twelve candles were placed around the edge of the top layer. Margaret stared at the cake while Edith prepared her supper dish.

"It's beautiful," Margaret said.

Edith glanced over her shoulder and smiled.

"Why, thank you, Luv. Your mum ordered it special. I wanted to make it nice for you."

Margaret looked at the empty chairs around the table.

"Am I to eat it alone?" she asked.

Edith bit her lip.

"Perhaps you'd like to share it with Toby."

Toby was the new stable boy. He'd been hired to replace an elderly man and had little experience, but his wages were lower.

"Father won't allow it," Margaret said.

Edith brought Margaret's dish and set it before her. She leaned down to Margaret's ear.

"Your father will be dining with his guests." Margaret smiled as Edith continued. "I'll fetch Toby. You come back here after the guests arrive."

Margaret ate her supper, and then she went up the backstairs to the second floor. She heard her father's voice echoing down the hallway and went to her mother's room, where she peeked through the crack between the door and its frame.

"You cannot do this to her," Eliza said.

"For God's sake, Eliza, she's a child."

"But she's been looking forward to this trip for ages. I can't tell her we won't be going."

"Then I'll tell her."

"Please, Reg, don't do this."

The silence that followed fed Margaret's imagination. Images of her father fisting his hands in a threatening manner appeared in her mind, and Margaret moved a few inches away from the door.

"We have to tighten our belts, Eliza."

"I can let some of the staff go. I can also alter the menus."

"And who do you plan to let go?" Reg asked. "We're down to the barest minimum now. No, we have to face facts. A trip to Paris is out of the question. I'll talk to Margaret. She's old enough now to understand."

Margaret thought of the new horse her father had bought, a powerful black stallion. She knew the horse had cost a fortune and understood that the horse had stolen her trip to Paris. She ran to the attic, threw herself on the divan, picked up her journal, and counted all the things that she had lost since her last birthday.

First, she had been taken out of boarding school. Margaret dearly missed her friends, but Eliza promised they would go to Paris. A tutor named Miss Blaine had been hired so that Margaret would not fall behind. Then, Eliza's Daimler had been sold. The new clothes she had ordered for Margaret were cancelled, and then Miss Blaine was dismissed. As Margaret looked at the list, she realized that her father had not sacrificed anything. He still had his car, his driver, and his valet.

Margaret's anger toward her father was always there, bubbling and brewing under the surface, even as she ran to embrace him when he returned home from London. It was as if she had two selves – the one who loved her father and the one who loathed him. These selves waged a daily battle for supremacy. Despite this, Margaret was always the dutiful daughter, for as Eliza reiterated time and again, you must never let anyone see how you really feel.

"Remember, Margaret," Eliza would say. "You represent us to the world. There are times the truth must be hidden away, or it could be used against you."

A missed birthday was now added to the litany of things Reginald Huxley had taken from her. Margaret sat up and wiped the tears from her eyes. She had a birthday cake, and Toby was coming to share it with her. Margaret pushed the anger she felt toward her father into a small box in her mind and tamped down the lid. Then, she got on her knees and thanked God for her nice home, her clothes, and the attic.

Chapter Three

THE STALLION NICKERED AND STOMPED HIS FOOT AS TOBY TRIED to saddle him. The boy, who stood no more than five foot two, was afraid of the animal, and his fear made his hands shake. Margaret watched him through the stable door and was happy *she* didn't have to put a saddle on that horse.

"He doesn't want you to do that," she said.

"Shut your gob," Toby said.

"You can't talk to me that way." Margaret stuck out her chin.

"Stop talking!" Toby cried.

The horse snorted, and Toby backed away.

"Please let me do this," he said softly.

"He can't understand you," Margaret said.

Toby shot her an angry glance, and then he took the saddle to the corner of the stall and dropped it.

"Your mum is plum crazy to want to ride this horse," Toby said.

"She's a fine horsewoman," Margaret said, repeating something she'd overheard a dinner guest say. "She's never been unseated."

"Well, I'm not sure 'e knows that."

Margaret eyed the horse. With his muscular legs, he could easily rear and throw a rider. Now, *she* feared what this horse might do to her sweet, petite mother.

Margaret ran to the house and went up the backstairs to her mother's room. Eliza was seated at her dressing table in her riding clothes, tying a scarf around her neck. She spied Margaret coming up behind her and smiled.

"Darling."

"Mummy," Margaret said.

"Yes, dear."

"I've just been to the stables. I don't think you should ride that horse."

Eliza put her hands to her sides and cocked her head.

"Now, why would you think that?"

"Because he's wild. I don't trust him."

Eliza smiled broadly.

"Oh, he just needs a firm hand. I've dealt with bigger than he, so don't you worry. I wouldn't mount him if I thought it was dangerous."

Margaret wasn't so sure. She'd seen her mother take chances before, and there was a time she'd nearly gotten her neck broken.

"So, has Toby been able to saddle him?"

"No," Margaret said. "He's afraid of him."

"Damn," Eliza said softly. "Old Ned would have had that horse in hand by now." She realized that an expletive had escaped her lips and turned to Margaret. "Please forgive me, darling. Mummy shouldn't use such words."

"Daddy uses them all the time."

"Yes, but I am the one who must set an example for you." Eliza stood, took one last look in the mirror, and then came to Margaret and put her hand on her daughter's shoulder. "We must be brave, my darling."

"Yes, Mummy."

Margaret followed Eliza down the backstairs and out the kitchen door. The stables were several yards away, but Margaret heard the horse nickering. Eliza strode toward the stables with vigor, forcing Margaret to up her pace. When they reached the door, Eliza stopped and put her hands on her hips.

"Is he saddled yet, Toby?"

Toby was sweeping the area in front of the horse's stable.

"No, milady."

"And why not?" Toby's downcast eyes stared at the floor. "Put that broom away. I'm going to show you how it's done."

Toby set the broom against the wall and watched as Eliza

went into the stable. The horse nickered, and she placed a hand on his side.

"There, there, boy."

The horse calmed under her hand, and Eliza saw the saddle in the corner.

"First, you take the horse out of the stables to saddle him."

Eliza took the bridle off the hook. The horse allowed her to put it on, and then she attached the reins and led him outside.

"Fetch the saddle," Eliza said to Toby.

Toby brought the saddle, and Eliza soothed the horse with her words while she placed it on him.

"That's how you saddle a horse," she said. Toby again lowered his eyes. "I expect you to learn how it's done by this time next week, or I shall have you replaced."

Margaret knew that Eliza couldn't replace Toby for no experienced horseman would work for such low wages, but Toby nodded.

"Yes, milady."

Margaret shuddered as Eliza mounted the horse, but he remained calm. Eliza sat tall and smiled at Margaret.

"See, darling? Gentle as a lamb."

"Please be careful, Mummy," Margaret said.

Margaret watched her mother ride toward the moor. He obeyed Eliza's every command, and the farther they went, the better Margaret felt about the horse. Her mother was right; she was able to handle the stallion.

As Eliza assessed the horse's personality, she had to admit that Reginald had made a good decision when buying the former racehorse. He planned to use the horse for stud services and would make the money he'd spent back in no time.

As they trotted along the well-worn trail to the river, Eliza allowed herself a moment to enjoy the ride and closed her eyes to feel the wind on her face. The horse felt good beneath her, and she relaxed her grip on the reins.

They sauntered along the path, and soon Eliza saw the river that ran between their property and Foster's farm up ahead. A steady rain had overflowed its banks, so she pulled a bit on the left rein, and the horse went left. As they approached the river, Eliza pulled back on the rein, and he slowed his pace until he stopped near the river's edge. It was a beautiful spring day, and the sound of the water rushing over the stones in the river's bed was soothing. Both she and the horse were content to stay there.

Eliza had some things on her mind. Her marriage for one, and her husband's temperament. The dinner with the Comstocks had been uneasy as Mr. Comstock was Lord Huxley's financial advisor, and he told Reginald that his financial situation was tenuous, and he would benefit greatly from selling the manor house.

"I'll be damned before I'll sell my legacy," Reginald said during a tirade that followed the Comstocks' exit. Eliza had tried to go to her room, but Reginald had kept her in the drawing room by blocking the door. He had a glass of whiskey in his hand, and his cheeks were red. He stumbled when he came toward her, spilling the liquor and staining the Oriental rug. "You must tell your father that we need some assistance."

Eliza backed away from him and went behind a chair.

"He gave you a dowry," she said.

"That was years ago. Surely you can convince him that it's in his best interest to keep his daughter in the style to which she is accustomed."

"His concern at present is for his unmarried daughter," Eliza said.

"She's a child," Reginald said.

"Who also has to find a suitable husband."

"Your father can afford to help you as well."

The conversation hadn't ended well. Eliza refused to agree to ask her father for money, and Reginald had hit her arm so hard that an ugly bruise appeared the next morning. It wasn't the first time, and if he continued his excessive drinking, it wouldn't be the last. Eliza had to decide if raising her daughter with such a man was something she was willing to do, and now, alone at the river, she made her decision. She would go to London and consult a solicitor.

The peaceful riverbank had lulled them both into a state of contentment, so when Eliza tugged on the reins to head home instead of turning, the horse jumped, his feet slipped on the wet ground, and his back legs crumpled beneath him. Eliza gripped the reins, but as the horse struggled to right himself, he threw her off his back. Eliza was thrown into the river, her head on a rock, and she lost consciousness as she slipped under the water.

When the riderless horse returned to the stables, Toby and Margaret ran toward the river. They found Eliza and pulled her from the water, but she wasn't breathing. Toby ran to get help as Margaret held her mother's cold hand. She wept so hard that her chest hurt. When help arrived, they placed Eliza on a stretcher and carried her away as Margaret clung to her mother's hand.

* * *

"SHE DROWNED, REG," THE DOCTOR TOLD REGINALD. "I'M SO sorry."

After the doctor left, Margaret sat at the top of the stairs and listened to her father's drunken expletives as he paced the sitting room floor. Sometimes he would cry out as if in pain, and then he would weep. After a while, Margaret ran to her attic sanctuary. Miss Tinsdale had been sacked two days before, and no other adult in the house came to console her.

Margaret sobbed into the arm of the comfy chair until it was soaked with her tears. She was alone with her father now. Margaret had seen the bruises on her mother's arms. She had heard the fights and her mother's sharp cries. But Eliza had borne the brunt of his anger. Without her to stand between Reginald and Margaret, would he abuse his daughter in Eliza's stead?

The funeral was a dreadful affair. It rained for three days, and when Eliza's coffin was placed in her family's tomb in Sussex, her father had stared at Margaret for a long time.

"She's not much to look at," he said to his companion.

Margaret blushed and turned her head away.

Eliza's sister and brother came to Margaret to offer condolences, and Margaret told them she missed her mother. They each told her they would write to her, and Eliza's brother gave Margaret his business card.

Following the interment, the mourners were invited to the manor house, and Lord Reginald met with the villagers to accept their condolences. He remained sober until the last guest left the house, leaving family members to share their memories of Eliza. The small gathering turned into an argument concerning Eliza's accidental death.

"That horse was dangerous," Eliza's father said. "You had no right bringing such an animal to my daughter's home."

"Eliza didn't think he was dangerous," Reginald said.

"Nevertheless, I hold you responsible for her death."

Reginald left them in the drawing room and refused to return until they had gone, and then he sent Margaret upstairs while he sat in the sitting room brooding over the loss of his wife with a bottle of brandy in one hand and a photo of Eliza in the other.

Margaret stayed in the attic for several days while her father ranted about the unfairness of life. Edith sought her out and brought her food, but Margaret only took a few bites before pushing the plate away.

"He's mad with grief," Edith said. "It's better you stay up here out of harm's way."

Margaret narrowed her eyes and pursed her lips.

"He's angry because she can't ask Grandfather for money anymore."

Edith' eyes widened.

"Margaret!" She put her hand on Margaret's shoulder. "Best to keep those thoughts to yourself."

"But it's true."

Edith leaned forward and looked into Margaret's eyes.

"Don't let bitterness harden your soul, Margaret. It would break your dear mother's heart."

Margaret pondered Edith' words during the days that followed. She didn't want to be bitter. She wanted to be carefree and loving as she had been when her mother was alive.

As the weeks passed, Edith encouraged her to go outside when her father was in London, and Margaret began to take walks around the estate. She also explored the rooms at the end of the hallway but found nothing of interest there. Then one day, she decided to go into the woods.

The gentle scent of lavender drew her deeper into the forest until she came upon a clearing. At its center was a marble altar littered with dead leaves and fallen branches. Such an altar had been mentioned in reference to Symond, and as Margaret swept the debris to one side, she searched for the bloodstains left by his sacrifices.

"Best ye not seek what ye cannot understand."

Margaret whirled around and saw a woman standing near

the edge of the clearing. She wore a blouse and skirt similar to those worn by villagers who attended the annual medieval festival in Dorley. Her thick braid of dark blonde hair hung over her left shoulder. Her blue eyes studied Margaret thoughtfully, which made the girl put her hands behind her back as if she had been caught stealing cookies.

"Who are you?" Margaret asked.

"My name is Rotrude. What is your name?"

"Margaret Huxley."

"Ah, a Huxley." Rotrude took a few steps toward Margaret. "And why did you come into the woods today?"

Margaret took a step back.

"I've never been in here before."

"So, curiosity brought you here."

Margaret nodded, and Rotrude came closer.

"Best you stay far from this place, lass."

"Is this where Symond sacrificed babies?" Margaret asked.

"So, you know about Symond." Margaret nodded. "Then you should know not to come here."

"He's been dead a long time. He can't hurt me now."

Rotrude tilted her head.

"Do you believe in spirits, lass?"

"I believe in God Almighty."

Rotrude raised her eyebrows.

"Aye, He is almighty. I've called upon him meself from time to time." Rotrude came to the altar and put her hands on the cool marble. "Twas Him that called me to this place so I would see what evil was taking place. For twenty years, Symond sacrificed his offspring to a Greek god, but was thwarted by a Huxley who discovered Symond's secret and reported him to the king."

"They cut off his head," Margaret said.

"Aye, they did, but they left this altar as a testament to the wee ones' sacrifices."

Rotrude's eyes welled with tears, so she turned her face away.

"Would you like to see where I live?"

"Is it far?" Margaret asked.

"Nay."

Margaret followed Rotrude through the trees to another clearing several yards away. Smoke rose from the chimney of the old cottage that had changed little since Rotrude and Greyson built it centuries before. Rotrude opened the door and let Margaret go inside first. The air smelled of spices and wood, and the walls were full of drying herbs and flowers.

"I'm getting ready for the festival," Rotrude said. "Each year, I go to sell my charms."

"I went with my mother last year," Margaret said. "We saw two men wielding swords."

"Pretentious morons. I've seen real knights wielding swords and not for sport. They wouldn't stop until they drew blood."

Margaret cringed as she watched Rotrude go to a cabinet with small drawers and pulled one out. She took something from the drawer and went to Margaret.

"I should sell this to you, but instead, I give it to you because you lost your mother."

Rotrude held out a disk on a gold chain. The disk had the image of a cottage etched on its surface.

"Is that your cottage?" Margaret asked.

"Aye, it is. Put it on if you ever find yourself in dire need."

"And what will happen?"

"I will help you."

"How?" Margaret asked.

"You ask too many questions." Rotrude looked out the window. "The sun is setting. You must go now."

"But I have so many questions."

Rotrude straightened her back and looked down at Margaret.

"I'll answer one."

"Where do you come from?"

"My brother and I were born here."

"You have a brother?" Margaret asked.

"Aye, a twin brother named Greyson. He's a kindly wizard."

"Your brother is a wizard!" Margaret cried. "Can he make things appear by magic?"

"No more questions."

"But you must tell me if he can do magic."

Rotrude put her hand on Margaret's shoulder again.

"If there is a dire need, put the chain around your neck."

With great reluctance, Margaret left the cottage. She dragged her feet to the path in the woods, and when she looked back, the cottage had vanished. She stared at the empty space for a long time before heading to the manor house.

When Margaret got home, she ran to the attic, put the disk under the cushions of the divan, grabbed her journal, and sat on the comfy chair. She opened the cover of the journal and went to the fourth page. After choosing a pencil from the mason jar, Margaret began to write the epic tale of *Greyson the Wizard and His Sister Rotrude.*

Chapter Four

1949

Every August, the village of Dorley would host a festival celebrating its history, and every year, the village would ask Lord Reginald Huxley if he would allow revelers to visit the ruins of Symond's Keep. Lord Huxley always refused their request. He also demanded that the village barricade the road that led to Huxley Manor.

The village would place two sawhorses across the road with a sign stating that the keep's ruins were privately owned, and the owner chose not to participate in the festivities. As a result, people would wander down Huxley Road out of curiosity and trample Lord Huxley's grass to find the ruins. The yearly battle between the village and the noble resident of Huxley Manor prevented his daughter from attending the festival.

This year, however, Margaret was twenty-two, and she had never forgotten her encounter with Rotrude. She decided to disobey her father's edict and go to the festival where she would seek out the "witch of the woods," an epithet used by the villagers to describe Rotrude for hundreds of years. Of course, no one believed she was the same woman their grandparents knew, and it was assumed that she was a descendant of the first witch, a healer whose name had been lost over time.

Margaret's bravado regarding her father's wishes might have been seen as bravery, but in truth, Lord Huxley had gone to Scotland to visit a colleague. He would be gone for the entire weekend, and Margaret didn't worry about the servants sharing this information with Reginald upon his return. The only servants they had now were the cook, Edith, and Finley, the butler, both of whom had encouraged her to spread her wings when her father wasn't about.

When Edmund Huxley created a road to shorten the journey to London, he built an inn with a public house and stables. When the plague drove the people to the country, craftsmen stayed at the inn, and many decided to stay. The descendants of those hearty souls built the Tudor buildings that lined the streets of Dorley during the 16th century.

Soon, Dorley was a seat of commerce boasting a smithy, a tailor, and a shoemaker. A bakery followed, and houses were built. Markets thrived, and the town grew. By the late eighteenth century, coaches boasted that the inn was a safe place to have a good meal and to spend the night. More merchants arrived, and the Earl of Dorley built a church for his brother, a vicar of high moral character.

The village enjoyed a long period of prosperity before it began its decline near the end of the nineteenth century. It fell further when the First World War began, and by the end of the 1920s, it had been reduced to the inn, the bakery, the smithy, the church, and a standalone pub. A doctor had an office on the first floor of his home, and the public library offered the village's main source of entertainment. The city's governmental body occupied a large building that had been donated to the town by a spinster named Quill. A plaque next to the entrance sang her praises.

It was a librarian who first suggested they hold a festival every year to lure people to the town and stimulate its economy. The village had a rich history, and old soldiers were encouraged to don chainmail and get out their old war swords to create demonstrations of swordplay and jousting. Vendors from neighboring towns brought wagons full of their wares. They lined the main road and paid a fee for the spot. Over time, the festival grew in popularity, bringing visitors from all over England, ceasing only during the war years as a show of respect for those losing their lives overseas. When it was revived following the Second World War, it was as popular as it had ever been, and the village prospered.

Huxley Road was one of four streets that met near the park

at an intersection. Baker Street was the main road through the village. Another was called Kelsey Dairy Road, which was the exit off the main motorway. Peterson Place was a rural road that brought visitors from the west. Peterson's farm hosted the jousting contests. Gas rationing kept the crowds small at first, but as things normalized, the need for parking grew, and Farmer Peterson provided that as well.

Displays of swordplay were presented there in the park, as were puppeteers performing Punch and Judy shows. The vendors who brought wagons in for the weekend offered goods reminiscent of the High Middle Ages or medieval times, especially the "witches" who offered charms, spells, and jewelry.

The Huxley name was on the church Reginald's ancestor built, and he had made his views regarding the pagan religions known to Margaret since she was a child. His forefathers had chosen to ignore the "witches" in favor of commerce, but Reginald felt it was his duty to protest the inclusion of such practices in the village celebration.

Reginald attended church services with Margaret and had urged the town fathers to ban the "ritualists" from coming to the festival, but the income derived from the wagons paid for civil improvements, so the village fathers, angered by his lack of civic responsibility with regard to the ruins behind Reginald's manor house, refused. While he spoke of protecting his daughter from spiritual confusion, the real reason he forbade her to attend the festival had more to do with the obstinacy of the town fathers than heathen worship.

Margaret felt a thrill as she walked down Huxley Road toward the village. She could barely handle her excitement as she saw the park come into view, or as she walked past the bakery and smelled the aroma of freshly baked bread.

The wagons were parked on Baker Street with a row on each side. Margaret quickened her steps when she saw the first one just past the bakery and approached it as if it were the Holy Grail. Her eyes sparkled as she gazed at the variety of items for sale, some from as far away as China, and she spent several minutes examining the wares so she wouldn't miss anything.

As she walked past the inn, she saw a caravan that resembled those used by Romanian "gypsies." The colorful wagon was decorated with flowers and gold trim, and seated on a stool next to a display of her goods was the witch of the woods, Rotrude. She looked beautiful, and she smiled at Margaret as she approached the wagon.

"I remember you," Rotrude said.

"And I, you," Margaret said.

Margaret reached into her pocket and pulled out the gold disk Rotrude had given her. Rotrude eyed the disk and tilted her head.

"Why do you carry it with you?"

"I thought I might see you here."

"You're disobeying your father by being here," Rotrude said.

Margaret blushed. "He's away in Scotland."

"So what he doesn't know won't hurt him."

"I don't agree with him," Margaret said.

Rotrude slipped off the stool, came to Margaret, put her hand on young woman's arm, and Margaret winced.

"And you pay when you disagree with him, don't you? How long will you hide the bruises?"

"I don't have bruises."

Rotrude squeezed Margaret's arm, and she gasped.

"Why have you not come to me?"

"I didn't know if you were still here."

Rotrude let go of Margaret's arm. She stepped back and folded her arms over her chest.

"I have a gift," she said. "I can read the human heart. If you stay with him, he will kill you."

Margaret swallowed hard as she tried to hold back the tears, but one rolled down her cheek.

"Come with me," Rotrude said.

Margaret followed Rotrude into the wagon. Rotrude sat on the bed and indicated that Margaret should sit beside her. The disk felt warm in Margaret's hand, and when she looked at it, she saw the cottage was glowing.

"Why didn't you come to me?" Rotrude asked.

Margaret bit her lip.

"I couldn't remember where you were."

"The disk remembers. It will bring you to me."

Margaret felt a tightening in her throat. Fear descended upon her, and her hands began to shake.

"Margaret, your father will not change, and you will not survive if you stay with him."

"I'm going to be married," Margaret said.

"Are you in love?"

Margaret struggled to keep her voice from quivering.

"It's my duty to marry him." She saw the look of disdain on Rotrude's face. "It's been arranged. I'm to marry him in December, and then I won't be with my father anymore."

"If you live."

Anger flashed in Margaret's eyes.

"And what would you have me do?"

Rotrude sat back and exhaled loudly.

"You are a stubborn woman," Rotrude said. "I must be getting old. I thought you would understand that all I wanted to do was to help you." She took something out of a drawer next to the bed. "Me brother and I thought Dorley was the most beautiful place in the world. Then Symond came and brought hell with him. When we were old enough to understand what he was doing, we knew we had to do something to help the people in the village." Rotrude held up the Silver Stag. "Greyson used his magic to create a world where people in trouble could go to get away from those who would hurt them."

Margaret touched one half of the silver coin.

"What is that?" she asked.

"It's called the Silver Stag. We use it to transport people to another world."

Margaret looked into Rotrude's eyes.

"I don't understand."

"This world is called Havenwood. It's a place where you can be free. Your father would never find you, and you would be safe."

"And this coin will take me there?"

"I will take you there using the coin," Rotrude said.

Rotrude studied Margaret's face. Her powdered cheek barely concealed another bruise, or the small scar above her eyebrow.

"Perhaps you need to see Havenwood for yourself," Rotrude said. "Come to my cottage after the festival."

"It disappeared…"

"People come looking for the witch of the woods, so I take precautions."

Margaret eyed Rotrude for a moment and then nodded.

"Should I dress warmly?" Margaret asked.

"There is no need. It's always warm in Havenwood."

Margaret got up and left the wagon as Rotrude put the Silver Stag back into the drawer. Rotrude left the wagon and found Margaret waiting for her by the display table.

"I won't have to stay if I don't want to," Margaret said.

"I will bring you back if that's what you choose."

Rotrude returned to her stool and watched Margaret walking toward the park. She hoped the girl would want to stay in Havenwood, but she and Greyson had agreed that all must come there of their own free will.

Chapter Five

LEAVING THE HOUSE AFTER DARK WAS MORE DIFFICULT FOR Margaret than leaving during the day. Out of concern for her, Finley would want to know why, but Margaret had learned how to escape unwanted attention and she was able to slip away after dinner while he was clearing the dining table. She'd left a torch in the sitting room and retrieved it before she went out the front door. Margaret was careful not to turn the torch on until she was near the edge of the woods, so neither Edith nor Finley would know what she was up to.

Margaret trained the torch's beam on the path she'd taken to the clearing where the altar still stood. She recalled the way to Rotrude's cottage, and when she stepped on the path leading to it, the disk on her chest grew warm. Its heat intensified as she got closer to the cottage, though not enough to burn her skin. When she entered the clearing, Margaret saw Rotrude standing in the doorway of the cottage.

"Hello," Margaret said.

"Hello." Rotrude took a few steps away from the door. "Did you feel the warmth of the disk as you approached?"

"I did."

"Will anyone be missing you tonight?"

Margaret stopped a few feet away from Rotrude.

"No one saw me leave. They will assume I've gone to my bedroom to read."

"Our journey won't take long."

Rotrude wore the Silver Stag around her neck. She took off one of the necklaces and gave it to Margaret.

"It's beautiful," she said.

"Put it on."

Margaret put the necklace on.

"You said this would take me to another world. Where is this other world?"

"I can't explain that to you," Rotrude said. "I must show you." Rotrude held up her half of the stag. "We have to press the sides of the Stag together, so they make the coin whole, then we will be transported in a whirlwind."

Margaret narrowed her eyes.

"A what?"

"A whirlwind. It will lift us up and take us to Havenwood."

Margaret stepped back.

"You mean like Dorothy in the *Wizard of Oz*?"

"I don't know who this Dorothy is," Rotrude said. She held out her half of the stag. "Shall we go?"

Rotrude pressed the edge of the stag against Margaret's, and a mighty wind lifted Margaret's skirt.

"Oh, my God!" she cried.

Rotrude stood firm as the wind grew stronger and louder, forcing Margaret to grab Rotrude's arm. When it lifted them off the ground, Margaret screamed as they went higher. She pulled at her half of the stag, but the bond holding the stag together was unbreakable. As her legs came up behind her, Margaret grabbed Rotrude's other arm and held on tightly until she was dropped from the sky onto a soft patch of grass. Rotrude landed a few inches away.

"Are you all right?" Rotrude asked.

Margaret was breathing hard and staring at the surrounding countryside. She looked at Rotrude as if in shock, but accepted Rotrude's hand when it was offered. She helped Margaret off the ground, after which she dropped Rotrude's hand and backed away.

"What have you done to me?"

"I've brought you to Havenwood."

Margaret's hands were trembling, and her lip quivered. Rotrude took her hands, but Margaret pulled them away.

"You've bewitched me," Margaret said. "This is some sort of magic spell."

"It's not a spell, Margaret. It's a real place. You are standing on solid ground."

"But this can't be!" Margaret cried.

Rotrude wasn't deterred. She folded her arms across her chest and watched Margaret shake her head in disbelief. Rotrude knew that in time, the atmosphere in Havenwood would sooth Margaret's nerves, so she sat on the ground and waited.

"Take me home," Margaret said.

Rotrude smiled.

"Can you feel it?"

Margaret clenched her teeth, but Rotrude persisted.

"The sun is very soothing." Rotrude smiled. "I asked Greyson to keep it in the sky so I could show you Havenwood."

"Your brother, Greyson," Margaret said.

Rotrude nodded. Margaret felt the warmth of the sun on her face. It *was* soothing, as was the pleasant scent in the air. For the first time, she noticed the green hills, the lush forest, and the leaves, which had already turned orange, red, and yellow.

"Why are the leaves changing in August?" Margaret asked.

"It's always autumn in Havenwood," Rotrude said.

"Why?" Margaret asked, but Rotrude's eyes were closed as she basked in the sun.

Margaret felt the tension in her shoulders melt away, reminding her of her childhood when Eliza was alive, and Margaret felt loved.

"How is this possible?" Margaret asked.

"My brother and I were born under a portentous star," Rotrude said. "We were given gifts. We decided to use them to help those who could not help themselves."

Margaret eyed Rotrude with the last bit of suspicion she could muster. She should be worried. She should run from this woman who obviously had enchanted her, but when Margaret looked at Rotrude, she knew with her whole heart that she had nothing to fear.

"Are you ready to see more?" Rotrude asked as she stood.

Margaret wavered for a second before nodding, and then followed Rotrude down a well-worn dirt path where dozens had followed her before. They went up a hill, and when they reached the top, Margaret saw the top of a circular stone building.

"That's Greyson's Welcome Center," Rotrude said.

They went down the other side of the hill, and the path continued until they reached a forest.

"Greyson created Havenwood using his imagination," Rotrude said. "His gift is to create something from nothing."

"And you can read the heart," Margaret said.

As they walked through the woods that stood between them and the village, Margaret heard birds chirping and small animals scurrying through the downed branches and leaves that littered the forest, but the forest had an odd light that gave it an ethereal aura. It, like the sun, soothed her spirit.

At the end of the path, the trees parted, and the first thing Margaret saw was the Welcome Center.

"That's where the town gathers for their evening meal," Rotrude said. "Though it's not required that you attend."

Rotrude walked past the round building and stopped at a place where three roads met. Margaret saw small houses lining the road in front of them, and shops lining the one to her right. She didn't see anything on the road to her left.

"There are farms down there," Rotrude said. "You won't see them from here."

"How many people are here?" Margaret asked.

"Not many. There used to be more, but now most of these houses are empty. If you choose to live here, you can live in one of them, or conjure yourself a new one."

"Conjure a new one?"

"When you live in Havenwood, you are able to conjure what you need. If you need a home, you make one. If you need food…"

"I conjure it."

"Hold out your hand," Rotrude said.

Margaret held out her hand.

"Now, think about something you want."

Margaret thought about a Frank Sinatra phonograph record she wanted. The record appeared in her hand, and she dropped it when she pulled her hand away.

"But this is impossible," Margaret said.

"This is why I couldn't tell you about Havenwood. You had to see it for yourself."

Rotrude began walking down the street in front of them, and Margaret picked up her record and followed. If felt real in her hands but it didn't make sense to her mind. She kept looking at the houses as they passed them, hoping to see a resident but saw none.

"Where are the people?" Margaret asked.

"Most live in the center of town over their shops," Rotrude said.

"Are all these houses empty?"

"Yes."

Rotrude sounded sad, but she perked up when a farm appeared at the end of one road.

"There it is," Rotrude said. "My brother's home."

"Does he live here all the time?" Margaret asked.

"He does. He likes people more than I do."

"You don't like people?"

"I prefer being alone," Rotrude said.

"I do, too."

"You can be alone here if that's what you want."

Margaret lifted her chin.

"I don't know why you think I'd want to come here."

Rotrude stopped walking and faced Margaret.

"Because your father hits you. You live in fear."

"I'm getting married," Margaret said.

"And what if your new husband slaps you? What will you do then, Margaret?"

Margaret stepped back.

"He won't…"

"You can't be sure, though, can you? You might be exchanging one monster for another, only this one can force you to…"

"Stop!" Margaret cried.

Rotrude clenched her teeth. She had heard the story many times before. Those who came to Havenwood lived while the others suffered, many unto death. She would never understand why they stayed with their abusers when they could live in paradise.

"When a threat to their safety is removed, the people who come here blossom," Rotrude said.

"I'm getting married," Margaret said. "I'm going to live in London. I'll have my own maid, and we'll give lovely dinner parties."

"Do you love him?" Rotrude asked.

"He is handsome."

"That's not what I asked you."

Margaret walked away from Rotrude, who followed her to Greyson's cottage. The first thing Margaret noticed was the garden that surrounded the wizard's home. Every flower, herb, vegetable, and fruit was represented there.

"GREYSON!" Rotrude shouted.

A moment passed before he appeared from behind the cottage carrying a basket. Greyson smiled when he saw them, and Margaret thought he was the most beautiful man she had ever seen.

* * *

GREYSON HAD THOUGHT LONG AND HARD BEFORE CONJURING HIS farm. He'd tried making one room at a time, but the building never looked quite right. Then, one of the residents drew a picture of a French cottage she'd seen in a painting, and Greyson knew he'd found his new home.

The first room as you entered was large with a broad stone fireplace that separated it from the kitchen in back. There was a loft above with stairs leading up, and everything about the place was peaceful. A long settee was centered so that you could watch the fire dancing in the fireplace, and one, large chair with soft cushions was against the wall.

Greyson wanted everyone and everything to live in harmony. His kind nature attracted goodness, and he was generous with his gifts. His belief in the goodness of human beings vexed his sister, who had seen the evil that men do, though secretly, she admired Greyson.

The kitchen exuded the pleasant scent of the herbs that dried on lines strung from one end to the other. He had a cast-iron stove at the back of the kitchen where pots were always bubbling on each burner. An oblong wooden table with benches on each side held rows of jars filled with Greyson's concoctions, leaving just enough space on the table for a teapot and a dinner plate.

Greyson smiled at Margaret before taking them inside. Margaret sensed a shift in Rotrude's attitude as they watched him conjure teacups and a plate of biscuits.

"So, you haven't introduced me to this lovely young woman," Greyson said.

"This is Margaret."

"Are you joining us?" Greyson asked.

Both Rotrude and Greyson looked at Margaret.

"I can't stay," Margaret said. "My father would blame Finley for my absence."

"Her father is abusing her," Rotrude said.

Margaret blushed bright red.

"He doesn't abuse me. He gets drunk and doesn't know what he's doing." Her eyes met Greyson's, and she saw the sad look in his eyes. "He would never hurt me if he didn't drink."

Greyson poured a cup of tea and handed it to Margaret.

"So, my sister is offering you a glimpse of Havenwood."

"She's to be married," Rotrude said. "She believes her marriage will save her."

"Are you in love?" Greyson asked.

"He is handsome," Margaret said. "He has a lovely town-house in London."

"Do those things speak to his character?"

Greyson handed a teacup to Rotrude. He wore a long tunic reminiscent of those worn by monks in a monastery in France. Margaret had seen photos of them in Life magazine. His calm nature was also like that of a holy man, and Margaret was overwhelmed by the desire to unburden her heart, but instead, she clenched her teeth.

"He is the son of Lord Bentley," Margaret said.

"I see," Greyson said.

"She has bruises on her arms," Rotrude said.

"Why do you protect him?" Greyson asked.

Margaret brought the teacup to her lips, took a sip, and then put it on the side table.

"He misses my mother," Margaret said. "He loved her very much."

"He's a brute who beats his child," Rotrude said.

Margaret's hands shook.

"He's lonely. He works hard, but he doesn't get the respect he deserves."

"He doesn't love you," Rotrude said.

A flash of anger brought roses to Margaret's cheeks.

"Of course, he loves me!" Margaret cried.

"Has he ever told you he loves you?" Greyson asked.

Margaret stared at him as she searched her mind for a moment of tenderness she had shared with her father. He had been kind to her before her mother died, but now, the only times he touched her was when he was inflicting pain. Tears formed in her eyes and rolled down her cheeks. She wiped them away, but she was unable to stop crying.

"Stay here, Margaret," Rotrude said. "I can protect Finley."

Margaret was sobbing now, and Greyson eyed Rotrude.

"May I speak to you for a moment?"

Rotrude didn't want to leave Margaret while she was so close to accepting their offer, but Greyson stood and beckoned her to follow. They went outside and stood a few feet away from the back door.

"You mustn't force her," he said.

"I saw how you looked at her," Rotrude said. "I've seen that look before."

"She's lovely," he said.

"She isn't lovely, Greyson, she's plain, which is why her father has arranged a marriage. It's also why I fear for her."

"You still can't bend her to your will."

"Then what would you have me do?"

"Wait, just as we do with everyone else we've brought here."

"I have waited. I gave her the disk years ago."

"Then you have to wait a little longer," Greyson said.

"And if she dies?" Rotrude asked.

"We must pray that she comes to you before that happens."

"Is that all you can say?"

Rotrude's cheeks were red. She fisted her hands and shook her head before turning on her heel and leaving him. Greyson thought about Margaret and, like Rotrude, wanted to make her stay, but that was not how things were meant to be.

He returned to the sitting room and saw Margaret looking

out the window. He came alongside her and studied her face. Rotrude was right; it was a plain face, but her heart was beautiful. She had been keeping it hidden away for a long time, and he hoped that she would choose to come to Havenwood so that she would once again allow herself to shine.

"We should be going back," Rotrude said when she appeared at the door of the sitting room. "It's late in Dorley."

"Yes," Margaret said. She smiled at Greyson. "Thank you for the tea."

"You're welcome."

"I like your world."

"I hope you reconsider coming to live here," Greyson said.

Greyson followed them out the door and stood in the yard as they walked away. When they returned to Rotrude's cottage, Margaret returned her half of the Silver Stag to Rotrude, and then turned on her torch before walking out the door.

The lights on the first floor of the manor house were off so she went to the back door. Finley must have noticed she was gone for he had left it open. She climbed the back stairs to the second floor and went to her bedroom without seeing anyone.

After dressing for bed, Margaret lay down and thought of Greyson. She felt the way she had the first time she saw Errol Flynn. Her heart had beat faster, and the memory of his handsome face stayed with her long after she left the cinema.

Chapter Six

1950

Euphemia Quince Delmer became a widow at the age of twenty-eight when her husband's plane was shot down over France. A childless widow, Euphemia returned to her father's house where, after a decent period of mourning, Euphemia's father, Humphrey, made a concerted effort to find her another suitable husband.

Euphemia was an attractive woman who could easily draw men to her side on her own, but Humphrey was determined that this time, Euphemia's marriage would give him the cachet of having a son-in-law with a title. Euphemia was, after all, twenty-eight, and there were questions about her fertility stemming from her failure to produce an heir during her marriage, so she knew that time was of the essence. She wanted to marry while she still had her looks, and with thirty peeking around the corner, she welcomed her father's intervention in seeking a proper mate.

Reginald Huxley had a title, but his always tenuous finances had taken a downward turn following the war, so when Humphrey approached him regarding his widowed daughter, Reginald welcomed the opportunity to court Euphemia. He introduced Reginald to Euphemia and then invited Lord Huxley to his home in Sussex.

Reginald visited their estate several times over the months following the introduction, and during his last visit, Humphrey took Reginald aside and told him that he was eager to see his daughter married.

"My daughter wants to marry while she is still young enough to have a child of her own."

"She's a lovely woman," Reginald said. "But, as I'm sure you are aware, my financial situation is somewhat precarious."

"How precarious, Huxley?"

"I am still recovering from the losses I suffered during the war."

Humphrey swirled the brandy in his snifter.

"You know, Reggie, I had to learn how to be a gentleman. I wasn't born to this life, but I've taken to it rather well. I would dearly love an introduction to the members of your club."

Reginald was more than happy to introduce Humphrey to several members of his club, after which he and Humphrey came to an agreement regarding a marriage between Reginald and Euphemia. The amount of the dowry took up a majority of their conversation, and in the end, Reginald was disappointed in the amount he would receive. Still, it would be enough to pay off his debts and spruce up the manor house, and Humphrey delighted in the idea of his future grandchild being a titled gentleman, perhaps a peer of the realm who would help guide England in the future.

Shortly after he arrived home from visiting the Quinces, Margaret suffered a terrible fall resulting in a broken ankle. Her father, drunk and angry over some trivial infraction she'd committed, had pushed Margaret down the stairs after striking her several times. He'd then poured whiskey over her and called the police. Their report reflected their assumption that Margaret had been tipsy when she lost her balance at the top of the stairs. The doctor at Brandmore Hospital, an old school chum of Reginald's, had put a hand on Reginald's shoulder and comforted him.

"She must get help, Reg, while she's still young."

Margaret was confused when she woke up to find a "friend of Bill W's" seated beside her bed.

"You're young, my dear," the woman said. "If you stop now, the damage caused by alcohol will be small."

Tears rolled down the sides of Margaret's face, and the woman, assuming she had reached the young woman with her own history of inebriation, put her hand on Margaret's and squeezed it gently. When visiting hours were over, she left

Margaret some pamphlets and encouraged her to attend a meeting at the church in Brandmore.

Margaret's time in the hospital, along with the assumption that it was she who had a drinking problem, helped her understand what it meant to be in dire need of help. She thought of Rotrude and always wore the silver disk.

Margaret had not yet set a new date for her wedding, and her fiancé, Lord Kenneth Bentley, seemed as reluctant as she to choose one. Though they had formally announced their engagement, Margaret rarely saw Kenneth except when he appeared in the social pages of the newspaper attending this party or that dinner. They had planned on a wedding in December, but with the holidays and Margaret's broken ankle, it seemed wise to wait a few months before resetting the date.

When she was released from the hospital with crutches, Margaret returned home, and her father told her that he was getting married. She was happy to hear the news as it meant he would have someone else in his life who would take his attention from Margaret.

"She's a lovely girl," Reginald said. "She's not much older than you. You should get on splendidly."

Margaret nodded. She wondered if this new wife would bear the brunt of his anger if she failed to produce a son. Her memories of Eliza's bruises had faded in time, and Margaret didn't recall any physical arguments between her parents. This led to her assumption that it was Margaret who ignited her father's rage, and now she wondered why. Was it because she'd been born a girl? Her answer came as if her father was reading her mind.

"And perhaps a year from now, you will have a little brother."

If I stay away from the stairs, she thought.

Margaret had no money of her own. Her mother had left her a trust, but she couldn't access the money until she reached the age of twenty-five. Her financial dependence on her father kept her bound to him, which is why Margaret had been elated when Kenneth Bentley asked her to marry him. It meant she would finally get away from her father, but now, as she thought of being Kenneth's wife, Rotrude's words came back to her.

"You might be exchanging one monster for another…"

A bed had been brought down to the sitting room so

Margaret wouldn't have to climb the stairs. She kept the doors closed and the radio on to help drown out her thoughts, for she couldn't stop thinking of Havenwood. She kept seeing Greyson's face and wishing she had stayed when Rotrude took her there, for it was too difficult to get to the cottage on crutches.

Unlike Margaret and Kenneth, Reginald and Euphemia set a date for their wedding. Two months after Margaret broke her ankle, Euphemia came to Huxley Manor to see if the home was suitable for the ceremony and reception. She was kind to Margaret and empathized with her for they had both lost their mothers at an early age. After Reginald introduced them, he and Humphrey went to Reginald's study, leaving the young women alone in the sitting room. The bed had been pushed to the wall and hidden by a screen, so they sat side by side on the settee.

"She died when I was seven," Euphemia said. "Father won't discuss it with me, so I've no idea what caused her death, but I do still miss her so."

"My mother was thrown from a horse," Margaret said, and Euphemia gasped. "I still miss her, too."

"Then we shall support each other," Euphemia said. She embraced Margaret. "We will have no secrets. You shall be as dear to me as a sister. Oh, Margaret, I have always longed for a confidante, and I am sure you are exactly what I've been looking for."

Margaret was a bit overwhelmed by Euphemia's exuberance and didn't understand why her father would find someone so cheerful to his liking. But she was happy because she believed Euphemia was sincere, and it would be nice to have someone to talk to. Margaret also prayed for Euphemia's safety.

The wedding was an extravagant affair. War rationing had eased a bit, and more food was available, providing their guests with a feast that hadn't been seen since before the war. Euphemia was radiant in an ivory silk gown, the same one she'd worn for her first wedding with a touch added here and there to alter its appearance. She asked Margaret to be her Maid of Honor, but it was still difficult for Margaret to stand for long periods of time, so a friend acted as Maid of Honor, and Margaret took a seat in the front row of the church.

While the bride and groom took their vows, Margaret touched the disk on her neck. The couple had spent the evening before their wedding apart, with Euphemia staying with her Maid of Honor. Reginald had taken a drink to calm his nerves, but one led to another, and soon, he was staggering around the drawing room, shouting expletives and berating Margaret for delaying her own wedding. She huddled in her bed in the sitting room hoping and praying he wouldn't come across the foyer. Margaret pulled the covers to her chin when she heard his voice grow louder. It echoed as he stumbled across the tiled foyer, and she closed her eyes and prayed that he would go away.

"You're a bloody coward!" he cried just before opening the sitting room doors. "You bloody bitch! You can't hide from me." Margaret shuddered as he stumbled through the doorway. "Bloody stupid girl," he said. "Didn't need you, did I? Just another burden to bear." A moment later, Lord Reginald Huxley, the Earl of Dorley, hovered over her and glared at her with bloodshot eyes. "Bloody bitch. Why did you live, eh? She should have put you on that horse." He started to cry. "She was so love-ly." Margaret tried to get off the end of the bed, but Reginald grabbed her by her hair. She gasped as he pulled her head back. "She was perfect," he said. He threw her against the wall next to the bed. "You're nothing, you know. Just a mistake."

Margaret was dazed as she fell back onto the bed. Reginald grabbed her hair again, but the need to save herself gave her strength. She fisted her hands and began punching his arms. Even drunk he was strong, and if she really hurt him, he just might kill her. She had to get away from him, but she couldn't get him off her hair.

"Bloody bitch."

Reginald let go of her hair and pushed her down. He punched her across the face with his fist, and Margaret saw stars. He went to punch her again, but this time, she slid off the bed, and he fell forward. Margaret crawled to the fireplace and grabbed the fire iron. Reginald was able to pick himself up and looked around the room. He spotted Margaret on the floor by the fireplace holding the poker out in front of her. The fierce look on her face warned him to stay away, so Reginald stumbled to the door and returned to the drawing room.

Margaret dropped the poker and began to cry. Edith and Finley had to hear what was happening, but neither came to her rescue. She looked at the telephone on a table near the settee and thought of calling the police, but they would agree with her father that Margaret had a problem and leave her to face the consequences the next time Reginald got drunk.

She limped to the small bathroom behind the coat closet and looked in the mirror. The red mark on her face would be a dark bruise in the morning, and she would have to find a way to conceal it before going to the church for the wedding where she would watch Euphemia marry that monster from the Huxley pew.

Margaret could object when the vicar asked if anyone knew of a reason they should not be wed, but who would believe her? The servants knew, but Margaret needed someone equal to Reginald to offer testimony. Unfortunately, they thought Reginald was a jolly good fellow. If she objected, she would be standing alone, and many could say she was jealous of her father's new bride.

Thoughts of Greyson drove the ugliness away for a while, but when Margaret put her hand to her throat, she didn't feel the gold disk. It must have fallen off when she was trying to get away from Reginald. She limped back to the sitting room and looked on the floor by the bed, but she didn't see the disk. Margaret got on her knees and crawled from the bed to the fireplace, and began to panic when she couldn't see it anywhere. Fear rose in her heart as she scanned the room hoping to see it on the settee or the chair, but the disk had vanished.

Had she waited too long? Had the disk returned to Rotrude?

Margaret pulled herself up on the settee and sobbed. She had survived by dreaming of Greyson, unable to make a decision, and worried that Finley and Edith would be blamed if she ran away. Now, as she put her face in her hands, she felt something against her arm and looked down. The disk was hanging on the lace of her nightdress.

Margaret grasped the disk tightly. Joy spread across her heart as she thanked God that she hadn't lost it. She felt her fear melt away as she opened her hand and looked at the disk. The clasp had broken, but the disk was unharmed. Margaret kissed the disk and then got back into bed with it clasped in her hand.

The next morning, Margaret saw a large bruise on her calf. She couldn't wear the tea-length dress she'd bought for the wedding. She chose another, a full-length dress she'd worn on her twenty-first birthday. Margaret covered the bruise on her face with makeup and hoped no one would ask her what happened.

Reginald was at the dining table when she came downstairs. He had no memory of the night before, but she remembered how she'd punched his arms and knew he must have bruises, too, which is why he glared at her when she entered the dining hall. She averted her eyes and decided not to eat.

Margaret drove herself to the church in Dorley and sat in the Huxley pew. The ceremony would be held in two hours, and she was happy to sit alone in the peaceful atmosphere of the church. When people began to arrive, those who recognized her came by to say hello. Everyone was polite, and she was grateful when the church was full, and the vicar came to the front of the church. Margaret held her tongue when he asked if anyone objected to the marriage, and she cursed her cowardice when she heard Euphemia say "I do."

After the ceremony, everyone headed back to the manor for a celebration. Margaret drove herself home but stayed in the kitchen with Edith and the staff that had been hired to help her with the reception. She sat at the table and picked at the hors d'oeuvres. Edith came to the table, looked at Margaret's face, and exhaled sharply.

"Any gent do that to me, and I'd call the coppers," she said. Margaret remained silent. "Does it hurt, pet?"

"No," Margaret said.

"You know I was wondering when you and that fiancé of yours are going to tie the knot. Why don't you talk to him and see if you can set a date?"

"He couldn't come today," Margaret said.

"He isn't here?"

"No. He had a previous engagement."

Edith sat near Margaret and put her hand on Margaret's hand.

"Listen, Luv, you don't deserve this."

"It doesn't matter."

"It does matter because you matter."

Margaret looked into her eyes. Edith cared for her, but she couldn't help her.

"Would you say I'm in dire need?"

"That's exactly what I'd call it," Edith said.

Margaret smiled and then got up from the table.

"I have to make an appearance," she said. "Does my face look all right?"

"You might want to powder your nose."

Margaret went to the small bathroom behind the coat closet. She checked her makeup and saw that the bruise was still quite visible despite several layers of makeup. The idea of making small talk with all those people made her stomach clench, and for the first time in her life, Margaret decided not to do what was expected of her. Instead, she returned to the kitchen and waited for Edith to be distracted by the hired help, and then Margaret grabbed one of the walking sticks in the umbrella stand by the back door, and slipped out before Edith saw her.

Margaret limped a bit as she walked to the woods. She had replaced the chain from the gold disk with a piece of string and felt it grow warm against her skin. As she entered the clearing, Margaret saw Rotrude sitting on a tree stump – her knees crossed, and her hands resting on her knee.

"So, what brings you here today?" Rotrude asked.

"I'm in dire need."

"Are you ready to go to Havenwood?"

"As fast as I can."

Rotrude pulled the Silver Stag from beneath her blouse and took off one half to give to Margaret.

"I'll let you press the pieces together," Rotrude said.

Margaret grabbed one-half of the Stag and held it up. Rotrude held out the other half and waited while Margaret said goodbye to Dorley. A moment later, Margaret pressed her piece against Rotrude's, and the wind began to blow.

James Huxley

1986

Chapter Seven

JAMES WILLIAM HUXLEY HAD SEQUESTERED HIMSELF IN THE attic after his father told him they would be entertaining a guest for the summer. A devoted introvert, James balked at the idea of spending his entire summer holiday with someone he didn't know, which was at odds with his own plans of rereading the *Lord of the Rings* trilogy.

At sixteen, James was a bundle of hormones dedicated to disobeying his father and ignoring his devoted governess, Miss Hettie Nithercott. He would often brood over the imbecilic nature of his father's arguments, which focused on James' academic failures, and would retreat to the attic to escape into his books. The last thing he wanted was to "entertain" some spoiled, American who would brag about his father's wealth and all the things he had at home that James didn't have in England.

James had also been dealing with the impulsive nature of his own body. The mere image of a healthy female drew an embarrassing response, and James had learned it was best to avoid such images. He stayed away from the telly and hadn't been to the cinema in weeks.

As he turned the page of the first Tolkien tome, he heard a car door slam in the courtyard. He got off the legless comfy chair, and went to the window. One of the panes in the mullioned window had cracked and a small piece fell out, allowing James a clear view of the drive in front of the manor house. He saw the top of Lord Harold Huxley's black Bentley.

The rear door opened and a figure emerged, and when they turned their face upward to look at the manor house, James realized that his guest was a girl.

He stopped breathing as panic set in. It was a *female* guest, and the realization produced paroxysms of despair. James' perfect plan to avoid unwanted erections would never work if he had to face her every day. His face burned as the blood raced to his cheeks. He felt awful, and when Miss Nithercott called up the attic stairs, he froze.

"James," she said, his name echoing up the old, wooden stairs. "Your father wants you to come down and greet your guest."

Miss Hettie Nithercott, James' governess, had been with him since his mother died. She raised James during his father's long absences and was a kind and patient authority figure. Though James was long past the age for a governess, he knew his father kept her on to keep a watchful eye on James.

"I know you're not eager to meet her," Miss Nithercott said, "but it's your father's wish that you come downstairs."

James came to the top of the stairs. He had grown taller and thinner during the past year, and his wavy dark auburn hair had grown over the collar of his button-down shirt. An attractive lad, James brilliant blue eyes were often admired by the old women in the village.

James shoved his hands into the pockets of his khakis and exhaled sharply.

"I'm coming!" he shouted.

He took the steps one at a time to the bottom where Miss Nithercott stood with her hands folded in front of her.

"I know how difficult this is for you," she said. "But it's important to your father that you make a good impression."

"Who is she?"

"She's the daughter of Arthur Wentworth."

Wentworth was a friend of Harold's and an investor in James' uncle's bank.

"She seems very nice. I'm sure you'll be just fine."

"I had plans," James said.

Miss Nithercott noted the edge in his voice.

"Maybe she likes to read as well."

James and Miss Nithercott went down the grand staircase to

the first floor. He kept his eyes downcast until his father addressed him.

"James, say hello to Mia."

James' eyes rose slowly from her flip-flops to the hem of her dress, to the color of her fingernails (frosted pink). His eyes rested on her breasts and the protruding nipples under the light material of her summer dress. When he lingered there too long, Harold reacted.

"James!"

James lifted his head and gazed at her face.

Mia eschewed the long, permed hair favoured by other girls her age and wore her light blonde hair in a pixie cut. James' heart skipped a beat when he saw her blue eyes peeking out beneath a fringe of blond bangs.

"Hi, James," she said.

Mia was small, a mere five foot tall, and she didn't wear makeup. She wore a light scent that didn't overwhelm, and her smile was genuine. Her sweet voice made his heart palpitate. It pounded in his ears, and he panicked as he feared he might pass out and fall at her feet.

"Where are your manners?" Harold asked.

James felt the weight of her hand as Miss Nithercott placed it on his shoulder. He took a deep breath, took a step toward Mia, and held out his hand. Mia took it, and the moment he felt her soft, warm skin, James knew he would love her until the day he died.

* * *

THE NEXT DAY, JAMES FOLLOWED MIA ABOUT LIKE A LOVESICK puppy as he tried to find the words that would make her fall in love with him. She was a talker who didn't mind sharing the intimate details of her life with him. They would go for long, rambling walks around the estate, and James was so attentive that he learned a great deal about her.

"My father has me during the summer," Mia said as they walked through the garden behind the manor house.

"So, your parents are divorced," James said.

"They broke up when I was twelve." Mia sat on a concrete

bench near the non-functioning fountain. "I hate living with my mother."

"Why?" James sat beside her but was careful to leave several inches between them.

"She wants me to be like her. She calls herself a free spirit." Mia looked into James' eyes. "She put me on birth control pills when I turned fourteen."

James lifted his eyebrows, and his cheeks turned red.

"She also told me if I ever became pregnant, I didn't have to worry because she would take me for an abortion. 'You're not going to make me a grandmother at thirty-eight.'"

James shuddered as he listened. No one had ever spoken so candidly to him before.

"But I could never do that," Mia said.

"What would you do?"

"I'd keep it." She looked at James' hand resting on the bench. "I'd go to court and emancipate myself so she couldn't force me to give it away."

"I wish I could emancipate myself," James said.

"What would you do if you could?" Mia asked.

"I'd go to Hong Kong to live with my uncle. He owns the Bank of Moreland."

"The one my dad works for."

"I'd work for him and have my own apartment."

"Do you want to be a banker?" Mia asked.

James imagined himself in a three-piece suit sitting behind a desk and cringed.

"Well, maybe I could find another job."

Mia stood and walked a few paces. "You haven't told me anything about yourself."

"There's nothing to tell."

James feared she would laugh at his penchant for fantasy novels.

"What do you like to do?"

"I…read," James said.

"What do you read?"

James bit his lip.

"Fantasy books," he said softly.

Mia came back to the bench and sat close to him.

"Fantasy books?"

"They're about imaginary places. They usually have a hero who has a quest, you know, things like that."

"What's your fantasy, James?"

James glanced at her and a warm sensation rose up his neck. Mia took James' hand in hers and brought it to her lips. He felt himself respond and shuddered.

"How old are you?" she asked.

"I'm almost seventeen."

"I just turned sixteen. We should celebrate our birthdays."

"We could go to town. There's a bakery there."

Mia smiled. "I was thinking of doing something else." She held his hand. "Where do you go when you want to be alone?"

The top of her dress was cut a bit low, and James could see the tops of her breasts.

"The attic," he said softly.

"Show it to me," Mia said.

As they walked back to the manor house, James stayed behind Mia, hoping she wouldn't see the bulge he was trying so hard to conceal. They went into the house and up the main stair-case. No one saw them as they went down the hallway to the attic door. James let Mia climb the stairs as he lingered behind watching her skirt move from side to side.

"Wow," Mia said when she reached the top. "You must really love books."

Six tall bookcases were against the wall across from the legless comfy chair.

"Most of these were here when I found this place," James said.

"So, this is where you come when you want to hide," Mia said. "I like it."

Mia sat on the divan and leaned forward, her hands gripping the edge of the cushion. James stared at her chest for a moment, and then Mia smiled.

"Come and sit with me."

James felt awkward and bent forward as he walked toward her. He was mortified by his body's reaction to her and wished he could run away. He finally made it to the divan and sat beside her, and then Mia leaned her head against his shoulder.

"This is nice," she said. "Maybe we can read to each other."

James stiffened as she put her hand on his arm, and he nearly burst when she kissed his cheek.

"I was surprised when I first saw you," Mia said. "I was afraid you'd be wearing thick glasses and have crooked teeth."

"I thought my father was bringing home a boy," James said.

"Are you disappointed?"

James shook his head.

"I'm ecstatic."

Mia put her hand on his cheek and turned his face toward hers.

"Your eyes are so blue," she said.

"My mother had blue eyes," James said.

"And this?"

She kissed his nose.

"I'm not sure where that came from."

Mia kissed his lips, and James held his breath. Mia had dated a boy during the school year and had some experience. She put her hands on his cheeks and continued the kiss as James wondered what to do with his hands.

Mia pushed him down and lay on top of him. James' eyes grew wide when he felt her touching him, and then he pushed her away as he lost control of himself. He got up and went to the stairs.

"Don't go," she said. "It's all right. It happens all the time."

James couldn't look at her.

"I…it's time for dinner."

James ran to his room to change his clothes while Mia came down the stairs. She stopped at his room and listened at the door, but decided it was best to leave him alone. Mia knew the Brits changed for dinner and went to her room to put on another dress. When she emerged from her room, she saw that James' door was open, and Mia heard him talking to Miss Nithercott on the first floor.

Mia joined them in the dining room. She sat across from James, who kept avoiding her eyes. Miss Nithercott had wine, but James was having a fizzy drink.

"Where's Lord Harold?" Mia asked.

"Gone back to London," Miss Nithercott said.

"Oh. I thought I'd ask him to take me to see my father."

James looked at her as if she had stabbed him in the heart.

"You're not leaving," James said.

"I haven't spent much time with him," Mia said.

"Dear, I believe you are to stay here for a few weeks," Miss Nithercott said. "It is my understanding that your father is going to Hong Kong, which is why he asked Lord Huxley if you could stay here."

"Oh," Mia said. "He didn't tell me that."

She looked a bit forlorn, and James grinned.

"So, you'll be staying,"

Mia attempted a smile.

"I guess you're stuck with me for a while."

"Well, then, shall we eat?" Miss Nithercott asked, and then she rang the dinner bell.

Chapter Eight

The following day, James asked Mia if she'd like to see the ruins, and she agreed. They went to the sitting room and walked out the French doors onto the patio.

"They're right over there."

James pointed to the far corner of the estate where the once-mighty fortress had stood. A lone tower remained amidst broken stonewalls and nature's debris. They walked through the garden and across the lawn until they reached a shallow stream.

"This used to be the moat," James said. "When they built the manor house, they tried to block the source of water, but it still pretty soggy when it rains."

He went across the stream and then held out his hand. She took it and tiptoed through the shallow water.

"Can we go inside?" she asked.

"I've been warned all my life not to," James said.

Mia gazed at the tower and the large courtyard. The jagged remains of three other towers were at each corner of the courtyard, and the foundation of a large room was on the left side.

"Wow," Mia said. "This is like what, Arthur and the round table?"

"It was built during William the Conqueror's reign," James said.

"Who did he conquer?" Mia asked.

"England for one," James said. "He also built a lot of castles."

Mia scanned the ruins.

"It must have been something once," Mia said.

They walked along the well-trodden path beside the ruins as they examined what was left. The massive fireplace in the great hall was still recognizable, and Mia wanted to get a closer look. She stepped over what was left of a wall and James grabbed her arm.

"I just want to take a look," she said.

"Maybe we should go back now."

"I'm just gonna take a quick look," Mia said.

She wrested her arm from his hands and walked toward the fireplace. The cooking hooks were still in place, as was the wooden mantel.

"Did they ever hang a stocking on this?" She smiled.

"I don't think they celebrated Christmas back then."

James was still on the outside when a piece of the fireplace fell at her feet.

"Please let's go," he said.

Mia looked down and then stopped to pick up what looked like a piece of paper.

"This was behind that brick," she said.

"Please come out of there," James said.

Mia went to James, and he looked at the paper in her hand.

"What is that?"

Mia held up the paper. Written in childish handwriting, the note read, "Mummy, I miss you. I need your help."

"This looks like something a kid wrote," Mia said.

"We're always finding kids from the village here. Maybe one of them left it."

Mia rubbed her thumb over the paper. The edges were green with moss.

"It's been there a while," she said.

"We should be heading back," James said.

"Can we look around again tomorrow?"

"If it doesn't rain."

They headed back to the house, and Mia took James' hand. He liked the feel of it and squeezed it gently. When they reached the patio, James opened the French doors and let her go in first. When he shut the doors, he turned and found her standing near him. She stood on her tiptoes and kissed him.

"I'm sorry if I embarrassed you before," Mia said.

"I wasn't embarrassed."

"Do you want to make out? No, wait, you call it snogging over here, right?"

"Yes, and…yes."

Mia took his hand and led him up the stairs. They looked down the hallway before slipping into her bedroom and then headed for the bed. Mia got on and moved to one side allowing James to lie on the other. Mia rolled onto her side and watched James, who was flat on his back. When he didn't move, she put her hand on his arm.

"So, why do they call it snogging?" Mia asked.

"I have no idea," James said with a smile.

Mia moved closer to him and put her head on his shoulder. James turned his head toward hers and felt his heart palpitating. Mia slid her hand across his chest, and she pressed her lips on his while she unbuttoned his first button, and he put his hand on her waist as his passion rose.

* * *

Mia woke up with James beside her. She glanced over her shoulder and saw him on his back, his hair over his eyes. She slipped out of bed and ran naked to the bathroom to brush her teeth.

Despite their awkward beginning, by their second coupling that afternoon, James was able to control himself, and things went off brilliantly. As Mia looked at her reflection in the mirror, she didn't notice any changes. Despite her assertive manner when it came to seducing James, Mia had never had sex before. She and her high school boyfriend had made out often, but she wasn't ready to go any farther.

James, though, was different. She'd been struck by his handsomeness when they met, and her affection for him was deepening. Now that they'd made love, she wanted to crawl inside his body where no one could find her.

James had been kind. He'd kept asking if she was all right, and his sweetness made her smile, for it meant he truly cared for her.

But how could he? They barely knew each other, yet the feelings she had were real compared to those she'd felt for other boys. And James wasn't like the boys she'd met in school, the ones who talked about girls in disparaging ways. James was attentive when she talked, and being with him felt as natural as breathing.

"Slow down, Mia," she said to her reflection. "You just met him."

But Mia knew she was head over heels for him, and as she put her toothbrush down, she hoped this wasn't just another crush. She wanted it to be real, and for him to feel the same way about her.

"Mia."

She pulled on a robe from a hook on the wall, went to the bathroom door, and saw James sitting on the edge of the bed.

"Are you all right?" he asked.

"Never felt better," she said.

"I can't believe I fell asleep."

She came and sat beside him.

"Will Miss Nithercott come looking for you?"

"She doesn't check on me anymore."

Mia bit her lip as she kicked her feet.

"Was I okay?"

"You were wonderful." He put his hand on hers. "What about me?"

"You were wonderful, too."

"Do you think you'll want to do it again sometime?"

Mia grinned.

"Yeah, I think so."

James leaned over and kissed her.

"Do you want to wait, or should we…"

Mia pushed him down and climbed on top of him.

* * *

IT RAINED THAT AFTERNOON, AND THE PAIR WERE FORCED TO STAY inside. Miss Nithercott seemed unaware of the intense glances that passed between them during dinner, and when she suggested they watch telly with her, Mia was quick to say that James had promised they would start reading one of his fantasy books.

"Oh, do you like that sort of thing?" Miss Nithercott asked.

"I do," Mia said. "I read them all the time."

James and Mia headed up the stairs, and then went to the attic because James feared Miss Nithercott, whose room was next to his, would go to bed early and hear them. Mia turned to James at the top of the stairs and pulled him toward the divan.

"Aren't you worried about…" James hesitated and blushed.

"About what, James?"

"About a baby."

"I'm on the pill. There's nothing to worry about."

Mia wore another light summer dress without a bra and James saw the outline of her nipples. Mia pulled the dress up over her head and lay down. Despite their intimacy, James still felt awkward. He sat with his back to her and stared at his books. His constant companions and the adventures they'd shared felt tame now, and as he felt her hand on his back, James closed his eyes and swallowed hard.

"We don't have to do it," Mia said. "You could read one of your books to me."

"I want to do it," James said. "It's just…do you really like it?"

Mia chuckled. "Of course I like it."

James turned his head to see her face.

"I have no idea what I'm doing," he said.

"Neither do I. We'll have to figure it out as we go along."

Something real was happening between them, and James felt its intensity. The emotion was one he had struggled with as he tried to define his relationship with his father, and now he understood the romantic poetry he was forced to read at school. Love. Miss Nithercott had often said that his father loved him, but James never felt loved, nor had he loved in return. Here, though, he felt it for this lovely girl, and understood that she would always be a part of him.

Mia sat, slid her hands around his waist, and hugged him. She felt a change in him and again felt the desire to crawl inside him.

"James," she said.

"Yes."

"What are you thinking?"

"Nothing."

She rested her head on his back, and he put his hand on hers.

"I don't want to push you," Mia said.

"You're not pushing me."

"You're really quiet."

"I'm just...it's only been two days and everything has changed."

"It's changed for me, too," Mia said.

"And you're okay with doing this?"

Mia giggled.

"Yeah. I like it."

James leaned his head back against hers.

"I love it," he said, and then Mia laughed.

"Then what are you waiting for?"

"For something terrible to happen. Things like this never seem to work out for me."

"You've done this before?" Mia asked.

"No, not this, but things, you know, good things that make me feel good. They always...end."

Mia squeezed him.

"I don't want this to end."

"Neither do I, but you will have to go home, and it will end."

"So, why don't we just not think about that? Let's just be together."

James exhaled loudly.

"It's not that simple," he said.

"It is if you want it to be," Mia said.

"I'm supposed to just do this without thinking about what I'll do when you're gone."

Mia released him and lay back.

"Yes, James, you're just supposed to do this without thinking. That's what people do."

"But don't you think about what will happen?"

Mia rolled onto her side, reached around his abdomen, and lay her hand on him. James felt himself respond and gasped. All other thoughts fled as she touched him, and he stood to take off his trousers.

Chapter Nine

AFTER BREAKFAST THE NEXT MORNING, MIA AND JAMES DRESSED and headed for the ruins. Mia was eager to see if the child had left any other notes, and James wanted to stay near her.

"They left one in the fireplace," Mia said. "So, where do you think we should look next?"

"The tower might have a loose stone," James said. "But you have to be careful."

Mia smiled and then took off her flip-flops so she could run. James followed her across the soggy ground and to the courtyard. The wooden door at the entrance to the tower was gone, and Mia peeked inside while she waited for James to catch up.

"Do you have a match?" Mia asked.

"No, I don't smoke, and please be careful," James said.

"I'll be careful." Mia looked at the trees surrounding the ruins. They blocked the sun. "It's too dark to see anything in there."

James went past her and peeked inside. He saw the stairs going up and looked at the stones at the base. He kicked one and then another.

"These are still stuck in place."

"Have you thought about who could have written that note?"

"Not really," James said.

"Maybe your father wrote it," Mia said.

"I can't imagine him being afraid of anything."

"Not even when he was a kid?"

James shrugged. "I don't think we're going to find out who wrote it." He leaned against the tower. "Do you feel like going to town? They have a bakery there."

"We just ate breakfast," Mia said.

"I'm hungry."

Mia put her hands on her hips.

"I can't believe you're hungry already." Mia looked inside the tower again. "Do you have a flashlight?"

"Flashlight."

"You know, it has a bulb on one end, and you put batteries in it."

"You mean a torch. Yes, we have a torch."

"Then, we can use that to look in the tower."

"You still want to look for more notes?" James asked.

"Of course I do."

James headed toward the old carriage house, which was now a four-car garage, with Mia at his heels.

"Where are you going?" Mia asked.

"I'm getting a torch."

"Oh."

Mia waited outside while James went to an old armoire at the back of the garage. He found a torch, and then she followed him back to the tower.

"Have at it," he said as he handed it to her. "Just be…"

"Careful. Yes. I got it."

Mia turned on the torch and it illuminated the staircase. The gloom was forbidding, and Mia imagined ghosts waiting to pounce on anyone who breached their domain. She doubted a child, let alone a frightened child, would wander up there, so she turned off the torch and handed it back to James.

"I'm done," she said.

"You're not going up there?"

"No." She walked past him. "So, what else is there to do around here?"

"I still want to go to town," James said.

"Right. You're hungry."

"And there are shops there."

"So, I should bring money."

"Yes."

James went into the garage and put the torch back into the armoire.

"We can ride to town," he said. "There are bicycles in here."

"I'll have to go inside and put on my sneakers," Mia said.

Ten minutes later, Mia came to the garage wearing trainers. She had a small purse over her shoulder and had changed from a skirt to a pair of shorts. James had taken the bicycles off the wall hooks and was sitting on one while he waited for her. Mia climbed onto her bike, and then James took the lead and headed down the driveway. Mia struggled to keep up with him, but he reached the park in Dorley long before she and was standing beside his bike when she arrived.

"Why did you have to go so fast?" Mia asked.

"I thought you were right behind me," James said.

"You never even looked back."

James blushed. The last thing he wanted to do was upset Mia.

"Sorry," he said.

She saw his reddened cheeks.

"Okay, but stay with me next time." She got off her bike and looked down the street. "This is the town?"

"This is Dorley. It was bigger in the nineteenth century before the wars. Now, it has more tourists than residents. We have a public library, a police station, a bakery, a pub, a chemist, and a variety store."

"Sounds fascinating," Mia said.

"We also have the Huxley church."

"You have a church?"

"One of my ancestors built it, and it has a sign on it with his name. We have a pew of our own, too."

"Do you go to church?" Mia asked.

"Not anymore. Miss Nithercott used to take me, but I kept falling asleep, so now she goes alone."

They walked their bikes to the bakery and left them outside. The scent of cinnamon and butter wafted through the air, and Mia had to admit that she wouldn't mind having some shortbread. James had a Chelsea bun. They sat at a table, ate their treats, and then got back onto their bikes and rode through the village.

James took her to see the church and the cemetery behind it.

He also took her to the variety shop where they each bought a fizzy drink.

"This is pretty much it, isn't it?" Mia asked.

"I'm sorry it isn't more exciting," James said.

"It's not so bad. Did I hear a train whistle while we were in the store?"

"Yes. The station is about a half-mile away."

"So, we could go to London if we wanted to," Mia said.

"We could go one day, bu..."

"But what?"

James was quiet for a moment.

"I don't have much money."

"I have money," Mia said. "I could buy us lunch."

James avoided her eyes as they walked their bikes down the street. His father gave him money during the school term but felt it unnecessary when he was home. It had been a bone of contention between them for years.

"Are you okay?" Mia asked.

"We'll have to talk to Miss Nithercott."

"Why? Mia asked.

"She's in charge while my father is in London. I don't want her to get in trouble."

Mia sensed a change in James' mood. She waited until they had walked to the next block before asking him her next question.

"Why do you still have a governess?"

James was thoughtful as they walked past the chemist's.

"I think my father is afraid to leave me on my own. He thinks I'll burn the place down or something."

"Would you?" she asked.

James' wan smile touched her heart.

"Maybe I should."

They stopped in front of the bakery and leaned against the window.

"So, what should we do now?" Mia asked.

"We could go up to the attic and read," James said.

"Is that what we're calling it?" James laughed, and she grinned. "Won't Miss Nithercott wonder what we're up to?"

"She's at her book club today," James said. "She won't be back until five."

"Then we'd better get going."

Mia got on her bike and took off before James could get on his, yet he still overtook her and was waiting at the front door when she rode up the driveway.

"Shouldn't we put the bikes back?" Mia asked.

"We'll put them away later," James said. He opened the door. "After you."

Mia dropped her bike, ran past him, and up the stairs with James close at her heels.

Chapter Ten

MIA SCANNED THE BOOKCASES AS JAMES DOZED ON THE DIVAN. She spied a slender book that seemed out of place amongst the thick, fantasy novels James had collected. She pulled it from the shelf and saw the word "Journal" in gold lettering on the cover.

Mia took the journal to the legless chair and pulled her legs up underneath her. She lifted the cover and saw an inscription on the first page.

"To my darling Margaret from your loving Mummy. Happy 12th Birthday, sweetheart. May, 1939."

Mia turned the pages and saw the neat handwriting of an adolescent who was writing something important. There were similarities to the note Mia had found in the ruins. While James slept, Mia read Margaret's journal, and by the end, she was convinced that Margaret was the author of the note.

The stories contained in the journal began with a fantasy tale similar to those in James' books, but then they took on a darker tone. Margaret's heroine, a girl of twelve, longed to overcome the circumstances of her life. The villain, an abusive man who drank too much, was the same in every story. The heroine, who was constantly subjected to his abuse, would always defeat him by plunging a sword into his heart.

Margaret also wrote about a wizard named Greyson and his sister, a witch named Rotrude. Her colorful descriptions made them seem real and Mia could see them in her mind's eye.

Mia glanced at James and then returned the journal to the

bookcase. She dressed, tiptoed downstairs, went down to the first floor, and then walked to Lord Harold's study. She looked around before opening the door and slipping inside.

Lord Harold's desk had been there since the early nineteenth century. It was the largest piece of furniture in the room and sat at its center. Bookcases lined the wall behind it, leaving a space for the window directly behind the desk. A fireplace filled the wall to the right, and two chairs were placed across from each other with a low table in between. A glass-topped display case was in the corner.

Mia started scanning the titles of the books from the left side of the room. Many of the books pertained to the history of England, and in particular, Dorley. Mia looked at each shelf seeking the Huxley name and discovered that each Huxley earl had either written a book or that one had been written for him. She took each of them from the shelf, put them on the desk, sat in the large, leather chair, and began to read.

* * *

James woke up alone in the attic and put on his clothes. He went to the first floor and looked into the sitting room. When he didn't find Mia, he looked in the kitchen, on the patio, in the drawing room, and finally found her in the study. She was sitting at the desk with a pile of books in front of her.

"I've been looking everywhere for you," James said.

Mia sat back and clasped her hands across her stomach.

"Have you ever read that journal in the bookcase upstairs?" she asked.

"What journal?"

"Margaret's journal."

James sat in one of the fireplace chairs.

"No. Who's Margaret?"

"She is the daughter of Reginald, the sixth earl of Dorley."

James narrowed his eyes.

"My father was an only child," James said.

Mia leaned forward.

"Reginald had a daughter. She went missing in 1950."

"Bollocks."

Mia got up, picked up a book, and took it to James.

"There are newspaper clippings in there all about the day she disappeared."

James sat forward and grabbed the book. It fell open to revealed several newspaper clippings.

"Lady Margaret Huxley Still Missing" read one headline. James glanced at the article and then shook his head. "This can't be true."

"Is that a real newspaper?" Mia asked.

The heading read Dorley Morning Gazette.

"I've never heard of it," James said.

"Does the library in town have an archive?"

"I don't know."

Mia looked out the window. "It's too late to go today." She eyed James. "That's what we can do tomorrow."

James shoved the clippings back into the book and threw it on the table.

"This can't be true," he said.

"Then who wrote that journal?"

"I've never seen it," James said.

Mia sat on James' lap and put her arms around his neck.

"Then, after dinner, we'll go upstairs, and I'll read it to you."

She kissed him, and he returned the kiss. He moved his hands to her waist and then up her back.

"Am I...all right?" he asked.

"What do you mean?" Mia said.

"I mean, am I doing this right?"

"Are you still worrying about that?" She put her hand on his cheek. "Not that I have anything to compare it to, but it feels right to me."

They kissed again and then heard Miss Nithercott coming through the front door.

"Hello!" she cried, and it echoed down the hallway. "Anyone about?"

Mia got up, took his hand, and pulled him out of the chair. They left the study and went to the foyer, where they greeted Miss Nithercott. Miss Nithercott observed their red cheeks and intertwined hands and decided that perhaps she should keep a closer eye on them from now on.

* * *

AFTER DINNER, JAMES AND MIA HEADED FOR THE ATTIC, BUT Miss Nithercott insisted they join her to watch the telly. The reluctant pair followed her to the sitting room and sat next to each other on the settee while Miss Nithercott sat in a big, comfy chair beside it. Mia and James watched Miss Nithercott, who watched the telly. From time to time, Miss Nithercott would glance at them and smile. James looked for signs that she might be getting sleepy, but her eyes didn't droop, or her head nod. Two hours passed, and Miss Nithercott was still awake, but Mia had fallen asleep with her head on James' arm.

"Well, wasn't that an interesting program?" Miss Nithercott said when she turned off the telly. "Oh, when did she nod off?"

"About an hour ago," James said softly.

"Well, I imagine she's still tired from all that traveling, poor thing." Miss Nithercott went to Mia and put her hand on Mia's shoulder. "Dear, it's time to go to bed." James moved his arm, and Mia opened her eyes. "It's bedtime, dear."

"Oh, what time is it?" Mia asked.

"It's past ten," Miss Nithercott said. "Come, I'll walk you upstairs."

James watched as Miss Nithercott helped Mia off the settee. She walked the sleepy girl out of the sitting room, and James followed them up the stairs. Miss Nithercott took Mia into her room and closed the door.

James went to his room and waited until Miss Nithercott knocked on his door to say goodnight. He listened to her close her bedroom door and then waited another fifteen minutes before leaving his room to check Mia's door. It was locked, so James decided to go up to the attic and read the journal alone.

Chapter Eleven

JAMES DRESSED HURRIEDLY BEFORE RUNNING DOWN THE STAIRS TO the dining room. Mia and Miss Nithercott were talking when he entered the room, and they both turned their heads his way.

"Good morning, James," Miss Nithercott said. "Did you sleep well?"

Mia suppressed a smile as James took a plate off the sideboard.

"Well enough," he said.

"I heard you going to the attic last night," Miss Nithercott said. "You will damage your eyes if you keep reading by that oil lamp."

"It's bright enough."

"Still, you need your rest. You're still growing."

James blushed as he filled his plate, brought it to the table, and sat.

"What were you reading?" Mia asked.

"Probably one of those fantasy books he's always going on about," Miss Nithercott said.

"It was a fantasy," James said as he looked Mia in the eye. "Nothing more."

Mia pursed her lips.

"A waste of time if you ask me," Miss Nithercott said.

"Have you ever heard of Margaret Huxley?" James asked her.

"You mean your father's sister."

James blushed again.

"My father doesn't have a sister."

"Oh, he did, but she ran away years ago, and his father chose to erase her from the family history."

"You're joking," James said.

"She was quite real, I assure you."

"Then why haven't I heard of her?"

Miss Nithercott sipped her tea. She put it down and exhaled loudly.

"When I came here after your mother died, your father told me about Margaret. He told me that his father had disowned her when she ran away and that you might hear about her one day, but until that happened, he didn't want me to discuss her with you."

"My grandfather disowned her," James said.

"I don't know details, James."

"Who would know why?" James asked.

Miss Nithercott's eyebrows rose.

"Well, there's the vicar in Dorley. He's so old I'm sure he would remember her."

"We could go there," Mia said.

Miss Nithercott put her teacup down.

"If you see him, tell the vicar that you are coming to him in confidence," she said. "Otherwise, he might tell your father."

James looked at his governess and smiled.

"I will," he said.

"You have a right to know about her," Miss Nithercott said. "And I can honestly say I didn't tell you about her until you asked me."

Mia eyed Miss Nithercott with surprise.

"I told him," Mia said.

"And how did you find out about her?" Miss Nithercott asked.

"She wrote a journal. It's in the attic."

"Blimey," Miss Nithercott said. "Good for her. She was smart enough to put it where his lordship wouldn't look." Miss Nithercott pushed herself away from the table. "Since you are going to town today, will you be so kind as to collect my medicine at the chemist for me?"

"Sure," Mia said.

"Then, I can spend some time in the garden."

Miss Nithercott left the room while James ate his food, and Mia thought about the journal.

"You read the journal," she said.

"After you went to bed."

"It was her handwriting on that note we found," Mia said.

James put his fork down.

"That wasn't my grandfather. I never saw him angry."

"Did you ever see him drunk?"

"Of course not."

"Then how do you know what he was like when he drank?"

"I just can't believe he would do...the sort of things she wrote about."

Mia sat back. "She might have exaggerated. Maybe they just didn't get along, and she wanted to hurt him by making him the villain in her stories."

"But you don't believe that," James said.

"No, I think he was a monster, but for your sake, I'll give him the benefit of a doubt."

James pushed his plate away and folded his arms on the table.

"What if it is true? Does it mean I could be like that one day?"

Mia tilted her head.

"I know I've only known you a couple of days, but you don't seem like an angry person to me."

"And if I drink too much?"

"We could always raid you're father's liquor cabinet and find out."

James smiled. "And if things turned ugly?"

"I think I could take you in a fight if I had to."

"Oh, really," he said. "You could take me in a fight."

Mia looked at his plate. "Are you done?"

"Not yet."

"Well, hurry up because I want to see the vicar."

Someone had put the bikes away the night before, and when they found them on the wall, each had a lock attached.

"Jesus," James said. He looked about the garage. "And of course, he's not here."

"Who?" Mia asked.

"Maynard. He tends the grounds. He's trying to teach me a lesson."

Mia spied a pair of shears on the wall on the opposite side of the garage.

"Will they work?" she asked.

James followed her gaze.

"They cut hedges," James said. He saw a set of keys hanging on the wall. "But he might have left us the keys."

"Then why bother locking them up?"

"Because I'm irresponsible. I've always been a lazy lout."

Mia scoffed as James went to retrieve the keys.

"This is too much."

"I agree."

James found the key and unlocked the bikes. He put the keys back as Mia shook her head.

"You should hide them," she said.

"He'd have a heart attack," James said. "That would be my fault, too."

James pedaled slower so they would arrive at the park together. They sailed past the park and down Baker Street, where they turned left onto Tinker Lane. The church was at the end of Tinker, and James was behind Mia when she got off her bike in front of the church.

"It's a nice church," she said.

James eyed the stone structure. Built in the nineteenth century to resemble a medieval cathedral, it loomed over the other buildings on Tinker Lane. Its spire rose 230 feet, and the stained-glass windows were handmade by a local artisan.

"It's another Huxley edifice built to remind me of my duty."

"Just you," Mia said. She elbowed him, and James suppressed a smile. "Poor James." She slapped his arm lightly, and he grinned.

"You have no idea what it's like," he said.

"James has such a miserable life."

He grabbed her and tickled her waist, and then remembered where he was and let her go.

They walked the stone walkway to the entrance, and James opened the door, allowed her to pass, and then followed her into the narthex. They walked past rows of pews, and when they got to the front of the nave, she saw two rows bearing plaques with the Huxley name.

"It's so quiet," Mia whispered. "Is this where you sit when you come to church?"

"I used to," James said softly.

James led her past the choir area to a door with a sign bearing the vicar's name. He knocked, and the vicar said, "Come in."

Vicar Greenway was sitting at an old, pine desk that bore the scars of countless scribblings. He looked up, saw James, and smiled.

"Lord Huxley," he said.

"You don't have to call me that," James said.

The vicar came around the desk and threw his arms around James. He saw Mia behind James and smiled broadly.

"And who is this enchanting creature?"

"This is my…friend, Mia."

"Well, Mia, welcome to my study."

They shook hands, and then the vicar went behind his desk.

"Sit, sit," he said.

James and Mia sat on hardwood chairs placed in front of the vicar's desk.

"So, to what do I owe the pleasure?"

James cleared his throat and then smiled.

"I came to you because I know that anything I tell you will be held in confidence."

The vicar looked from Mia to James, and then he shook his head.

"Oh, children," he said. He cast his sad eyes on Mia. "Are you with child?"

Mia's eyebrows rose. "No, no, it's not anything like that."

"Oh, well, then, I assure you that anything you tell me shall not leave this office."

James bit his lip before speaking.

"Mia and I found a journal written by a girl named Margaret, and then Miss Nithercott told me Margaret was my father's sister. I'd never heard of her, so Miss Nithercott suggested I come to you and ask you if you knew anything about her."

Vicar Greenway sat back and clasped his hands over his stomach.

"Aye, I knew Margaret. She was your father's sister, but she left town before your grandfather remarried, and your father was born."

"My grandfather remarried?" James said.

"Aye, he did. His first wife, Lady Eliza, was thrown from a horse. She died, and Lord Reginald raised Margaret." He took a thoughtful pause. "Margaret left Dorley the day of the wedding. I was there to assist the vicar. I remember Margaret hobbling around."

"Why was she hobbling?" Mia asked.

"She'd fallen down the stairs and broken her ankle a few weeks before."

Mia cringed, and James narrowed his eyes.

"How?"

Vicar Greenway ran a finger over the edge of the desk.

"Lord Huxley told the constable that Margaret had been drinking when she fell down the stairs."

"Margaret drank?" James asked.

"It wasn't the first time the constable was called to the manor house. Margaret had fallen before and broken her wrist. As to your question, James, it would seem the most likely excuse for her losing her balance at the top of the stairs."

"Unless someone pushed her," Mia said.

"You do have a vivid imagination, Mia," Vicar Greenway said.

James shot her a look, but Mia refused to back down.

"Margaret wrote about him hitting her all the time," Mia said.

"She did?" Vicar Greenway tilted his head forward. "Did she say it was Lord Huxley?"

"She didn't give him a name," Mia said. "But she started writing about him when she was just a kid. Who else could it be?"

"She could have just made it up," James said.

Mia glared at him as James looked at the vicar.

"Do you know where Margaret went?" James asked.

"She didn't share her plans with me."

"When did she leave?"

"As I said, it was the day of the wedding."

"Did they still get married that day?" Mia asked.

"They did."

"You're kidding," James said.

"No one knew she was gone. The ceremony went on as planned, and by the time they realized she was gone, the day was nearly over."

"And you never saw her again?" James asked.

"Everyone searched for her, in the woods, and on the moors - we all searched. The police in London were advised to keep watch for her on the trains. Her photo was posted. Everything that could be done was done to find her, but Margaret had simply vanished."

"There are no pictures of Margaret in the house," James said. "It's like she never existed."

"Perhaps it was too hard for his lordship to see her every day." Vicar Greenway sighed. "Old Vicar Welch told me that when his wife died, Reginald fell into a terrible state. He drank heavily. He was a broken man." He sat back. "It's possible that he might have mistreated Margaret, but I cannot attest to that as I never saw him hurt anyone."

James nodded, and Mia clenched her teeth.

"I wish I knew more, James," Vicar Greenway said.

"It's all right," James said. "At least I know more now than I did when I came."

"Have you tried looking through the newspaper archive in the public library?" Vicar Greenway asked.

"We were going to do that after we saw you," Mia said.

"Thank you, Vicar."

"I hope you find what you're looking for."

The aged vicar didn't get up when James and Mia stood. Mia walked in front of James and quickened her pace when they left his office. She was out the door before James and on her bike with a frown on her face when he reached her.

"She broke her wrist, too," Mia said. "She wasn't drunk."

"We don't know that," James said.

"Bullshit."

"I can't...it just doesn't make sense. None of this makes sense."

Mia tempered her anger and forced a smile.

"Come on," she said. "Let's go to the library. Which direction?"

James pointed to the building next door.

"So, we can leave the bikes here," she said.

She got off her bike, took James' hand, and pulled him toward the library.

Chapter Twelve

THE DORLEY PUBLIC LIBRARY HAD BEEN THE RECTORY OF A Catholic cathedral, which Henry the Eighth had decimated during his reign. Bits of the old cathedral still lay behind the library. During the Middle Ages, when the village began to attract merchants from London, the rectory had been used as a town hall. It was turned into a library when a new seat of government was built in 1954. The current vicar lived in a stonewall house built to match the present faux medieval church.

The entrance to the library led to a foyer with a large umbrella stand. The heart of the library was a large stucco room with exposed wooden beams. A brick fireplace filled the wall at one end, and a staircase against the right wall went to the second floor.

The building was empty but for a serious woman wearing half-glasses perched on the end of her nose. She sat at a desk just past the foyer but before the rows of bookcases. The elderly woman had a cup of tea in front of her, and she raised her eyes when James and Mia approached her.

"Hello," James said. "Where can we find the newspaper archives?"

"They're all on microfiche," the woman said, and James cringed. "Ordinarily, I would get them for you, but I trust that you will abide by the rules."

"Absolutely," James said.

"Go up those stairs." She indicated the stairs with a tilt of her head. "They're in the loft. They are in order, and I expect them to be that way when you leave."

"We'll be careful," Mia said, and then whispered, "That woman scares me," as they walked away.

Old monk's cells occupied the loft. One of these contained the microfiche reader and file cabinets. The reader sat on a small desk with one chair.

The files for the *Dorley Morning Gazette* were in order by year, and James and Mia focused on the years 1925 through 1950, which was when the local paper shut down. James stood behind the chair while Mia sat and threaded the machine. Fortunately, the local newspaper issued papers with less than ten pages each week. Mia cycled through them quickly, searching for marriage, anniversary, and birth announcements. She stopped when she saw the name Huxley.

"It's a birth announcement for a child named Margaret Anne born on May 10, 1927. Father, Reginald; Mother, Eliza."

"Eliza," James said. He tried to picture his grandfather's first wife. "Let's see if we can find Eliza's obituary."

Mia scrolled past twelve years and found a headline reading, "Lady Eliza Huxley Dies in Tragic Accident."

"The life of our beloved Lady Eliza Huxley was tragically cut short on May 15, 1939, when she was thrown from her saddle while riding a new stallion. Lord Huxley had only recently announced that he had acquired a racehorse, a black stallion named *Once in a Lifetime*. The animal was put down following the incident."

"She died when Margaret was twelve," Mia said.

"She's not in our mausoleum."

"That's weird, isn't it?" Mia asked.

"Not if her family wanted her placed in their family tomb. Shit. Another relative I've never heard of." James leaned toward the machine to read the obituary. "Lady Huxley was an accomplished horsewoman who was well-known in equine circles as a gifted rider."

"She knew how to ride," Mia said.

"Something might have spooked the horse."

Mia scrolled past several ads for the Festival in Dorley as she searched for the name Huxley.

"That festival must have been some big deal," Mia said.

"It still is. People come from all over the country and spend lots of money."

James scanned the pages of the newspaper. He caught a glimpse of the name Huxley and put his hand on Mia.

"Back up," he said, and then he read the headline. "Police Respond to a Call at Huxley Manor."

The article was dated the 3rd of April, 1950.

"The constable was called to Huxley Manor Sunday evening when Lady Margaret Huxley tumbled down the grand staircase. Lord Reginald Huxley led the officer to his daughter, Lady Margaret, whom he had found lying at the bottom of the stairs. An ambulance was dispatched, and Lady Margaret was taken to Brandmore Hospital where she was treated for cuts, bruises, and a broken ankle resulting from the fall. Lady Margaret was conscious and told police that her foot slipped out of her shoe at the top of the stairs causing her to lose her balance. Police investigated and concluded that the fall was accidental."

"Bullshit," Mia said. She rolled the tape back to see if there had been any other headlines regarding the Huxleys. "Here's one from 1946."

"Lady Margaret Huxley stumbled when she was walking on her own through the woods. The groundskeeper heard her shouting for help and came to her rescue. He brought her home, and the family physician was summoned to Huxley Manor. Margaret suffered from cuts, bruises, and a broken wrist."

"I don't believe she was just clumsy," Mia said.

"Maybe she was. The constable said it was accidental."

"Your grandfather was a lord, right? The constable might have believed him because of who he was."

"You really believe my grandfather shoved his own daughter down a flight of stairs."

"So what, she slipped out of her shoe at the top of the stairs?" Mia said. "Seriously, James, do you really believe that?"

James couldn't reconcile the memories he had of his grandfather with the angry drunk in Margaret's journal. He folded his arms over his chest and leaned against the file cabinets. Mia continued to look for any mention of the Huxley name. She found a small article buried near the back of the paper.

"Reginald was arrested in 1946," Mia said. James didn't move. "The constable was called to the manor by a maid who said that Lord Huxley was inebriated and was threatening to harm his daughter, Lady Margaret."

Mia paused, but James remained unmoved.

"He was drunk and threatening to hurt her," she said.

"I'm done," he said. "I'll meet you outside."

Mia continued her search and found the article describing Margaret's disappearance in 1950. It was just as the vicar said - it was the day of her father's wedding to Euphemia Quince. They discovered that Margaret was missing after the ceremony. Lord Reginald and his new bride postponed their honeymoon. Searches were made of the woods surrounding the manor, and the Metropolitan Police displayed flyers in train stations.

Mia put the films back and looked through another paper's archives for any news after 1950. She found the birth announcement for James' father and the obituary for Euphemia Quince Huxley. This news sent a shiver up Mia's spine. Women didn't fare well in the Huxley household.

Mia left the library and found James astride his bicycle near the curb.

"We should go to London and look for her," Mia said as she climbed on her bike.

"What?" James asked.

"We should go to London and see if we can find her."

"How?"

"We'll hire a private detective."

"With what? I get five pounds a month allowance when I'm at school."

"You're kidding," Mia said. "That's pitiful."

"Harold believes it builds character."

"Harold is a cheap son of a bitch."

Despite his gloomy mood, James laughed out loud.

"We all have relatives who embarrass us," Mia said.

"Have any of yours turned out to be brutal monsters?"

"My mother's brother creeps me out."

James smiled, and then he leaned toward her and kissed her.

"Do you think she died?" he said when they parted. "Do you think he killed her and hid her body somewhere?"

"I don't feel like she died. I feel like she's hiding somewhere."

"Maybe she had some money," James said.

"Maybe she took her mother's jewelry," Mia said.

"And pawned it in London."

"But that would have left a trail."

"Right, so it would have been cash."

"Wherever she is," Mia said, "I'm sure she's happier than when she lived here." She touched James' cheek. "So, let's go and get Miss Nithercott's medicine, and after that, we can go home and sneak into the attic."

James blushed. "I was hoping you would say that."

Chapter Thirteen

Miss Nithercott was nowhere in sight when they returned, so Mia took James' hand and led him up the stairs. They tiptoed down the hallway to the attic door. Mia closed it as James went upstairs, and she put Miss Nithercott's medicine on the first step before joining him.

James was sitting on the divan when she reached the top step. He was fully dressed, and Mia smiled. She loved that he was shy and didn't grope at her the way some of the boys she'd dated had the first time they went out.

"Why are you still dressed?" she asked as she pulled her shirt over her head.

Mia wasn't wearing a bra, and James averted his eyes. She slipped off her shorts and panties and then sat beside him.

"Your turn," she said.

James began pulling his shirt up, but he was too slow for Mia. She grabbed the bottom of the shirt and pulled it over his head, placing her breasts in close proximity to his eyes. He turned his head, and she giggled.

"You've seen me," she said.

"I know. I'm just not used to this."

"Do you want to stop?"

"No, I just, can we go a little slower?"

Now, Mia blushed.

"I'm sorry," she said. She held his shirt in front of her. "I'm acting like a slut."

"No, you're not a slut, it's just that you're the first one I've ever been with, and I keep thinking I'm doing it all wrong."

"You're the first one I've been with, too."

James looked into her eyes.

"You seem like you have more experience than me."

"You must think I'm terrible."

"No, not at all," James said. "In fact, I wish I could be more like you."

"We're pretty loose in my house," Mia said. "What my mom calls clothes optional. I'm used to being naked around other people."

James lifted an eyebrow.

"Are you nudists?"

Mia laughed. "No, just hippies. We don't go outside the apartment that way." Mia hugged his shirt. "I really like you, James. This isn't like the way I felt with other boys." She turned her face toward his. "This is different. I just want to be with you all the time."

"Me, too."

Mia ran her hand down his smooth chest.

"We have to find a way to outsmart Miss Nithercott," she said. "I want to sleep with you."

"I can sneak to your room after she goes to bed."

"How do you know she's in bed?"

"She used to sleep in my room when I was young. She usually fell asleep within a few minutes, then I would get out of bed and play with my toys."

"And she never knew?" Mia asked.

James shook his head.

"And she's a heavy sleeper."

Mia smiled and kissed him. He hesitated before putting his hand on her arm. She let go of his shirt and wrapped her arms around his chest. When they parted, he put his hand on her cheek, and James looked into her eyes.

"I love you."

She smiled.

"I think I love you, too."

* * *

J<small>AMES AND</small> M<small>IA SPENT THE AFTERNOON ENTWINED IN EACH</small> other's arms, and an hour or two before dinner, Mia sat up and looked at James.

"If Margaret lived here, she would have had a bedroom." James stretched. Mia smiled. "Don't you agree?"

"She would have had a bedroom," James said.

"Right, so why don't we look for it?"

"Because there are no photos of her anywhere in the house. Don't you think he would have cleaned out her room, too?"

"Maybe, but who knows?" Mia said. "Maybe he hoped she would come back and left it the way it was when she ran away."

"You really think we'll find her bedroom?"

"It's worth a try."

After they dressed, James and Mia began their search with the rooms next to theirs. These were guestrooms, and they were all decorated in a similar fashion. When they tried to open the one next to Miss Nithercott's room, it was locked.

"Do you have a master key?" Mia asked. James shook his head. "Do you have a screwdriver?"

"You think you can break it open," James said.

She grinned at him. "I learned how to open my mother's bedroom door when she wasn't there." Mia laughed. "You should see your face."

"We don't keep any tools in the house, but we might have something in the garage."

James left her to run to the garage, and ten minutes later, he returned with a flathead screwdriver smiling triumphantly.

"I found one!" he cried.

"It doesn't take much to make you happy, does it?"

Mia grinned as she took it from his hand. She went to work on the lock while James looked over her shoulder. A few minutes later, she turned the knob and opened the door.

"Nothing to it," Mia said.

The musty smell caused Mia to take a step back, but James felt for the wall switch and turned on the lights. They scanned the room and saw a Victorian-era dollhouse, a four-poster bed with a canopy, a white chest of drawers, a child's table with a tea set and four chairs, and a white dressing table. Photographs decorated the walls and the dresser.

They walked inside and went to opposite sides of the room.

Mia looked at the photos on the dresser. One depicted a young girl and a woman posed in front of a large, black stallion. Another depicted the girl on the brink of womanhood and must have been taken the year Margaret graduated from school. There was a wedding picture hung on the wall. James recognized his grandfather, but the woman by his side was unfamiliar.

"What did he think?" Mia asked. "That he could lock the door and forget she existed?"

James joined her at the dresser and looked at the photo of Margaret and Eliza in front of the horse.

"The woman is very pretty."

"I don't recognize her," James said.

Mia studied James' face.

"What was your grandfather like?" she asked.

"He was tall. A proper English gentleman."

"And your grandmother died when your father was born, so, Lord Harold didn't have a mother either."

James picked up the other photo on the dresser and looked at Margaret at eighteen.

"She's not very pretty," he said.

"What happened to your mother?" Mia asked.

"She died when I was young."

"Women don't live long around here," Mia said.

James pondered this. "My mother had cancer." He put the photo back.

James went to the hallway and waited for Mia to come out of the room. She took one last look around and then joined him in the hall. James was quiet as they went downstairs and remained so as she followed him to the sitting room.

"You okay?" she asked.

He sat on the settee and turned on the television.

"I'm fine."

"You're really quiet," Mia said as she sat beside him.

James laid his head back and stared at the ceiling.

"I never thought much about my family when I was young," he said. Mia put her hand on his. "And I never even knew about Margaret or her mother." He looked at Mia. "My roommate at school always talked about his ancestors. He liked to remind me that he was in line for the throne. I thought he was full of shit because I never cared about my ancestors. I never even asked my father about them. They were all just names in the family Bible he keeps in the study. They weren't real to me, but those photos of Margaret, she was real."

Mia laid her head back.

"We have to find out what happened to her," Mia said.

"How?"

"Like I said, we have to hire a private detective. I have some money."

"I don't want to use your money," James said. "And besides, what will they be able to do that we haven't already done? And what if she doesn't want to be found?" James sat up. "Let's just find out if my father knows anything about her."

Mia sat up, glanced at the clock on the mantel, and then put her head on his shoulder.

"We still have an hour until dinner," she said. She ran her finger up his arm. "Do you want to watch TV?"

James smiled.

"I could read one of my books to you."

"The ones in the attic?" Mia asked.

James nodded. Mia stood, held out her hand, and James let her lead him up the stairs.

Chapter Fourteen

JAMES CLOSED THE FIRST BOOK IN THE *LORD OF THE RINGS* trilogy and waited to hear what Mia would say. He had started to read it to her after they made love, and he thought she might fall asleep, but when he put the book on the old end table next to the divan, she squeezed him and kissed his cheek.

"I like it," Mia said.

"I love his stories," James said.

"It will take us all summer to read all of them."

"How long are you staying?"

"I'm supposed to be here until the end of August," Mia said. "But if my mom finds out he dumped me here, she might tell me to come home."

James had his arm around her shoulder. He put his other arm over her as he lay on his side.

"Don't tell her," he whispered into her ear.

"I won't."

James lay his forehead against her head and exhaled sharply.

"I can't stop thinking about you," he said.

Mia smiled and turned to face him.

"Me, too."

They kissed, and then kissed again, and then pulled apart when they heard a car stopping in front of the house. James got on his knees and looked out the window.

"Miss Nithercott is home."

"We'd better get dressed."

By the time they dressed and went downstairs, Miss Nither-cott was at the dining table awaiting their arrival. She noted Mia's disheveled hair and the roses in their cheeks. Miss Nither-cott had seen them the day before as well when she returned from her book club.

"So, what were you two up to while I was gone?"

They sat on opposite sides of the table and smiled at Miss Nithercott while she eyed James. He was a moody boy, and she feared that the discovery of a heretofore unknown aunt would summon his black dog, a depressive state that she referred to as Alfie, named for the character played by her favorite actor, Michael Caine. James had wrestled with Alfie since early child-hood, and when he lost his way, it could be weeks before he found his way out.

"I think we should all go to the cinema this weekend," Miss Nithercott said.

"I want to go," Mia said.

James perked up a bit.

"I would love to see *Labyrinth*," he said.

"Oh, yeah, David Bowie," Mia said.

"Is that one of those awful fantasy things you drag me to all the time?" Miss Nithercott asked.

"Yes, but it's supposed to be very good," James said.

"I'd rather see *My Beautiful Launderette*." Miss Nithercott pursed her lips. "But if you insist."

"Do you have multiplex theaters here?" Mia asked, and James' eyes lit up.

"There's one in Milton Keynes."

"But that's miles from here," Miss Nithercott said.

"But then we could go see whatever we want," James said.

"I can't believe you want me to take you all the way to Milton Keynes to see a film." Miss Nithercott rolled her eyes. "Very well. But only this time."

"We won't ask again," James said.

James could hardly control his joy. He'd been looking forward to seeing the film since he saw the trailer, and now he was rocking in his seat. Mia was eager to see it, too. She stuck her foot out to touch his leg, but it didn't reach. She ended up kicking the tabletop, which drew Miss Nithercott's attention.

"What was that?"

"Nothing," Mia said.

"So, what else did you do today?" Miss Nithercott asked.

Now, both of them blushed, and no one spoke as Hughes brought the first course to the table. When he left, Mia shifted in her seat.

"We read the Lord of the Rings," she said.

"Oh. Did you like it?"

"I like the way it was written," Mia said.

"How many times have you read it, James?" Miss Nithercott asked.

"I've lost count," he said.

Miss Nithercott was happy to see him smiling. The black dog had been held at bay for now.

"Well, we should go to London next week and see if there isn't some other book you might want to read. You need to expand your horizons, my boy."

"Fantasy books do expand my horizons," James said. "I can go anywhere, be anything when I read them."

"And they're interesting," Mia said.

"Oh, you don't mean that, dear," Miss Nithercott said.

"I do. Tolkien was a good writer."

The rest of the dinner went smoothly as they discussed their plans for the weekend. An early show, and then supper at a local restaurant. And all agreed it would be nice to get away from Huxley Manor for a few hours.

Miss Nithercott was once again able to keep the two lovers with her in the sitting room, and once again, Mia fell asleep on James' shoulder. When her programs were over, Miss Nithercott roused Mia and went up the stairs behind her, while James lingered in the sitting room. After they had gone, he went to his father's study.

The family Bible was in the display case in the corner of the study near the fireplace. James lifted the top and put on the white gloves kept under the Bible. He lifted the cover and turned the next page. A list of births and deaths began on the second page.

James struggled to read the faded entries, but the dates were easier, and when he got to his father's name, he noticed that a piece of paper was glued to the page to conceal whatever was above his father's name. He could not lift it without tearing the page, but he knew what it was. It was Margaret's name. What else could it be?

James closed the Bible and took off the gloves. He shoved them beneath the Bible, closed the lid, and looked at the bar at the other end of the study. James had never been tempted to drink before, but his anger made his hands shake, and he wondered if a shot of whiskey would calm his nerves.

"Hey." He was startled when he saw Mia at the door. "I think she's asleep."

James smiled. "I'm right behind you."

Something else was good for calming the nerves, and as he watched Mia go up the stairs in front of him, her hips swaying beneath her sleepshirt, his hands stopped shaking.

Chapter Fifteen

THE SUMMER PASSED WHILE THEY LINGERED ON THE DIVAN IN THE attic. Miss Nithercott tried in vain to keep them busy, but they always managed to sneak away when she was otherwise occupied. By the middle of August, they were hopelessly in love, and closer to the end of Mia's stay.

The old divan in the attic was now covered with a sheet. James stole two pillows from the guest rooms, and sometimes they slept there at night. The hours spent there brought them closer, and soon, neither could imagine a life without the other. Then the black dog worked its way into their happy union, and Mia was unprepared for its arrival.

James would often slip from one mood to another without reason, but when Alfie came to visit, Mia had a hard time waking James so they could go to their respective rooms before Miss Nithercott woke up. The first time James swatted her away and cried, "Go away!" when she pulled on his arm, Mia was stunned. She backed away and stared at him for a while, and then went downstairs alone.

Mia was with Miss Nithercott when James came down to breakfast the first time. Miss Nithercott recognized Alfie right away, and she saw the sad look on Mia's face.

"It's Alfie, luv," she said softly as James filled his cup with coffee. "It's not you."

"Whose Alfie?" Mia whispered.

"The black dog. His dark mood."

Mia watched James sit at the table, his eyes dull, and his shoulders slumped. He drank the coffee but didn't eat anything.

"You need to eat something," Miss Nithercott said.

"I'm not hungry," James said.

"You have to eat, James. You're too skinny as it is."

"I'll eat later."

Mia watched him for a long time as she waited for Miss Nithercott to leave the table. If she was with him alone, she knew she could talk him out of his dark mood. Miss Nithercott stayed a while, for she, too, still believed that the right word might snap him out of it, even though attempts to do so in the past had failed.

His doctor had suggested medication, but James didn't like the way it made him feel. Besides, the mood would right itself in time – a day, a week, or a month – if James went to his room and read a book.

Miss Nithercott glanced at Mia. She was quiet, which was unusual for the lass.

"Are you all right, luv?"

"I'm not hungry, either," Mia said. "My stomach is upset."

"I can take you to the clinic in Brandmore if you like."

"Maybe if it doesn't go away."

"You let me know then," Miss Nithercott said as she got up. "I've got an errand in town. I'll be back in an hour or so."

Mia kept watching James, but he was resting his head on the table. She worried that he might be like this until it was time for her to go.

"She's gone for an hour," Mia said.

James grunted, but he didn't lift his head.

"We could go to the attic," she said.

James lifted his head now and saw her eyes. He sat back and held onto the edge of the table.

"I'm sorry," he said. "I just don't feel like it right now."

"Is it something I did?" Mia asked.

"No. Not at all. Why would it be something you did?"

"I don't know. I just…I've never seen you this way."

"I get this way sometimes."

"Do you want to go for a walk?" Mia asked.

James peered at her through half-closed eyes. He had a duty

to entertain their guest. His father's voice rattled around in his head, and James tried to block it out.

"Okay," he said.

James got up and followed Mia out the front door. She headed toward the woods, and he walked a few feet behind her. The clouds threatened rain as they entered the woods, following a natural path that ended at a clearing. An old, marble altar sat at the center, and James recalled something a fellow student had said when he heard James' name.

"Huxley? Are you from Dorley?"

"Yes," James said.

"Your ancestors practiced a pagan religion."

"What are you talking about?" James' anger rose as the boy adopted a cheeky smile.

"They sacrificed babies and drank their blood."

"That's a lie."

"It's true. Ask St. John."

Peter St. John taught history. He knew each noble line and where they originated. He had told James that one of his ancestors had built the largest port in England. He had said nothing about them drinking blood.

James went to St. John the next day, and the man put a soothing hand on James' shoulder.

"It was a man called Symond. He was the first Earl of Dorley until it was discovered that he was practicing blood sacrifices. The king cut off his head, and he was replaced by Edmund Huxley."

James went to the altar and searched it for traces of blood. Mia came alongside him and put her arm through his.

"What is it?" she asked.

"Nothing," James said.

"What's it doing out here?"

"Must have been one of my crazy ancestors. Who knows why they did anything?"

Mia looked up through the trees.

"It looks like it might rain. We should go back."

They walked back to the house arm in arm, and then, as they stood at the door, James wrapped his arms around Mia.

"I'm sorry," he said.

"For what?"

"For this. For being such a shit to you this morning."

"I forgot about that. Don't sweat it."

He pulled away and put his forehead on hers.

"I try not to let it get to me, but sometimes it just takes over."

"It's okay. You do what you've got to do. You don't have to entertain me."

"But I want to be with you."

She laid her head on his chest.

"You're with me now."

James' mood lifted a couple of days later, and Miss Nithercott thanked God for Mia's presence as she believed that the girl was able to help James find himself again. She eased up on them a bit, allowing them to be alone more often, and hoped she wouldn't regret her decision.

When James and Mia noticed that Miss Nithercott wasn't as watchful, they began spending more time in the attic. They would settle on the divan, make love, hold each other, and then fall asleep, but one night, James woke to find Mia sitting cross-legged in the legless chair.

"Something's wrong," he said. Mia's downcast eyes warned him to proceed cautiously. "What is it?"

"It's almost time for me to go home," Mia said. "I don't want to leave here."

"Why don't you ask your father if you can stay?"

"I have to go home. It's the custody arrangement, and he's perfectly happy with things the way they are."

"Maybe he would ask her if you could stay," James said.

"Have you seen him visit me once since I've been here?"

"He's been working."

"Bullshit. He just doesn't care about me. He never has."

"Then why bring you here at all?" James asked.

"Because my mother insists he spends some time with me so she can be alone with whoever she's sleeping with." Mia got up and walked to the bookcases. "Did I tell you what she said when she heard that there was a boy here? 'Don't get knocked up.'"

"Jesus."

"Not, hey, love you, miss you. Just don't get knocked up."

Mia came to James, lay beside him, and snuggled against his chest.

"I don't want to leave you," she said softly.

"We could get married."

"We're not old enough."

"We are if we get their permission."

Mia pulled away and looked into his eyes.

"And your father would give you permission to marry me? Aren't you supposed to marry some lady or something?"

"We could run away."

"And what would we live on? Neither of us has any money."

"I could sell my collections," James said.

James was referring to his book collections, and Mia chuckled.

"God, James, you are so sweet, but no one wants your collections, and even if they did, they aren't worth much." Mia got up and went to the legless chair. "We can't run away."

Her words stung, but they were true. He looked at the bookcases and the rows of fantasy books.

"We could get jobs. With both of us working, we could afford a flat."

"I'd have to get a work visa," Mia said. "Would I need my father's permission for that?"

"You'd need a sponsor," James said. "My father might be willing to do that."

"Doesn't he want you to finish school?"

"Right." James shook his head. "Screw him. I'll drop out."

"And do what? What kind of job would you get? Or me, for that matter? We'd barely make enough to feed ourselves, let alone pay rent."

"So, you're ready to just give up on us?" James said.

"I'm not giving up on us," Mia said. "I'm just being honest."

"James!" Miss Nithercott's voice echoed up the stairs. "It's getting late."

"We'll be right down!" James shouted. He looked at Mia. "We aren't done talking about this."

Mia watched him dress and head to the stairs. She got up, pulled her dress over her head, and followed him. They parted ways in the hall. He waited to see if she would look at him before closing her door, but she closed it without a backward glance. He wouldn't give up his post until he heard the lock turn.

Chapter Sixteen

JAMES TOSSED AND TURNED UNTIL THE LIGHT FROM THE RISING sun brightened his windows. He got out of bed, washed up, and then went to the hallway. Mia's door was still closed, so he went downstairs.

The newspaper was on the front stoop, and he brought it inside. A large advertisement for the Festival in Dorley was on the second page. It was to be held in two days, and James had been looking forward to taking Mia, but now he wasn't sure she would want to go.

An hour later, Miss Nithercott came to breakfast and found James lingering over his coffee.

"Why you're up early," she said. "Happy birthday!"

James had been so worried about Mia's departure that he had forgotten about his birthday.

"It is my birthday, isn't it?"

"It is indeed."

Miss Nithercott went to the kitchen while James cast his eyes on the ceiling. When Miss Nithercott returned, she sat and waited for breakfast to be brought to the sideboard. She saw James looking up and leaned forward.

"She's still asleep."

"How do you know?" James asked.

"I didn't hear her moving about when I passed her door." James exhaled sharply. "James, I heard some of what you said last night."

"You were listening.

"I didn't intend to, but when I heard you talk about getting a flat...Mia is right. You can't leave school."

"She doesn't want to go home."

"She is too young to have a choice. Her parents are still the responsible parties."

"Her mother is a selfish twat who doesn't care if Mia lives or dies," James said vehemently.

"James!" Miss Nithercott cried. "Mind your tongue."

"I can take care of her."

"You're too young."

"I'm seventeen today. I can get a job."

"But you can't sign a contract," Miss Nithercott said. "Or the lease on a flat, and you know your father would never do it for you. Now, get this nonsense out of your head. Just enjoy the time you have with her."

James got up and left Miss Nithercott alone at the table. He glanced up the stairs, and then went out the front door. He walked around the estate, across the "moat," and past the ruins. He ended his sojourn at the patio, sat on a sun lounger, and closed his eyes. He awoke an hour later to find Mia in the lounger beside him.

"I thought you'd never wake up," she said. "Why didn't you tell me it was your birthday?"

"I forgot about it."

"Bullshit. No one forgets their own birthday."

"Well, I did." He glanced at her. "I've been focusing on something else."

Mia leaned toward him.

"I saw the ad for the festival."

"It's on Saturday," James said.

"I'd like to go if you still want to."

"I would."

Mia stared at the sky for a few moments.

"James, I'm sorry about last night. I just don't think we can make it on our own."

"Neither does Miss Nithercott," James said.

"How does she know..."

"She heard us talking."

"And she listened?"

Mia's eyes were wide as she leaned toward James.

"She didn't hear much. Just the bit about us getting a flat."

"Oh." She sat back in the chair. "Are you still mad?"

"I'm not mad. I'm frustrated."

"In two years, we'll both be eighteen, and we can do whatever we want."

"But you'll be in America. You'll have some other bloke you want to be with."

Mia smiled. "You really don't know how I feel about you, do you?"

James frowned. "No."

"I can't believe after all the time…after all the things we did, that you don't know how much I love you."

James sat up and stared at her.

"Why didn't you say it before?" he asked.

"I did say it before. I said it a few days after I got here."

James thought back to the day Mia arrived, and he remembered the rainy afternoon they'd spent on the divan. Mia had put her arm across his chest and whispered, "I think I love you."

"You said you thought you loved me," he said.

"It's the same thing," Mia said.

"No, it isn't."

"Well, then, I'm telling you now that I do." Now, Mia sat up to face him. "It's your turn."

James gazed at her for a moment.

"I adore you. I'll never love anyone the way I love you." He reached for her hand. "No one else, not ever."

He saw tears in her eyes as she put his hand on her chest.

"Can you feel that?" Mia asked. James nodded. "My heart is pounding in my ears."

"We have to find a way to be together," James said. "You have to talk to your father."

Mia smiled, and then she let go of his hand.

"What are we doing for your birthday?" she asked.

James shrugged. "Miss Nithercott will probably have them make me a cake."

"Do you get presents?"

"If my father is here, he usually gives me a pat on the back, and Miss Nithercott gives me a new shirt."

"Then we have to go to town. I want to get you something."

"You don't have to do that," James said.

"I want to."

"All right then. I'll go and let Miss Nithercott know, and then I'll meet you in the garage."

* * *

As James had predicted, Miss Nithercott had ordered a cake, and it was at the center of the table when she called James and Mia to dinner. Mia was wearing a gauze dress with spaghetti straps. The pinks in the flowered pattern made her cheeks look rosy, and James found it hard to focus on his meal with her sitting across from him. The gauze didn't conceal her breasts, and James found himself responding to the sight of them as Miss Nithercott was apologizing for the absence of his father.

"He wanted to come, James," she said. "He asked me to convey his regrets."

"Did he really say that?" Mia asked. "He wanted you to convey his regrets?"

"Lord Harold can be a bit too proper sometimes," Miss Nithercott said. "I'm sure he's upset that he couldn't be here."

James never heard a word. He wanted to be alone with Mia.

"So, Mia, what did your father say?"

James did hear this and turned his head toward Miss Nithercott.

"He said Lord Harold would be here on Sunday, and I was to return to London with him on Monday morning." James' mouth fell open. "I have to be home when school starts."

"Well, I will miss you," Miss Nithercott said. "It's been nice having another female about the house."

"Why didn't you tell me?" James asked.

"I didn't have time," Mia said.

"You could have told me as soon as you found out."

"James, Mr. Wentworth called just before dinner."

"I was coming to your room when Miss Nithercott told us to come to the table."

James stricken appearance concerned Miss Nithercott, but she carried on, and when dinner was over, she put some candles on the cake, lit them, and then switched off the light.

"Shall we dispense with singing *Happy Birthday*?" Miss Nithercott asked.

"I think so," Mia said. "James can just blow out the candles."

James glared at her and then blew out the candles. Miss Nithercott clapped and switched on the light. She cut the cake and handed pieces to James and Mia. She cut one for herself and sat.

"James, you are seventeen today, and I thought you deserved something more exciting than a new shirt." Miss Nithercott went to the kitchen and returned with a large box wrapped in paper. She put it on the table near James, who had not yet touched his cake. "Open it."

James ripped the paper off the box. It contained a boombox, one he had admired in the variety store window. His eyebrows rose, and the color returned to his cheeks.

"It's…I can't believe you bought me this."

"Well, I wanted to get you something special. It works with batteries so you can take it outside."

"We can take it out later," Mia said. She slipped something across the table to James. "This is my present."

James picked up the small box and ripped off the paper. It was a cassette by Madonna.

"We can listen to it later," Mia said.

"Oh, isn't that nice, James?" Miss Nithercott said.

"It's wonderful," James said. "I can't believe it."

"I'm so happy you liked it," Miss Nithercott said. "Now, don't let that cake go to waste."

James and Mia stayed at the table until Miss Nithercott rose to leave. They waited for her to go to the sitting room to watch the telly, and then Mia went upstairs to grab a blanket from her bed. James took the boom box to the garden behind the house.

The fountain at the center was surrounded by grass and cement benches at four corners. Mia lay the blanket on the grass so they could lie down and watch the moon rising over the woods. James lay down and watched her put the cassette tape into the boombox. Soon, violins heralded the beginning of *Papa Don't Preach*, and Mia began to dance. The large moon in the navy blue sky was behind her as James watched her gyrating with the music. Mia was a good dancer, and she entertained him doing a moonwalk like Michael Jackson. James saw her breasts moving under her dress and wanted her to come to him, but Mia stayed just out of his reach until the song ended. When the next song came on, Mia came to James, unbuckled his jeans, and straddled his body. She lifted her dress over her head, let it fall behind her, and placed James' hands on her breasts.

"Happy Birthday," she said.

She kissed him, and James put his arms around her.

Chapter Seventeen

MISS NITHERCOTT ROSE WITH THE SUN. IT WAS FESTIVAL DAY, and she was eager to attend. She had already made arrangements to meet a friend at the pub for it was the only day she allowed herself to drink a pint or two. She put on her sensible shoes and went down to the dining table.

James and Mia were in his bed, and James winced as he heard Miss Nithercott walking by his room. He held his breath, half-expecting her to pop in to remind him it was festival day, and he didn't breathe again until she heard her footsteps fade away.

Mia slept soundly, and he watched her chest rise and fall. They had two more nights together before she went home, and he was still trying to find some way to keep her in England. She turned on her side and opened her eyes for a second before closing them again. James reached for her, but it was still early, so he got out of bed and took a shower.

When James came out of the bathroom, Mia was gone, so he got dressed, thinking he would see her at breakfast. James knocked on Mia's door, and when she didn't answer, he opened it and peeked inside. Mia was sitting on the edge of the bed with a tissue in her hand.

"Are you all right?" he asked.

"I'm fine. I'll be down in a minute."

James closed the door, listened for a minute, and then headed downstairs. Miss Nithercott was fixing her plate at the sideboard, so he sat and waited for her to sit.

"I think Mia is crying," he said.

"She's upset about leaving," Miss Nithercott said.

"Is that all?"

"Why, yes, James. What else would it be?"

"I'm not sure." He cocked his head toward the foyer. "Would you be upset if we didn't go to the festival with you?"

"Oh, James, you love the festival, and Mia has never been so you must share it with her."

"I'd rather spend the day alone with her," James said.

Miss Nithercott poured some milk in her tea and bit her lip as she stirred it.

"You promised to take her. I think she's excited to go."

"She didn't say that to me," James said.

"Well, she said it to me, so let's just have a nice breakfast."

James got up, filled a plate, and then Mia appeared.

"So, are we still going to the festival?" she asked.

"We don't have to," James said.

"I'd like to go," Mia said. "Miss Nithercott tells me it's not as boring as it sounds."

"It's not boring at all," Miss Nithercott said.

"It's just a lot of local sods getting drunk and slashing swords about," James said.

"It's nothing of the sort." Miss Nithercott's withering gaze amused Mia, who put just one slice of toast on her plate.

"I would still like to see it," Mia said. "And I want to see it with you." Her eyes met James,' and he smiled.

"Fine, but I'll make you see it all."

"I'd better wear my sneakers."

When they'd finished breakfast, Miss Nithercott went to the garage and brought the old Rover to the front door. James and Mia got in the back seat and held hands.

The car park in front of Peterson's farm was already half-full when they turned off the road. The farm was a mile away from town, and everyone got out and walked to Baker Street. Miss Nithercott was sweating by the time they reached the park, and she sat on a bench while Mia and James walked down Baker Street where the annual vendors had set up their wagons.

"I usually go to the demonstrations in the park," James said.

"The swordsman," Mia said.

"Yeah."

"I'll go with you."

James stopped in front of the bakery and leaned against the window.

"I'm not really in the mood," James said. "Let's just walk for a while."

The vendors were animated as they tried to whip up enthusiasm for the same wares they hawked every year. Those who'd been to the festival before walked by with nary a glance, but first-timers strained their necks to see what was being offered. A charm wagon was parked in front of the chemist's, and James spotted it before Mia.

"See that charm wagon?" he asked. "My family has been trying to get her banned for years."

"Why?" Mia asked.

James stood straight and put his hand on his chest.

"The Church of England does not tolerate this pagan nonsense." He grinned. "I used to buy things from her just to piss off my father."

"He doesn't seem very religious," Mia said.

"He's not. He just feels that since the church was built by a Huxley, he has to protect his reputation."

They stopped in front of the charm wagon, and Mia smiled at the woman sitting on a stool behind a table of charms. She had warm eyes and smiled.

"You're an American," the woman said.

"How did you know?" Mia asked.

"I have a gift."

Mia missed James' smirk and went up to the table.

"I am Rotrude," the woman said.

"I'm Mia. This is James."

Rotrude studied James' face.

"You are a Huxley."

"That's not hard to guess," James said. "Everyone around here knows me."

Rotrude focused her attention on Mia.

"So, you have been staying at the manor house," Rotrude said.

"Just for the summer."

Mia saw a rack of necklaces and took one off the rack. She held up the gold disk and saw a cottage etched on its surface.

"This is cute," Mia said.

"The disk chooses its owner," Rotrude said.

"Bollocks," James said softly.

"You're a skeptic." Rotrude slid off her stool and walked up to James. "What do you believe in, James?"

"I don't believe in your bloody magic if that's what you're asking."

"James!" Mia cried.

"What do you know about me, James? Did you know that I was here when the king cut off Symond's head and gave the earldom to a Huxley?"

"So, you're crazy, too," James said.

"Symond was a monster. He performed blood sacrifices. The altar is still in the woods. The bloodstains have washed away, but the cries of those who died can still be heard when the moon is full."

"Oh, for God's sake," James said.

"We saw that altar," Mia said. "You remember that altar, James."

Rotrude tilted her head back and looked up at James with a sly smile, and then she grew serious.

"She's still alive, you know," Rotrude said.

Mia stared at Rotrude, but James looked down the street.

"Who's still alive?" Mia asked.

Rotrude put her hand on James' cheek and turned his face toward hers.

"She came to me because she had no choice."

"Who are you talking about?" Mia asked, and then her eyes lit up. "Margaret. You're talking about Margaret."

"People come to me when they have no choice," Rotrude said. "People come because they are desperate." Rotrude put her hand on James' arm. "It's important that you understand this."

James shook her hand off and walked across the street. Mia watched him go and then looked at the necklace.

"Where is she?" Mia asked.

"Somewhere safe," Rotrude said.

"Can she come back if she wants to?"

"She isn't a prisoner."

118

Rotrude took the necklace from Mia's hand.

"I want that," Mia said as she reached into her purse for her wallet.

Rotrude went behind the table and slipped it into a brown bag. She brought it to Mia, put it in her hand, and wrapped her own hand around Mia's.

"This is a special disk," Rotrude said. "If you ever find yourself in dire need, put it on and let the disk lead you to the cottage in the woods."

"How much is it?" Mia asked.

"It's a gift," Rotrude said.

James returned, grabbed Mia's arm, and led her away from the charm wagon.

"Hey!" Mia cried.

"She's a fake," James said.

"Let go of me."

Mia shrugged off his hand and looked back at Rotrude. She saw a tear roll down Rotrude's face.

"She gave me the creeps," James said.

"I liked her," Mia said.

James saw the bag in Mia's hand.

"You didn't buy that thing," he said.

"No. She gave it to me."

"You're not going to keep it, are you?"

Mia stopped, forcing James to turn and look at her. Her mouth was set in a hard line.

"I like it, James, and I'm going to wear it."

Mia took the necklace out of the bag and put it on. James saw a faint glow outline the cottage, and a chill went up his spine.

"Take it off," he said.

"No."

"Please, Mia."

She walked past him, and James wanted to grab her arm but stopped himself. They wandered down Baker Street and found Miss Nithercott sitting at a table outside the pub with the librarian, Miss Naugle. She smiled and waved, and they walked over to her.

"Hello, James," Miss Naugle said.

"Hello," James said.

"Your friend misfiled those spools."

Mia blushed.

"I'm sure Mia didn't mean anything by it," Miss Nithercott said. "She's a good girl."

"I'm sure," Miss Naugle said.

"We're just having a pint." Miss Nithercott held up her mug. "I shouldn't be more than half an hour."

"We can walk home," James said.

"Then I won't look for you," Miss Nithercott said.

Miss Naugle looked down her nose at Mia as they walked away.

"She had to say I misfiled those spools," Mia said.

"She's a miserable twat," James said.

Mia giggled. "Be careful, or she'll hear you."

"I don't care if she does." He glanced at Mia. "Are we okay?"

"As long as you stop trying to control me, we'll be fine."

"I wasn't trying to control you. I just got this creepy feeling when I saw…"

James hesitated, and Mia stopped walking.

"When you saw what?"

James smiled.

"Nothing. I just didn't like the way she looked at me."

He put his arm around Mia as they walked past the park and onto the road leading to Huxley Manor. Other strollers passed them walking toward the village, and James realized that no one had been stationed by the ruins to keep visitors away.

"Shit," he said.

"What?"

"We forgot to hire guards to stand by the ruins. If someone gets hurt, we could be liable."

"I wondered what they were doing down here."

"My father will have a fit when he finds out."

"Who is supposed to hire the guards?" Mia asked.

"Miss Nithercott. It's not like her to forget."

"He won't fire her, will he?"

"I hope not, but I am seventeen now. He might have planned to do it anyway."

"So this will give him an excuse," Mia said. "What will happen to her?"

"She'll find another position." James let his arm fall to his side. "But he might not give her references. She's been with me since I was six. He has to give her a good reference."

Mia took James' hand and squeezed it.

"Race you to the end of the road," she said.

Mia took off before James, but he had longer legs, and he soon passed her. He stopped at the drive and waited for her as she jogged to the finish line. She fell into his arms and wrapped her arms around him.

"Let's go to the attic," she said.

"You're not too tired?" he asked.

"Never."

James put his arm around her, and she leaned against him as they walked to the house. When they got inside, he pulled her arm as they walked up the stairs, and then again as they went up to the attic. He even helped her take off her trainers, her blouse, her shorts, and her panties. As Mia lay down, she smiled sweetly.

"I love you," she said.

James saw the necklace on her chest and cringed, but he forced a smile.

"I love you, too."

He lay beside her, and she snuggled against his chest. The disk fell onto his chest, and James felt its heat. Was Mia aware of it? Fear kept him from saying anything for he didn't want them to fight again. These were their last hours together. He didn't want to spoil them with a row.

They fell asleep in each other's arms and didn't wake until Miss Nithercott called up the stairs to let them know that Lord Harold had arrived and that they had to come to the dinner table.

Chapter Eighteen

WHEN JAMES CAME DOWN TO BREAKFAST THE FOLLOWING morning, he was in a sullen mood. His father's presence in the house had kept them apart, and he hadn't seen Mia that morning. If felt as if a part of him was missing.

Harold was sitting at the table with Miss Nithercott. His lordship didn't look up from his newspaper, but Miss Nithercott smiled broadly.

"Good morning, James!" she cried, causing Lord Harold to shift his gaze from his paper to his son standing at the entrance to the dining room.

"It's about time," Lord Harold said.

James went to the sideboard, poured a cup of coffee, and then held the cup as if it had magical powers. He sat across from Miss Nithercott, who seemed a bit off balance.

"Miss Nithercott tells me that she forgot to hire guards to keep onlookers away from the ruins during the festival," Harold said.

"No one was here when I came home," James said.

"But it's standard procedure. Someone might have gotten hurt. You're seventeen-years-old now, James. You should have reminded Miss Nithercott about the guards."

James closed his eyes and gripped his cup.

"Right," James said.

Harold put his newspaper down and glared at his son.

"And what does that mean?"

"Nothing. It means nothing."

Harold looked at his own empty teacup and rang the bell beside his plate. Hughes emerged from the kitchen, grabbed the teapot from the sideboard, and filled Harold's teacup. He then returned to the kitchen, and Harold returned his attention to his son.

"I know how you've spent your holiday. Miss Nithercott has brought me up to speed. But that is over now. You will begin preparations for the new term tomorrow, and I expect a better performance this year. It's your last term. I've spoken to a friend at Cambridge about you. As my son, you will be considered, but you must rise to the occasion, James. The things you do over the next few years will determine the rest of your life."

"Your life, you mean," James said.

Harold's lower lip trembled, and he tore his newspaper when he set it down.

"This is all a joke to you, isn't it? You sit up there in your little tower reading those ridiculous books without giving one thought to the example you set. You represent this family, James. I don't care about what you want, is that clear? It has never been about what you want, but about our heritage."

"Does that include Margaret?"

Harold's face grew red, and Miss Nithercott feared he would have a stroke.

"This conversation is over."

Harold got up and left the room while Miss Nithercott eyed James with compassion.

"You are seventeen now, James."

"He doesn't give a shit about me," James said.

"Language!" she said, and then shook her head. "Lord Harold must think about the future of this house."

"Then, he should have another son."

"James."

"Seriously. He should remarry and have another son. He's never been happy with me."

"I'm sure he loves you in his way," Miss Nithercott said.

"Bollocks," James said softly.

"James, please."

"Sorry."

Miss Nithercott clasped her hands on the table.

"Have you seen Mia this morning?" she said softly. "Is she still sleeping?"

"She's in her room, packing."

"Look, I know how hard this is for you, but don't ruin your last day together by brooding about your father. Take her to town. Have a nice lunch."

Miss Nithercott took a ten-pound note from her pocket and slid it across the table.

James looked at the note for a moment, and then took it from her.

"I'll tell her it's from you," James said.

"That's not why I gave it to you…"

James stood. "I'm going back upstairs."

"You didn't eat your breakfast."

James left the dining room and climbed the stairs two at a time. He went to Mia's room and found her still in her night-gown, sitting on the edge of the bed next to her suitcase. She had the gold disk in her hand.

"Hey," he said.

She looked up, and he saw that her eyes were red.

"Hey," she said.

"I just saw my father. He's a right bastard that one."

Mia smiled wanly.

"Come and sit by me," she said.

James went to her and took the suitcase off the bed. He sat beside her and put his arm around her.

"When you're done, we should walk to town. I have money for lunch."

"That sounds nice," Mia said.

"And then we can go to the attic."

Mia snuggled against him.

"To read your books."

"Of course." James kissed her forehead. "We left Frodo and Sam on Mount Doom."

Mia began to sob into his shoulder, and James put both arms around her.

"I'll come to America," he said.

"You can't."

"I'll find a way."

"You have to finish school," Mia said between sobs.

"I don't give a shit about school."

"Please, James, stop." She pulled away and wiped her eyes with the back of her hand. "I'm gonna get dressed so we can walk to town."

Mia got up, grabbed some clothes from a chair, and took them into the bathroom. James looked inside her suitcase and saw the gauze dress she'd worn on his birthday. He ran his hand over the fabric and remembered how her breasts swayed when she danced. The ache in his heart grew, as did his anger at his father.

Mia came out of the bathroom and went to the chest of drawers. She brushed her hair and pinched her cheeks.

"That will have to do," she said.

"You look beautiful," James said.

She smiled. "You're just being nice."

James came to her and wrapped his arms around her.

"You are beautiful," he said.

Mia lay her head on his chest.

"We could just go to the attic," she said.

"If that's what you want."

They went up to the attic and lay on the divan in semi-darkness. Gray clouds prevented the sun from brightening the room, but the gloom matched their moods. It was oddly comforting.

"My father talked to someone at Cambridge," James said.

"That's a good school."

"I dread going there."

Mia lifted her head and looked into his eyes.

"Why?"

"Because he will view it as a competition that I am destined to lose. It will satisfy him to see me fail."

"That doesn't make sense," Mia said. "You are the next in line, right? Wouldn't he want you to do well?"

James studied her almond-shaped blue eyes and the fringe of light blond bangs above them. Her full lips and pink cheeks invited a kiss, but James resisted as he memorized her face.

"Yes," he said. "I guess he would."

"I'm graduating in June," Mia said. "I'll be seventeen, but once I'm out, I'll come back."

"And I'll be waiting."

"I'm counting on it."

Now, James kissed her, a long, passionate kiss that they held onto for dear life. As he responded to his physical desires, Mia let him take off her blouse and kiss her neck. She ran her hand over his hair as tears rolled down the sides of her face, and she moaned when James kissed her breasts.

Chapter Nineteen

DINNER WAS A SAD AFFAIR WITH JAMES AND MIA STARING AT EACH other, and Harold unaware of the emotions that crisscrossed the table. Miss Nithercott, however, saw something that she hadn't believed until this day. It wasn't just a crush or puppy love between the two, it was real love, and the pain they were going through was so palpable that Miss Nithercott found Lord Harold's indifference unbearable. She wished she could save them, to find them a place of their own, and take them from the adults in their lives who seemed unwilling or unable to care for them. But Miss Nithercott didn't have the means to save them, so she tried to keep Lord Harold's attention on something other than his disappointment in James.

"The constable told me that he had posted a man in front of the ruins yesterday," she said. "He said he thought I had contacted him as I always do, so he sent a man to keep an eye on things."

"Well, then, I guess he's pulled both of you out of the fire," Harold said.

"Yes, indeed," Miss Nithercott said.

As each course was served, Lord Harold would make some inane remark, but no one at that table heard him, for they were caught up in the drama unfolding as James and Mia thought about her leaving in the morning. Miss Nithercott feared how James might react when she walked out the door and hoped that the black dog would stay away. She remembered what happened when his mother died. He had been inconsolable for months.

"I'm expecting you to be dressed and ready to leave the house at six," Harold told Mia. When she didn't reply, he focused his gaze on her. "Mia. I'm speaking to you." At the sound of her name, Mia turned her head toward Harold. "Six. I expect you to have your bag at the door by six tomorrow morning."

Mia's hand shook as she lifted her fork and moved her food around on the plate.

"I'll be ready."

James clenched his teeth and fisted his hands under the table.

"I want to go with you."

"Don't be ridiculous, James," Lord Harold said. "I'm not returning until the end of the month, and you have work to do."

"I want to go to the airport."

Harold put down his fork.

"Get over it, boy. Say your goodbyes and let her go. You're both far too young for this nonsense."

"Nonsense!" James cried. "You stupid, bloody, bastard. I love her."

"What did you call me?" Harold's face was bright red.

James stood. "You can't understand us because you've never loved anyone."

"Mind your tongue, boy," Harold said. "Why, I should put you out of this house."

"Do it. Do you really think I'd care?"

"Get out of my sight." Harold saw Mia rise from her chair. "Let him go. You stay and finish your dinner."

Mia glared at him and then ran after James. She overheard Harold threatening to send James to Hong Kong to live with his uncle before following James up the stairs.

Mia thought he would go to the attic, but James went to his room and slammed the door. The sound echoed down the staircase, which Harold was sure to hear. She turned the knob on James' door, but it was locked, so she sat on the floor beside the door.

"James," she said. "Open the door."

Miss Nithercott came up the stairs and saw Mia on the floor. She took a key out of her pocket and unlocked the door.

"Make sure he's all right," Miss Nithercott said.

Mia opened the door, went inside, and closed it behind her. James was lying on his bed, facing the window. The gray clouds hadn't lifted, and the room was dark. Mia got into bed, put her arms around his chest, and leaned her forehead against his back.

"Miss Nithercott is worried about you," she said.

"I'm fine."

"This is my last night here, James. Please don't do this."

James rolled onto his back and put his hand on her cheek.

"I hate him," he said.

"I know."

"I can't stand being here."

"It's only one more year. Finish school, and you can get a job."

"He won't let me go," James said.

"I heard him say he would send you to Hong Kong."

"No, he won't because he knows that would make me happy."

Mia got up on one elbow.

"Let's go upstairs."

"We could stay right here and lock the door," James said.

"But upstairs is our place. I want to spend my last night here where we fell in love."

She slid off the bed, and he followed her to the door. Mia peeked into the hallway and then took James' hand and led him to the attic. He struck a match and lit the wick in the oil lamp before joining Mia on the divan.

They fell asleep, and when James woke, it was still dark. He found Mia sitting on the legless chair. She'd turned off the oil lamp and the moon cast its light on James' face. She'd been watching him sleep, but all he could see was her foot in the moonlight.

"How long have you been awake?" he asked.

"A long time."

"Come back here."

"I need to tell you something," Mia said.

James rolled onto his back.

"Okay."

"I didn't tell you before because you kept telling me you wanted to marry me, and that you wouldn't let me go, and I knew if I told you this, you'd do something crazy, and I can't let you do that."

James got up on one elbow.

"What is it, Mia?" James sat on the edge of the divan. "What haven't you told me?"

Mia bit her lip.

"My mother has boyfriends."

"You told me that."

"Don't talk, just listen. She has boyfriends, and she brings them home to live with us. They...look at me. I even woke up one night and found one standing over my bed. When I told my mother, she told me not to walk around the house in my night-gown. When I told her about the one near my bed, she told me to keep my door locked."

"Shit."

"None of them has ever touched me, but now, well, I look like this." She cupped her breasts. "You couldn't keep your hands off me."

James reached out and put his hand on her arm.

"Kick them in the balls," he said.

"I'm not big, James. I don't know if I could stop them, and my mother would blame me if anything happened."

"Tell your father," James said.

"My father. How many times has he come to see me while I'm here?" James sat and exhaled loudly. "I worked hard, James. I did really well in school. It was something *I* wanted, and now I want to graduate with *my* class. I'm not gonna let them take that away from me."

"Why did you wait so long to tell me this?" James asked.

"Because I knew you would get all weirded out, and we would just fight over it all the time." She leaned closer to him. "I just wanted us to be happy."

James exhaled loudly.

"Do you have someone you can go to, like an aunt or uncle?"

Mia shook her head.

"If I did, I would have already." She picked up James' hand and kissed it.

"I *will* come to America," James said. "I'll stay with you and keep them away."

"Do you know how ridiculous that sounds?" She let go of his hand and sighed. "I'll just have to keep my door locked."

James hung his head, and Mia put her hand on his cheek.

"I'll come back next year. We'll both be out of school. We can get jobs, and we'll get our own flat."

"And no one can stop us." James kissed her palm and then looked into her eyes. "I love you."

"I love you, too."

"I want to save you."

"I know. I'll be all right."

Mia went to the divan. James lay down, and she curled up beside him. The warmth of her body was the sweetest thing he'd ever known, and his heart ached as he thought of her leaving in the morning.

James fell asleep with her in his arms. He dreamed of slashing swords and bloody lords, one bearing Lord Harold's head. He opened his eyes when he lopped off Harold's head and reached for Mia, only to discover that she had gone.

James Huxley

1996

Chapter Twenty

BIXBY'S BREWHOUSE WAS ON HAVERTY ROAD IN MORSETON, just off the main motorway. Its clientele consisted of pensioners and working men who stopped by for a pint on their way home. The atmosphere was congenial, and the patrons attributed the pub's renewed success to publican James Huxley.

When Calvin Bixby was diagnosed with lung cancer, he worried about who would run the pub when he was gone. It had belonged to the Bixby family since 1925. His diagnosis forced Calvin to make a decision, the hardest he had ever made. His only child, a daughter named Maryanne, believed that the pub would one day be hers, but Calvin, like many men of his age, feared she would marry or be unable to handle the responsibility of a business and placed an ad in the Sunday Times seeking a buyer. He kept this from Maryanne, a spirited young woman who wasn't afraid to speak her mind, for had she known what Calvin was planning to do, Maryanne would have made what was left of Calvin's life unbearable.

James Huxley, future Earl of Dorley, had been at loose ends following a contentious divorce, and he asked his father for a loan that would enable him to buy a pub he'd seen advertised in the Times. The conversation had taken place in Harold's study after a rather large Christmas dinner.

"A pub?" Harold said. "This is what you want to do."

"I need something of my own," James said. "I talked to Uncle Billy, and he said it seems like a sound investment."

"Of course, William would say that. He's always had a soft spot for the working class."

"There's nothing wrong with work," James said.

"If it's work you want, you can finish your education so you can take my place when I retire."

James slumped in his chair and then straightened his back.

"I've no desire to return to school, and you know better than anyone how ill-suited I am for a position in the bank." James felt his chest tighten as he fisted his hands. "This is something I can do. I'd have my own business. It comes with a flat, and Uncle Billy says I could pay you back within a year."

"Bloody William," Harold said. "Why doesn't he lend you the damn money?"

"He's given me half of the twenty-five thousand I need. It includes the land, Father. It's a good deal."

"It's foolishness, but if you are determined to make a bloody fool of yourself, then I won't stop you. I'll give you the money, and I expect it to be paid back in a timely manner." Harold leaned forward. "But that's all you'll be getting from me, James. Don't come back here looking for more."

James left the manor house with a check and an admonition that he not use the family name in connection with the pub.

With the money in hand, James bought Calvin Bixby's pub and signed a contract stating that Maryanne Bixby would always have a job there as long as she wanted one. James didn't mind having Maryanne for she knew everything about the business, and the patrons knew her. What he didn't know was that Maryanne had a temper that made grown men shiver in their boots. Sometimes, he was happy to let her handle the more difficult patrons, and at other times, James would find things to do that allowed him to keep his distance from her.

James paid his father back in one year, and his Uncle Billy in three. He found the life of a publican suited him. The men he served liked James, and work kept him focused for the first time since Mia Wentworth disappeared.

* * *

TEN YEARS HAD PASSED SINCE MIA LEFT HIM. THE YEARS HADN'T softened the pain he felt whenever she came to mind, and his memory of her had cost James his marriage to a woman he'd met in college who chose not to compete with the memory of James' perfect girl and filed for divorce after three months.

But when he was in the pub, James felt at home. The patrons respected him and called him "mate." He sang when they sang, and hoisted a pint with them when their football team won. It was a good life, and James loved it.

One rainy Wednesday in October, James went to unlock the door when he spied something sitting on the concrete stoop. It was a package, and it was heavy when James picked it up and took it inside. It had been sent from Woollcott.

James recalled seeing the exit for Woollcott on the motorway. It was halfway between Morseton and Dorley. He sat at a table with the box between his feet and examined the name of the package sender, a Lily Profitt, someone unfamiliar to James. He took out his penknife, slashed the tape, and lifted the flaps on the box. A handwritten note sat on its contents.

DEAR JAMES,

MY NAME IS LILY PROFITT. I WAS HETTIE NITHERCOTT'S landlady. Hettie passed away on October 2 after suffering a heart attack.

I was very fond of Hettie. We would often take tea in the afternoons, and she would tell me about her "children." You were a particular favorite of hers. She had talked about traveling to Morseton many times, but she was never in the best of health.

This box contains Hettie's possessions. I was hoping you might know how to get in touch with her family. Her sister is in a care home, but I thought you might know if she had other relations. Also enclosed is an urn containing her ashes.

James, she often said she was proud of the man you'd become. I believe she would have wanted me to tell you. Again, I offer my deepest condolences.

YOURS SINCERELY,

LILY PROFITT

. . .

AFTER JAMES READ THE NOTE, HE RECALLED THE LAST TIME HE saw Miss Nithercott. It was in Dorley shortly after his divorce. She was living in a small flat above a business, and he visited her before leaving for Morseton. She had no tea or cookies to offer him, but they spent an hour talking about the past.

When he left her, he promised her he would try to help her find a new position. He was unable to find one, and he thought of giving her a job at the pub, but Maryanne was all the help James could afford at the time. He kept meaning to call Miss Nithercott but was always in the midst of something he couldn't ignore, and soon she disappeared from his thoughts.

Hettie Nithercott had been good to him when he needed someone to be kind. James had lived with the black dog since childhood, and Hettie had always found a way to comfort him. She helped him deal with those dark emotions, and now he felt the black dog beckoning, but James refused to entertain him.

James shook the dog off and did what he had learned to do whenever his emotions tried to control him – he replaced them with happier thoughts and a shot of whiskey. Sometimes it worked; other times, he would have to push through the exhaustion until the darkness lifted.

James picked up the box and put it behind the bar. He poured a shot of whiskey and held it up.

"To you, Miss Nithercott," he said before draining the glass.

James eyed the box. He knelt down, flipped the lid, and went through its contents – some clothes, a few books, and old photographs. The sad remains of a life spent in service to others. As he went to close it, he saw something shining at the bottom of the box. He lifted a plastic bag out of the box and held it up. It contained two necklaces fashioned from one silver coin. Each half of the coin had a hole at the top and a black leather strap for a chain.

James opened the bag, pulled one half out, and examined the picture embossed on its surface. It was the head of a stag with an eight-point rack. He turned the coin over and saw half an inscription.

This is the Silver Stag
and cast by Greyson.

James pulled the other half out and read the back.

fashioned by Rotrude,

Use with caution.

Rotrude had been the witch who ran the charm wagon during the festival in Dorley. James had visited it one time with Mia. Rotrude had given Mia a gold disk. James couldn't find the disk with her belongings after Mia...

The bell on the front door rang, and James put the necklaces back into the plastic bag and dropped the bag into the box. He shoved the box under the bar with his foot.

Artie Caraway, a local pensioner and retired headmaster who lived two houses away, came through the door. He hung his cap and jacket on a stand by the door, took his place on his stool, looked at the bar, and then stared at James.

"Crisps?" Artie said.

James saw the empty bowl. He reached for a new bag of crisps from underneath the bar, filled that bowl, and then filled the others on the bar. Another one of James' "boys" came in. Eighty-six-year-old Devon Brady hung his hat and coat on the stand. James filled two pints from the tap, placed one in front of Artie, and placed the other in front of the adjacent stool.

Chapter Twenty-One

James was leaning against the back of the bar with his arms folded across his chest. The old men watched him and then exchanged glances.

"I know that look," Artie said.

"'e's got somethin' on 'is mind," Devon said.

"I'll bet it's a woman," Artie said.

"Aye, that's the look. Tell us 'er name, James."

James smiled. "Wouldn't tell you lot." He grabbed a towel from his waist and wiped the bar. "You gossip like a bunch of old hens." James threw the towel over his shoulder, placed his hands on the bar, and then leaned toward them. "It's not a woman. I've just found out that a dear friend has passed away."

"Oh," Artie said. "Sorry, mate."

The door opened, and Old Smythe shuffled in. He hung his things on the stand and hobbled to the bar to take his place next to Devon.

"What can I get for you?" James asked.

"You need to ask?" Old Smythe said.

Devon looked at Old Smythe's dirty shirt and pursed his lips. He also caught sight of a car driving by the window.

"Brace yourselves, boys."

James smiled as they all hunkered down, awaiting the storm to come. A few minutes later, Maryann Bixby came through the kitchen door. A short woman in her early twenties, Maryanne struck fear in the pensioners' hearts. She was James' enforcer, the one who made sure their bar bills were paid in full. Any patron who failed to pay their bill in full by week's end was banished until they received their monthly allotments.

Maryanne had a booming voice and long brown hair. She wore jeans, T-shirts, and trainers to work every day and rarely smiled. Now she put her hands on her hips and eyed the pensioners.

"It's the same cluster of miscreants and layabouts I see, is it? Well, it's the end of the week, lads, and you lot know what that means." She went behind the bar, reached for something, and then held up the accounts book with a gleam in her eye. "So, who wants to go first?"

Grumbling ensued as the boys reached into their pockets. Crumpled bills and coins were put on the bar. Maryann tilted her head back so she could look down her nose, and she tapped her foot for good measure. She gathered the money and entered the amounts into her ledger.

"You're two-pound short," she told Artie. "You're cut off until you're paid in full."

"But I don't get my pension till the end of the month."

"And what's that to me, eh?"

The scene would play out with each man who arrived until she had settled all the accounts.

When Maryanne went back to the kitchen, Devon and Old Smythe were smiling, but Artie looked sad as he nursed his pint. When Maryanne returned, James tilted his head toward her.

"You know they don't all get paid at the same time, luv," James said softly.

"They know the rules," Maryanne said.

"But what harm would it do to let them go once in a while," James said.

"You're too soft. They take advantage of you."

"But some of them…this is all they have."

Maryanne came close to James. The top of her head reached the center of his chest, but when she stared into his eyes, he took a step back.

"Me Da never let them get away with it. You grow a backbone, James Huxley, or you'll be begging for beer from me when I take this place away from you."

"You don't mean that," James said.

"Try me." Maryanne took a step back. "Did the mail come?"

James pulled envelopes from beneath the bar and handed them to her. She returned to the kitchen, and James felt the men's eyes on him.

"Why don't ye knock 'er down a time or two?" Old Smythe asked.

"Aye," Devon said. "Ye can take 'er."

James put his hands on his hips and smiled.

"Forget it, mates," he said. "She scares the daylights out of me."

The men laughed and shook their heads. The bell on the door rang, and a young man came in. All heads turned, and Artie nodded at the man. He came to the bar and sat at the end away from the kitchen door.

"Who's he?" James whispered to Artie.

"You'll see."

The men whispered and glanced at the stranger while James went to take his order. He was about to open his mouth when Maryanne burst out of the kitchen. She let her gaze drift past the old boys and stopped when she saw the young man. The pensioners were transfixed as they watched her walk to the other end of the bar. She stopped a few feet away from him, and then Maryanne put her hands on her hips.

"So, what's it to be today?" she asked. She glanced at the pensioners. "Sandwiches or fish and chips?"

"Where do you get your fish?" the young man asked.

James was standing between the man and Maryanne when he saw the look on her face.

"Why do you need to know?" she asked.

"Because I know the markets hereabouts, and I know which ones I can trust."

"And you think I don't?"

Maryanne took a few steps toward him. The young man didn't cower. He straightened his back and looked her in the eye.

"Which market?" he asked.

Maryanne's lip quivered, and her hands fisted.

"Bloody cheek," she said.

The young man tilted his head forward.

"Which market?"

The pensioners were riveted as they watched the young man

defy Maryanne. She was pressed up against James' back, and when she tried to move around him, James moved to block her path.

"You listen to me," Maryanne said. "I've been buying fish since I was six-year-old. No one has ever gotten sick in my pub."

The young man smiled and tilted his head back.

"Well, then, I vote for fish and chips."

James relaxed when Maryanne took a step back. She gave the young man one last withering look before returning to the kitchen. The young man smiled as he looked at James.

"A half-pint of bitters."

James grabbed a mug and filled it while sizing up the young man.

"So, I haven't seen you here before."

"It's been a while," the young man said.

"I'm James by the way."

"Kirby. Tom."

They shook hands.

"And that charming lady was Maryanne."

"Charming, is it?" Tom smiled.

"Aye." James looked over his shoulder. "She can be when it suits her. So, do you live around here?"

"I was born here. I live on Regency Hill."

"Why haven't I seen you before?"

"I wasn't sure how she'd feel about it," Tom said.

James' eyebrows rose.

"Maryanne?" James smiled. "You and Maryanne?"

"We went together when her father owned the place." Tom took a sip of his beer. "I can honestly say she hasn't changed a bit."

"She was always like this?" James asked.

"Aye, she was."

"Why did you break up?"

"She caught me with her friend and cracked me over the head with a glass ashtray."

James cringed. "Aye, mate, that would do it then."

"I guess she's still mad at me," Tom said.

"I wouldn't think she'd be one to hold a grudge," James said.

He winked, and Tom smiled.

"She's a right angel she is," Tom said.

The pensioners laughed, and James nodded his head. They reminisced about Tom and Maryanne's relationship, which had begun while they were in school.

"She were sixteen," Devon said.

"Sixteen?" James asked.

"Aye," Tom said.

"Was she like this when she was sixteen?"

"Aye." Tom winked. "I liked the challenge."

A half and hour later, Maryanne burst through the door with a plate of fish and chips, which she slid across the bar to Tom so hard that some of the chips landed in his lap.

"I'll 'ave some," Devon said.

Maryanne glared at poor old Devon and then stomped back to the kitchen.

"You take your life in your hands sometimes, Dev," James said.

"I'm 'ungry."

"Ye should 'ave waited a bit before pokin' the dragon," Old Smythe said.

"I'm not afraid of 'er," Devon said.

James and Old Smythe exchanged glances, and then James pretended to wipe the bar when Maryanne burst through the kitchen door and tossed the plate at Devon. The old man was quicker than anyone thought he could be and managed to catch the plate with the food still intact. Old Smythe suppressed a smile, and James turned his head away until they heard her go back through the kitchen door.

"'ow'd ye catch that?" Old Smythe asked.

"Me wife throws plates," Devon said.

"I don't understand why you all come here," James said. "You could go to Hannigan's and avoid the abuse."

"We like the publican 'ere," Old Smythe said.

James smiled, put one arm across his waist, and bowed.

"I aim to please."

The afternoon passed with a few changes in the clientele, but by seven, the pensioners were gone and the working men had taken their places at the bar. They were a rowdy bunch who bought more beer and kept James on his toes. At eleven, Maryanne would sit on a stool at the end of the bar sipping wine and tallying the day's receipts. By two, the working men were gone, and James was sweeping the floor and counting the darts in the dartboard.

"What's this?" she asked.

"What's what?"

"The box under the bar?"

"Someone died and left it to me," James said.

"Who died?"

"Someone I knew."

"And who was that?"

"Jesus," James said. "It's none of your bloody business."

"Then it shouldn't be under the bar."

"I didn't have time to take it upstairs."

"So, who died?"

James placed his hands on the edge of the bar and hung his head.

"My old governess."

Maryanne smiled broadly.

"Oh, so it's his lordship's *governess*."

James glared at her.

"Yes, my old governess. Go ahead and laugh. Get it out of your system."

Maryanne's smile faded, and she tilted her head.

"Sorry she died."

"Yeah, me too," James said.

"I didn't know you had a governess."

"I didn't know you had an ex-boyfriend."

"That bastard," she said.

"So, maybe we should just talk about something else."

Maryanne finished counting the till and shut it with a bang that echoed off the lino. She slipped off the stool and went to the kitchen. James took the box upstairs and set it down near the settee. A few minutes later, Maryanne shouted up the stairs.

"I'm leaving."

"Make sure the doors are locked," he said.

"You could come down and watch me get into me car."

James' shoulders ached, but he went downstairs and stood at the back door while Maryanne got inside her car. When she drove away, James went to the office to check the balance in the accounts book. The pub was making enough to keep it open, but he wouldn't see a raise this year. Still, he loved the place and wouldn't change it for the world.

James went upstairs, washed up, and then went to bed. For the first time in a long time, he dreamed of Mia, the love of his life, and when he woke up, there were tears in his eyes.

Chapter Twenty-Two

JAMES STUMBLED OUT OF BED AND WENT TO THE LOO. IMAGES OF Mia flashed through his mind, and he tried to remember the day they went to the festival. He remembered the gold disk Mia got from Rotrude, the witch of the woods.

James sat on the settee, took the plastic bag out of the box, and looked at the Silver Stag. He didn't remember seeing it that day, but maybe it had been on the table with all Rotrude's other pendants.

The memories of that summer were mixed up with the memories of what happened after Mia disappeared. The day he woke up to find her gone, James didn't remember Mia getting up and leaving the attic. He went to her bedroom, and her bags were there, as was her purse with her passport. James went down the back stairs, through the kitchen, and out the back door. He into the woods where they had found the altar. James went to the ruins and the forest behind it, but she was nowhere to be found. He returned home in a panic and told his father and Miss Nithercott that Mia was missing. Miss Nithercott kept weeping, but James was angry. Why would Mia run away and not tell him?

The police interrogated James in his father's library. They questioned him several times, and since he could answer them honestly, his story never changed. Tabloid journalists camped out on the road for weeks, hoping to get a glimpse of the young man who claimed he had no idea where his American girlfriend was.

They took his picture, and followed him to school, making his final term intolerable. His former mates eyed him suspiciously. They had all seen the photo of Mia, a cute pixie with a winning smile, and they imagined James burying her body in the woods surrounding Huxley Manor.

After a few weeks, the clamor to find Mia Wentworth died down. James spent his nights tossing and turning as he imagined all the terrible things that might have happened to her. He didn't pass his exams and had to take them the following summer.

James finally passed and was able to go to college, where he met his wife, Vera, a small, blue-eyed blonde. They dated for three months before marrying against their parents' wishes. Her parents bought them a flat in London. Vera had her own money and, at first, was sympathetic regarding his notoriety, but eventually it became clear that James had been less than honest with her about his feelings for Mia. Had she understood the depths of his passion, she wouldn't have married him. Their marriage was over three months after it began.

The divorce, however, took two years. Vera's lawyer argued that she had been in love with James, a man who had misstated his intentions, which persuaded Vera to marry him; therefore, she was the injured party, and as such, entitled to a portion of James' future earnings. James' lawyer, Martin Collier, a corporate lawyer who worked for his uncle's bank, argued that the length of the marriage should be a factor in determining any financial outcome.

"They were married for three months," Collier said. "They signed an agreement stipulating that any assets accumulated during the marriage would be divided equally. There was nothing in the language of the contract concerning my client's future income, or his right to her future income."

But Vera's solicitor had tried to argue that Vera was devastated when the marriage ended. She had suffered greatly, and therefore, was entitled to compensation. The judge disagreed. He dissolved the marriage, gave Vera the flat in London, and told each party that they should "think long and hard" before contemplating marriage in the future.

Harold let James return to Huxley Manor at Uncle Billy's request. One day, James was walking in Dorley when he saw Miss Nithercott. It was the first time James had seen her since his father sacked her when James was seventeen. She took him to her flat, and they parted with promises to keep in touch.

The black dog was always sniffing at James' heels, and after his divorce, James allowed the dark pooch to form a cocoon around him. Sequestered in the attic, James reread his fantasy books and pined for Mia. For years, James lived under a cloud unaware of the passage of time, and ignored by his father. Then, one day in the fall of 1991, the black dog ran away, and James went to the breakfast table after he saw his father's car drive away.

He saw an ad for the festival in the newspaper. James thought about the charm wagon and Rotrude and recalled the way she had talked to Mia. He remembered Mia saying Margaret's name, and then took his first, tentative step back into the real world.

James walked to the end of the drive where he was accosted by a reported named Jem, a wily young woman who had slept in her car, awaiting the opportunity to talk to James Huxley.

"Are you James Huxley?" she asked when she saw him. James flinched and tried to turn around, but Jem blocked him. "What do you think of the reward being offered for the safe return of Mia Wentworth?"

"Reward?" James asked.

"The one her father posted in the Times. He's offering a hundred thousand pounds to anyone who can produce his daughter."

"I don't know anything about that."

James tried to go around her, but Jem was quick. She got to the door of the manor first and blocked him from going inside.

"Do you know where she is, James?"

James' jaw twitched and his hands fisted.

"No."

Jem must have seen something ominous in his stance, for she moved out of his way and let him pass, but she stayed outside for the rest of the day. As soon as James was inside, he went to his father's study and found a copy of the Times. He saw the ad and the photo of Mia in her school uniform.

James decided to go to the festival and look for Rotrude. The festival hadn't changed at all. The same vendors were there along with the same swordsman giving a demonstration in the park, but James was focused on the line of wagons parked along Baker Street. He stood by the bakery and scanned them for the colorful charm wagon, and then began to walk down the center of the road.

James' frustration grew as he made his way past the vendors and didn't see the charm wagon. He stopped at each vendor on the way back asking if they'd seen her, and each told them that they hadn't. Rotrude hadn't come to the festival that year, and James went home in despair.

For the next week, he searched the woods surrounding Huxley Manor, looking for her cottage. He found a clearing and the remnants of a firepit, but nothing else to suggest Rotrude had been there. James almost fell into despair again, but fought to keep himself in the light.

Then Mia's father hired a private detective.

Peter Barret was a retired police officer. He was a short, dark man with squinty eyes and a long nose. Many thought he resembled a mole, but Pete's appearance belied a canny knack for investigation. He had worked the Wentworth case as a copper – now he would work it as a private dick.

Pete was an honest guy who hated a bent copper, but now that he was out from under the restraints of the Met, he was going to go after James Huxley like a pit bull after a bone. He arrived at Huxley Manor one morning shortly after Harold had left for London, and he persuaded Hughes to let him in. Hughes left Pete in the drawing room while he fetched James, and that gave him an opportunity to study the family photos. His trained eye noticed a lack of pictures of little James, or adolescent James, or any James for that matter. When James appeared at the entrance, Pete observed the dark circles under James' eyes and his gray pallor.

"I'd like to ask you a few questions," Pete said after introducing himself. "Can we sit?"

James nodded, and then they sat on the settee. Pete took a pad and pen from his pocket and then smiled at James.

"I've been hired to find Mia Wentworth," Pete said. He saw James wince. "I read the police inquiries and know that you were the last one to see her alive."

James' lip trembled, but he looked Pete in the eye.

"I was asleep when she left."

149

"And you didn't feel her moving away from you?" James shook his head. "So, you two were close at the time?"

"We were."

"You were shaggin' her, right?"

Anger brought roses to James' cheeks.

"I loved her. I still do. We made love."

"Right. You made love. Two teenagers."

"What do you want?" James asked.

The edge in his voice surprised Pete. James was younger and taller, so Pete got up and moved across the room.

"I told you. I've been hired to find Mia Wentworth."

"I've already told the police everything I know."

"Everything, James?"

"Everything. Several times."

Pete paced the floor a couple of times, and then stopped, looked at James, and smiled.

"What was she like, eh? Was she good, James?" James clenched his teeth. "I remember what it was like to be seventeen. I can't blame you. Get her out of her knickers."

James stood. His body trembled as he took a step forward.

"It wasn't like that."

"Then what was it like? Explain it to me so I can understand why a girl like Mia would just up and run away without so much as a kiss goodbye?"

"I don't know."

"But I think you do know. I think you had a row, and you hit her. I think she died, and you buried her in the woods."

James came at him with such force that Pete was pushed up against the wall before he knew what had happened. James' eyes were wild, and Pete had trouble dislodging James' hands and pushing him away.

"She was alive when I went to sleep," James said. "And she was gone when I woke up. I looked for her everywhere."

James shuddered and backed away from Pete. Tears formed in his eyes and he brushed them away. Pete saw something in James' eyes he hadn't expected to see – the truth. James didn't know what had happened to Mia.

After Pete Barret told Arthur Wentworth that he was unable to locate Mia, Arthur tried suing Harold Huxley, but the case never saw the light of day following Arthur's mild stroke.

After that, James tried to find work, but his fame was still an issue for some employers. They, like many others, assumed James had gotten away with murder and wouldn't even give him an interview.

Now, sitting in his flat above the pub, James pulled the pieces of the Silver Stag from the plastic bag and held one in each hand. He turned them over, put them next to each other, and read the inscription again.

This is the Silver Stag, fashioned by Rotrude, and cast by Greyson. Use with caution.

Sparks flew from the edges as the pieces touched, and James pulled them apart. It freaked him out, so he put them back in the plastic bag and dropped the bag into the box.

The black dog kept sniffing at James' heels that day. It would be easy to let it take over, to wallow in the misery of lost love and grief, but James had a business to run, and the boys would be knocking on the door in less than an hour.

James got up, dressed, and went downstairs, but he still felt the black dog breathing down his neck. James felt drained and wanted to go back to bed, but Artie was at the door, and he had to rally himself.

"You look knackered, mate," Artie said.

"I'm all right," James said.

"I found a five-pound note in my light jacket."

Artie handed it to James, but he held up his hand.

"Give it to her," James said.

"Right."

Artie hung up his things and went to his stool. He watched James set up clean glasses under the bar. A few minutes later, Devon came in.

"Hi, mate," Artie said as Devon took his stool. He tilted his head toward James. "I told him he looks knackered."

"Aye, right knackered," Devon said.

"I'm fine," James said.

"You don't look fine." Devon clasped his hands on the bar. "You look like you could use some sleep."

James poured them each a pint and set it in front of them. Old Smythe came through the door, and Artie waved at him.

"Just seen 'er driving 'round to the back," Old Smythe said.

Artie took the five-pound note from his pocket and laid it on the bar. He glanced at Devon.

"I found it in my light jacket."

Devon nodded. Old Smythe hobbled to his stool and patted Artie on the back. James placed his hands on the bar and leaned forward.

"Bitters?" he asked Old Smythe.

"Aye." Old Smythe looked at the empty bowls on the bar. "Crisps."

James grabbed two bags of crisps from under the bar and set them in front of Old Smythe. He collected the bowls and placed them in front of the pensioner, too.

"Fill 'em up, would you?" James said.

James went through the kitchen door just as Maryanne was walking in from the back door.

"You look like something the cat dragged in," she said.

"So I've been told."

"Well, you do."

"I didn't sleep well last night."

Maryanne took her coat and purse to the office and got the till out of the safe.

"Artie's got a fiver for you," James said.

"Found it in a jacket, I suppose," Maryanne said.

"Aye."

"These old codgers are always finding money tucked away. So, why didn't you sleep well?"

"I kept thinking of my friend, you know, the one who passed away."

Maryanne took the till to the register at the bar, and then came back to the kitchen.

"Is there a funeral?" she asked.

James exhaled sharply as Maryanne waited for a reply.

"James!" she cried.

"What?"

"Is there going to be a funeral?"

James raised his eyebrows. It was an excellent excuse to take a day off and visit the woman who sent him the box of Miss Nithercott's things.

"Aye," he said. "It's tomorrow."

"So, take the day. I can handle things here."

"You're sure you'll be all right?" James asked.

"I'll be fine. Decide now before I change me mind."

"I'll go. I'll have my mobile if you need to call me."

All that day, James thought about the Silver Stag and hoped Lily Profitt could tell him what it was and how Miss Nithercott had come to own it. By two a.m., he was eager to lock the door and get to bed so he could get an early start in the morning. He waited until Maryanne went home to withdraw money from the safe, but he left a note for her so she wouldn't get upset when she found it missing.

James went upstairs and threw some things into a rucksack in case he ended up spending the night away. He put the plastic bag holding the Silver Stag in it, too.

The next morning, James took his road map out of the kitchen drawer, locked up his flat, and got into his ten-year-old VW Jetta. Before he got into the car, he took the Silver Stag out of his rucksack and put it in his pocket.

Chapter Twenty-Three

WOOLLCOTT, A CHARMING LITTLE VILLAGE ESTABLISHED DURING the sixteenth century, was just off the motorway. A large, Anglican church dominated its circular town square, which had imposed a ban on vehicles sometime in the 1960s. Shops, cafes, and pubs competed for the random tourist who happened upon the village while searching for Cambridge. Still, its proximity to the railway attracted commuters, which led to the gentrification of the abandoned Victorian townhouses occupying the main roads in the village, but it also turned the close-knit community into a preppy haven with coffee houses and tony shops the long-time residents couldn't afford.

Lily Profitt lived at 169 Beacon Place. According to his map, Beacon Place was a right turn off King's Crossing, the exit road off the motorway. Number 169 was a narrow building with a date stone embedded in its red brick façade that read "1867." Three stories high, it was the centerpiece in a line of decrepit townhouses that had somehow escaped gentrification.

A stone walkway nearly buried in dirt led to the entrance of the house. All the homes on Beacon Place had a small garden. The ubiquity of plastic gnomes suggested, in James' opinion, a lack of imagination, but he did smile when he walked past the garden at 169. The gnomes were a romantic couple bent toward each other in anticipation of a kiss.

James knocked, waited for a bit, and then knocked again. A tall, elderly woman opened the door, her gray hair pulled into a bun, and curls surrounding her kindly face. Her simple black dress with its high neck and long sleeves reminded James of a Victorian mourning gown.

"We're full up, pet," she said.

"Oh, I'm not here for a room. I'm James Huxley. Are you Lily Profitt?"

"Aye, luv," she said. "I'm Miss Profitt. Why look at you. Hettie talked about you all the time. Come in, James."

The phrase *faded gentility* came to James' mind as she led him to a pleasantly appointed sitting room. A dusty chandelier hung from the high ceiling, and two tall windows looked out on the pitiful garden. The heavy, red velvet drapes were dusty, too, and the lace panels beneath them were frayed at the edges. Water-stained wallpaper curled at the corners of the ceiling, and the place smelled of wet wood, mildew, and arthritis ointment.

A period settee was against one wall, and a comfy chair was placed facing an ancient black and white TV console on the opposite wall. A rolling cart with a tea service was sitting beside the comfy chair as if the lady of the house had been expecting guests. Miss Profitt sat in the comfy chair, and James sat on the settee. She poured his tea.

"Cream and sugar?"

"Just cream," James said.

Miss Profitt added a bit of cream and then handed the cup and saucer to James.

"I was beside myself when Hettie passed. She and I would often have afternoon tea together." She shook her head and frowned. "It hasn't been the same since she's gone."

"I was so sorry to hear of her passing," James said. "I was curious to know…how she passed."

Miss Profitt glanced to her right as she summoned her memories of dear Hettie Nithercott.

"Two months ago, she began having chest pains. The doctor took some tests and found that her heart was weak. She was given medication and told to rest, but that wasn't Hettie. She liked to visit the care home in Brakenshire and spend time with her sister. She used to take the bus there once a week, but I persuaded her to go once a month." Miss Profitt cast her sad eyes on James. "I tried to persuade her to stop altogether, luv, but she insisted."

"Your letter asked about other relations she might have had," James said. "I didn't even know she had a sister."

"Oh, dear. Yes, Hettie was the younger sister. Mary was the eldest."

James set his tea on a side table.

"I wish I'd known she was ill," he said.

"I'm not surprised she didn't share it with you." Miss Profitt smiled. "Hettie wouldn't want you to worry. She was quite proud of you, you know."

"She was like a mother to me." James glanced at the photos on the wall behind her. "Miss Profitt, I was wondering about something I found in the box you sent me."

Miss Profitt put down her cup and saucer, folded her hands, and straightened her back.

"And what is that, pet?" James pulled the plastic bag out of his pocket. "Oh, yes. I found it in the top drawer of her bureau." Miss Profitt blushed. "Behind some of her intimates."

"Had you ever seen it before?" James asked.

Miss Profitt shook her head.

"She never showed it to me. I thought it was a trinket she'd saved from her childhood or some such thing. Odd that it was broken in half like that."

"Yes, it is odd."

James put the plastic bag back into his pocket.

"When did she move here?" James asked.

Miss Profitt put her finger on her cheek and pursed her lips.

"It was about five year ago. Maybe six. It was shortly after Mary entered the care home."

"And she never showed you that coin?"

Miss Profitt shook her head. "She did talk about her children, though."

"She had children?" James said.

"You, luv, and the others she cared for."

"Oh. Of course."

"The children grew up, and all Hettie had left were her memories," Miss Profitt said.

"Did she work while she was living here?" James asked.

"Aye. She had a job in a shop, but her legs were bad, and it didn't last."

"What shop was that?"

"The ladies' wear on Boynton Road."

James scanned the room and then looked at Miss Profitt. He sipped his tea and glanced at the large clock on the wall. After what he felt was a reasonable amount of time had passed, he drained his teacup and set it down on the end table.

"Well, I must be going," he said.

Miss Profitt stood and grabbed his hand.

"Again, luv, I'm so sorry for your loss," she said.

"Thank you," James said. "And you, too."

They walked to the foyer, and Miss Profitt opened the door.

"Be careful on the road, pet," she said as he walked past her.

"I will."

Miss Profitt watched James walk to his car before closing her door, and he saw her peeking out the window as he drove away. He drove to town and stopped at a pub for a sandwich and a pint, and then called Bixby's Brewhouse.

"You should have told me you were taking money out of the safe," Maryanne said.

"Hello to you, too," James said.

"So, how's the funeral?"

"It's okay. I met her old landlady. So, how are things going?"

"The same. Old sots and young hooligans."

"They're our best customers, Maryanne."

"Is the funeral over?" Maryanne asked.

"No. There's a wake. I'm not sure when I'll be back."

"Well, you better be back soon cause I'm fixing to kick Old Smythe out on his arse."

"Why? What did he do?" James asked.

"He's giving me lip about paying his bill."

"But I thought he was all caught up."

"Just get back here," Maryanne said.

Maryanne hung up without a goodbye. James folded his phone and stuck it in his pocket. He couldn't imagine what the old man had done to rile her, but he'd worked with her long enough to know that she was probably trying to get James to come back sooner rather than later. He rubbed his eyes and looked out the pub window where he saw a street sign for Boynton and Harrow at the intersection.

James finished his lunch, and then he walked up Boynton and found the ladies' wear. A large window displayed the latest foundation garments for the "modern woman," but James doubted any women of his age had ever crossed its threshold. He went inside and saw an older woman sitting behind the counter filling out a ledger. He smiled as he approached her, but her face remained passive.

"Can I help you?" she asked, though she didn't get off the stool.

"I was told that a Miss Nithercott used to work here."

"Hettie Nithercott? Yes, she worked here." She folded her arms across her chest. "And before you ask, she was only here for a month, and we didn't share our personal lives."

"Right. Well, then, thank you for your time."

James went back to his car. Miss Nithercott had lived in Dorley after she left the manor house. Maybe someone would remember her. She'd been friends with the librarian, Miss Naugle, when she was James' governess. Maybe Miss Nithercott had shown her the Silver Stag.

Chapter Twenty-Four

A WAVE OF NOSTALGIA WASHED OVER JAMES AS HE DROVE INTO Dorley. Nothing had changed except that the town had a paved car park now and charged a quid for each spot. James drove into town and cruised until he saw an empty spot on Tinker Lane. As he got out of his car, he saw the old church and wondered if Vicar Greenway was still there.

James walked to the center of town and peeked through the bakery window. He didn't want to go inside; he didn't want anyone to remember him. He had grown too fond of his anonymity. James doubled back and went to the new library on Baker Street. He walked into the lobby, which smelled like fresh carpeting, and saw a large circular desk in the center of the room. Miss Naugle was also there, and James was grateful he wouldn't have to go looking for her.

James pulled out the Silver Stag as he approached the desk. Miss Naugle looked up, and then she narrowed her eyes.

"James Huxley," she said. "I haven't seen you for ages."

"I live in Morseton now," James said.

"I was just thinking about Hettie the other day."

"Miss Nithercott passed away," he said.

"Oh, I am sorry. We lost track of each other when she moved away."

"Actually, she's the reason I'm here," James said. He put the Silver Stag on the counter. "Have you ever seen this before?"

Miss Naugle touched the plastic bag and shook her head.

"Can't say as I have."

"She had it when she died. So, she never talked to you about it?"

"No. Like I said, we lost touch."

Miss Naugle turned over the bag and saw Rotrude's name.

"That's the name of the witch who used to come to the festival," she said.

"Used to come?"

"Yes. We were talking about her during the last festival, me and the other ladies here, we all noticed that her wagon wasn't there, and then we realized that it hadn't been there for a long time."

"Have you any idea what happened to her?"

Miss Naugle shook her head.

"Don't know how we would. She only came during the festival, and I doubt she told anyone where she lived. She was a strange one, that Rotrude." Miss Naugle looked at the coin again. "Who's Greyson?"

"I've no idea." James glanced toward the inside of the library. "Do you have any books here about Dorley in the old days?"

"Old like what, the eighteenth century, nineteenth?"

"Older."

"Are you interested in the Huxleys?" Miss Naugle asked.

"I'm interested in her," James said, pointing to the coin. "Rotrude."

"There might be something in the *Occult* section. If I remember correctly, there was a man who wrote about the Celtic religion, and he came here asking about Symond. He wanted to know where the altar was." Miss Naugle smiled. "Well, I told him it used to be in the woods near the old keep, but I doubted it was still there."

James chose not to mention that he had seen the old altar in the woods.

"What was his name?" James asked.

"Can't remember his name. I only saw him the one time, and I only remember it because of Symond's name. We don't get that many inquiries about him anymore, so it stuck out."

"But you think there might be something in *Occult*?" James asked.

"That's where it would be, yes. You can do a search on the computers. We have a row of them now."

"Thanks."

James walked away from the desk and saw the row of computers in the center of a vast room that served as the main library. Rows of bookcases filled both sides and nooks for children and teenagers had round tables and chairs. He had to wait for one of the computers to be free, but it didn't take long. The whole catalog was now available at his fingertips.

The *Occult* section contained all aspects of the supernatural, and it wasn't hard to find books on Dorley. One, *The History of Witchcraft in the United Kingdom,* mentioned Symond and Rotrude. It hinted that she had lived for centuries, which reminded James of something Rotrude said when he and Mia were at her wagon.

"…I was here when the king cut off Symond's head…"

James scoffed and put the book back on the shelf. He found another on medieval witchcraft and found their names listed again. Her story remained unchanged; she lived in a cottage in the woods near Huxley Keep and was known as a healer. She and her twin brother, Greyson, helped protect the villagers when Symond held sway over Dorley. He practiced blood sacrifices and found his victims in Dorley.

A footnote added beneath this passage read: There was a spate of unexplained disappearances at this time. Symond only required one girl for his purposes each year, but a traveling monk recorded that many girls and women had vanished during Symond's time.

James reread the passage. "…girls and women vanished..." Did Rotrude and her brother have anything to do with this? James recalled something else Rotrude had said that day, something he had ignored.

"She's still alive, you know."

Mia had guessed it was Margaret, and if that's what Rotrude was referring to, it would mean that she had something to do with Margaret's disappearance, too.

The author mentioned Rotrude one more time in the Afterward when he wrote, "Many say she still comes to the village of Dorley once a year to sell her charms, but I believe someone who read the legend comes to Dorley each year to carry on her legacy."

James put the book back on the shelf and wondered how many people had gone missing from Dorley since the eleventh century. He thought of Margaret and Mia. Was Mia with Margaret now? He remembered going through the newspaper archives with Mia and returned to his computer. He searched for the newspaper archives. They were listed as "under construction."

"Bollocks," James said.

Newspapers had their own websites, but many of them were "under construction," too. The local newspaper was The Journal, and its office was on Baker Street. James logged off the computer, waved at Miss Naugle as he passed, and went down Baker Street.

* * *

THE JOURNAL'S OFFICE WAS LOCATED IN AN OLD RESIDENCE, similar to the one Miss Profitt occupied. The archives were stored in a back room. A computer had been set up so they could be put on the paper's website, and once a week, a student would come in and scan the old documents into the computer.

"You're welcome to look in the computer," the editor, a man named Gil, said. "He's done the nineteenth century. I think he started the twentieth."

"And if it's not on the computer…"

"It's there."

He pointed to racks of old newspapers.

"They are in order, at least most of them are."

"Thanks," James said.

"I'll be at my desk if you need anything."

James turned on the computer and opened a file on the desktop called "Archive." The records were in order by year, and James figured he could start anywhere since Rotrude had been visiting Dorley once a year since the festival began. The last time he attended the festival, which was with Mia, it was celebrating its one hundred year anniversary. He clicked on the file marked "1886."

James checked the paper for references to missing people. He found an article regarding a fifteen-year-old girl named Hannah Blaine who had gone missing from her father's farm. James looked for her in subsequent articles, but she was never mentioned again. He then clicked on 1896. A woman named Jilly Bristol went missing after the constable was called to the house by her husband, who complained that his wife had become "contrary." Jilly had gone to the constable to complain that her husband had caused her to lose her unborn baby. She wanted them to arrest him for murder. When the constable went to see Mr. Bristol, he told him that Jilly was "sulking and refused to perform her wifely duties."

James looked for a follow up to the accusation of murder but found none. He went back to 1886 to see if Hannah Blaine had been a victim of abuse, but he couldn't find anything preceding her disappearance.

In 1900, he found another missing woman who had complained that her husband abused her, but since there were no laws broken, the constable had suggested she "go home and do your duty as a wife and mother." There was another in 1904 and another in 1910. James kept finding missing women and girls who were simply forgotten over time. It was no surprise to him now that Margaret had also been overlooked.

James sat back, exhaled sharply, and then remembered what Miss Naugle said about Rotrude not being at the festival for a long time. The computer files ended in 1950, so he turned to the racks and looked for recent copies starting in 1992. James only read copies printed in August when the festival took place, but he couldn't find any mention of Rotrude or the charm wagon. He did notice the name of a woman who had written reviews of the festival and jotted it down on a scrap of paper.

The editor was typing when James came out of the room.

"Find what you were looking for?" Gil asked.

"Sort of. Can you tell me where I can find a woman named Harriet Crawly?"

"Harriet writes special articles for me," the man said. "She lives on a farm a few miles from here."

"Do you think she would talk to me?" James asked.

"Maybe on the phone. I don't know you, or I'd give you her address."

"On the phone would be fine."

"I'll see if she's home," Gil said.

James sat on a wobbly wooden chair while Gil dialed Harriet's number. She answered on the third ring.

"I have someone here who asked if you could talk to him for a minute about..."

Gil looked at James.

"The festivals in Dorley," James said.

"The festivals in Dorley. Right. Okay, here he is."

James took the receiver from Gil's hand.

"Hello. Yes, I was wondering if you could tell me anything about Rotrude, the witch."

"You mean the charm lady," Harriet said.

"Yes. She had a wagon."

"Let me think. I haven't seen her for a while."

"Can you remember the last time you saw her?" James asked.

"I'm not sure. It might have been four years ago."

"Have you any idea why she stopped coming?"

"No. In fact, I remember talking to the mayor about her. She was a fixture at the festival, and people were asking where she was. The mayor couldn't answer me, so I asked his secretary, and she told me that Rotrude hadn't applied for a license that year."

"Did she say why?" James asked.

"No. There was no way of knowing, really. She just didn't apply."

"Did she come back the next year?"

"No. Like I said, not for at least four years, maybe five. You could ask at the town hall. They can tell you the last time she applied for a license."

"Right," James said. "Good idea. Thanks for your help."

James thanked Gil and left the office. He walked to the town hall, which was next to the library. A woman at the reception desk told him that Rotrude hadn't applied for a license since 1991.

James remembered when he went looking for Rotrude in the woods and couldn't find anything but an old firepit, though he couldn't remember what year that was.

As James walked back to his car, he wondered why Rotrude had suddenly stopped coming to the festival. Of course, she couldn't be the same Rotrude who had been around when Symond was in Dorley, but as far as he knew from what he'd read that day, there had always been a witch named Rotrude in

Dorley since the eleventh century. If there were women who took on the mantle in her name, what had happened to the woman he and Mia met in 1986?

As he rode down Baker Street, he saw the road leading to Huxley Manor. He hadn't been there in years and didn't want to go there now, but he stopped at the intersection and gripped the steering wheel. It was afternoon, so his father wouldn't be there, and there were books in the attic he'd left behind when he moved out.

James crossed the intersection and got onto the familiar road that led to Huxley Manor. He turned onto the drive and rode to the front entrance of the grand old house. When he got out, he looked up at the attic window and recalled waking up alone the day Mia Wentworth went missing.

A brisk knock on the door brought a butler to the door; a new man James had never seen before.

"May I help you?" the man asked.

"My name is James Huxley."

"I recognize you, sir."

"Is my father here?" James asked.

"His lordship is in London."

"Shit." James took a deep breath. "Is Caroline still working here?"

The butler raised his eyebrows.

"Indeed, sir."

"May I come in and speak to her?" James fisted his hands. "Or has he told you not to let me in?"

"You may come in, sir."

James stepped into the foyer, and the butler went to fetch Caroline. She had been the Huxleys' cook since James was small. As he waited, he glanced at the parlor where a large portrait of his mother was hung over the fireplace. He hadn't seen her face since leaving Dorley, and the sight it brought tears to his eyes.

"Lord James!"

He turned to find Caroline coming toward him. She took his hands.

"Oh, it's so good to see you."

"You, too. You're looking well."

"From your lips to God's ears."

James smiled. "I was wondering if we might talk for a moment."

"Of course."

"I wouldn't mind seeing the kitchen again."

Caroline smiled, and then he followed her to the kitchen. Nothing had changed here, either, and James took his old seat at the large table where he'd watched Caroline preparing meals for most of his early childhood. It also smelled the same, which comforted James.

"So, what brings you to Dorley?" she asked as she brought a bowl to the table.

"I was wondering how much you knew about Miss Nithercott."

"Hettie?"

"Aye. She died recently, and her landlady sent me her things. She thought I might know if Miss Nithercott had other relations."

Caroline bit her lip.

"Poor Hettie, may she rest in peace."

"Did she ever talk about her family?" James asked.

Caroline picked up a bunch of carrots and a knife.

"Not that I recall. I do remember her telling me that she had been a policewoman, but nothing about her family. Of course, that don't mean she didn't have any, just that she never talked about them."

"Aye. She was a private person. And you said she was a policewoman?"

"Aye. That's why your father engaged her. He wanted someone who would keep you safe."

"She never told me that."

"It was after your mum died," Caroline said. "I think he was afraid something might happen to you."

"Do you remember anything else about her?" James asked.

"Just that she loved a good joke."

James sat back in the chair.

"Where did she work as a policewoman?"

"Not sure exactly. Maybe London."

"The Met should have a record of her," James said.

"They should." Caroline sliced a carrot and then cast her

eyes on James. "You look so handsome, James. You take after your mum."

"I was looking at her portrait in the parlor," he said. "I'd forgotten how beautiful she was."

"Did you take pictures of her when you left?" Caroline asked.

"No. I was in a bit of a hurry that day."

"Then you should take one now. You're entitled to a photo of your mum."

"Wouldn't what's his name object?"

"Oh, you mean Bruce. He's all right. He won't say anything to his lordship."

"And how is his lordship?" James asked.

Caroline stopped slicing.

"He's a bit off his game these days."

James frowned. "Why is that?"

"He's not as spry as he used to be. It's probably just old age coming on."

"But he's not that old," James said.

"He's past seventy," Caroline said. She glanced toward the entrance to the kitchen. "I heard the doctor tell him he has to slow down."

James exhaled sharply.

"I guess I should come by and see him."

"He's here on weekends," Caroline said. "He doesn't go out much anymore."

"Then, I'll come by some weekend." James stood and took a business card from his wallet. "This has my number on it. Let me know…"

"I'll call you," she said.

"Thanks, Caroline. For everything."

"You're welcome, Lord James."

He left the kitchen and went to the parlor. A long table was set against the back wall, and it held family photos. James went to the table and reached for the photo of his mother and him taken when James was three. He slipped the picture out of the frame and into his shirt pocket.

Chapter Twenty-Five

It was three in the afternoon, and James wasn't sure what to do next. He thought about his books and went to the stairs. Bruce came down the hallway from the kitchen and saw James halfway up the stairs.

"Caroline suggested you might want to stay the night, sir."

James stopped and looked at Bruce.

"She did?"

"His lordship won't be home until Friday evening."

"I doubt he would approve," James said.

"He doesn't have to know, sir."

James smiled.

"I would appreciate it, Bruce."

"Caroline also said dinner is at six."

Bruce left him on the stairs and disappeared down the hallway going toward the kitchen. James ran up the stairs and walked down the hall, glancing into each bedroom as he passed. His room hadn't changed, nor had the room where Mia stayed. Time had stood still at Huxley Manor.

He climbed the attic stairs two at a time and stopped at the first bookcase. A box of clothes was on the divan, so James dumped the clothes onto the divan and took the box. He filled it with his books and then took them to the boot of his car.

James knew he had to call Maryanne and tell her he was spending the night in Dorley, but he also knew what she would say, so he left that task until he'd finished collecting his things.

After shutting the boot, James went to the sitting room, sat on the sofa, pulled out his phone, looked at it for a while, and then dialed Bixby's Brewhouse.

"Bloody hell," she said. "You'd better be back tomorrow. And I'm leaving the floor the way it is."

"Fine. You can even stay in the flat if you want," James said.

"Oh, don't you worry. I'll stay in the flat."

She hung up without another word, and James laid his head back and closed his eyes. He thought about what he had learned since leaving Morseton and wondered what he should do next. Miss Nithercott's sister came to mind, so he decided to stop in Brakenshire on his way home.

James' hand rested on his pocket, and he felt the Silver Stag. He pulled the plastic bag out of his pocket. James opened the bag, took the two necklaces out, and put them around his neck. He held one of the halves of the coin up and looked at the stag. Sparks had flown from them the last time he put the halves close to each other, and James' curiosity led him to try it again. Sparks flew, but this time, James kept them close.

The halves were drawn to each other and soon came together despite James' efforts to keep them apart. Wind swirled around him, lifting him up in the air. James tried to pull the halves apart to no avail, and as the wind blew harder, he got closer to the ceiling. He was inches away from the ceiling when the roof faded away.

James was under the open sky now, encircled in a tornado that threatened to tear his body apart. He screamed as it whirled and tried to grab the Silver Stag, but his arms wouldn't bend. A moment later, he felt the wind diminish, and he was able to move his arms, but he still couldn't get hold of the coin.

Then, as quickly as it began, the wind was gone, and James was dropped to the ground. He landed on his ass and then lay on his back, looking up at the bluest sky he'd ever seen. The manor house was gone; he was at the center of a clearing in the woods.

As he regained his composure, James was able to stand. He looked for a road and saw an opening in the woods the width of a single-lane highway. James walked down the path and came to a village. At its center was a large, circular building, which acted as a hub for the streets emanating from it like the spokes on a wheel.

There was a large sign on the circular building that read, "Welcome Center," but James saw no signs of life as he walked around the building. A church bearing a strong resemblance to the Huxley church on Tinker Lane was on the corner of a street bearing the same name. A cemetery lay beside the church, and as James passed, he saw something that made him stop in his tracks. He stared at the name on the headstone, and a chill went up his spine.

Margaret Huxley
Born May 10, 1927
Died June 15, 1991

"It can't be," James said.

He searched the other headstones for familiar names and saw one for Hannah Blaine and Jilly Bristol. Again, a chill went up his spine, so he began walking again.

James examined houses across the street; quiet, empty places still bearing evidence of the lives once lived there. Wash still hung on the line behind the house facing the church. An empty drinking glass was on the porch step as if the person drinking from it had left it there while they got up to collect the mail from the mailbox marked, "Cramer." The grass was brown and the shrubbery, dead. James took a few steps toward the house and stopped at the porch steps. The door was open, so he went inside.

More evidence of life was found in the parlor, where books lay open on the settee. In the kitchen, a pot was on the stove, and a place setting was on the table. James stood at the backdoor and looked out at the empty backyard. The grass there was brown, too, and a large tree was rotting near the center of its trunk.

James returned to the road in front of the house and noticed all the other rotting vegetation as he walked past the houses. The stench of decay was strong, and dead leaves blew across his path. He didn't hear the sounds of birds or other animals. The silence was haunting, and James felt the black dog smiling. This was his kind of place, a place where he could insinuate himself without notice until it was too late to stop him from gaining a foothold over James' mind.

James stopped and put his hand over the Silver Stag. He should go back to the clearing, press the coin together again, and leave this place, but curiosity kept his feet moving. He passed more houses with dead and dying foliage, and then came to a farm. The walls of the dilapidated house were barely standing. The garden consisted of patches of misshapen tomatoes and green peppers. A man wearing a monk's robe was bent over a patch picking tomatoes off a vine and putting them into a basket.

The man had long white hair and a long white beard. James immediately thought of Gandalf, the wizard in *Lord of the Rings*. The man's slender form looked frail, but when he stood, he straightened his back and held his head high. As he looked at another patch, he saw James at the edge of the yard.

"Are you real?" he asked.

"Yes," James said.

The man picked up his basket and came to James with a smile.

"How did you get here?"

James held up the Silver Stag.

"How…?" the man said. A tear ran down his face, and he wiped it away. "I am Greyson."

"Oh." James smiled. "I'm James."

Greyson eyed James for a moment, and then he put his hand on James' arm.

"How did you find it?"

"The woman who raised me died, and I found it in her belongings."

Greyson squeezed James' arm. His wizened face was ruddy from the sun, and his hands gnarled from years of hard work, but his grip was firm.

"Let's go to the Welcome Center and have some tea."

James followed Greyson back to the Welcome Center. The large room was a jumble of books, papers, and dead plants. A long, rectangular table with a bench on each side was at its center. James sat on a bench and watched Greyson go to a large stove and light a flame beneath a teakettle.

"It's been so long since I've entertained a guest," Greyson said. "I never expected to see anyone new again."

"What is this place?" James asked.

Greyson sat opposite James.

"This is Havenwood."

"Havenwood," James said. James looked into Greyson's eyes. "Am I still in England?"

Greyson smiled.

"No, James. Havenwood is not in England."

"Then, where am I?"

"In another world."

James closed his eyes and exhaled loudly.

"What does that mean?"

"Have you ever heard of Rotrude?" Greyson asked.

"Yes. She was the witch of the woods."

"She was my sister, and we created Havenwood as a safe harbor for those in trouble."

James cocked his head.

"You said she *was* your sister."

Greyson lowered his head and clasped his hands on the table.

"She died some years ago," Greyson said.

That's why James couldn't find her.

"How did she die?"

"Boris Black killed her."

James saw Boris Black's face in his mind. The notorious gangster had lived in the London borough of Croydon. He had died in 1991 under mysterious circumstances. A young woman had crawled out of the woods with a bullet hole in her side. A search of the woods led to the discovery of Boris Black's body. He had a bullet in his gut.

"She was my twin, you know," Greyson said as he stood. "We were born under a portentous star."

"How do you know Boris Black killed her?"

"How do you take your tea?"

"With cream…" James watched as Greyson put leaves in teacups. It was obvious Greyson didn't want to talk about Rotrude. "Why is there a tombstone for Margaret Huxley in the cemetery?"

Greyson sighed as he poured water into the teacups. He brought them to the table.

"I'm sorry I don't have cream." He put one in front of James and returned to his seat. "Margaret lived here for over forty years." Greyson raised his eyes. "We were very close."

"This makes no sense," James said. "How did she get here?"

"You are wearing the Silver Stag and sitting at my table."

"How did *she* get the Silver Stag?" James asked.

"Rotrude brought her here." Greyson brought the tea to the table. "She used the Silver Stag to bring Margaret here."

"This is insane," James said as he shook his head. "I must be going mad."

"I've been told that you read fantasy books," Greyson said. "Is that true?"

"Who told you that?"

"Is it true?"

"I read classic books," James said.

"And these classic books, do they have wizards and fairies?"

James eyed the old man.

"It's fiction," he said.

"But when you were a boy, did you think it was real?"

"What does it matter what I believed? I'm not a boy anymore."

Greyson set his teacup down.

"I'm too old to argue with you. If you can't believe your own senses, then there's nothing I can do to convince you that Havenwood is real."

James rubbed his eyes. He was exhausted.

"Is Mia here?" James asked.

It was barely a whisper, but as Greyson's eyes met his, James knew. His pulse jumped.

"Is she?"

"She was."

"Was," James said. His lip trembled. "She...was..."

"She was taken from us," Greyson said.

"She died?" Tears formed in James' eyes.

"No, James. Mia was kidnapped."

"Kidnapped!" James cried. "Who kidnapped her?"

"Boris Black."

"The man who killed Rotrude?"

"Why don't we take a walk?" Greyson said as he rose from his seat.

The wizard moved quickly for one so old, and James had to run to catch up to him. Greyson took him down the road and past the church. They walked past houses until they came to the end of that road, and then Greyson stopped. A beautiful, sparkling sea lay before them, and Greyson sat on the ground.

"Sit," Greyson said. James stood still. "Please."

James looked out at the sea for a moment, and then sat beside him.

Chapter Twenty-Six

Greyson inhaled sharply and then exhaled.

"My world, the world Rotrude and I created, is dying," Greyson said. "My powers alone aren't enough to sustain it. As twins, our lives were intertwined. This world depends on us working together."

"And when she died...," James said.

"It began to die, too."

"Did the people living here die?"

"No, but when they saw what was happening, they asked me to take them back to England." Greyson pulled something out from under his robe. It was another Silver Stag. "I used it to take them home."

"They were brought here because they were in trouble," James said. "How did you know they'd be safe?"

"I didn't, but if they had stayed here, they would have perished. I did the best I could to ensure that they would be all right. I had them conjure money so they would have enough to live on. I took them to safe places, so they could make a fresh start."

"Why not just do that instead of bringing them here?"

Greyson gazed at the water.

"That world isn't without danger. We wanted a place they could live in without fear."

"That's why Margaret came here," James said.

"Her father...she was afraid."

"She could have come back when my grandfather died."

"Margaret was my wife."

James stared at him in disbelief?"

"You and Margaret?"

"We fell in love. I…it wasn't the first time I had feelings for one of our…guests. But Margaret was different. She was the love of my life."

James thought of the love of his life.

"What did Mia tell Rotrude?"

"Mia was afraid to go home."

"I know, and I told her I would marry her so she wouldn't have to go, but she turned me down."

"And you've been angry ever since," Greyson said.

"Not angry, just hurt."

"Your hands are fisted. You're angry."

James took a deep breath.

"I just don't understand why she didn't trust me." James got up on his feet. "I loved her. I still do. I would have protected her."

Greyson stood and eyed James. He took a deep breath and smiled.

"Why don't we take a walk?"

"I thought we already had," James said.

"Then we shall go for another walk."

Greyson led a reluctant James back down the street and past the Welcome Center. James contemplated ditching Greyson so he could return to the clearing, but curiosity kept him following the old man. Greyson took him to a road that had one house, a small version of a Queen Anne-style home. It was pink, had two floors, a large porch with a swing, and a rocking chair near the front door.

"Why is there only one house here," James asked.

"People were allowed to conjure their own dwelling. Mia created this one. She chose to live alone."

James looked at the house and then went to the porch. A swing was suspended from the ceiling and had two pillows shaped like cats. The door was white, as were the window frames and gingerbread trim. James opened the front door and went inside.

Plush chairs with overstuffed cushions were on one side of

the sitting room. A rocking chair was in one corner, and under the windows, a divan just like the one in the manor house attic. James went to it, put his hand on it, and gripped it tightly.

Greyson came in and stood at the foot of the stairs leading to the second floor.

"Mia invited me here when she had finished decorating," he said. "She was quite proud of her achievement."

"Why did you bring me here?"

"I thought you would want to see where she lived."

"I have." James went to the door, but something kept him from leaving. "This is you, isn't it? Let me go."

"Are you sure you don't want to go upstairs?"

"I'm sure. I just want to go back to Dorley."

"We should have some tea."

"I don't want any bloody tea!"

Greyson walked toward the back of the house. James exhaled loudly before going after him. Greyson was standing near a stove, putting a light under the teakettle when James came in.

"Mia was like so many we had brought here. A lot of the people chose to live alone. I think it was the first time many had been given a choice, and they didn't want anyone interfering with it."

"Is that why she came here?" James asked.

"No, James. She truly feared going home."

"But she didn't have to go home," James said softly.

"That's the thing you never understood. All of Mia's choices had been made for her. Coming here was the one she'd made for herself."

James sat at the small, round table.

"And then Boris kidnapped her," James said. "I read something in a book in Dorley. It said that Rotrude had a very long life as if she were immortal."

"If we were truly immortal…I just kept living, as did she."

"What did you mean when you said you conjured money?"

"Rotrude and I were given gifts. I can conjure objects, and she could read the human heart. When people came to Havenwood, they, too, could conjure what they needed."

"If Rotrude could read hearts, why didn't she see Boris coming? Why didn't she save herself?"

"I have asked myself that question for many years. The only

explanation I can find is that for some reason, she trusted him and let him get too close."

James ran his finger along a crack in the wood.

"How did he even know about Rotrude?"

The teakettle whistle blew, and Greyson made the tea. He brought the cups to the table and sat.

"I have also contemplated this, and the only thing that makes sense is that one of our residents, a girl named Marie, heard that her abuser had died. She decided she wanted to go home to be with her mother. I believe she met Boris and told him about this place."

"Why would she do that?" James asked.

"It's a mystery." James slumped in his chair as Greyson looked around the kitchen and smiled. "She liked pastels. Everything in this house is bright and cheerful." He sighed. "Would you like to stay the night? I would enjoy the company."

James watched the smile fade on the old man's face as he waited for James' reply.

"I can't. I have to get home. I have a pub and if I don't get back soon...well, let's just say it might not be standing in the morning." James looked at Greyson. "I'm grateful for what you told me."

James saw Greyson smile as he looked past James. His eyes were twinkling, and James wondered if he was having a stroke.

"Are you all right?" James asked.

"Jon," Greyson said. "Come and meet James."

The boy walked past James and stood beside Greyson, and James saw that the boy had brilliant blue eyes.

Mia Wentworth

1986

Chapter Twenty-Seven

MIA AWOKE WITH A START AND RAN FROM JAMES' ROOM TO HER own. She made it to the bathroom in time to retch in the loo, and then sat on the floor. She was vomiting every day, and it was getting harder to keep it from James.

Mia laid her head back against the bathroom wall and cried. Her stomach churned as she thought of her mother and the words she'd heard since she got her first period when she was twelve.

"I'm making an appointment with Dr. Warner."

"Why do I have to see him?" Mia asked.

"Because now you can get pregnant. You have to go on the pill."

"What pill?"

Paula rolled her eyes and shook her head.

"The one that keeps you from getting pregnant."

Mia, who had only recently learned from a friend how to have sex, was horrified.

"I would *never* do that," Mia said.

"Well, you say that now, but just wait till you start kissing a boy, and things get out of hand."

"I couldn't."

It had shocked Mia, and as time went on, Paula would repeat those sentiments over and over, saying that if Mia ever came home pregnant, she'd arrange for a trip to a private clinic "where they will get rid of it. You're not going to turn me into a grandma."

Mia had also overheard her mother talking with a friend one night after Mia had gone to bed.

"But what if it's too late?" the friend asked.

"Then we'll have to give it up for adoption. There's no way in hell I'm going to be a grandmother at my age. Besides, white babies are always in demand."

Dr. Warner had discouraged Paula when she asked him to put Mia on the pill.

"She's a bit young," he said. "Bring her back when she's fourteen."

Paula had taken her back, and she'd been taking the pills ever since. Paula doled them out every morning with Mia's orange juice. Mia had brought them with her to England – a three month supply – but without Paula's watchful eye keeping track of the pills, Mia had missed a few during those first days she'd been at Huxley Manor.

Mia wanted to share her fear with James, but he had already said he would marry her just to keep her from going home, so she couldn't imagine what James would do if he found out she might be having his baby. She loved James, really, truly loved him, and would marry him in an instant if they were older, but she didn't want him to marry her out of guilt or obligation.

As she sat on the bathroom floor, Mia wanted to run away somewhere she could have her baby, but she had no money. She put her hands on her stomach and wept. A few minutes later, Mia got up, opened the door, and found Miss Nithercott sitting on her bed.

"Have you told James?" Miss Nithercott asked.

Mia blushed. "No."

"Are you going to tell him?"

Mia went to the armoire and began pulling clothes out and throwing them on the floor.

"I have to wash some clothes," Mia said.

"Listen, this isn't something you can hide, and if James is responsible, you need to tell him."

Mia found what she was looking for, pulled her nightgown over her head, and put on a loose, peasant dress.

"Mia, please talk to me."

Mia turned her face toward Miss Nithercott and glared at her.

"I'm not telling James. I'm not telling anyone."

"But you're just a lass. Have you any idea how hard it is to face something like this on your own?"

Mia's shoulders drooped.

"I can't tell him. He'd want to marry, and I can't...I don't want to be married that way."

"Marriage isn't the only way he can help you," Miss Nithercott said.

"He doesn't have any money," Mia said. She glanced at Miss Nithercott. "I'll figure something out. Just promise me you won't tell him."

Miss Nithercott got up.

"I won't tell him." She took Mia's hand and looked into the girl's eyes. "You need to eat a proper breakfast. Especially since you're vomiting. You need to drink water, too, lest you become dehydrated." Miss Nithercott let go of Mia's hand. "There's a clinic in Brandmore. I'll take you there so they can run a proper test. That's the only way you'll know for sure."

Mia bit her lip. "Don't tell Lord Huxley, either."

"It's not my place to tell anyone. I'm James' governess, not yours. Now, get dressed and come down. We have to find an excuse to go off on our own."

Miss Nithercott left the room, and Mia sat on the bed. She wept for a while, and then went to the bathroom, splashed some cold water on her face, and went downstairs to join James at the breakfast table.

James was waiting for her and saw how pale Mia looked. He had noticed that she'd lost weight when he ran his hand over her ribs and had thought of taking his concerns to Miss Nithercott, but in loyalty to Mia, he kept this to himself. Instead, he kept an eye on her and watched to make sure she ate something each day.

The next morning, Mia and Miss Nithercott drove to Brandmore, and Mia had her suspicions confirmed. There was no doubt.

She'd had a brief moment of relief when she woke that day and hadn't vomited. She was, in fact, feeling really good, so when the nurse told her that she was pregnant, her heart fell, and she almost fainted. The drive back to Dorley was quiet, but Miss Nithercott held her hand and reassured her that everything would be all right.

"He's a good lad," Miss Nithercott said. "Trust him, Mia. Tell him. He has a right to know."

But Mia feared the black dog when she saw how it affected him, and news like this could throw him into the abyss.

"I know he's good. I just…I can't tell him this."

Miss Nithercott respected Mia's wishes and kept her secret. On the day of James' birthday, Miss Nithercott ordered pizza and had Caroline bake a cake. Mia ate well, and James couldn't stop smiling as he opened his presents, especially the Madonna cassette that Mia bought him.

Then dinner was over, and the cake was taken away. James and Mia went to the sitting room and slipped out the French doors to the garden. The moon was rising in the navy blue sky, and James put the cassette into the slot on the boombox. She was wearing a gauze dress that clung to her in a seductive way, and she knew James was admiring the way her breasts moved beneath the fabric.

They walked to a spot far enough away from the house to ensure privacy, and Mia put the cassette into the boombox. When the song *Papa Don't Preach* came on, it felt particularly relevant to Mia, and she began to dance. She had the cassette at home and sang along, knowing every word emphasizing the phrase about keeping her baby. James was enthralled as he watched her body move and he didn't notice the vehemence in her voice. For that moment, Mia felt free and powerful.

When she stopped dancing, she looked at James' face in the moonlight and felt the pull of love so strongly that she shuddered. When the next song came on, Mia went to James, unbuckled his jeans, and straddled his body. She lifted her dress over her head and placed James' hands on her breasts.

"Happy Birthday," she said.

She leaned over and kissed him, and then James put his arms around her and pulled her close.

* * *

MIA HELD THE GOLD DISK IN HER HAND AS JAMES SLEPT. THEY

had been to the festival the day before. Mia met the witch of the woods, Rotrude, and she gave Mia the gold disk. Mia looked at the cottage etched on it and remembered Rotrude's words.

"If you ever find yourself in dire need, put it on and let the disk lead you to the cottage in the woods."

James was sleeping on the divan and she was thinking about going home. Mia closed her eyes and felt what it would be like to be in her old bedroom. She saw the poster of Madonna on the wall next to the mirror over her dresser. She saw blinds on her window. Her closet door was open and her laundry hamper was overflowing. Then she saw her mother burst through the door, her face red, and her eyes bulging.

"You stupid bitch! I warned you. I warned you what would happen if you got knocked up."

Mia wrapped her arms around herself and her lips trembled. The thought of going to a clinic and having someone take this baby from her frightened her more than anything had ever scared her before. She looked over at James' face and longed to snuggle up next to him and bury her head in his chest, but then a light flashed in her eye and she saw that the outline of the cottage on the gold disk was glowing.

Mia put it on the table near the oil lamp. James wanted to marry her. Why couldn't she just marry him and stay in England? He was good to her. He loved her, and his father was hardly ever home.

Mia was set to graduate next year. She would have her diploma, but she wouldn't have any money, and Paula would have seen to it that she had no baby, either.

So, what would Mia do? She couldn't go home. That left marrying James.

Mia didn't want to get married. She wanted to graduate from high school, party with her friends, be young for as long as she could, but as she ran her hand over her stomach, she understood that that life was over.

James had no idea what it meant to be married either. He had told her he'd never even had a girlfriend before and that he was shy around girls. While she didn't doubt his love for her, Mia believed he had found something with her that he'd never had before – a companion. James had been alone most of his life and when she appeared, the missing part of his soul came with her.

That's why he wanted to marry Mia, because he didn't want to lose her.

It was getting dark, which meant it was near dinnertime, and Mia had to dress for dinner. Lord Harold had badgered James during breakfast and she didn't want another scene. It was their last night together and Mia wanted it to be a good one.

Chapter Twenty-Eight

DINNER THAT EVENING WAS STRAINED. MISS NITHERCOTT WAS nervously explaining how she had forgotten to hire a guard and Harold Huxley told Mia he wanted her ready to leave at six the next morning. James wanted to go to the airport with her, but Harold denied his request. James called his father a "stupid, bloody bastard" and left the table.

Mia heard James slam his bedroom door shut as she climbed the stairs. She turned the knob on James' door, but it was locked, so she sat on the floor beside the door.

"James," she said. "Open the door."

James didn't respond, and Mia pressed her ear against the door. She'd seen his dark moods and feared he might do himself harm. Miss Nithercott had followed Mia up the stairs. She saw that the door was locked, and she gave Mia the key.

"Make sure he's all right," she said.

Mia opened the door, saw James' still form on the bed, and walked across the room. She crawled into the bed and pressed her forehead against his back. She wrapped her arms around him, and soon, James turned to face her. He saw the gold disk and his body stiffened.

"I can't believe you're wearing that thing," he said.

"I like it," Mia said.

"It's bollocks," James said. "There is no cottage. I've been in those woods a million times, and I've never seen a cottage."

"Well, I'll never know anyway because I'm leaving tomorrow."

James repeated his arguments as he tried to get her to change her mind and stay, and Mia repeated her reasons for going home.

"Let's go upstairs," Mia said.

"We could stay right here and lock the door," James said.

"But upstairs is our place. I want to spend my last night here where we fell in love."

Mia got up, and James followed her up the attic stairs. James lit the oil lamp while she went to the divan. Mia turned on her side and waited for James to come and lie down behind her. When he did, he put his arm around her and she snuggled against his chest. When she felt James arms loosen their grip on her, she slipped out of bed and went to the legless chair.

Mia's mind was in turmoil. When Mia met Rotrude, it was as if the witch could read her mind. She told her to come to her if Mia was in dire need. Mia *was* desperate, and time was running out. She put on the gold disk and felt it grow warm against her chest.

Mia longed for a safe place to have her baby. She needed time – time to think, time to give birth in peace, and time to let her and her baby grow old enough so that her mother would no longer be a threat. Mia closed her eyes and imagined herself sitting in a rocking chair with her baby in her arms. The scene caused the disk to grow warmer, and with that image in her head, Mia heard James stirring on the divan.

"How long have you been awake?" he asked.

They talked about how Mia had felt when one of her mother's boyfriends had stood beside her bed one night. It had made her feel powerless, which is how she felt now. Mia had decided to go to Rotrude and she hoped that by telling James this story, it would help him understand why she had to go. James told her he loved her, and Mia returned to him, lay on her side, and he put his arm over her. Soon, she felt his breath on her neck and knew he had fallen asleep. She lifted his arm, got off the divan, and went downstairs.

Mia had packed most of her clothes in the big suitcases, but had put her favorites, along with a photo of James, into a small carryon. Mia went to her room and grabbed that bag. She listened at Miss Nithercott's door and heard her rhythmic snoring. She then stopped by Lord Harold's door. He was snoring, too.

Mia went down the back stairs and slipped out the back door. The moon illuminated her path as she walked through the garden to the woods. The gold disk felt warm against her skin as she entered the woods, and then she noticed that the light from the disk was bright enough to show her the narrow path. Soon, Mia came to a clearing where the light was as bright as day. A small cottage with a thatched roof sat at the center of the clearing and for the first time in a long while, Mia felt safe. As she approached the cottage, the front door opened, and Rotrude stepped outside.

"I'm in trouble," Mia said. "You said if I was in dire need, you could help me."

"Come in," Rotrude said.

Mia followed Rotrude into the small cottage. Logs ablaze in the fireplace lit the room. A round table with four chairs sat in the middle, and Rotrude pulled a chair out for Mia. Mia put her bag on the floor and sat.

"What is your trouble, Mia?"

Rotrude went to a trunk pushed against a wall on the other side of the room. She lifted the lid, took something out, and came back to the table.

"I'm pregnant," Mia said. "I'm afraid to go home because my mother will want me to get rid of the baby."

Rotrude sat and held up a pair of necklaces, each bearing half of a silver coin on a thin leather strap. She put one on and looked at Mia.

"You want this child."

"More than anything," Mia said.

"What are you willing to do to keep this child?"

Mia's forehead creased.

"What do you mean?"

"Are you willing to leave James?"

"If...yes."

Rotrude lifted the leather strap around her neck to show Mia her half of the coin.

"Many years ago, my brother and I created a safe harbor for people in dire need. We called this place Havenwood." Rotrude held the halves so Mia could see what was on the coin. "This a Silver Stag. We use it to transport people to Havenwood."

"Is that where Margaret went?"

Rotrude raised her eyebrows. "You understood."

"That you were talking about Margaret when we were at the festival."

Rotrude smiled.

"She was hard to convince, but the pain became too much to bear."

"Is she still there?" Mia asked.

"She is married to my brother," Rotrude said.

Mia bit her lip.

"What if I want to come back?"

"You can come back whenever you like," Rotrude said.

"When the baby is grown so my mother can't take her away."

"It's your choice."

"Can James come with me?"

Rotrude studied Mia's face.

"Maybe you're not ready."

"I'm supposed to go home tomorrow morning. I don't have any more time. Please, can James go with me?"

Rotrude put her hand on Mia's.

"Does James know about the child?"

"I haven't told him." Mia sat back and lowered her eyes. "Because he wants to marry me."

Rotrude stared at Mia for a long time.

"You love him. I feel the love, but I also feel fear."

"I'm terrified," Mia said.

"You don't want to be poor," Rotrude said. Mia began to cry. "You don't want to be hungry. You want to raise your child in a safe, beautiful place."

Mia closed her eyes.

"It's been so hard," she whispered.

"And you want things to be easy," Rotrude said.

"But I want James, too."

Mia stared into Rotrude's eyes as a tear rolled down her cheek.

"I feel a whirlwind in your soul. You are young. You think that whatever you do today will be for the rest of your life, but you have so many years yet to live. Mia, come to Havenwood. You will be safe. Have your child. You can return to Dorley anytime you like and bring your child with you."

"He will be devastated," Mia said.

Rotrude sat back and studied Mia's heart.

"He is stronger than you think," Rotrude said. "But he is still a boy. In time, he will become a man." Rotrude paused. "Do you really want James to be with you in Havenwood?"

Mia opened her eyes and gazed at Rotrude. She remembered his dark moods and how hard he had begged her to marry him. Rotrude was right – James was still a boy. If Mia stayed in Havenwood until James grew up…

Mia got up and looked into Rotrude's eyes.

"Take me to Havenwood."

Chapter Twenty-Nine

MIA LOOKED AROUND HER AFTER THE WIND DIED DOWN. SHE HAD landed on her bum, and Rotrude was standing above her.

"Welcome to Havenwood." Rotrude said.

She held out her hand, and Mia got up, picked up her bag, and then followed Rotrude down a path through the woods. The air was sweet and the sky clear. No sound other than the birds' songs filtered through the trees, and for the first time in her life, Mia felt free.

When they emerged from the woods, Mia saw the circular Welcome Center and fell behind Rotrude. She clutched her bag in her arms and looked around. Rotrude hadn't said another word as she led Mia to the door of the Welcome Center, but now she stopped and turned to Mia.

"My brother's name is Greyson. He and his wife will help you understand life in Havenwood."

Rotrude opened the door and held it for Mia. Mia was still clutching her bag as she walked inside, and she kept it close as Rotrude walked past her to a door on the other side of the room.

"Is this a shortcut?" Mia asked.

"I thought Greyson would be here," Rotrude said. "I'll have to take you to his home."

When they went outside, Mia noticed that the streets were like the spokes of a wheel, and that a church like the one in Dorley occupied the corner of a street called Tinker Lane. She followed Rotrude and soon Mia saw the perfect patches of land that comprised Greyson's farm.

"My brother has always admired the farmers," Rotrude said. "You will learn that there is no need to grow your own food here, but Greyson does it for pleasure. It boggles the mind."

"It's beautiful," Mia said. "Everything is so perfect here." She glanced at the houses. "Where are the other people?"

"We don't have as many these days. Those we do have live in the center of town."

"So, these houses are empty?"

"For now."

A large stone cottage sat in the middle of Greyson's farm. It was taller than it looked from a distance, and surrounded by a garden where flowers from every country grew. A large apple tree stood beside the cottage, and a cow grazed beneath its branches. As they walked down the stone walk to the cottage, the scent of baking bread reminded Mia that she hadn't eaten in a while, and her stomach grumbled.

The door to the house was open, so Rotrude took Mia inside. There was no second floor in the house, which consisted of one large room with a peaked roof. A round table sat at the center of the room, and a large, cast-iron stove was against the wall to Mia's left. A fireplace filled the right wall, and, much to her surprise, a small, green dragon lay on the floor in front of it.

"That's Henny," Rotrude said. "He's very old, and he's lost all his teeth."

Mia cast a wary eye on Henny as they walked past him and out the back door. The branches of a large tree had been used to form a heart-shaped clearing behind the cottage, and two chairs sat side by side in the space. An young man and an older woman were holding hands when they saw Rotrude and Mia approaching them.

"Rotrude!" the man cried.

"You were supposed to meet us at the Welcome Center," Rotrude said.

"You didn't tell me we had a new arrival," the woman said.

"It must have slipped my mind," he said.

The man got up and then helped the woman to her feet. She held onto his arm while they waited for Rotrude and Mia, and then he smiled broadly at the small girl.

"This must be Mia," he said.

"This is Greyson, Mia," Rotrude said. "And this is his wife, Margaret."

Mia stared at Margaret as she tried to see past the wrinkled skin and gray hair. She recognized her from the photos she'd seen when she and James searched the newspaper archives.

"You're Margaret Huxley," Mia said.

"I used to be."

"I read about you in the paper. Have you been here all this time?"

"I came to Havenwood in 1950."

"James and I read about you."

"James?" Margaret asked.

"James Huxley. He's your nephew."

Margaret tilted her head. Greyson waved his hand, and two more chairs appeared.

"Why don't you sit down?"

They all sat, and Rotrude narrowed her eyes.

"I told you I was bringing her today," she said.

"It was my fault, Rotrude," Margaret said. "I was unwell this morning."

Greyson's eyes were on Margaret, and Mia's were on Rotrude. The witch of the woods was annoyed with her brother, and she didn't try to hide her feelings.

"I depend on you to handle things here," Rotrude said.

"I know, and you're right," Greyson said. "I should have sent someone in my stead."

Mia observed Greyson's long, dark blond hair and beard, his robe, and his deep, brown eyes. His presence made her feel safe.

"Mia is with child," Rotrude said. "You will have to keep an eye on her."

"Of course, Rotrude," Margaret said. "Agatha taught me all she knew before she passed." She looked at Mia. "Agatha was a midwife before she came to live in Havenwood."

"Her husband liked to burn her with cigarettes," Rotrude said.

"Is that necessary, sister?" Greyson asked.

"It's the truth. She should understand that her trouble is minor compared to those we've helped in the past."

"Why should she understand that?" Greyson frowned. "Do not diminish her dilemma. It's unfair to judge her that way."

Rotrude looked up at the sky and exhaled sharply.

"You're too soft, Greyson."

"And you have been hardened by what you've seen."

Rotrude stood.

"I've delivered her. I leave her to you."

Mia was shocked by Rotrude's words, for she had thought the witch was sympathetic to her situation. When she had gone, Mia turned to Margaret with a mouth set in a hard line.

"Rotrude is a good woman," Margaret said. "She's just seen too many women suffer at the hands of men."

"It has changed her," Greyson said. He took Margaret's hand. "So, we should explain to Mia how things work in Havenwood."

Greyson stood and helped Margaret to her feet. He waved his hand, and a walking stick appeared in her hand.

"Let's take a walk," Greyson said.

Mia, still clutching her bag, got up, and Margaret smiled at her.

"You can leave that here if you like."

Mia left the bag on her chair and followed them past the cottage and onto the road leading to the center of town. When they arrived at the Welcome Center, Greyson stopped and glanced at Mia.

"You will need a home to live in while you're here." He pointed toward the church. "Tinker Lane is popular with those who make crafts." He indicated another. "Yardley has several houses." He nodded toward another. "But Huxley road is fairly new. There are no houses on it yet."

"Can I look at that one?" Mia asked.

They walked in the direction of Huxley with Margaret hobbling along beside Greyson. Mia wondered if her broken ankle hadn't healed well, which meant her father's abuse had left her with a permanent, physical scar. Despite her past, though, Margaret seemed serenely happy. She gazed at Greyson as if he were the sun, and she Venus spinning in his orbit.

James was on her mind when Mia walked down Huxley Road. She wondered what he would do when he woke up to find her gone. Remorse over her decision not to tell him reared its ugly head, but Mia refused to let it take hold of her. She maintained the hope that James would mature and be ready to accept the responsibilities of fatherhood when she returned with their child.

"Here in Havenwood," Greyson said, "we conjure what we need. You will have the gift to conjure as long as you live here, so the first thing you must create is a home. Have you ever thought about what type of house you would like to live in?"

Mia remembered a visit to the Jersey shore and the old Victorian houses that lined the streets of small towns like Avon by the Sea.

"I like the old Victorian houses," Mia said.

"Oh, I like them, too," Margaret said. Her eyes lit up, and Greyson gazed at her with love.

"You never told me that, my dear," he said.

"I'm content with our cottage," Margaret said.

"We can always rearrange it if you like."

Margaret stroked his cheek.

"I told you that I am content. There is no need to rearrange our home."

Mia found it hard not to stare at them, for they seemed to glow with love. She wondered if she and James appeared that way to those around them.

Greyson held out his hands as he leaned his head toward Mia.

"When you need something, just imagine the thing in your mind and..."

Mia watched as an apple appeared in his palm. He held it in his hand for a second before giving it to Margaret.

"Now you," he said to Mia.

Mia lifted her hand, thought of an apple, and one appeared in her hand.

"Oh, wow," she said. She held it up and grinned.

"Now, try making something bigger," Greyson said.

"What do I do with my hands for something bigger?" Mia asked.

"Wave them as you imagine it."

Mia thought for a moment and then waved her hand. A rocking chair appeared on the ground in front of her.

"Holy shit," she said softly.

"And now, imagine a home," Margaret said.

Mia imagined a pink, two-story Queen Anne-style home with a large, white porch. When nothing happened, she looked at Greyson.

"Are you imagining a house?" he asked.

"Yes," Mia said.

"Sometimes, the larger things take a minute to manifest."

A moment later, the house appeared before them.

"Holy shit!" Mia cried.

"It's beautiful," Margaret said.

"It's amazing," Mia said. "I have to make furniture."

"Why don't we leave you alone so you can finish it up?" Margaret asked.

"Yes, we'll leave you alone now," Greyson said. "We have a communal dinner every evening at the Welcome Center, and we'd love to see you there."

Mia smiled and nodded her head.

"I'd love to come."

Mia watched Greyson and Margaret walk away, and then she scanned the land around her new home. Since hers was the only house on Huxley Road, she would make it a showplace.

Chapter Thirty

Mia wrapped her arms around her belly and sighed. She'd added a pillow to the rocking chair on the porch, but still felt uncomfortable when she sat. A girl named Marie was folding baby clothes and biting her lip.

"Why not just conjure them when it's born?" Marie asked.

"Because I want everything to be ready when she comes."

"How'd you know it's a girl?"

"I feel it," Mia said.

Marie eyed her for a moment, and then put the folded clothes in a box to be taken upstairs. She had been a resident of Havenwood for two years and still bore the physical scars of an abusive dad. Mia waved her hand, the box disappeared and then Marie sat on the porch floor, put her hands behind her, and smiled.

"You look like you're about to pop."

"Margaret said she will come soon. I can't wait to get her out of my body."

"Is it awful?" Marie asked.

"No, just uncomfortable. I can't find a way to sit without having pain in my back."

"I'll bet you wish that bloke was carryin' 'im instead of you."

An image of James came to Mia's mind, but she replaced it with one of the baby's room.

"So, what do you think of her room?" Mia asked.

"I like the paintin' on the wall."

197

Mia had imagined a scene out of Cinderella riding the pumpkin coach to the ball.

"I'm trying to think of what else I can put in there for her."

"Me mum never 'ad the money to fix up our room."

Marie's face fell as she thought of her mother. She had told Mia the story of her father's abuse and her mother's fear, of how she cowered when he beat his children, and it broke Mia's heart to think that Marie had run for her life to Havenwood after going to the festival in Dorley.

"I took the train to Dorley on me own. I 'ad a black eye and bruises on me arm, so when Rotrude saw me, she gave me the disk. I waited until it was dark and followed it to 'er."

Mia met other survivors of abuse in Havenwood, and those meetings left an indelible mark on her soul. The women in Havenwood had suffered, and Mia felt like an intruder, for she hadn't been the victim of physical abuse, just poor judgment, and when she looked at Marie, she tried to imagine the horror Marie had gone through. The girl was so small that a stiff breeze could knock her over, but she had repeatedly taken a punch from a large man.

Mia was always shocked by the way the women talked about the men who hurt them. Some defended their actions, while others missed them. Mia recoiled from the idea of being hit by a blow that sent you to the floor, but to these women, it was part of a life they remembered with fondness. Even Margaret would voice her regret over the decision she made when she was away from Greyson.

"I should have said something." Mia and Margaret were sitting behind the cottage when Margaret began talking about her father. "Maybe he would have stopped."

"Do you really believe that?" Mia asked.

"I believe anything is possible."

Mia shuddered as she thought about the accounts in the paper. The police thought Margaret was a drunk. Her reputation had been ruined so her father could save face. It disgusted Mia, and saddened her that Margaret still believed her father could have changed.

But when Marie talked about the beatings she'd endured, it meant more to Mia because they were the same age. She didn't understand when Marie complained of being bored, or would talk about her father as if he might have undergone some incredible change while she was gone. Mia worried that Marie would leave Havenwood too soon and return to her old life.

"He might be missin' me," Marie said.

"Who?" Mia asked.

"Me dad."

"You're kidding, right?"

"I'm not kiddin'. He was right fond of me. I know he misses me."

"He hit you all the time, Marie."

"So, a person can't change?" She sat up. "People change."

"Yeah, they do, but I doubt your father has changed."

Marie got up and went to the steps.

"He loves me," she said softly.

"How can you say that? He gave you a black eye. He broke your arm."

Marie turned to face Mia with fisted hands.

"What do you know about it anyway, miss la-di-da. You've had everything your whole life just handed to you. What do you know about anythin'?"

"I know what love feels like," Mia said as she held her stomach. "I could never punch her no matter what she did."

"Miss la-di-da. We'll see what happens when it's born."

Marie went down the porch steps. She glared at Mia before heading down the road, and Mia watched Marie walk toward the town. Mia had nothing in common with the women who lived in Havenwood and would often find herself alone during the communal dinner. She'd sit at the end of the big table in the Welcome Center watching them laugh as they looked in her direction, and then Margaret would come to her and put a loving arm around her, but it did little to ease Mia's pain. She longed for a friend, and she missed James terribly.

Mia got up and walked to the porch railing. The baby was due in six weeks, but she'd been having pains for days. Margaret said they were false labor pains, but that didn't ease her concerns. What she feared most was being alone when her time came, and she would often test Margaret by imagining her. Margaret would then reassure Mia that it was still false labor.

Now, as a pain rolled across her back, Mia tried to ignore it, but when she felt something trickling down her leg, she looked at the floor and saw a puddle.

"Margaret!" she cried.

Mia closed her eyes and focused on Margaret, but another pain ripped across her back. It was worse than the false labor she'd been having, and Mia gripped the railing. A moment later, Margaret appeared on the porch.

"I felt you calling me," she said. She saw the puddle beneath Mia. "Your water broke. You should change into something more comfortable."

Margaret held onto Mia and conjured them to Mia's bedroom. She helped Mia change into a nightgown and sat her on the bed.

"You don't have to lie down until you want to," Margaret said.

"It hurts so much," Mia said.

Margaret observed Mia for a moment and sensed her fear.

"Just keep reminding yourself that it will pass, and when you're done, you'll have a lovely baby to cuddle."

Mia tried to smile, but another pain ripped across her back, and she cried out.

"They are coming fast," Margaret said. "That's unusual for the first time. Lie down and let me look at you."

Mia obeyed, and Margaret checked the baby's position. Mia was already fully dilated.

"This is strange," Margaret said.

"What's strange?" Mia cried.

"That you are almost ready to deliver."

For a moment, Margaret wondered if Havenwood had anything to do with the rapid labor, but other women had given birth there, and there was nothing unusual about their labors. Perhaps Mia was just one of the lucky ones whose travail would pass quickly.

A few more moments passed, and Mia screamed again. Margaret lifted the blanket and saw the baby's head crowning.

"You must push now, Mia."

Mia pushed twice, and the baby was born. Margaret held him up and showed him to his mother.

"He's beautiful," Margaret said.

"It's a boy," Mia said. "He is beautiful. Can I hold him?"

"Let me clean him up first."

Margaret tied off the umbilical cord and conjured a warm bath in a basin. She cleaned the baby's nose and mouth, washed his eyes, and then his body. She wrapped him in a soft blanket and put him in the basket beside her bed that Mia had conjured for him.

"We have to finish here before I give him to you."

"What do you mean?" Mia had not finished the sentence when she felt the mild labor pains again. "Is there another one?"

"It's the afterbirth."

Once she had delivered the afterbirth, Mia held out her arms for the baby. Margaret brought him to her, and she gazed at him in wonder.

"He really is beautiful," Mia said.

"Aye. He is that. What will you name him?"

Mia had chosen a name for a boy and a girl. She smiled at her son and glanced at Margaret.

"Jon. Without an h."

"It's a good, solid name."

Mia pressed her head to his and closed her eyes.

"I can't believe how much I love him," Mia said.

Margaret's wan smile went unnoticed by Mia. She picked up the basin, and instead of conjuring it away, she held it and conjured herself to the kitchen. There, she conjured the basin away and held onto the sink as tears rolled down her cheeks.

As a young woman, Margaret had longed for a child, but it was not to be. She envied those who could have them, and now she wanted nothing more than to find solace in Greyson's arms. But Mia could not be alone, and the other women in town were not as fond of Mia as Margaret was. No, Margaret would have to dry her tears and tend to Mia for a day or two. She would smile and coo over the baby, and remind herself that instead of a child, she'd been given a wonderful man, one who loved her unconditionally. The thought comforted her as she sat near Mia's bed and watched her snuggle her newborn son.

Chapter Thirty-One

MIA CUDDLED JON AND COOED IN HIS EAR. HER FASCINATION with her young son brought a smile to Greyson's face, and Margaret saw how he looked at the boy. As he stood at the end of the bed, Margaret slipped behind him and went out the door.

In the kitchen, Margaret put the teakettle on and sat at the dining table. When Margaret came to Havenwood, she had little expectations save the absence of an abusive father and the avoidance of a loveless marriage, but that was before she fell in love with Greyson.

At first, she was standoffish and was careful not to be alone with him. It was easy, too, for she was nursing her ankle and would stay in the small house she'd conjured. Greyson respected her wishes. When her ankle healed, Margaret began taking walks around Havenwood, and discovered its wonders on her own. She didn't know that Greyson was watching her from a distance.

When he felt the time was right, Greyson approached her and asked if he could walk with her. A reticent Margaret accepted his company, but she balked at leaving the constraints of the village where the other women of Havenwood would serve as quasi-chaperones. She needn't have worried – Greyson's intentions were always honorable.

Their courtship was sweet, and their conversations, congenial. Margaret began to look forward to their afternoon strolls, and soon they were walking the entire width and breadth of Greyson's creation. Then one day, Greyson kissed her. It was the

202

beginning of love, an emotion that, for her, had always involved pain, so she kept her distance from him for several days.

After a week, Margaret found herself longing for his company, and took her first tentative steps toward trust. She made a decision to let Greyson into her heart and went looking for him at his farm. When he saw her, the warm look in Margaret's eyes sealed her acceptance that this man would never hurt her. A month later they vowed to honor each other until death separated them.

The teakettle whistled, and Margaret made herself a cup of tea. She could have conjured one, but there was comfort in the ceremony. Margaret put leaves in her cup and then filled it with the water from the kettle. Steamy tendrils scented with jasmine rose in the air bringing the comfort she so longed for.

Margaret wanted to be happy for Mia, but her inability to have a child left her bereft. She would often sit with women who had been forced to leave their children behind when they fled to Havenwood and took solace from their shared pain. Those women could eventually go home and see their children; Margaret would not.

Greyson's laughter echoed down the stairwell, bringing a new wave of pain to Margaret's heart. He had never complained that he had been cheated out of having a son, but that didn't quell the ache.

It didn't help that he still looked like a young man. His magical longevity kept him from aging like an ordinary man, but Margaret was sixty. She looked too old to be his wife now, even though Greyson seemed unaware of changes to her appearance. She wished she could embrace her "golden years," but it was hard when every year, Rotrude would bring another woman to Havenwood, and they were always younger now.

"Margaret."

Margaret started when she heard his voice behind her.

"Yes," Margaret said. "I'm having some tea."

Greyson came and sat across from her. He conjured a cup of tea and saw the look on her face.

"You look lovely today, my dear."

Margaret blushed.

"I look tired," she said.

"Not at all."

He reached for her hand and squeezed it.

"The child is healthy," Greyson said. "And Mia is happy."

"He's beautiful," Margaret said.

"And Jon is a fine name."

"It is."

Greyson sat back and exhaled softly.

"We missed our afternoon stroll yesterday," he said. "Perhaps we can spend tonight on the beach."

Margaret smiled as she recalled the first time they made love.

"It's been a long while since we watched the sunrise over the water."

"I agree."

The baby cried, and they both looked toward the stairs.

"I'll go and see how she's doing," Margaret said. She eyed Greyson. "And then we'll go to the beach."

Greyson winked at her, and then she went upstairs. The baby was still crying, and Mia was trying to soothe him, but Margaret saw how agitated she was. She went to the bed and put her hand on Mia's arm.

"Perhaps he's hungry," Margaret said.

"I tried, but he won't do anything."

"Place him near your breast."

Mia brought Jon to her bare chest.

"Now what?" Mia asked.

"Let him find your nipple."

"I tried that…"

"Mia, relax."

Margaret reached over and rubbed Jon's cheek, and he turned his head toward Mia's nipple. He shook his head with an open mouth and was rewarded when he found it. He latched on, and Mia smiled broadly.

"He did it!" she cried.

"Indeed he has," Margaret said. "The secret is to relax and let him do the work."

Mia held him close as he satisfied his hunger, and Margaret was able to take some joy from the scene.

"He's really lovely," she said.

"I can't believe how beautiful he is," Mia said.

"I'm going to ask June to stay with you. I want to go home and get some rest."

June was an older woman and was one of the few who had accepted Mia's presence without rancor, for she had brought her children to Havenwood when she came.

"Okay," Mia said. "Will you come back later?"

"I'll come back tomorrow," Margaret said.

Mia's face fell, but Margaret patted her hand and left her alone with Jon. She had learned long ago that if she let them, those in need would consume her. She found Greyson at the bottom of the stairs, and he waved his hand toward the door, it opened, and they went outside.

"We have to stop at June's before we go," Margaret said. "Mia needs someone for a day or two."

"And June has been kind to her," Greyson said.

"Yes." Margaret glanced at Greyson. "Do you think Mia will stay now that her baby has been born?"

"She feared that her mother would give her child away, so I think she will stay for a while."

"She's had a hard time adjusting to Havenwood," Margaret said. "The other women don't think she belongs here."

"She is just as deserving as they are," Greyson said. "She was in dire need."

"But she wasn't afraid of dying."

"Rotrude made the decision to bring her here. She must have felt Mia belonged here."

"Yes, Rotrude decided, and you always go along with whatever Rotrude wants."

Greyson stopped walking, and Margaret took a few more steps before turning to look at him.

"I do because Rotrude judges the heart, Margaret. She sees what we can't, and she believed Mia should come to Havenwood."

Margaret blushed and then smiled.

"Yes, she can read the heart." She started walking, and Greyson followed her past the Welcome Center and down Yardley Road. June's house was the second on the left side of the street. "It's so quiet now that the children have grown and gone."

"I was surprised June chose to stay," Greyson said.

"She said Havenwood is her home now, but she plans to visit them from time to time."

"Does Rotrude know that?"

"You have a Silver Stag, Greyson. You can take her if she asks you."

"I could, indeed."

Margaret smiled at him.

"Did you forget you had one?"

"It's been so long since I used mine that I guess it slipped my mind."

"Do you know where it is?" Margaret asked.

"Oh, yes, it's in that chest of drawers in our bedroom. I remember putting it there three hundred years ago."

Margaret put her hand on his.

"Three hundred years ago, and you don't look a day over twenty-five."

Greyson smiled.

"Neither to do you, my dear."

Margaret smiled, and for a moment she believed him. She kissed him and then left him while she went to the front door of June's house.

Chapter Thirty-Two

As Jon grew, Mia coped with loneliness. She missed James and wanted to go home, but feared what would happen if her parents found out about Jon. When she turned eighteen and was finally out from under her parents' autonomy, she still hesitated as she recalled Rotrude's words when she spoke of James.

"…he is still a boy. In time, he will become a man."

Had enough time passed? Had James become a man?

Mia was contemplating these thoughts while she sat cross-legged on the porch playing with Jon. Marie walked up to the porch steps and offered Mia a sad smile. She had been angry at Mia for a long while, but had missed talking to someone her own age and began stopping by in the afternoon when she knew Mia would be on the porch with Jon. Marie glanced at Jon and didn't try to hide her indifference toward him. She climbed the steps, conjured a rocking chair, sat, and crossed her legs.

"I'm goin' home," Marie said.

Mia tilted her head toward Marie.

"You are?"

"Me dad is dead, and I'm goin' to live with me mum."

"Are you okay?"

"He was a bastard."

"Are you excited?" Mia asked. Jon came to her and fell into her arms as he giggled.

"Not really. Me Mam will just take up with some other punter who likes to use his fists."

"Then why not stay?"

"Because I'm sick of this place," Marie said. "I want to see somethin' else."

"I'll miss you,' Mia said.

"You won't even notice I'm gone." Marie nodded toward Jon. "You've only got eyes for him."

"Well, that's true, but that doesn't mean I won't miss you."

Marie stood and went to the railing.

"It is a bit lonely out here. You could move to town."

"I've thought about it, but the others don't want me there."

"Suit yourself." Marie went to the steps. "I just wanted to tell you the news. Rotrude is comin' tomorrow to fetch me."

"Rotrude will be here?" Mia asked.

"Aye. Greyson didn't say when."

"I'll ask him."

Marie folded her arms over her chest and pouted.

"I guess that's it then," she said.

"I'll find out when you're leaving so I can be there," Mia said.

"Whatever."

Mia watched Marie go down the steps and walk away. She had been the closest thing to a friend Mia had in Havenwood and she would miss her.

As Mia watched Jon toddle across the porch to retrieve a stuffed bear, she wondered again if it was time to go home. She knew she was hiding in Havenwood, avoiding real life in favor of the fantasy she was living, but fear gripped Mia every time she pondered the idea. How would she look James in the eye after what she had done?

Her hand shook as she reached for Jon's ball, and she watched it for a moment. Mia was waking up in the middle of the night, her heart palpitating, and her hands shaking. It reminded her of the time she woke up and found her mother's boyfriend standing next to her bed. Mia froze, and when her mother called his name, the boyfriend had left her alone.

Now, Mia fisted her hand and wrapped her other hand around it.

"Mummy," Jon said.

His blue eyes studied her. He came to her with his hand extended, Mia took it in hers, and kissed it. She peered at his small face, a miniature version of James', and her heart ached, but she managed a smile.

"What is it, my darling boy?" Mia asked.

"Bear."

Jon held it out to her.

"Yes, bear."

She pulled him to her and wrapped her arms around him. She smelled his toddler scent and snuggled him. Jon pulled away and put his tiny hands on her cheeks.

"Mummy."

"Jon," she said.

She wasn't ready to go home. Mia wanted her son all to herself. She wanted to read to him and teach him how to write his name. Mia wanted her son to know she loved him unconditionally.

Mia put all thoughts of leaving aside for now. The time would come when she had to take Jon to Dorley, but until then, she would be the best mother she could be, and she persuaded herself that when it happened, James would understand.

* * *

Greyson didn't know when Rotrude would come for Marie, so Mia brought Jon to the Welcome Center in the morning to wait for Rotrude's arrival. As they always did, the other women congregated around the table, but June had left space for Mia at the end. She and Jon sat by a window instead and watched the birds pecking in the grass as Mia tried to ignore the others.

At noon, Rotrude came down the road. Mia saw her and felt her heart skip a beat. All Mia's decisions flew out the window as she thought of Marie going home. All she had to do was ask Rotrude to take her with them. Mia got up and took Jon's hand. He had his teddy bear with him, so why not join Marie?

"Because there are only two parts to the stag," Mia said aloud. She looked down at Jon. "But maybe if I ask her, she'll come back for us."

Mia's heart kept leaping back and forth as Rotrude and Greyson greeted each other. Marie arrived a few minutes later with a small bag in her arms, and Mia took Jon across the floor to greet her. It was an awkward goodbye, and Mia was surprised when Rotrude took her by the hand and led her outside while June watched Jon. They stopped a few feet from the entrance.

"You know I can read the heart," Rotrude said. "I see your struggle. You long for James."

"I want to go home but I'm scared."

Rotrude folded her arms over her chest.

"James is married." Mia backed away from her and shook her head. "He met a woman in college and they married."

"I don't believe you. You're just trying to get me to stay here."

"And why would I do that? It is of no concern to me if you stay or go."

Mia's lip trembled as her heart broke. He had moved on. He was no longer waiting for her to return.

"I can take you back to Dorley if that's what you want," Rotrude said. "Your father wants you to come home."

"My father wants me?" Mia shook her head again. "He never wanted me."

"You have judged him wrongly. Perhaps you should give him another chance."

Mia had trusted James, and he hadn't waited for her. She had never trusted her father, so why should she believe he had changed?

"I'll stay here until Jon is old enough for school," Mia said.

"It is your choice."

Mia left Rotrude and went inside the Welcome Center. She took Jon's hand, gave Marie a kiss on the cheek, and then took Jon home. They ate a small dinner, and Mia read to Jon until he fell asleep.

When she climbed into bed, Mia lay on her back and looked at the moon outside her window. Tears rolled down the sides of her face as she thought of James in the arms of another woman. Had he ever really loved her?

Mia turned the pillow over when she turned on her side. She had Jon, and he loved her. If he was the only one who ever needed her, it would be enough.

Chapter Thirty-Three

Seasons didn't change in Havenwood – it was always autumn, Rotrude's favorite time of year. The trees were full of colorful leaves that didn't leave their branches, and the crops were continuously ready to be picked. Some would argue that the sameness of it all could be stultifying, but in truth, it was soothing.

At the beginning of June during Jon's fifth year, Margaret had complained of a pain in her jaw, and then she fell while walking with Greyson along the beach. He carried her home to their bed and stayed with her through the night until she recovered her senses and seemed to heal. Two months later, though, she collapsed during a communal dinner, and this time Margaret didn't recover. She passed away in Greyson's arms.

Greyson buried her in the church graveyard and conjured a headstone. Mia and Jon stood by his side, and the other residents came to pay their respects. The community had dwindled in recent years, and only twenty-five women lived there now. Rotrude came to Havenwood to offer her condolences and stayed for the wake that followed Margaret's burial. Mia approached Rotrude after they had finished dinner. She hesitated for a moment, and then Rotrude spoke.

"He is no longer married," she said.

Mia's eyebrows rose.

"What?" she said.

"The marriage failed. He lives with his father now."

"At Huxley Manor?"

"Aye."

"You read the heart, Rotrude. Why did his marriage fail?"

Rotrude eyed her for a moment and then smiled.

"James' wife was unhappy. She said she didn't want to compete with a ghost."

"Me," Mia said. "I'm the ghost, right?"

Rotrude smiled again, and Mia felt her heart skip a beat. He hadn't gotten over her. His marriage failed because he still loved Mia.

"But he's still struggling with the black dog," Rotrude said. "He doesn't leave the attic."

"Who's James?" Mia hadn't seen Jon come to her side. "Why won't he leave the attic?"

"James is the man in the picture on the mantel," Mia said.

"My dad?" Jon asked.

"Yes, your dad."

"I'd like to meet his black dog."

Mia bit her lip, but Rotrude put her hand under his chin and studied his face.

"This one will never meet the black dog."

"But I want to meet him," Jon said.

"It's not a real dog, Jon," Mia said. "It's an expression people use to describe someone who's sad."

"My dad is sad?"

"Sometimes."

"I'll be back next month if you want to go to Dorley," Rotrude said.

"Are we going back to Dorley?" Jon asked.

Mia narrowed her eyes as she looked at Rotrude.

"Someday."

"When?" Jon asked.

"I haven't decided yet."

At five years, Jon was a bright boy who read every book that Mia could conjure. He was a cheerful soul who was eager to learn everything. Sometimes, though, Mia felt guilty about keeping Jon from the real world where he would be starting school. Greyson, who at first had championed their return, was now reluctant to see the boy go for Jon had become Greyson's dearest companion.

The old wizard was an exceptional teacher and took Jon all over Havenwood so Greyson could share the wonders of his world. Greyson began to believe he could teach Jon a deeper magic, but Mia wanted her son to have a normal life.

"He's not going to be a wizard," she said.

"But he's gifted, Mia. You must let him spread his wings."

"His wings are just fine the way they are." She peered at him from underneath her bangs. "Besides, I've been planning to take him back to Dorley soon."

So many others had left Havenwood in recent weeks that Mia had been reluctant to mention this to Greyson. Many were homesick, while others had found out that their abusers were no longer a threat. While they loved Havenwood, they also missed their families, and one by one, the houses emptied. Though it was the normal cycle of things in Havenwood, to Greyson, it felt different. He feared Havenwood was coming to an end. He kept his thoughts to himself while he sat with Mia at her dining table, but when she said she was planning to leave, he knew his thoughts were coming to fruition.

"It's what's best for Jon," Mia said.

"Rotrude told me that James is alone," Greyson said. "Is that why you're thinking of leaving?"

"He's gonna hate me for doing this."

"I don't think he will hate you."

"But he'll be mad, and he might not want to see me ever again."

"Mia, what do you want to do?"

"I want to give Jon the best life possible."

"And do you think you can do that here?"

Mia sat back and glanced at the window over the sink.

"He needs to be around other people. He needs friends his own age."

Greyson nodded and exhaled loudly.

"Then you should go. It's been six years, and I believe you're ready."

Mia folded her arms on the table.

"I don't have any money, Greyson. I didn't graduate high school. I won't be able to get a decent job, and I can't just conjure things there like I do here."

"He has a father, Mia."

"So, I'm gonna spring Jon on him, and he'll go, oh, I have a son, and even though Mia ran away and never told me he existed, I'm gonna accept my responsibility and pay her child support for the next ten years. That oughta go over big."

"You think so little of James," Greyson said. "I am sure he will rise to the occasion and embrace his fatherhood."

Mia frowned.

"I do not think little of him. I just know how men are when it comes to their kids."

"Not all men are the same, Mia."

"My father hardly spoke ten words to me even though I came all the way to London to see him. Me. I came. He never came to New York to see me."

"I'm sorry your father cared so little for you," Greyson said. "But you cannot paint James with the same brush."

"Look, I know James is a good guy, but he's also a dreamer. If he's spending all his time in the attic, then he's reading those fantasy books he loves. He'd rather be fighting a dragon than raising a kid."

"I don't think that's what's holding you back," Greyson said. Mia eyed him. "You see James as he was when he was a boy, but I think you are the one who's afraid to grow up."

"You don't think I've grown up?" Mia asked. Her eyebrows rose. "I got a big shove into adulthood, Greyson, so don't tell me I'm not grown up."

"Then take Jon to his father."

Greyson got up, patted her shoulder, and then went to Jon's room to bid him goodnight. The old wizard felt a bit defeated when he left Mia's house, so he went to the Welcome Center and looked at Jon's drawings that covered its walls. The communal dinners were discontinued after Margaret passed away, increasing the sense of an ending that permeated Greyson's thoughts, but as was his nature, he tried to remain optimistic. Still, when he left the Welcome Center and went toward the woods, he noticed that some of the leaves had fallen off their branches. It puzzled him, and he summoned Rotrude. When the night passed without hearing from her, Greyson went to the chest of drawers in the bedroom and withdrew his Silver Stag.

* * *

A BREEZE BILLOWED THE CURTAINS IN MIA'S ROOM, AND IT tickled her hand as she dozed. Jon was asleep in his bedroom, but Mia was restless. After Greyson left, she sat on the porch for a long time, trying to imagine what James looked like now. What would he think of her if he saw her again?

Mia thought about her conversation with Greyson. He was right – Mia had been hiding long enough. It was time to face the music and introduce Jon to his father. Mia had to give James a chance to step up and be a father. She would pack a small bag for each of them and go to Greyson first thing in the morning.

Mia noticed a strange scent the air when she pulled her blanket up to her chin. She opened her eyes and saw a shadow at the end of her bed. Terror filled her heart as the shadow move to the side of the bed and a hand grabbed her arm. It gripped her tightly and pulled her to her feet.

The man wasn't much taller than Mia, but his strength outmatched hers. He pushed her out the bedroom door, and when she protested, Mia felt the barrel of a gun in her back.

"Go," he said. "Down the stairs."

Mia glanced at Jon's room as she prayed he would stay asleep. She was halfway down the stairs when she saw someone else near her front door, a familiar face that appeared to be as frightened as she.

"Marie," Mia said, but the man hit the side of Mia's head with the butt of the gun and she fell to the floor.

"Shut your gob," he said.

Mia saw stars, but the man grabbed her arm again and pulled her to her feet. She felt blood run down her cheek and wiped it away. Mia looked at Marie. She had a gun in her hand, too.

"Why?" Mia asked.

"I said shut your gob!" The man raised his gun again, but Mia ducked, and he missed. "Out the door, now."

Marie moved toward the door.

"Not you," he said. "Just her."

"You're not leavin' me here," Marie said.

"I told you I'd come back for ya," he said as he gripped Mia's arm.

Marie thrust out her chin.

"You ain't gonna leave me here."

Marie had her back against the door. The man raised his gun, and Marie flinched.

"This isn't fair," Marie said. "I told you where she was. I told you about her. You can't leave me here."

"Move," the man said. "I told you I'd come back for you, now move." He gripped Mia's arm so tightly she gasped. "I'll kill you. You know I will."

Marie moved aside, and they went out the door. She went out after them and followed them down the porch.

"I can hold onto her," Marie said. "I can hold onto her arm when you put the pieces together."

The man kept walking, pulling Mia along as she dragged her feet.

"She can hold onto me," Mia said.

"Another word." He held up the gun. "Dead or alive, it said."

Dead or alive? Mia thought.

The gunman continued to pull her down the road.

"You can't leave me here!" Marie cried.

Mia tried looking behind them for Jon, but the man kept pulling her, and she feared falling down. Dead or alive. She took his meaning and didn't want to give him a reason to shoot her.

The man was ahead of Mia as they made their way down the road. Marie kept following them, begging him to take her with them. They went past the Welcome Center, and Mia strained to see if anyone was about, anyone who could help her.

"Please, Boris, don't leave me here."

"That's your name?" Mia asked. "Boris?"

Boris stopped and backhanded Mia. She fell to the ground, and then he yanked her up by her arm. Boris kept going until they reached the clearing where Rotrude had landed when she brought Mia to Havenwood. Marie was close when he took off one half of the Silver Stag and put it around Mia's neck.

"How do you have that?" Mia asked, and he slapped her.

Marie grabbed Mia's arm, and Boris hit her across the face with the butt of the gun. Marie fell, and Mia saw blood trickle from Marie's lip.

"You wouldn't have even known about her if it wasn't for me," Marie said.

"Shut up, you stupid cow," Boris said. "For Christ's sake, I told you I'd come back for ya."

Marie hung on Mia's arm.

"No you won't," Marie said. "Me Mum knew. She knew what you were."

Boris pulled Mia away from Marie and pushed Marie to the ground. He got behind Mia, held up his half of the Stag, and put it in Mia's face.

"Grab your piece," he said.

Mia didn't move, so he held the barrel of the gun to her cheek.

"Hold it up!"

Mia picked up her half and held it in front of her. Boris held the gun over Mia's shoulder and aimed it at Marie.

"Please, Boris," Marie said. "You can't leave me here." Marie tried to get up, but she faltered. "Damn you, Boris. Damn you to hell."

Mia held her half of the Stag up, but not high enough to meet Boris' half.

"I said hold it up!"

She raised her hand, and Boris pressed his half against hers. The wind began to blow. It blew Mia's hair across her face, and she didn't see Marie raise her gun.

* * *

Greyson heard the shot as he was putting the Silver Stag around his neck. He ran out of the cottage and toward the Welcome Center. He saw Jon a second before the boy saw him.

"Greyson!" Jon cried. "I can't find Mummy!"

A chill ran up Greyson's spine, and then he saw June running toward them.

"What on Earth was that?" June asked.

"I don't know," Greyson said. "But Jon can't find his mother."

"Are you all right?" June asked Jon.

"I heard something and went to find Mummy, but she wasn't in her bed."

"June, you must take care of Jon. I have to go and find Rotrude."

June put her arm around Jon's shoulders, and they watched as Greyson pulled the Silver Stag from beneath his robe. He pressed the halves together, and June and Jon were knocked back by the wind as it lifted him into the air.

Greyson landed in the woods bordering Huxley Manor. He was near Symond's marble altar and went to the path that led to Rotrude's cottage. There was no smoke rising from her chimney, and the door was open. He tried to sense her spirit but felt nothing.

Greyson stood at the door and scanned the room as his eyes adjusted to the dark. He saw Rotrude's colorful skirt lying on the floor a few feet away. He took two steps inside and saw her blouse. When he was closer, he saw dust near the hem of her skirt, at the bottom of the sleeves, and near the neck of her blouse, but there was something odd about the dust. There was nothing above the neck.

Greyson felt his heart lurch as he understood why - her head was gone. He forced himself to look across the room. A dark blonde braid lay in a pile of dust in front of the fireplace. Greyson ran from the house and fell to his knees. Rotrude had met a terrible end, and now he understood why the leaves had fallen off the trees in Havenwood.

Their magic had created another world. It worked because they had done it together – and Rotrude was at its heart. He wailed in pain. Havenwood was dying, and that meant that he, too, would die. Whoever had done this had ended their dream.

The pain was replaced by rage as he imagined Rotrude's last minutes on Earth. They must have surprised her, but how? She would have reacted if she sensed danger was near. She would have cloaked the cottage – unless she knew them. Someone whom she had trusted.

There had been so many transported between the worlds that Greyson had no idea whom it could be. How could one of their women do such a horrible thing? And why? It made no sense to Greyson, and if he stood there trying to figure it out, he would lose precious time, for whoever had done this might have taken Mia against her will, and Greyson had to find her.

Greyson went outside and walked a few feet away. He faced the cottage, raised his hands, waved the house into oblivion, and then walked through the woods toward Dorley. He was near the edge of the woods when he saw someone lying on the ground.

The man was lying on his stomach. Blood stained the back

of his jacket, and when Greyson felt his neck, there was no pulse. Greyson looked around for Mia, but all he saw was a trail of crushed leaves with traces of blood leading away from the scene. Greyson followed the trail until he reached the edge of the woods.

He saw a crowd gathered, and people were yelling at each other. He waved his hand and cloaked himself so he could approach them unnoticed. They were surrounding a form lying on the ground, and Greyson went past the people until he saw what they were looking at. It was Mia, and she had a large bloodstain on her nightgown.

"She's been shot," a man said.

"Did anyone call the police?" another said.

"I'll go and get the constable," a woman said.

Greyson hovered near them until the police came, and was there when a vehicle took Mia away. He then followed the police into the woods where they found the body of the man.

"I know who that is," a policeman said. "That's Boris the Butcher."

"It can't be," another said. "He's still locked up."

"He got out a few weeks ago."

Another man in a plain suit came up to the group and looked at the man's body.

"Boris Black," he said. "I'll be damned."

"That girl must have been with him," the first man said.

"What girl?" the man in the suit asked.

"The one they took to Brandmore. Looked like she'd been shot."

"Right. I'll go to Brandmore, and you get his body to the morgue."

Greyson leaned against a tree and felt the weight of grief rest on his shoulders. He didn't know if Mia had died, or why this man, this Boris Black, had taken her, but he had to go home. He had to make sure that Jon was safe. As two men came into the woods with a large, black object and laid it beside the body, Greyson lifted the halves of the Silver Stag and pressed them together.

Chapter Thirty-Four

Hettie Nithercott was having a bad day. She'd been sacked from her job and had few prospects on the horizon. The rent was due on her small flat, and her shoes hurt her feet. She was at the end of Baker Street and looking down the road that led to Huxley Manor when she spied a small gathering near the entrance to the park. Her curiosity urged her to join them, and when she did, she was shocked by what had brought them together.

A young woman lay on her stomach on the ground, and the nightgown she wore was stained with blood. A woman was kneeling beside her.

"Should we turn her over?" the woman asked.

"No," another said. "Wait till the ambulance comes."

"But I'm worried she can't breathe," the first woman said.

"I can see her breathing, " a man said.

Hettie stared at the young woman and pursed her lips. There was something familiar about her, and Hettie strained to recall where she had seen her. Then, with remarkable clarity, Hettie knew who it was. In an instant, she remembered the headlines and the way the media had hounded James Huxley. Her natural instinct was to protect this girl, and so she said the first thing that came into her mind.

"That's my daughter!" Hettie cried. "Oh, Mary."

She pushed her way through the crowd and bent over Mia.

Mia's cheek was cut, and Hettie recoiled at the sight of the blood.

"Mary," Hettie said. "Oh, my sweet daughter."

Where had you been all these years? Why are you in Dorley?

The local constable asked people to stand aside as he came to Mia's side.

"Move back, madam," he said to Hettie.

"She's my daughter," Hettie said.

"What's her name?"

"Mary Nithercott."

"Have you any idea what happened here?" he asked.

"She ran away years ago. I haven't seen her in all that time. Oh, Mary."

Hettie's concern for Mia was real, and the constable didn't question her claim that she was the victim's mother.

"Why did she run away?" he asked.

"She was sixteen. Who knows why a sixteen-year-old does what they do."

"Aye, I can agree with that," he said.

A siren broke through the chatter of the crowd, and people stepped aside to let the male and female paramedics through. Now, Hettie moved back and let them tend Mia. She watched them gently turn her over and place her on a stretcher. All was done within five minutes, giving Hettie little time to plan her next move. As they put Mia in the back of the ambulance, Hettie's instincts kicked in.

"I want to go with her," she cried. "I'm her mother."

The female paramedic helped Hettie into the back of the ambulance and showed her where to sit. Hettie held Mia's hand as they drove away, and the woman placed an intravenous line in Mia's other arm. Hettie looked at Mia's pale face.

"Why is she bleeding?"

"She's been shot," the woman said.

"Oh, dear lord," Hettie said.

"She's lost a lot of blood, but it looks like the bullet went straight through."

"And that's good?" Hettie asked.

Before the woman could answer, the ambulance was pulling into the lot behind the emergency entrance to Brandmore Hospital.

"Take the necklaces off and put 'em in your purse," the woman said. "Otherwise, someone might nick 'em."

Hettie hadn't noticed the leather straps around Mia's neck. She took them off and saw that they held two halves of a silver coin. Hettie then slipped them into her purse.

The paramedic helped Hettie down and told her to go to the waiting room. She watched them take Mia through a set of double doors before finding an empty chair in the waiting room. It was the first time she'd had time to contemplate the events of the past hour, and now she remembered that Mia had been pregnant when she ran away.

"Oh, lord," Hettie said. *What happened to the baby?*

Hettie saw a woman with a clipboard come through the double doors.

"Ms. Nithercott?" the woman said.

"I'm Mrs. Nithercott," Hettie said.

The woman came and knelt down in front of Hettie.

"Hello, luv. I'm so sorry about your daughter."

"Is she all right?" Hettie said, panic rising in her voice.

"Oh, sorry, yes, well, they're operating on her now."

"Oh, my God, you made it sound like she died."

"Sorry. So, I must ask you to fill out this form and give me her NHI card so I can make a copy."

"I'll have to look for it when I go home," Miss Nithercott said. "She ran away years ago."

"Oh, well, in that case, we can look her up," the woman said. "Just give me her full name and birthdate."

Hettie blushed and bit her lip. She'd been a copper in her younger days and Hettie remembered a couple who were arrested for child abuse. When Hettie looked for the child's birth record, she couldn't find it and asked the couple why they hadn't registered the birth.

"We live off-grid," the man told her. "We don't have any papers."

Hettie kept her eyes on the ground and softened her voice.

"She was born off-grid," Hettie said. "She doesn't have a birth certificate or an NI number."

The woman tapped her pencil against the clipboard.

"Really? I've heard of that, but I've never met anyone who actually lived off-grid. You'll have to get it sorted right away."

222

"I'm not sure how to do that," Hettie said.

"They should be able to help you at a registry office. So, luv, just fill out the papers the best you can, and I'll come back for them."

Hettie looked at the first page. She wrote "Mary Jane Nithercott" as the patient's name and then stared at it. What if Mia woke up and told them her real name? Would Hettie be arrested for making false claims?

She left the lines asking for the address blank and made up a date for Mia's birth with the correct year of 1970. She had no idea what childhood illnesses Mia had suffered and feared if she entered false information it might affect her treatment, so she left that blank, too. If they asked, she'd feign memory loss due to her "hippie lifestyle," which included "smoking too much marijuana."

Hettie took a small notepad and pen from her purse and began a list of things she would have to do for Mia until she woke up and could speak for herself. Applying for official documents would be the last thing on the list for Hettie didn't fancy doing something illegal, and hoped to have Mia sorted before anyone insisted upon seeing them.

As she waited for news of Mia, Hettie thought of James. He should know that Mia had been found, but was it her place to tell him? Mia had run, whether from James or something else Hettie didn't know, but it was up to Mia to make a decision to see him again. For now, Hettie would continue the ruse of being Mia's mother until they could decide what to do next.

Hours passed before a doctor seeking Mrs. Nithercott came through the double doors.

"I'm here," Hettie said, raising her hand.

The doctor looked serious but not grim, and she smiled a bit when she came to Hettie.

"She was fortunate," the doctor said. "The bullet entered the front of her body just below her left shoulder and went out the back. I was able to stop the bleeding and stitched the wounds. I also stitched a cut on her head, and there are bruises on her arm and wrist as if someone held her tightly."

"Oh, thank God," Hettie said. "Can I see her?"

"She's recovering. Someone will come and get you when they move her to a room."

An hour passed before someone came and took her to Mia's room. Mia was being monitored by a machine and hooked up to an intravenous drip. She looked small and pale, and Hettie's eyes filled with tears. She sat beside Mia's bed and again thought about James as she took the girl's hand.

"Keep out of it, Hettie," she said.

It was hard not to tell him, for she knew that James had loved Mia. Perhaps he still did, and keeping this from him was wrong. She willed Mia to wake up so she could talk to her, to get her permission to let James know she'd been found, but the girl was as still as death. Hettie kept looking at the monitors to make sure Mia was still breathing.

In the evening, a nurse came in and stood at the end of the bed reading Mia's chart.

"So, this is your daughter?" she asked.

"Aye. Mary Jane."

"I heard they found Boris Black's body in the woods near where they found her. She must have fallen in with a bad lot, poor thing."

"Boris Black?" Hettie said. "No one mentioned him when we found her."

"It's what I heard," the nurse said. "It's on the news."

Hettie had read newspaper accounts of Boris Black's crimes, and the thought of him touching Mia made her shudder. He had been released from prison amidst protests against it from the families of his victims, and Hettie knew he had lived in Liverpool. Had Mia been in Liverpool all this time?

"I've read about Boris Black," Hettie said. "He's a bad one."

"Well, he won't be hurting anyone now." She put Mia's chart down. "I'll be checking on her again before I leave tonight."

When the doctor left, Hettie put her hand on Mia's. What had Boris Black done to her? Was she forced to do things…?

Hettie closed her eyes and shook her head to drive the thoughts away. Her back ached from sitting too long, and it was getting dark. She didn't want to leave Mia, but she had to go home and get some sleep.

Hettie wrestled with her thoughts of James when she went to bed that night. She had seen him a few weeks ago when they met on the street, and she'd shown him her flat. He had been struggling with the black dog again, but he had bought a pub and hoped he could stay out from under Alfie's dark sway.

"It has a flat, and I won't have time to brood," James said. "You should come and see me. It's near the train station."

James had given her a card with the name of the pub and its address, and she'd stuck it in the top drawer of her bureau. She took it out when she got back to her flat, where she also found a notice of eviction on her door. She had seven days to vacate the flat.

While Hettie grappled with her own dire situation, Mia fell into a coma. When Hettie came to see her the next morning, she found the nurse lightly pinching Mia as they tried to rouse her.

"We haven't been able to wake her," the nurse said.

"She wasn't in a coma when I left last night," Hettie said.

"Well, she did suffer a head injury. I'm sure the doctor can tell you more when you see her."

Hettie sat beside the bed and held her purse on her lap. It contained all the cash she had in the world – five pounds and sixpence. Hettie had nothing of value, no jewellery to sell, or money hidden away in some safety deposit box. Her shoulders slumped as she felt the weight of her dilemma bearing down on her.

Hettie recalled reading an ad in the Journal that appeared on the day of the festival. Mia's dad had offered a reward for any information that would lead to her recovery. He wanted to know what had happened to his daughter and wanted to know even if the news was terrible. At the time, Hettie had felt sorry for the poor man and wished she knew where Mia was so she could end his suffering.

Now, she realized that she did know and that the reward money would go a long way to solving Hettie's problems. She imagined herself calling the number and telling Mr. Wentworth that his beloved daughter was in Brandmore Hospital. One hundred thousand pounds would allow Hettie to buy a small cottage somewhere. Her needs were few, and that money might support her for the rest of her life.

Then, Hettie remembered the day she confronted Mia about the pregnancy. Mia had been adamant about keeping the baby a secret, and Hettie had given her word that she wouldn't tell anyone. Her word was her bond, and that meant that she couldn't go to Mr. Wentworth or tell anyone else – not even James – that she had found Mia Wentworth.

Mia remained in a coma for three days, and each day Hettie came and sat by her bed. The nurses told her to talk to Mia, and she spun a yarn about their lives and the years they lived off-grid. It was nice to imagine what it would have been like to raise a little girl for all Hettie's "children" were boys. As she watched Mia, Hettie willed her to wake up, and one day, Mia opened her eyes.

A week passed as Mia continued to shake off the coma. She was moved to a room with other patients, and it had a vinyl-covered sofa under a window near Mia's bed. Mia looked at Hettie when she came to her bed and always had a look of wonder on her face. Hettie kept their conversation light and generic with no mention of Huxley Manor or James.

Seven days passed, and Hettie packed her things and left her flat for the last time. Everything she owned filled one large suit-case, which she brought with her to Mia's room. Hettie didn't know what she would do when visiting hours were over, but she'd cross that bridge when she came to it. For now, she had a place to be.

When Hettie arrived, she put her suitcase on the floor and sat on the sofa. Mia was wearing a nightgown one of the nurses brought from home when they learned that Mia didn't have any clothes. Her cheeks were pink and her eyes bright.

"They're sending me home tomorrow," Mia said, and Hettie panicked.

"Oh, luv."

Mia glanced at the door and then turned her attention to Hettie.

"I know you're not my mother," Mia said softly. "Why did you tell them you were?"

"Because I was afraid for you."

Mia sat on the edge of the bed so she could face Hettie.

"I remember you."

Hettie smiled.

"And I, you."

"I just can't remember why I know you."

Mia winced when she moved to stand.

"They told me I was shot, but I don't remember it."

"You had quite a shock," Hettie said.

"The doctor wants me to go to a care home for a week, but the nurse said I don't have an NHI card." Mia took a few, wobbly steps, and Hettie shook her head.

"I'm not sure what to do. I don't have any papers for you. I told them you were born off-grid and they told me I would have to get you registered, but I'd have to lie, and I'm a terrible liar."

Mia stared out the window for a moment.

"Was I born off-grid?"

Hettie eyed Mia.

"You don't remember?"

"It's all a jumble what I remember. I'm having trouble making sense of it."

"Well, I'm sure as time goes by, you'll sort it."

Mia smiled at Hettie.

"Who am I?"

Hettie looked at the door and at the other patients.

"Your name is Mia Wentworth," Hettie whispered. "You're American."

Mia tilted her head and then smiled broadly.

"Mia Wenworth," she said. "I remember being on a plane." She grinned. "I came to visit my father." Her eyebrows rose. "You're Miss Nithercott!" Her grin faded. "James."

Mia went back to the bed and sat on the edge. She stared at the tiled floor as she remembered James and her feelings for him.

"There's something…James…something I can't…" Mia looked at Hettie. "There's something about James I can't remember."

"I'm sorry, dear. I haven't seen you in years."

Hettie thought of the baby, but she couldn't bring herself to ask. It was better to let Mia's mind come back on its own.

"I told them your father was American, and that's why you talk like you do."

"You thought of everything," Mia said.

"Once you start lying…"

By nine, a reminder that visiting hours were over announced, and Mia had fallen asleep. The sofa was soft, and the room was dimly lit. Perhaps if Hettie put her legs up and feigned sleep, they would let her stay overnight. She lay down and closed her eyes. Soon, Hettie drifted off and was sound asleep when the nurse came to check Mia's vital statistics at midnight.

"Mrs. Nithercott," the nurse said as she shook Hettie's shoulder. "Perhaps it's time you went home."

Hettie put her feet on the floor, but she remained on the sofa.

"I've nowhere to go," Hettie said.

The nurse looked at the suitcase and then at Hettie's face.

"I shouldn't do this, but they can't see you from the door, so just stay here for now."

Hettie's gratitude shone on her face, and it touched the nurse's heart, but there was little else she could do for Hettie.

The lure of Mr. Wentworth's money beckoned her again as Hettie sat on that sofa. She didn't want to go into social housing with drug dealers and prostitutes. Hettie wanted a nice, clean, quiet place where she could enjoy her sunset years. She never imagined that she would end up like so many domestic workers who gave the best years of their lives to the care of others only to find themselves alone and penniless when their physical strength was gone. But here was Hettie, penniless and alone, and all she had to do was make one telephone call...

"Stop," she said softly.

Honor meant everything to Hettie. It was the way she had lived since becoming a police officer, and then a governess. She taught her children the importance of giving your word and standing by it. Hettie had reinforced its importance over and over until the children tired of hearing it, but her words had left an impression that would stay with a child for life.

No. Hettie couldn't break her own word, no matter what the cost.

Chapter Thirty-Five

THE NEXT MORNING, A YOUNG WOMAN NAMED JOAN CAME TO THE room and sat next to Hettie. Mia was eating her breakfast. Joan had a clipboard and pen, which she held over the clipboard as she asked Hettie questions.

"One of the nurses called our office and said you were in a spot of difficulty," Joan said. Hettie bit her lip. "She said your daughter is scheduled to leave hospital today but that you don't have anywhere to go, is that correct?"

"It is," Hettie said softly.

"Well, let's see if we can sort this before she's discharged."

Joan made a note on her clipboard. "So, Mary's paperwork doesn't list a place of birth. Where was she born?"

"In Northumberland. We were on a large farm."

"The name of the town?"

"I think it was called Whalton. I'm not sure anymore. It was more than twenty years ago."

"Can you remember the name of the hospital?" Joan asked.

"She was born at home," Hettie said.

"And you never had the birth recorded?"

"It was against our beliefs," Hettie said.

"And no one in Whalton ever asked you about it?"

"Why should they? We kept to ourselves and farmed the land. It was easy to hide a baby."

The flow of lies was astonishing for a self-proclaimed "terrible" liar, and Mia smiled.

"You said Mary ran away when she was sixteen. Why?"

"We would fight about boys and such, and one day I woke up and she was gone."

"And you never reported her missing?" Hettie cast her eyes to the floor. "Why didn't you report her missing, Mrs. Nithercott?"

"I was ashamed. She was sixteen. I'd run off when I was sixteen."

"So, you just let her go," Joan said.

"I had no husband. I could barely keep myself together, let alone a sixteen-year-old girl."

Joan's mouth set in a hard line. Hettie's story was the same as many Joan had heard before. She jotted something on the clipboard and then exhaled loudly.

"And now you don't have a place to live," Joan said.

"I lost my flat because I couldn't work for coming here."

Joan eyed Mia.

"We were able to arrange a few days in Brakenshire for you. The care home will help rehabilitate you." Joan turned to Hettie. "She needs to heal if she's to take care of herself." Joan took a slip of paper from her pocket. "My great-aunt owns a rooming house in Woollcott. She believes in helping others who have fallen on hard times. What is your income right now?" Hettie pursed her lips. "Mrs. Nithercott."

"I don't have an income right now."

"How old are you?" Hettie remained silent. "Please, Mrs. Nithercott. I need to know so I can help you."

"I'm sixty."

Too young for a state pension. Joan sat back and hugged her clipboard.

"The rent Aunt Lily charges is well beneath what she could ask for. Sometimes, she takes in someone who can't pay at all. We, that is the family, aren't happy about it, but it's her house, so we leave it alone." She glanced at Hettie. "I'll see if she has a room available."

"I don't have *any* money," Hettie said softly.

"You won't need any, at least not for a bed. You'll have to pay for food, but Aunt Lily won't let you starve."

"Why are you doing this?" Hettie asked.

"Because you're between a rock and a hard place, and I'd

want someone to do it for me if I ever found myself in your situation."

Joan left them alone, and Hettie exhaled loudly.

"Well, that was a surprise," Mia said.

"You never know, do you?"

"Now, I just have to figure where to go when I leave the care home."

"We still have a few days to sort that," Hettie said. "You just focus on getting better."

"Miss Nithercott?" Mia asked.

"Yes, dear."

"Thank you."

"You're welcome, luv."

* * *

HETTIE AND HER NEW LANDLADY, A SWEET, VICTORIAN LADY named Miss Lily Profitt, got along famously. Every afternoon, Lily would make tea, and they would drink it in the sitting room while sharing the gossip of the day. Lily helped Hettie secure a position in a ladies' wear in town, which paid little but gave Hettie the means to travel to the care home in Brakenshire.

Mia's memory was still giving her trouble. She had also been experiencing symptoms of Post Traumatic Stress Syndrome and was seeing a counselor. Since her time at the care home was limited, the counselor recommended a halfway house and had been able to place Mia in one in Brakenshire a block away from the care home.

"Are you worried about this traumatic stress thing?" Hettie asked Mia one day while they sat in front of the halfway house.

"A little," Mia said. "I have nightmares that scare the hell out of me."

"But there's a counselor there who should help you."

"They teach you how to cope," Mia said. "That's about all they can do."

"And how's your memory coming along, dear?"

"It's coming back. Not as fast as I'd like it to, but the doctors are happy with my progress."

"I've been thinking about James," Hettie said. Mia furrowed her brow. "Have you thought more about talking to him?" Hettie waited for a reply, but Mia stared at the lawn. "Would you like me to tell him that you're all right?"

"I don't know," Mia said. "Do you think he'll remember me?"

"He was in love with you. How could he forget?"

"I just, it's just that it's been so long." She stood. "And after what I did, I don't think he'll ever forgive me."

"He can't if you don't give him a chance," Hettie said.

Mia wrapped her arms around herself and sighed.

"I can't see him yet," she said. "I'm not ready."

"Okay, dear. When you're ready."

They walked back to her room and were met by a woman named Glynis, who had been trying to help Mia find a place to live when she was released from the halfway house.

"Hullo," Glynis said.

"Hi," Mia said. "I don't think you've met my mother."

"Hello, dear," Hettie said.

"We've been trying to find a place for Mary because we need her bed for one of our returning soldiers."

The halfway house had been established to help the soldiers returning from the Falklands. Mia's acceptance had always been temporary.

"Oh, those poor lads," Hettie said.

"Indeed," Glynis said, "and so we must find our Miss Mary a place as soon as possible."

Hettie had been concerned about this herself, and then one day, she was making a list of things Mia could do to earn a living when something came in the post. It had been forwarded from an address she'd left two years before and had somehow found its way to Miss Profitt's boarding house. It was from one of Hettie's "children," a boy named Sidney Jackson whose great-grandfather had made a great deal of money mining tin. Sidney had used one of his family's estates to build an animal refuge, and on a whim, Hettie called him and asked if he needed help. Sidney was thrilled to hear from his old nanny and said that yes, indeed, he was looking for an assistant.

"I can't pay much, but there's an old hermitage on the property. We put in a bathroom so whoever gets the job can live there."

"I think I have the perfect person for you. She's…my niece. Her name is Mary."

"Why don't you bring her up, and we'll all have lunch?"

They arranged to meet the following Wednesday, and when Hettie told Mia, she suggested Mia pack a bag.

"If you come with a bag, how can he say no?"

"Don't you think that's being a little pushy?" Mia asked.

"Would you rather live on the street?"

"No, but I don't want to force him to accept me."

"You're not forcing him to do anything. I saw a lady on the telly talking about something called The Secret. She said if you focus on something, the universe will give it to you, at least that's what I got out of it, so, if you take a bag, you're just being positive so you can get the job."

"I still don't know…" Mia said.

"Listen, luv, you don't have much of a choice right now, do you? Bring a bag. Sidney's a good bloke and the job is taking care of animals. You can do that now, can't you?"

"I do like animals."

"There, now, bring a bag and I'll meet you at the train station bright and early."

Chapter Thirty-Six

MIA MET HETTIE AT THE RAILWAY STATION AFTER LEAVING THE halfway house, and Hettie purchased two tickets to Plankton in Yorkshire. It was a long ride, but Mia enjoyed the passing scenery as the train rumbled through one small town after another. They reached Plankton before noon, and Sid was waiting for them when they stepped off the train. They arrived at the refuge half an hour later.

The refuge had been created when Sid inherited the estate, one of the first his great-grandfather had owned. Cyrus Jackson renovated the manor house and used the hermitage for its intended purpose by installing a hermit named Bledsoe, who entertained Jackson's guests with his stories. The manor house was in dire need of repair, and the hermitage had to be updated for modern living before Sid could receive his new "guests," so he used his entire savings to bring the place up to speed.

The manor house was not grand, but it was stable, and the hermitage had been given a facelift and a new bathroom. It was across a dirt road from the horse stables and a barn. A tiled dog kennel and newly built "cat house" occupied a large area behind the stables. The noise from the barking dogs echoed across the land, and Sid worried that it might be hard for Mary to ignore it while she was trying to sleep.

"Do you like animals?" Sid asked as they turned onto the drive leading to the refuge.

"I love animals," Mia said.

"Do you mind the noise they make?"

"I haven't thought much about it."

"Well, if you find it's too much, we can give you a room in the house."

They passed a car park, a booth for selling tickets, and then stopped at a gate. Sid used a small remote control to open it.

"All the money we earn goes to the animals," Sid said. "We take in any animal in need of a place to stay, but lately, we've had a spate of neglected horses."

"Oh, that's so sad," Hettie said.

"They're expensive to board, and farmers don't need more than one to pull a plow."

"Do farmers still use plows?" Hettie asked.

"Smaller farms do, especially with the cost of petrol."

Sid parked the car in a spot next to the stables. They all got out of the car, and Sid held out his hand toward the hermitage.

"Your new home," he said.

The front of the small house had one window and a red door. Mia went to the window to peek inside while Hettie went to look inside the stables. Sid took a key from his pocket and opened the hermitage door.

"This place didn't have a loo when we came here," Sid said. He looked Mia in the eye and winked. "And it's not as big as a London flat."

Mia smiled, and they went inside.

"Oh, my God, I love it," she said.

"Gloria did the decorating," Sid said. "She'll be happy to hear that you love it." Sid handed the key to Mia. "I'll leave you to it, then."

Mia took a good look around. The room was a large, single space with a counter, sink, and window on the left wall, a small round table with two chairs in the centre, a bed and chest of drawers against the back wall, a bathroom hidden by a curtain, and a large, overstuffed chair next to the front window. The walls were painted white, and the moldings around the windows were dark blue. The pallet of colors used reminded Mia of the ocean – green, blue, and a light tan.

Hettie and Sid appeared at the door.

"So, this was a true hermitage," Hettie said. "I pity the poor blokes who lived here."

"The man who lived here when my great-grandfather owned it was well-treated," Sid said. "He had food and a warm place to sleep."

"But he was still considered an ornament," Hettie said. "Not much more than a slave."

"He could have been a beggar on the street, Miss Nithercott." Sid exhaled sharply. "At least he had a roof over his head."

Hettie bit her lip.

"I didn't mean to offend you," she said.

"I'm not offended," Sid said. "It was a different time." Sid put his hands on his hips. "So, we don't follow the rules out here. Lunch is at noon and dinner at five. She's expecting you for dinner, so make your way up to the house when you're ready."

"Thank you, Sid," Hettie said.

"Let's take a walk," Mia said.

The refuge was tucked into a valley surrounded by moors, but the manor house was built on a hill. The stable was the former carriage house, and the whole refuge was overseen by the manor house residents. It had been built to house five horses with room for two carriages and a wagon. A paddock was behind the stable, and a path from the stables to the woods passed between it and the farm. A pigpen and chicken coop were outside the barn where a sad, skinny cow also lived.

As they walked past the pigpen, Hettie grabbed Mia's hand.

"This is such a nice place," she said. "I'm so excited for you."

"I'm excited about having my own house."

"Can you imagine living here a hundred years ago? Those poor men. I'll bet they didn't even have a pump for water."

Mia tilted her head.

"It really bothers you, doesn't it?"

"More than I thought it would when Sid told me about it. I guess seeing it, how small it is, well, I guess I see a bit of myself in them."

Mia hugged her.

"Why don't you stay here with me?" Mia asked.

"Oh, I'm fine, dear. I'm just feeling a bit peckish. I should have eaten before we came."

Mia pulled away.

"Why didn't you eat?"

"I left before dawn. I usually eat whatever Miss Profitt is having, but she was still in bed when I left."

"She doesn't have bread for toast?" Mia asked.

Hettie stopped at the pigpen and looked at the piglets.

"I didn't have time. I had to catch the train."

"Then, let's see if there's anything in my house."

When they got into the house, Mia went to the small fridge and looked inside.

"They bought me food." She pulled out a quart of milk and then saw a tin of tea on the shelf above the sink. "Why don't I make some tea?"

Mia filled the teakettle with water, lit a flame under it, and then took her rucksack to the bed. She sat and bounced a bit before smiling broadly.

"It's much softer than the one I've been sleeping on."

Hettie came over to the bed and sat beside her.

"I hope you give this a chance, Mia." Hettie caught herself. "I mean, Mary."

"Of course, I will. I want this to work out."

Hettie reached into her purse and took out a business card. "There's something I wanted to talk to you about." She pressed it into Mia's hand. Mia looked at it and then at Hettie.

"It's James' pub," Hettie said.

"Is James a bartender?"

"He's the owner," Hettie said. "We call him a publican."

Mia read the card again.

"How far away is Morseton?"

"Not far. We passed it on the train."

Mia stared at the card as if she could summon James by reading his name. Miss Nithercott put her hand on Mia's arm.

"He's been through so much, Mia."

"Because of what I did," Mia said.

"And because of the bad choices he made, but I think he has a right to know you're here."

"I'm not ready to see him yet," Mia said.

"Can I at least let him know that you're all right?"

"Will he come looking for me?"

Hettie sighed. "Right, well, perhaps it's best I let you handle it."

The teakettle whistled.

"Do you want tea?" Mia asked.

"I think I'm going to head up to the house."

"Okay. I think I'll put my things away and come up in a little while."

Mia watched Hettie go out the door, and then looked at the business card. Seeing his name brought his image to her mind, and then tears to her eyes. Mia wiped them away before they could fall.

Mia's memories had returned like a tsunami one night after she had a nightmare about Boris Black. She'd seen his photo on the TV in the common room, and her hand began to shake. When she went to bed, the nightmare started, and she woke up screaming. She remembered Jon and Havenwood and how Marie had betrayed her. She also remembered how much she still loved James.

Then Mia put her hand to her throat and remembered the Silver Stag. What had happened to it? Boris had put half of it around her neck, but what happened to the other half?

Mia thought about it over and over as she tried to remember what had happened after she and Boris landed in Dorley. She remembered Marie, how Boris had made her hold up her half of the Stag, and the wind, but that's where her memories ended. She must have been wearing her half when they took her to the hospital. Had someone taken it?

Mia had read the police report. It said that she had crawled out of the woods, so it might have come off when she and Boris were dropped in the woods. If so, there was a chance that it might still be there.

But what would Mia do with one half of the Silver Stag?

"Oh, Jon," she said as she looked at the business card. "I love you, sweetheart."

Mia went to the bed and slipped the card into the pocket of her rucksack. Before Hettie left for the train, Mia would ask her about the Stag. If Hettie hadn't seen it, Mia would find a way to get to Dorley so she could search the woods.

"Rotrude!" she said aloud.

Mia didn't have to find her half of the Stag. All she had to do was go to Rotrude's cottage and the witch of the woods would take her to Havenwood.

With a lighter heart, Mia left the house and climbed the stairs leading to the manor house. She hadn't realized how hungry she was until Sid opened the door and invited her into the house where the scent of garlic and tomatoes filled the air.

Chapter Thirty-Seven

JAMES 1996

James stared at the boy behind Greyson. He'd seen photos of himself as a child and recognized the blue eyes and wavy auburn hair. She hadn't run away from him – she'd run to Havenwood to have their child.

James got up, went to the boy, knelt down in front of him, and embraced him. The boy looked up at Greyson, who smiled and nodded his head.

"James is your father, Jon."

James pulled away and smiled at Jon.

"He's beautiful," James said.

"He's more than that," Greyson said. "Jon is a very capable child, and he's been a fine companion."

"And he's been here with you since she was taken away?"

Greyson nodded. "Many times, I thought of taking him to Dorley, but I was afraid Mia would return for him."

James backed away from Jon, and the boy went to Greyson's side. Like James when he was a boy, Jon was small for his age, and his naturally slender form was exaggerated by the lack of food. He was pale, but his eyes were curious.

"You understand who this is, don't you, Jon?" Greyson asked.

"His picture is on the mantel," Jon said.

"What picture?" James asked.

Jon pointed to the sitting room, and James went to the fire-place where the photo Mia had brought to Havenwood was, indeed, on the mantel. It was a photo of James Mia had taken when they were walking around the estate. He recognized the edge of the patio in the background. Mia had taken him with her after all.

James returned to the kitchen and sat at the table. Greyson still had his arm around Jon.

"How old are you, Jon?" James asked.

"I'm nine years old."

James looked at the boy's ill-fitting clothes and bare feet.

"Would you like to come home with me?"

Greyson smiled, but Jon clung to the wizard's sleeve.

"I can't leave Greyson," Jon said.

James sat back and eyed Greyson.

"You should come with us, too."

Greyson shook his head.

"There is nothing for me there. This is my home."

"I won't leave him," Jon said. "He needs me."

Greyson took his arm away, turned, and looked into Jon's eyes.

"This is not your home, Jon. You belong in the real world."

"You need me," Jon said.

"You have done all you can for me, and your father needs you now."

Jon's lip trembled, but he didn't cry.

"Please come with us," Jon said softly.

Greyson put his forehead against Jon's.

"I've never said no to you before, but I must say it now." He put his hands on Jon's cheeks. "I am giving you a quest. You must go with your father to Dorley and help him become the man he was meant to be."

A single tear rolled down Jon's cheek.

"I accept this quest," Jon said.

"That's a good lad," Greyson said. He looked at James. "This boy will honor his quest, and you must honor this boy."

James was solemn as he watched the scene. It felt as if he had fallen into one of his fantasy books, and he understood what Greyson expected him to do.

"I will honor this boy," James said.

"And I will honor this quest," Jon said.

Greyson stood and took Jon's hand.

"It is time."

Greyson led Jon to the front door with James following close behind.

"Wait," Jon said.

Jon ran up the stairs, and a moment later, he returned carrying a stuffed bear. He took Greyson's hand and held his head high.

"I'm ready now," Jon said.

The trio walked to the clearing where James had arrived earlier that day. Greyson smiled at James and held out his hand.

"May I have Jon's half of the Silver Stag?"

James took one of the necklaces from around his neck and handed it to Greyson. Greyson put it on Jon and then put his hands on Jon's cheeks.

"You are a brave warrior, Jon Huxley. You've been charged with a noble quest. As I place this talisman around your neck, I impart these things as well – wisdom, strength, and courage. Go forth, my good knight."

"And may I bring you honor always," Jon said.

Greyson put his hand on James' shoulder.

"I've lived for a thousand years. I've seen good men and evil men, but this boy is the best I've ever known. Do you understand what I'm telling you?"

"That I can't let him down," James said.

Greyson held the half coin from James' necklace and then held the one on Jon's. James watched Jon's face as he watched Greyson. He loved the old wizard, and James wanted to put his hand on Greyson so they would all go together, but he knew Greyson was right. His time was over, and now James would determine the rest of Jon's life.

"To a safe journey," Greyson said as the edges of the coin met, and the wind began to blow.

* * *

James and Jon landed on the sofa in the sitting room of Huxley Manor. James got up and took Jon's hand.

"We have to go."

He led Jon to the door, peeked outside and down the hallway, and then took Jon to the front door. He remembered he had told

Caroline that he would stay the night, but how would he explain Jon?

James opened the door and pulled Jon through behind him. The Volkswagen's chrome bumper gleamed in the setting sunlight, and James looked down at Jon.

"This is my car," James said. "Have you ever seen one before?"

"No."

Jon's solemn expression touched James. He put his hand on Jon's shoulder and smiled.

"It's something we use to get from one place to another." James opened the passenger door. "You sit inside."

Jon slid onto the seat. When he shut the door, James took a deep breath before going to the driver's side. He opened the door, sat, and then glanced at Jon.

"Are you hungry?" James asked.

"Yes."

James looked at his watch.

"It's past lunch, but we could get supper."

He started the car's engine and heard the boy gasp, but Jon was honoring his promise to be brave and said nothing. James saw Jon gripping his knee as the car moved, but he still remained silent.

"There's nothing to be afraid of," James said.

"I'm not afraid."

"Right. Well, let's go and see if we can find a place to eat."

James went down Huxley Road and drove to the motorway. Halfway to Morseton, James saw a sign for food and lodging and pulled off at the next exit. A large, Tudor-themed building appeared on the left side of the road, and James turned into the car park. The place was called McMurray's Pub and Inn. James got out of the car and went to the passenger side.

"See the little handle on the door?" Jon looked at the door and nodded. "Pull it, and it will open the door.

Jon pulled the handle, and the door opened. He got out, and then James closed it.

"See? That's all you have to do."

They went into the pub, and James took Jon to a table by the window. The publican was a large woman with a broad smile.

She came over to their table, put her hand on Jon's cheek, and looked into his eyes.

"Those eyes," she said. She eyed James. "So blue, just like your Da's." She pursed her lips. "You know he shouldn't be in here without his shoes."

Jon's forehead creased, and James blushed.

"Aye. He took them off when we were in the car, and I forgot to remind him."

"Well, since you're the only ones here, I'll make an exception." She nodded toward a large chalkboard behind the bar. "Make your choices. I'll be back."

"So, what do you like to eat?" James asked.

"Vegetables," Jon said.

James looked at the board, which listed standard pub fare. He chose fish and chips with carrots on the side and hoped Jon's system would be able to handle fried food. When the food came, Jon picked at his carrots but left the rest.

James was tired, and he wasn't ready to go to Bixby's Brewhouse, where questions would be asked that he wasn't prepared to answer. He asked the bartender if there were any rooms available, and then she directed him to a portly, balding man with a quick smile.

"Aye," he said. "Is it just the two of ya?"

"Yes, me, and my…son."

The man eyed Jon for a moment and then grinned.

"There's no denying that lad is yours." James smiled, and then the man led them up the stairs to the second floor. "This place was built over two hundred years ago, so the rooms are a wee bit small."

The room *was* small, but there were two beds and a small table with a lamp between them. James could see the motorway out the window.

"The loo is down the hall," the man said as he handed James the room key. "After eleven a.m., we charge for another day."

"Thanks," James said. After the man left them, James went into the room, but Jon stood at the door for a minute. "You all right?"

"Aye," Jon said.

Jon continued to stare at the room, and James wasn't sure what to do next. He hadn't been near children since he was a lad himself, so he took off his jacket and lay on the bed, hoping Jon would understand.

"Is this where we live?" Jon asked.

"No," James said. "I'm tired is all. It's only for one night."

Jon went to the other bed. He sat with his back to James, and a few minutes later, James saw the boy's shoulder shaking.

"It's all right, mate," James said. "I know it's hard…"

James got up from his bed, sat beside Jon, and the boy began to sob. He buried his head in James' chest. James held him tightly and felt Jon's pain.

"It's all right, luv."

Jon wept for a long time, and James held him.

"I can't imagine how hard it's been for you," James said. "Things will be very different here. Anything you need to know, you just ask me."

Jon pulled away from James.

"I'd like to brush my teeth," Jon said.

"We'll have to get you a toothbrush before we go home."

"Where is home?" Jon asked.

"It's in Morseton," James said. "A flat above a pub."

"What's a flat?"

"It's a place, a room up the stairs from the pub. It has a bathroom, a bedroom, and a kitchen."

"Where will I sleep?" Jon asked.

James hadn't thought of where Jon would sleep. He only had one bedroom.

"You'll sleep in the bedroom," James said. "I'll sleep on the settee for now."

Jon leaned against James' arm.

"I miss Greyson."

"I know."

"Will I ever see him again?"

James wondered if he should lie or tell Jon the truth. He remembered Greyson's words about honoring the boy.

"No," James said. "He gave you this quest because he knew he would never see you again."

Jon exhaled loudly and sat up.

"I'm tired, too."

James moved so Jon could lie down. He saw the boy's dirty feet, and his heart ached. How long had he been without shoes?

Within minutes, Jon was asleep, and James was alone for the first time since he'd gone to Havenwood. He sat on his bed, watched Jon breathing, and thought of Mia. James remembered the things Mia had told him about her mother, how she had threatened Mia with abortion if she ever came home pregnant, and he understood why Mia had done what she did. But why hadn't she trusted him? James had offered to marry her without knowing she was pregnant. He would have done anything for her.

But James had no money. He was seventeen and still in school. He wouldn't have been able to take care of her.

Now, as then, he had little to give Mia or his son, and that is what Mia had tried to make him understand. Going to a magical place where she didn't need money to raise her child must have seemed like the only choice she had.

James lay back and stared at the ceiling. He again thought of Greyson's words.

You must go with your father to Dorley and help him become the man he was meant to be.

Even Greyson had understood that James still had a long way to go before he would be a man Jon and Mia could depend on.

Chapter Thirty-Eight

THE NEXT MORNING, JAMES WOKE TO FIND JON STARING OUT THE
window.

"Did you sleep well?" James asked.

"Aye," Jon said.

"Are you hungry?"

Jon glanced at James.

"Aye."

"Do you fancy a raspberry tart?"

"I don't know what that is," Jon said.

"Well, then it's high time you found out."

After tending to their needs in the loo, James and Jon left the
pub and drove back to Dorley so James could show Jon the
bakery. He bought Jon a raspberry tart and a cup of coffee for
himself. They sat at an outdoor dining table, and James was
happy to see Jon eat the whole tart.

"I like this," Jon said. Jon looked at his empty plate. "Can I
have another one?"

"Are you sure? Maybe you should let your stomach get used
to it, or it might make you sick."

Jon sat back. "I don't feel sick."

"I'll tell you what. I'll buy another one, but we'll take it with
us so you can have it later."

"All right." Jon eyed James. "I know your name is James, but
Greyson said you're my father. Do I call you Father?"

"You can call me dad if you like," James said. "Jon, I have to talk to you about something."

"What?"

"We can't tell anyone about Havenwood."

"Why not?"

"Because they wouldn't understand." James leaned his head toward Jon. "People in this world don't believe in magic. They will think you're daft if you talk about it."

"Oh," Jon said. "Will they ask me where I came from?"

"They might. If they do, tell them you lived up north."

"Where up north?"

"Just up north, so it's easy to remember."

James saw the edge of Jon's sleeve as he pushed his plate away. It was ragged, and the sweater he wore threadbare.

"How would you like to get some new clothes?"

"I've never had new clothes." He looked down at his shirt. "Greyson found these in an abandoned house. He said the boy who wore them had gone home."

"Well, then, let's go and get that tart, and then we'll go clothes shopping."

James looked in his wallet when he paid for the tart. He hadn't much left after spending the night at the inn, so he took Jon to a charity shop. One of the volunteers recognized *Lord* Huxley and rushed over to greet them. The woman was well past her seventies, but she was spry and heavily made up.

"Why I 'aven't seen you in ages," she said. Her name badge said, "Millie."

"My er...Jon here needs some clothes."

Millie narrowed her eyes as she assessed James. She noted the quality of his clothes and concluded that James must have fallen on hard times. She had heard that the old lord was not pleased when his son got a divorce and had cut him off. Apparently, those rumors were true.

"Well, 'ow old are ya, pet?" she asked.

"I'm nine years old."

"Not very tall, though, is he?" Millie said, and then she waved her hand. "Oh, but that's no matter. I'm sure we can find something for ya."

James clenched his teeth as the old woman shuffled toward a rack of clothes. He didn't like the way she talked about Jon's height the way schoolmates had taunted him for being the shortest boy in his class.

James glanced at the racks Millie was searching. She pulled a pair of jeans from the rack and held them up to Jon.

"What do you think, mate?" James asked. Jon nodded, and James glanced at Millie. "Where can he try these on?"

"In the back," Millie said.

Jon followed James to the fitting room, and James handed him the jeans.

"Go inside and put them on," James said.

Jon did as he was told, and James pulled the curtain across the doorway. A few minutes later, Jon peeked around the curtain looking grim.

"They won't stay up," he said.

James pushed the curtain aside and saw that the jeans were a bit large, but a belt would fix that. He pulled up his own shirt to show Jon his belt.

"We'll get you one of these. It will hold them up until you grow into them."

James smiled as he recalled Miss Nithercott saying this very same thing to him when he was a boy.

"Can you get me a belt now?" Jon asked.

"Aye, I'll see if they have one."

Millie was still looking through the racks when James began searching for a belt. She had some shirts over her arm, and when she saw James, she went to stand beside him.

"These'll do very nicely," she said.

"He needs a belt," James said.

Millie held up one finger. James followed her to a wall full of hooks where Millie took a belt off and added it to the shirts. James took them to Jon and showed him how to put on the belt.

"That should do it," James said. "Now, try on the shirts."

Jon put on a shirt and came out to show it to James. Millie had chosen a variety of button shirts suitable for church, but not for play. James grabbed the others and took them back to the rack. He chose T-shirts with the names of football teams, striped cotton pullovers, and one checkered button shirt with large black and white checks. James took these to Jon and hung them on a hook in the fitting room.

"Try the ones you like," James said.

Jon pulled the curtain shut. James heard him changing and hoped the shirts would please Jon.

"How's it going in there?" James said.

"All right."

"Can I see them?"

Jon stepped out of the fitting room and stood before James. He looked like a smaller version of James, further proof of his fatherhood.

"You look good, mate."

Jon grinned. "I like them."

"So, did you try on the others?"

"Aye. I like them all."

"Good. So, all we have to do is find some trainers."

"What are trainers?" Jon asked.

"Shoes, like for sports, but we wear them all the time." James scanned the shop. "They must have them here." He went into the fitting room and grabbed the shirts Jon had tried off the floor. He saw Jon's old clothes shoved into a corner. "Do you want your old clothes, mate?"

"No," Jon said.

James picked them up and dropped them into a small bin near the front counter. He handed the shirts to Millie, who sat on a stool behind the counter.

"Is 'e going to wear them 'ome?" she asked.

"Aye, but we have to find him a pair of trainers."

"Shoes are on the other side of the shop," she said. "Do you need me to show ya?"

"I think we can manage."

"Wait," Millie said, and they stopped. She took a pair of socks from a bin and brought them to James. "Put these on 'is feet first."

He put his hand on Jon's shoulder as they walked. Several shoe racks stood in a row with adult sizes on the first rack. James followed the signs to the kids' shoes and had Jon sit on the floor with his foot up while James measured the shoes against Jon's foot.

"Put these on," James said as he handed the socks to Jon. He waited until Jon was ready and then slipped the trainer on Jon's foot. "Looks good. How do they feel?"

"I can move my toes."

"Hallelujah," James said. He helped Jon put the other shoe on and was happy to see that Jon could tie the laces. "So, is there anything else you need?"

Jon cast his eyes on the floor.

"I don't have any pants on."

James suppressed a smile.

"Aye. I don't think they sell pants at the charity shop. We'll see if we can find them on the way home."

Millie eyed Jon as they approached the counter.

"So, you're wearing 'em home, are ya? You look real nice."

"Say thank you, Jon," James said.

"Thank you."

"Aye, you're a good lad," Millie said. She cocked her head back. "I didn't know you 'ad a son, Lord 'uxley."

James paid for the clothes without responding to her comment. They left the shop and walked to the car in silence, but as soon as they got inside the Volkswagen, Jon waited until James had started the car before looking up at him.

"Why didn't you tell her I'm your son?"

James put his hands on the wheel and kept his eyes on the road while he pulled onto the street.

"Because my father is an important man and people are nosy. If they find out about you, they will put it in the paper, and everyone will want to take a picture of you and ask about you, and I don't want them chasing you on your way to school."

"They would do that?" Jon asked. He thought for a moment. "I'm going to school?"

"Aye, you're going to school, and I want you to have a normal life, so I didn't tell that *woman* you were my son."

"Oh," Jon said. "I've always wanted to go to school. I read all the books in Greyson's library. I'd like to read something new."

James thought of his father's study and all the books he'd been forbidden to touch.

"I'll get a bookcase, and we'll fill it with all the books you want," James said.

"We will?"

"Aye, as many as you want. That's a promise."

As Jon grinned, James realized he had better be careful when it came to making promises to his son.

Chapter Thirty-Nine

MIA 1991

THE OLD, CHESTNUT STALLION EYED MIA SUSPICIOUSLY. HIS emaciated form had alarmed Mia the first time she saw him, and Sid explained that she would have to approach him with caution.

"He doesn't trust us yet," Sid said. "I don't want you to touch him until he grows accustomed to you. I want you to bring his food to him for a while, so he thinks kind thoughts toward you."

"How could they do this to him?" Mia asked.

"People are capable of the most egregious things," Sid said. "You'll see things here, well, you have to grow a thick skin if you want to help these poor creatures."

"Where do they come from?"

"The RSPCA refers us. When I get a call, I go and pick them up, usually after the police have been there."

Mia looked into the horse's large, brown eyes.

"He's so sad."

"He will probably look that way for a while," Sid said. "Like I said, you have to develop a thick skin, Miss Mary, or you won't be fit to care for any of them."

"I'll try to remember that," Mia said.

The chickens provided eggs, and the goats provided milk that Sid sold to help support the refuge. Sid would hold a fundraiser once a year, too, so his wealthy friends could donate according to their conscience. His family disdained his efforts, but Sid chose to ignore them in favor of doing what he believed was right.

Mia admired Sid and Gloria for putting their money where their mouths were. She watched Gloria muck out a stable and saw Sid assist a cow birthing a calf. They weren't anything like her parents, and Mia found herself looking forward to getting up every morning and seeing their smiles. To them, she was like one of the neglected animals, and their affection for her was genuine.

"What's his name," Mia asked.

"Galahad," Sid said. "The owner was calling him Shite. I tell you, Mary, if I ever met one of them, I'd be hard-pressed not to beat them to death." Mia raised her eyebrows. "But if I were to do that, I wouldn't be able to help fellows like Galahad. When the court needs testimony, Gloria appears. She's better able to compartmentalize her feelings. Besides, she's very good at telling the court what these animals were like when they arrived."

"I wish I could do that with my feelings," Mia said.

"It's a gift. I'm convinced of it." Sid put his hands on his hips. "So, let me show you what to feed him."

Sid had taken Mia all around the refuge the first day, but each animal's needs were different. Sid would go over what to feed, how much, and how often with each new arrival. Mia quickly learned not to question him, for Sid had a knack for sussing out what was best for each new animal in his charge.

Every day, Mia would feed the pigs and chickens. She spent time with the kittens in the barn and ran over the moors with a pair of Great Danes who had come from an abusive home. Mia discovered that she, too, had a gift, one she'd been unaware of her whole life – a gift of empathy. She would spend time with an animal and understand its heart. They took to Mia as they would a mother, and she would often curl up next to a new arrival in the barn and sleep with them. The animals acclimated to their new surroundings faster, and it helped them adapt when people came to see them on weekends.

Mia was also dealing with the symptoms of Post-Traumatic Stress. Sid had noticed her hand shaking on more than one occasion and commented on it one day when they were mucking out stalls.

"I've seen men with Post Traumatic Stress Syndrome," he said. "They shake, sleepwalk, have headaches all because their bodies don't know how to handle what their minds have been through." He waited for her reply, but Mia remained silent. "Miss Nithercott didn't tell us why you were unable to find work."

Mia stopped raking and looked at Sid.

"I was shot during a…robbery," Mia said.

"Oh, Mary."

"I have nightmares sometimes."

"Why didn't you tell us?"

"I don't like to think about it."

Sid pursed his lips and shook his head.

"Well, I hope you know you can come to us for anything you need."

"Thanks, Sid."

"And if you don't want to talk about it, that's okay, too."

"I appreciate that."

Hettie had promised to visit that month. She had also promised not to tell James she had found Mia, and she hoped that Hettie had kept her word. Mia wanted to go to Rotrude first and bring Jon back to Dorley before seeing James. Once he saw their son, Mia knew he would be able to forgive her.

As she lay in bed the night before Hettie's visit, her mind raced, and she felt as she had when she woke up in the hospital. Her heart was beating fast, and her hands shook. The anticipation of seeing a new face was enough to bring on her symptoms, and she tried using the yoga techniques her counselor had taught her. When she finally calmed down, she fell asleep but awoke to find herself standing near Galahad's stall. He was in the corner shaking.

"Did I say something, boy?" she asked.

Had she yelled at the poor animal? Had she frightened him?

"I'm sorry, Galahad," she said. "I didn't mean to scare you."

Mia went back to her tiny home and sat in the big chair by the window. This was the first time she had walked in her sleep. The next morning, Mia approached Sid while he fed the chickens and told him what had happened. She asked him to feed Galahad, for she didn't want to stress the horse again.

"So, you're walking in your sleep now," Sid said.

Mia bit her lip. "I've never done it before."

"Isn't Miss Nithercott coming to visit today?"

"She said she'd come in the afternoon," Mia said.

"Then maybe you're just excited to see her."

"But what if it happens again? What if I wander off and fall into a ditch?"

Sid stared at her for a moment and then went to put the pail he had used away. Mia followed him and waited for his reply.

"I can put a lock on the door," Sid said. "But I don't want to put you in danger if there's a fire or something."

Mia pondered this and then spotted a barrel against the barn wall.

"What if we put something in front of the door that I can't move easily? Something that wouldn't keep you from getting inside in an emergency?"

"That seems a bit dodgy." Sid's jaw tightened, and then he smiled. "What about a net?"

"What, like a fishing net?"

"No, like the ones they use in football. They kick the ball in, and the net stops it."

Mia narrowed her eyes.

"They don't have nets behind a football goal."

Sid eyed her for a moment.

"Are you talking about American football?" he asked.

Mia blushed. "Oh, yeah, I know what you mean."

"You hang it in front of the door when you're ready to go to bed. You can rip it down in an emergency."

"I can rip it down in my sleep," Mia said.

"Maybe, but it's better than nothing," Sid said.

"All right. Let's give it a try."

Later that morning, Sid rode into town and bought a football net and two large hooks. When he returned to the refuge, he spent a half-hour installing the hooks and showing Mia how to hang the net in front of the door.

Mia eyed the space under the net. "I could just crawl under it."

"I doubt you'd do that in your sleep," Sid said. "Just give it a try. Otherwise I'll have to install restraints."

Mia cringed at the thought.

"Yeah, okay."

Sid looked at his watch. "I checked, and the train from Woollcott is due at two. I'd better get going."

Mia wanted to go with him, but Sid wanted her to try

approaching Galahad again to see how he would react. She waved as Sid drove away and then went to Galahad's stable. He was standing at the gate when she came in, and he didn't back away when she approached the gate.

"Hey, buddy," Mia said. "Have you forgiven me yet?"

Galahad let Mia open the gate, put on his reins, and lead him out of the stable. They walked toward the path that led to the woods, and he balked a bit. She let him calm down before proceeding, and he was fine for the rest of the walk. Mia was grateful that she hadn't ruined their relationship forever.

When they returned from their walk, Mia rubbed him down and brushed his coat before putting him back in his stable. She heard Sid's car coming and ran outside. Hettie was in the front seat with a big smile on her face. She waved, and Mia waved back.

"Oh, it's so good to see you, Mary," Hettie said as she embraced Mia.

"Gloria wants us up at the house for lunch," Sid said. He looked at Hettie. "You look a bit winded. Can you make it up the stairs today?"

"Oh, I'm in tiptop shape," Hettie said, but when she reached the top of the stairs, she was covered in sweat.

"You should sit down," Sid said.

"I'm fine, luv."

"You don't look fine," Mia said.

"It's warm today is all. We'd better go inside. Don't want to spoil Gloria's lunch."

Mia kept her eye on Hettie while they ate lunch. Hettie's cheeks were flushed, and she kept coughing. By the end of the meal, both Gloria and Sid were watching Hettie, too.

"That cough doesn't sound good," Gloria said. "Have you seen a doctor?"

Hettie waved her hand.

"All they do is give you pills. I'm fine. It's the horses. I'm a bit allergic."

"You never told me you were allergic to horses," Mia said.

"Oh, I am, dear. Have been since childhood."

"I rode horses when I was a child," Sid said. "I don't remember you coughing then."

"Now, listen, all of you, I'm fine, and I don't want to hear another word about it."

Sid glanced at Mia, and she lowered her eyes. Gloria bought a small cake to the table and cut a slice for each of them. Hettie continued to cough, but no one mentioned it again.

Chapter Forty

JAMES 1996

JON KEPT HIS EYES ON THE SCENERY AS THEY TRAVELLED TOWARD Morseton. James' guts were in an uproar as he passed the last exit before his own as he tried to find a way to explain Jon to the people at Bixby's Brewhouse.

When James bought the pub, Maryanne had grilled him regarding Mia's disappearance. She had read every tabloid account and knew all the details of James' life, literal and fictional, and he wasn't keen on going through that again.

As he imagined different scenarios, the only one that felt right was the one that teetered on the truth, that James had been contacted by an old girlfriend who asked him to take care of their son because she was sick. It would keep questions to a minimum and might appease Maryanne.

It was late in the afternoon when they pulled into James' spot behind the pub. There were two sets of stairs leading to the second floor – one inside and one outside. Now, they took the outside stairs to the flat. Maryanne's bag was on the sofa, and his bed was unmade. Jon was holding his teddy bear and the bag of new clothes as he stood at the door with his eyes on James.

"You'll be sleeping in that room," James said, nodding toward the bedroom. "I'll change the sheets for you, just take your things in there for now."

Jon went to the bedroom and put his things on the bed. His stomach rumbled, and he glanced at James, who was looking in the fridge.

258

"Is there anything to eat?" Jon asked.

"You just ate your raspberry tart."

"I know, but I'm still hungry."

"Well, there's nothing in here," James said. "We'll have to go shopping before I introduce you to the people downstairs."

They returned to the car and drove to the supermarket. Jon eyed the vehicles in the car park and clasped his hands.

"Are there lots of people in there?" he asked.

"Probably." James noticed Jon's hands were shaking. "You don't have to come inside if you don't want to."

"I want to," Jon said.

James got out, walked around the car, and waited for Jon. The boy opened the door but took his time getting out. When he did, he stood by the car for a moment until James began walking toward the store.

"First, we need to get a trolley," James said as he grabbed one and pushed it toward the entrance. Jon followed James and stopped when they were inside to stare at the displays. He also looked at the people and moved closer to James as they went up and down each aisle. James held up an item now and then for Jon's approval, but otherwise, he stuck to the basics – bread, milk, butter. James also put a toothbrush for Jon in the trolley. Jon liked the pictures of food on the boxes and kept adding them to the trolley.

"Easy, mate," James said. "I'm low on cash."

"What does that mean?" Jon asked.

"It means I might not have enough to pay for all this."

"I've never heard that word."

"Which word?" James asked.

"Pay."

"When we buy something here, we have to pay for it with money. We can't just conjure it out of thin air."

"How do you get money?" Jon asked.

"Most people work for it. They have jobs, but some people are born with it."

"What kind of people are we?"

"We're the ones who have to work for it."

Jon puzzled over this for a while, and then took some of the items out of the trolley and returned them to the shelves.

"Why are you doing that?" James asked.

"I don't have a job."

James bent over so he would be eye to eye with Jon.

"You don't need a job, mate. You have me. I will pay for the food until you're old enough to pay for it yourself, okay?"

"Okay," Jon said.

"Now, go get those things back so we can go home."

Jon brought everything back to the trolley, and then they paid for the food and took it to the car. Jon's eyes were always watching and exploring his new world. Most of it was familiar, as Havenwood's residents had created things they were used to, but the noise from the automobiles was new to him.

"It's very loud here," Jon said.

"You'll get used to it."

"Are you sure?"

"To be honest, I'm not sure of anything." James put his hand on Jon's arm. "But I know what it's like to be in a strange place. It takes time to get to know things."

"Do you like it here?" Jon asked.

"Well enough. It's a good place to live."

"I wish we could take some food to Greyson," Jon said. "But I have to honor this quest."

James heard the sadness in Jon's voice and it broke his heart. The boy was still worried about the old wizard, and nothing James did would make it easier on Jon. He pulled out of the car park and Jon read the signs as they passed them.

They drove home, and Jon helped James take the groceries upstairs. They put them away, and then James took a deep breath. He exhaled sharply and looked at Jon.

"I'll make those dinners we bought, and then we'll go downstairs."

"What's it like downstairs?" Jon asked as James put the frozen meals into the microwave.

"It's loud. There are lots of people there who come in for a pint or two before going home. Some play darts."

"Do I have to go down there?" Jon asked.

"I want to show you off to my mates," James said. "I'm that proud of you."

The microwave stopped, and James put the meals on the dining table. He showed Jon where to find the utensils, and then they sat at the table.

"Remember what I told you at the inn?" James asked.

Jon's mouth twisted as he thought.

"No."

"That you can't talk about Havenwood."

"Oh, yes, I do."

"Right. So we have to make up a story about how we met."

"You mean we have to lie," Jon said.

"Just a white lie," James said.

"Is that better than a regular lie?"

"It's…we're doing this because…just don't tell anyone about Havenwood."

"I will tell them I come from the north," Jon said.

"Right, the north. Your mum was sick, so she asked me to take care of you. And if anyone asks you a question you don't want to answer, just look at me, and I'll think of something to tell them."

"Okay."

"And let me tell them you're my son. I want to break it to them myself."

"Just like that lady in the charity shop."

"Exactly."

Jon put his fork down.

"Do you think she died?"

"Who?"

"My mum."

James held his fork aloft for a second, and then put it down.

"I don't know, Jon."

Jon raised his eyes to meet James'.

"I don't think she died. I still feel her."

James nodded.

"I think I do, too."

"Can we look for her?"

"We'll talk about that after we're settled, okay?"

"Okay."

When they were done eating, James tossed the empty containers into the bin, and then he looked at Jon.

"We have to go downstairs now."

"I'm ready," Jon said.

"I'm glad you are, mate, because I'm not."

James put his hand on the knob. He stood there for a moment.

"Dad," Jon said. "Are we going?"

"Aye."

James turned the knob and opened the door. The noise from the pub rose up the stairs.

"It's very loud," Jon said.

"It's another thing you'll have to get used to, I'm afraid."

James went down the stairs, and Jon followed at a slow pace. When the people saw James coming down the stairs, they started clapping, and some whistled.

"He's back!" Artie said.

"It's about time his lordship made an appearance," Maryanne said.

Every stool at the bar was taken, and some lads were throwing darts. Maryanne was behind the bar, and she looked frazzled. She caught sight of Jon standing behind James.

"And who's this then?" she asked.

James put his arm around Jon's shoulders.

"His name is Jon," James said.

"And where did he come from?"

All eyes were on James.

"He's...my son."

Jon's eyes grew wide. James had told them the truth.

Maryanne came over to Jon and cocked her head to one side. She wasn't much taller than the boy, and when she came close, she put her hand on his chin and peered into his blue eyes.

"He favors you," she said. "And all this time, you never told me you had a son."

"His...mother contacted me and asked if I could keep him for a while."

"So, where's he been then?"

Maryanne put her arm around Jon's shoulders and walked him to the bar.

"Up north," James said.

"So, why call you now?" Artie asked.

"She's been ill and can't take care of him right now."

"And you're just gonna hand him over when she gets better?" Maryanne asked.

"I'll cross that bridge later," James said.

"So, it's Jon is it," she said.

"Right, but it's spelled J O N."

"Of course, his lordship's son's got a fancy name."

"It's not fancy," James said. "It's a good, solid name."

"I like it," Jon said.

Maryanne's face softened, and she squeezed Jon's arm.

"Well, then I guess it's all right." She leaned on the bar. "So, you're the reason your da abandoned me for days without a word."

"I didn't abandon you," James said.

"I've been runnin' the whole show meself, and you didn't call. What would you call it?"

"Look, I'm sorry I didn't call."

"You promised."

"I know, but…there was no service where I was."

"Likely story," Maryanne said. "Well, we'll see how you do on your own tomorrow."

"Does that mean you won't be coming in?" James asked.

"I think I'm due," she said.

"Right. You take the day. I'll take care of things here."

The lads at the bar were sniggering. Artie caught James' eye and nodded.

"Glad you're back," Artie shouted.

James smiled, and then he caught the look of disdain in Maryanne's eyes. He'd seen it a few times before, and it always caught him off-guard. She left Jon's side to go upstairs, and she wasn't seen again that night.

Chapter Forty-One

MIA 1992

HETTIE SUFFERED A MILD HEART ATTACK SHORTLY AFTER Christmas, so she hadn't come for a visit in several months when Mia saw the ad in the Times for the festival in Dorley. Mia had saved most of her salary and had enough for a train ticket to Dorley, with one stop in Woollcott to see Hettie. As the day approached, Mia was tempted to tell Sid that she wouldn't be back, for Mia intended to go straight to Rotrude's wagon when she got to the festival but kept stammering when it came time to talk to Sid. How could she ever explain Havenwood to him?

When the day arrived, Mia put her things in her rucksack and went to say goodbye to Sid and Gloria in the stables.

"All ready for the festival?" Sid asked.

Neither questioned why she was taking her rucksack. They must have thought she was using it as a purse.

"Yup. I'm really excited about it, actually."

"Well, have a good time," Gloria said. "And take your time. No need to rush back."

If Mia found Rotrude, she could get Jon and take him to Morseton. She would call Sid and Gloria to explain everything. Of course, they would understand.

"Thanks. Well, I'll see you later."

Mia blushed as the words left her lips, but they had already returned to their tasks and didn't see her cheeks. Mia walked to the train station and arrived with minutes to spare. Her hand shook as she watched the scenery go by, and heart palpitations caused some alarm as she passed the Woollcott station. Mia didn't stop to see Hettie. She just couldn't wait to get to Dorley.

The train was full and most of those on board were getting off in Dorley. Mia walked to the center of town and remembered the day she and James came to the festival just before she left for Havenwood. Rotrude's wagon had been in front of the Chemist's shop, which was halfway down Baker Street. Mia walked past the bakery and strained her neck to see over the heads of the people filling the street. She arrived at the Chemist's but didn't see Rotrude's wagon. Her heart beat a little faster as she kept walking past it, and it beat more when she reached the end without seeing the charm wagon.

Mia looked around and backtracked up the street checking each wagon she passed. Panic rose inside her, which agitated her condition, and her hand started shaking again. She shoved it into her pocket and went to the park. The spot where she had been found a year before was to her left, but she kept her eyes straight ahead. The urge to go to Huxley Manor came and went as she walked down Huxley Road and turned into the woods.

Mia hadn't come to Rotrude's cottage from that direction the first time the disk brought her to Rotrude, but she thought she could find it anyway. Mia walked through the trees and broke boughs as she made her way deep into the woods. She wasn't sure she was going in the right direction, but Mia breathed a sigh of relief when she came upon the old marble altar for she knew Rotrude's cottage wasn't far away. She turned left and followed the overgrown path until she came to an empty clearing.

A blackened spot marked the place where the cottage had been for a thousand years. The firepit still held the ashes of Rotrude's last fire, but little else spoke of her existence. Mia's muscles tightened around her chest, and she couldn't breathe. She fell to her knees and tried to scream for help, but couldn't make a sound.

Yoga. She closed her eyes and did her yoga exercises, which helped calm her, and her breathing returned to normal. She sat on the ground and shook her head as she looked at the empty spot. What had happened to Rotrude? Where had she gone?

Mia thought of the Silver Stag. Boris had worn one half and she the other. Mia got off the ground, went back to the road, and then walked to town. She entered the woods where she had crawled out after she and Boris landed and began searching under the leaves for the necklaces. Maybe hers had fallen off while she crawled. Maybe Boris' had, too, and they were only feet apart. Mia clung to the hope that it was here, buried in the tangle of leaves and branches, for if she didn't find them...she couldn't contemplate never seeing her son again.

It was darker in the woods, so there was no light to reflect off the silver, which made it much harder to find the Stag. By the time she made it back to Rotrude's clearing, her knees hurt, her palms were rubbed raw, and she hadn't found either half of the Silver Stag.

A dejected Mia emerged from the woods as the festival was ending. She sat on a park bench for a long time watching people go by on their way home. Her mind was numb, and her body exhausted. And when Jon came into her mind, she began to cry.

The sun set and it grew dark. Mia got up and walked to the train station. She had nowhere to turn, and no one could help her. All she could do now was go back to the animal refuge and try to make some kind of life worth living.

Mia saw the Woollcott station and thought of Hettie. She should ask her if Mia had been wearing the Silver Stag when they took her to the hospital, but what good would one half of the necklace do? Mia needed both halves to travel to Havenwood.

As she rode toward Plankton, she thought of James. If she went to see him now without Jon, she would have to tell him why she had robbed him of a son he would never meet. Mia lay her head back as they passed Morseton and closed her eyes. She had already broken James' heart once. She wasn't going to hurt him again.

When she got to the refuge, Mia went into her tiny house and threw her rucksack on the bed. She had a home, a job, and had the animals in the refuge, many of which had lived lives that mirrored her own, disjointed life. They were kindred spirits, and Mia was grateful to have them.

Mia went to the stables and switched on the lights. She went to Galahad's stable, and he stayed at the gate when she approached him. She stroked his soft muzzle and laid her fore-head against it.

"I lost my son today," she said. "I'm never going to see him again, Galahad, and you're the only one who will ever know."

Mia stroked him again and then went home. She slipped into bed, turned on her side, and if she hadn't been exhausted, she would have tossed and turned all night. Instead, for the first time in years, she instantly fell into a deep, dreamless sleep.

Chapter Forty-Two

JAMES 1996

When the wall clock struck ten, James looked around the pub for Jon. He found him at the top of the stairs fast asleep. He shook him gently, and Jon opened his eyes.

"Do they stay here all night?" Jon asked.

"Only until two or three," James said.

"When do they sleep?"

"Come on," James said. "Up with ya. It's time you went to bed." James opened the door to the flat and followed Jon inside.

"Go on now and brush your teeth. I'm going to change the sheets on the bed."

Jon went to the bathroom while James checked the bedroom closet for a clean set of sheets. He found a flat sheet and one pillowcase. It would have to do until he could buy a full set. James was tucking the corners when Jon came into the bedroom.

"You'll have to use the blanket on top 'til we get you some new sheets."

James saw the sad look on Jon's face and put his hand on Jon's shoulder.

"You all right?"

"I miss Greyson."

James sat on the bed so he could look Jon in the eye.

"He must miss you, too."

"Will you stay with me until I fall asleep?" Jon asked.

"Aye."

Jon lay on the bed, and James put the blanket on top of him.

He sat on the edge of the bed as Jon held his teddy bear and stared at the ceiling.

"My house had higher ceilings," Jon said.

"I grew up in a house with high ceilings, too. The house we were in this afternoon, in fact. My room was the size of the bar downstairs."

"Do you have parents?" Jon asked.

"My father is still alive. My mother died when I was a boy."

"Why don't you live there in that house anymore?"

"I wanted to see if I could take care of myself."

"Can we go back there someday?" Jon asked.

"Maybe."

Jon yawned. "I feel sleepy."

"Then close your eyes," James said.

"What if I wake up and you're gone?"

"I'll be right downstairs if you need me."

"All right then," Jon said.

Jon closed his eyes, and two minutes later, he was snoring. James got up and watched Jon for a minute before going downstairs. It had been a long day, and James' back ached. James lifted his arms over his head and circled them as he tried to loosen the muscles in his back, but the ache persisted, so he went to the bar and poured himself a shot of whiskey.

Tom Kirby sat at the end of the bar. He nodded to James when he caught his eye, and James nodded back.

"He's been comin' in while you were gone," Artie said.

"You're here late," James said.

"I've been staying late hoping you'd come back. I wanted to see how you were after the funeral and all."

"I'm fine, mate." James tilted his head toward Tom. "So, what's the story here then?"

"She's mellowed toward him."

"I'll believe that when I see it."

"So, how old's the lad?" Artie asked.

"He's nine," James said.

"And you are what, twenty-six? That would make you a dad at seventeen. You randy little punter."

James shrugged his shoulders and smiled.

"The girls just love me."

"So, is she really sick, or has she scarpered?" Artie said.

"No, she's sick." James put his hands on the bar and leaned on them. "He's gonna have to go to school."

Artie was a retired headmaster.

"Aye, that he will."

"What will I need to get him started?" James asked.

"Just give them the name of his old school. They'll transfer his records. They'll ask for a record of his vaccinations, too."

James picked at his fingernail.

"What if I don't have his records?"

Artie tilted his head forward.

"What are you sayin', James?"

James leaned on the bar on his elbows.

"His mum didn't have any records. She had him at home."

"And he's never been to school," Artie said. "Then you'll have to apply for a birth certificate. You'll need that for school, and you can't get him his NHI card without it."

"So, how do I do that?" James asked.

"Make an appointment with the registry office in Beverly. Tell them he was born off-grid and the mother is gone. You might have to take a paternity test, too."

"Shit."

Artie arched his brows.

"You're not sure he's yours," Artie said.

James leaned back against the counter and folded his arms.

"You saw him. What do you think?"

"He's the spittin' image of you." Artie sipped his beer. "But the registry office will require documentation. And I would take care of this now." Artie took his wallet out. "You know, with your name, you could send him to any school in England. He could go to Eton."

"I'm not sending him away," James said. "Besides, do you know how much it costs to go to Eton?"

"Talk to your dad." James glowered at Artie. "Don't let your pride stand in the lad's way."

James leaned toward Artie.

"He doesn't know about Jon, and I want to keep it that way."

Artie took a fiver out of his wallet and put it on the bar.

"I've got some books at home that will help Jon prepare for his exams." Artie stood. "They're gonna want to test him."

"Can you help him?" James asked. "Give him a leg up so he can be with kids his own age."

"I'll bring the books by tomorrow. We'll talk about it then."

By the time James shut the door on the stragglers, it was after three, and the ache between his shoulder blades was worse. He left the chairs on the floor and turned off the lights. As he climbed the stairs, he was aware of each creaking board and hoped that Jon was a heavy sleeper.

He tried to be quiet when he pushed open the old, warped door, but it still creaked as he pushed it forward. He lifted it to keep it from squeaking again as he shut it, and then went to the kitchen to get the torch he kept in the drawer. He went to the bedroom and turned on the torch, but he didn't see Jon on the bed. James panicked and went to the other side of the bed where he found Jon curled up on the floor in a fetal position clutching the teddy bear in his arms.

Chapter Forty-Three

James awoke on the settee with a start. His head hurt, and his back was stiff. He sat up, rubbed his eyes, and then noticed that the flat was quiet. He got up, went to Jon's bedroom, and grew fearful when he saw the empty bed. James went to the settee, grabbed his jeans off the floor, and was putting them on when he saw a piece of paper on the dining table.

"Dear Dad, Maryanne is taking me to the park. Jon."

James sat at the table, threw his head back, and sighed. His pulse returned to normal, and he reread the note. The only other time in his life that he'd felt like this was when he lost Mia.

James held his head for a while before getting up to make coffee. He was surprised to find that the percolator was already set up. James put it on the cooker turned it on. He took a quick shower and dressed. He had to clean up the pub before the pensioners arrived, but his whole body ached. James grabbed the bottle of aspirin off the shelf above the sink and took four.

James turned off the cooker and poured a cup of coffee. As he sipped it, he looked around the flat. It had served his needs, but if they were to stay there, James would have to put a bed in the sitting room.

He took a mental inventory of his belongings. They were pitiful indeed. The furniture had been there when he bought the pub. If he left them there, he could rent the flat out so James would have money to pay rent on a two-bedroom somewhere nearby. It, too, would have to come furnished.

James stuck a piece of bread in the toaster, and Mia came into his mind. She had been taken from Havenwood against her will. Greyson had no idea what had happened to her after that. Was she in Dorley, and if so, why hadn't she come looking for James?

And then there was Miss Nithercott. She had the Silver Stag when she died. It was unlikely that she stumbled upon it on the street, so how had it come into her possession? Had Mia come to Miss Nithercott looking for James? No, because if Mia had the Silver Stag, she would have gone back to Jon.

"She's dead," James said aloud.

It was the only explanation that made sense. Mia had died when the man brought her back to Dorley.

But that still didn't explain how Miss Nithercott came to have the Silver Stag.

"How did you get it, Miss Nithercott?" he said.

The toast popped, and James buttered it. He ate it as he went downstairs, got the broom from the backroom, and started sweeping in the dining area. Mia stayed his mind as he swept the floor.

Mia's last name had been Wentworth. Her disappearance had been front-page news. Her reappearance would have triggered some sort of announcement, but James hadn't read a newspaper since leaving Huxley Manor.

"Harold," James said.

He stood for a moment. Mia's father was Harold Huxley's friend. If Mia had returned, Harold would know, but he cringed as he thought of asking his father about Mia.

James hurried through his sweeping and then got the till from the safe before unlocking the door. He'd have to put these thoughts aside until later.

* * *

Maryanne ran a finger over Jon's cheek.

"You look like your dad, all right," she said.

Jon watched a seagull standing at the end of their picnic table as he licked his vanilla ice cream cone. Melted ice cream covered his hand and the sleeve of his shirt.

"You've got more on you than in you," Maryanne said. "I'll be back in a minute."

Maryanne went inside the seaside ice cream parlor and asked the girl at the counter to wet a paper napkin. When she returned to Jon, she saw that he had given the seagull his ice cream. He jumped when she came up behind him and began wiping off his face, hands, and sleeve.

"That's better," she said. She tossed the napkins in the bin, returned to her place across from him, and folded her hands on the table. "So, you like school?"

"I've never been," Jon said.

Maryanne's eyebrows rose.

"You've never been to school?"

"No." He tilted his head back and peered at her through his lashes. "Greyson said that his school would teach me all I needed to know."

Maryanne narrowed her eyes and cocked her head.

"Who's Greyson?"

"He was…" Jon remembered James' admonishment not to talk about Havenwood. "He took care of me."

"What was he, like your grandfather?"

Jon bit his lower lip.

"He was my friend."

Maryanne lifted an eyebrow.

"What kind of friend was he?" she asked.

"I don't know what you mean," Jon said.

Maryanne sat back and studied Jon's face.

"Do you like James?"

"Yes."

"Did he visit you a lot?" Maryanne asked.

Jon felt her eyes on him and blushed. He was unaccustomed to lying.

"No."

"So, when he came for you, it was the first time you'd ever seen him?"

"Yes."

"It must have been hard, leaving your mum. Where does she live?"

"In the north."

"Where in the north?"

Jon pursed his lips. "Can't remember."

Maryanne sat back and folded her arms across her chest. This kid was just like his da. James would always clam up whenever the conversation turned personal.

"Do you miss her?" Maryanne asked.

"Yes," Jon said.

Jon's downcast eyes almost brought Maryanne to tears.

"I'm sorry," she said. "I miss me mum, too."

Maryanne tapped her fingers on the table. His hair looked as if it hadn't been trimmed in ages.

"Would you like to get your hair cut?" she asked.

Jon nodded. "The scissors broke, so Greyson wasn't able to cut it for me."

"Well, then, it's a trip to the barber for you," Maryanne said. "Let's go."

They got into Maryanne's car and drove to the village of Morseton. Maryanne parked on the street in front of the barber and took Jon inside. The barber took one look at Jon's hair and shook his head.

"How long has the lad been like this?" he asked.

"I'm not sure," she said. "His mum's been sick."

"Well, then, why don't we just take it down with the clippers and start all over again, eh?"

Maryanne watched the barber run the clippers over Jon's hair, leaving about half an inch all around. Jon smiled as he rubbed his hands over his head.

"I've never felt my head before," he said with glee.

"Enjoy it," Maryanne said. "It'll grow back soon enough."

Maryanne and Jon returned to the car and got inside. She rubbed her hand over his head and smiled.

"You look happy," she said.

"I like the way it feels," Jon said.

Maryanne had cousins Jon's age, a rowdy bunch of boys who would sass their mum. They paid little heed to anything the adults in the room said, and never spoke a word of gratitude to anyone. Jon was nothing like them, and as Maryanne looked at his innocent smile, she feared what would happen to him if he was placed in a class with them. The more she thought about it, the more apprehensive Maryanne grew, so by the time she reached the pub's car park, she had made up her mind that the boy would be better off with a private education.

When they walked into the pub, James' eyes widened.

"I hardly recognize you," James said. "You got his hair cut without asking me."

"It had to be done, and you'd have never gotten 'round to it," Maryanne said.

"I would too."

"No, you wouldn't, and besides, he likes it."

They sat at the bar, and Maryanne folded her arms and leaned on them. Jon followed suit.

"So, where were you all day?" James asked.

"Maryanne showed me the ocean," Jon said."

"We drove to Whitby," Maryanne said. "I bought him an ice cream."

"It was good," Jon said.

Jon began to kick the bar, and Maryanne put her hand on his arm.

"Don't kick the bar." He stopped and then looked at James. "And don't go looking at your father." Maryanne glowered at James. "He already knows you're a soft touch." Maryanne touched Jon's arm. "Go upstairs and change your clothes."

"Why?" he asked.

"Because you got ice cream all over you. Now, go."

"Don't go ordering him around," James said.

"Someone has to." Maryanne waited while Jon climbed the stairs and didn't talk until she heard the flat door close. "That boy is too soft for a public school."

"That's what you think, is it?"

"Aye, it is."

"I don't recall making you part of the decision," James said.

"I made meself part of it," she said.

"And for your information, I got my ass kicked plenty when I was in private school."

"Is that what made you the man you are today?" Her wicked smile made him blush. Maryanne exhaled sharply and gazed around the room. "Where's Artie?"

"Haven't seen him," James said.

"Didn't he used to teach?"

"Aye." James folded his arms and leaned on the bar.

"Well, maybe he can help us decide what to do."

James stood and straightened his back. "There is no us, Maryanne, there's just me." James rubbed the back of his neck.

"So, you think you can do this all on your own, do ya?" Maryanne slid off the stool and came around the bar. She stood in front of James and put her hands on her hips. "Like you've done such a great job with your life so far."

"What's wrong with my life?"

"You're spoiled is what. You've never had to do nothing on your own, and now you have a kid to think about."

"Why are you yelling at me?"

"Because you have to put the boy first!" she cried. "He's a good lad. He deserves a good dad."

James ran his hand through his hair. He was still tired from driving the day before and sleeping on the settee. For a moment, he longed for his old life where he had his own bed and didn't have to deal with things like a child's education, but then Jon came downstairs wearing one of James' shirt. The sleeves were too long, and the hem hung around the boy's knees.

"What the devil do you have on?" Maryanne asked.

"I couldn't find my clothes," Jon said.

"They're still in the bag," James said with a smile. "I forgot to take them out when we got home."

"Well, you look bloody ridiculous," Maryanne said. "Let's go up and find you something else."

As James watched Maryanne follow Jon up the stairs, he wished he had a dragon to slay or a ring to deliver to Mordor. At least he knew how to wield a sword.

Chapter Forty-Four

Artie arrived for his afternoon pint and sat on his favorite stool.

"I've been wondering where you were," James said.

"I went fishin'," Artie said. "Waste of time that. Not a bite to be had." James poured him a pint and set it on the bar. "You look knackered."

"I haven't been sleeping well."

"Lots on your mind."

"I need to get him registered," James said.

"Call 'em now. Make the appointment."

"Won't they ask me what happened to his mother?"

Artie sipped his beer as he eyed James.

"Tell them the truth. It's easier to remember."

Jesus, James thought. *The truth.*

James leaned on the bar on his elbows and clasped his hands.

"Will they want to talk to her?" James asked.

"Tell 'em that the girl left him on your doorstep with a note," Artie said. "It wouldn't be the first time somethin' like that happened. The fewer people you have to remember, the better."

"But you just said that the truth is easier to remember."

Artie tilted his head forward.

"You're making this harder than it needs to be," Artie said.

"I'm making it harder." James shook his head and then looked at Artie. "I don't know if I can do this."

"Do what?" Artie asked.

"This." James glanced at the stairs. "Take care of him. Make decisions about his future. I can barely take care of myself."

"Get over it," Artie said. "You have a son. He needs you."

James hung his head. "So, I can't just run away and leave him with Maryanne."

"No boy deserves that."

James smiled broadly.

"Well, then, I guess I'd better call the registry and find out what I need to get him sorted. Can you watch the bar for a minute?"

"Aye, mate."

James went to the office and looked for the directory. He looked through the desk drawers until he found it, but he also found a letter addressed to him from a law office in London. The postmark was a year old. James found the number for the registry office in the directory and made an appointment for the following week. When he hung up, he opened the letter.

"DEAR LORD HUXLEY;

I REPRESENT YOUR LATE MOTHER'S ESTATE, AND IT IS MY DUTY TO inform you that you are the beneficiary of a discretionary trust. It was your mother's desire that you should have full access to the trust once you reached the age of twenty-five years. Please contact my office regarding this matter.

YOURS TRULY,

HENRY DANVERS, ESQUIRE

JAMES STARED AT THE WORDS "DISCRETIONARY TRUST." HIS mother had left him money. Depending on the amount, it might mean the difference between putting Jon in a public school or finding a place where he wouldn't be bullied, if such a place existed.

James dialed the lawyer's office and made an appointment

there, too. Maybe he would take Jon with him, and James could show him London. He'd have to be nice to Maryanne so she would agree to watch the bar...

"Why did she hide this?" James said aloud.

James got up, shoved the letter in his pocket, went outside, and went up the backstairs to the flat. Jon and Maryanne were looking through Jon's clothes, and when she saw the look on James' face, she straightened her back and looked him in the eye.

"What?" she asked.

James pulled the letter out of his pocket.

"Why didn't you give me this?"

Maryanne went to him and took the letter out of his hand. She looked at the envelope and the postmark.

"I don't remember this," she said.

"It was in a drawer under the directory."

Maryanne shook her head.

"I don't remember it. Maybe it got stuck on something."

"It's from a lawyer. I have to go to London next week. I'll need you to open."

Maryanne opened her mouth to protest, but she saw that James was distraught.

"Fine," she said.

"Did you do it on purpose?" he asked.

"No, and why would I?"

"I don't know."

"Well, think before you speak, *Lord* Huxley."

Maryanne tossed him the letter, went back to the bed, and continued to sort through Jon's clothes. James fisted his hands and then returned to the bar. Artie saw James' red cheeks and raised his eyebrows.

"What happened now?"

"I found a letter in one of the drawers in the office. It was sent to me a year ago, and she says she doesn't remember it."

"What's it say?"

"It says my mother left me a trust."

"Then I'd say the timin' is just right," Artie said.

"I'm still mad at her."

"Choose your battles, James."

"So, I should just forgive her and go on? I could have used this money."

"For what? You do all right."

"Well, I could have done better," James said.

Artie waved his hand.

"Let it go." He leaned forward. "You know you need her."

"I could hire someone to do what she does."

"No, you couldn't. She knows this place. She swallowed her pride when her father sold it to you. She always believed she was gettin' it. She had no idea her da had put it up for sale."

"And she never lets me forget it," James said. "It's been five bloody years, Artie."

Artie shrugged and then tilted his head.

"Then why don't you sell it to her?"

"What?"

"Sell the pub to *her*."

"Why would I do that?" James asked.

"Your mum left you money. You don't need this place anymore, so sell it to her."

"I don't know how much money there is. For all I know, it's just enough to put Jon in school for a year."

Artie rubbed a spot on the bar.

"Didn't you say your uncle owns the Bank of Moreland?"

"Last time I looked," James said.

"Was your mum his sister?"

James folded his arms across his chest.

"She was."

"Odds are, she had shares, and now those shares belong to you."

"Maybe."

"They could be worth a fortune," Artie asked.

The Bank of Moreland had branches everywhere. Artie was right – those shares would be worth a fortune.

"Then I might think about selling this place."

"To Maryanne."

Maryanne and Jon came down the stairs before James could answer. He watched as they sat at the bar and Artie admired Jon's clothes. James also watched Maryanne run her hand over Jon's head and his shoulder to smooth a wrinkle. She could be so nice when she wanted to be.

Chapter Forty-Five

JAMES OPENED HIS EYES AND LOOKED AT THE WALL CLOCK. IT WAS past ten. He listened for sounds of Jon and didn't hear any, so he sat up, and the stiffness in his back was worse than the day before.

"Jon!" he cried. "Where are you?"

Jon came out of his room and stared at James.

"I'm here."

"Are you all right?"

"I'm a little hungry."

"Right. I'm getting up."

"I can make breakfast," Jon said.

"Do you know how to work a toaster?" James asked.

"I had one in my house."

"Then have at it."

Jon went to the kitchen counter while James went to the loo. Jon heard James turn on the shower as he put two slices of bread into the toaster, and then took butter and jam from the fridge. Jon also put a light under the teakettle, got two mugs from the shelf over the kitchen sink, and put tea bags in each.

James was dressed when he came out of the loo and was surprised to see the table set and the tea made. Jon smiled as James sat.

"This is lovely," James said. "No one has made me breakfast in years."

"I made breakfast for Greyson," Jon said. Jon bit his toast. "Do you think we can look for my mum?"

James lifted his mug and held it aloft. He set it down, sat back and studied Jon's face. A warm feeling washed over him and he knew he would do anything to make the boy happy.

"I don't know where to start, Jon."

"Can we ask someone to help us? Maryanne has a radio in her car and I heard a man say he was the finder of lost things. Mum is lost, so maybe he could find her."

"Your mum is not a thing. And that just sounds like an advertisement for a private detective."

"So, can we hire a private detective?" Jon asked.

"I can't promise you anything until after we see the solicitor," James said.

"Why?"

"Because we have to pay them," James said.

"Like in the store. You have to pay them with money."

James smiled. "Aye."

"And we will see the solicitor tomorrow," Jon said.

James nodded. He looked at the clock and drained his tea.

"I've got to get going."

"I can help," Jon said.

"Okay. Clean up the breakfast and meet me downstairs."

James didn't have time to do more than put the till in the cash register before he heard a knock on the front door. Old Smythe was grinning at him when he opened the door.

"I'm the first today."

"Aye, mate," James said.

The usual parade of pensioners arrived and took their stools while James set up their pints. Maryanne had taken the day off because James and Jon were going to London the following day, so James was glad to have Jon to help with the little things like fetching clean bar rags and putting glasses in the dishwasher. James winced when he moved the wrong way, and a twinge of pain ran from his waist to his neck. Old Smythe noticed and shook his head.

"Young lad like you shouldn't be in pain."

"It's nothing," James said.

"It ain't nothing, son. Take me word for it."

"It's just that I'm sleeping on the settee, and it's hard as a rock."

"Then get yourself a decent bed, mate."

James smiled. "In time."

"The longer you wait, the worse it will be."

Artie came in and sauntered over to the bar. He saw James bent forward with his hands on the bar.

"Your back is acting up again," he said.

"It's the settee," James said.

"You need a proper bed," Artie said.

"I know. In time."

"Did you talk to Maryanne about her buyin' the pub?"

"Is Maryanne buyin 'the pub?" Old Smythe asked.

"No," James said. He looked at Artie. "And I'll talk to her when I'm ready."

"Wouldn't like it if'n she owned the place." Old Smythe shook his head. "Not one bit."

"I haven't decided what I'm going to do," James said.

Jon came downstairs and climbed onto the stool next to Artie.

"Hullo," Artie said.

Jon smiled.

"Hello."

"He almost sounds American," Old Smythe said.

"His mum was…is American," James said.

"Is she now?"

"Aye," Artie said.

"And how would you know?" Old Smythe said.

"Because I've got ears, don't I? James told me about it."

"When did I tell you she was American?" James asked.

"Don't remember when," Artie said.

"I told you," Jon said.

Artie nodded. "That's right."

"Why didn't he tell me about it?" Old Smythe asked.

"Because you can't keep your gob shut."

Tom Kirby came into the pub and sat at the end of the bar. Artie nodded toward him.

"You should think about getting someone in to help out when Maryanne's off," Artie said.

James leaned with his hand on the bar.

"D' you think?"

"Aye, mate, you look positively knackered."

"Jesus, I know!" James cried.

James sighed, grabbed a bar towel, and wiped off the bar.

"He needs a bed," Artie said.

"They've got nice beds at Anderson's," Old Smythe said.

"We weren't talking about a bed," James said. "We were talking about hiring someone."

"You should talk to Maryanne about buyin' the pub," Artie said.

James stopped wiping and closed his eyes while he thought about strangling Artie. When the feeling passed, he went to each table and wiped it down.

"So, Tom, what's new?" Artie asked.

"Nothin'," Tom said.

"You workin'?"

"Laid off. They're calling us back in a month's time."

"Bloody bastards," Old Smythe said.

"I've been picking up work here and there."

"James just said he could use some help," Artie said.

James came back to the bar, leaned against the back counter, and folded his arms across his chest. He glanced at Jon.

"Go see if the glasses are done," James said.

Jon slid off the stool and went through the kitchen door.

"How do people do it?" James asked.

"Do what?" Artie asked.

"Raise kids alone."

"I've seen 'em do it," Artie said. "It's hard."

"I don't know if I'll ever get used to it," James said. "There's so much to remember."

"Let him help you. Give him chores."

"I'd let him work the bar if I could get away with it."

"Is she here today?" Tom asked.

"She's out today," James said. He eyed Tom. "So, what's the story with you two?"

"We used to go together. We stopped."

"Yeah, so you said before. She 'as a temper that one." James' eyes lit up. "She hit you with a glass ashtray!" Tom smiled and raised his pint. James put his hands on his hips. "If I can find a way to pay you, would you like to work here a couple of days a week?"

"She'd bloody kill you, mate," Tom said.

"Yeah, she would, wouldn't she." James grinned. "So, what do you say?"

"Just let me know when."

"You're playing with fire, James," Artie said.

"You were the one who said I needed help." James took a deep breath. "I'll tell her I have to spend more time with Jon."

"Speaking of Jon, I found the books he needs to prepare for his exams."

James nodded. "And you said you would help him."

"I'll tutor him."

"How much do you get for tutoring?" James asked.

"Free beer for a month," Artie said.

"Deal. And I'll square it with Maryanne."

The kitchen door opened, and Jon walked through with a plastic tub filled with clean glasses. He set it down on the floor in front of the bar and put them in order underneath.

"Good job, mate," James said. "Now, go and ask that man at that table what he'd like to drink."

James watched Jon scurry over to the large man. A moment later, Jon returned with a grin on his face.

"A pint, please."

"A pint it is," James said as he put a mug under the tap. "But, I have to deliver it."

Jon's smile faded, and then Artie touched Jon's shoulder.

"Come outside with me. I've got some books for you."

Jon followed Artie to the car park to retrieve the school books. James watched them from the door and saw Jon grin again. The boy was always so thankful for anything he was given, and James hoped Jon's gratitude would rub off on him one day.

Chapter Forty-Six

THE SOLICITOR'S OFFICE WAS IN A TALL, MODERN, GLASSY structure in a building complex called Canary Wharf. Jon's mouth was agape and his eyes wide as he and James walked past the shimmering edifices. The lift was another new adventure, and James warned him off playing with the buttons, but he loved seeing the world through Jon's eyes.

When the lift doors opened, they were greeted by an older woman who introduced herself as Mr. Danvers' assistant.

"Lord Huxley." She stood with her hands clasped in the manner of elderly ladies and smiled benignly at them. "I'm Miss Reade. Mr. Danvers is waiting for you. Would the boy like to watch the telly?"

James looked down at Jon, who took his hand. This was his opportunity to shield Jon from learning about the Huxleys before he was old enough to understand, but Jon tightened his grip on James' hand.

"Can he come with me?" James asked.

"Of course."

Jon's eyes swept left to right as they followed Miss Reade down a wide corridor banked on each side by offices. Hushed voices could be heard behind the nameplated doors, and the air of solemnity was a marked contrast from the pub's noisy conviviality.

"Is this a church?" Jon whispered.

"No," James whispered.

Mr. Danvers' office was the last on the right, and when they reached the office, Miss Reade opened the door and announced James' arrival.

"Lord Huxley."

James felt Jon tighten his grip again. He smiled at Mr. Danvers, a tall, slender man in a custom made suit who extended his hand in greeting and cast a leery eye on Jon.

"Perhaps the boy would prefer to wait outside?"

"Jon wants to stay with me," James said.

"Very well."

Mr. Danvers led them to a group of chairs in front of the windows. He sat, and James followed suit as he pointed to one for Jon. Mr. Danvers picked up a black leather portfolio with the name "Horton" embossed in gold lettering on the cover from the end table.

"I remember the day your mother came to see me," Mr. Danvers said. "She was eager to create a trust in your name. I'm not sure what your father has shared with you regarding the financial arrangements between the Hortons and Lord Huxley."

"I'm not aware of any financial arrangements," James said.

"She shared her fears with me regarding Lord Huxley's situation and felt it wise to keep this money in trust until you turned twenty-five." Mr. Danvers looked at the folder. "If I may talk plainly."

"Go on," James said.

"Your mother felt that your father would influence you. She worried he would persuade you to give him the money." Mr. Danvers paused. "She wanted to ensure your future."

James' downcast eyes settled on Jon's trainer. The boy's foot moved back and forth like a pendulum.

"Well then," Mr. Danvers said. "Shall we proceed?"

"Please do," James said.

"As you know, we sent you a letter regarding the trust on the occasion of your twenty-fifth birthday. The details regarding the trust are as follows."

Mr. Danvers put on his half-glasses and turned a page in the folder. He scanned the page and then closed the folder.

"There are thirty pages here." He smiled at James. "Why

don't we dispense with the legal nonsense. I'm sure you'd just like to know what you've inherited."

"Please," James said.

"Celeste was a dear friend, James. It surprised everyone when she married your father. She was a free spirit, and Lord Harold was a bit of a stick, but your Grandfather Horton believed that marriage to an Earl would tame Celeste. I always thought she did it to please her father." Mr. Danvers paused with his eyes downcast, and then perked up. "Be that as it may, I promised her that I would protect your interests, and I can say here and now that I have personally seen to your trust for the last twenty years. As of now, the trust itself is worth several hundred thousand dollars."

James felt his throat constrict. His hands gripped the arms of the chair as he stared at Mr. Danvers.

"Are you all right?" Mr. Danvers asked.

"Water," James gasped.

Mr. Danvers went to the bar and poured James a glass of water. He handed it to James and watched him drain the glass.

"Several hundred *thousand*," James said.

"Yes. As I said, I've watched over it personally."

"I never imagined…" James looked at Jon. "It's a lot of money."

"It is indeed." Mr. Danvers tilted his head. "If you'd like, I'd be honored if you'd allow me to administer it for you. We could also set up a trust for your son."

"Yes, definitely. And I would like to have you administer it for me."

"Wonderful, then if you'll excuse me, I'll ask Miss Reade to draw up the papers."

After Mr. Danvers left the office, Jon turned to James.

"We never needed money in Havenwood," Jon said.

"Well, we need it here, mate, and now we have more than we need."

James glanced at the door and then went to the folder and lifted the cover. He searched through the papers for a figure, and when he found one, he felt his throat tighten again.

"Oh, my God," he said.

"What is it?" Jon asked.

"The amount. I never dreamed…"

Mr. Danvers returned, and James went to his seat.

"Why don't we go to the desk so we can go over these documents?"

"Stay here," James told Jon.

The desk was on the right side of the room with two chairs in front. James sat in one while Mr. Danvers went behind the desk. He laid the papers in front of James.

"We can use the same model to set up Jon's trust," Mr. Danvers said. "You always have the option of changing it later on."

"It should be fine," James said.

Mr. Danvers eyed James.

"I know this must be a bit overwhelming, James. You don't have to sign anything today. Take the papers home and read them."

"I trust you."

"It's not a matter of trust. It's a matter of you understanding what's involved."

"I understand that my mother trusted you. That's all I need to know."

Mr. Danvers sat back and studied James. He looked at Jon and saw the stark resemblance between them. He also noticed that Jon was older than one would expect.

"How old is Jon?" he asked.

"Nine," Jon said.

"He was born when you were…"

"Seventeen," James said. He focused on the papers while his cheeks turned red. He raised his eyes to meet Mr. Danvers'. "I wasn't married to his mum."

Mr. Danvers clasped his hands on his stomach.

"Is she liable to ask for support?"

"No. She's…not in his life right now."

"But if she hears about the money…"

"I'll deal with that if it happens," James said.

"We should deal with it now, James. You have to consider your future, Jon's future."

"We're making a trust for him."

"Where is the mother?"

"Mum is lost," Jon said.

James glanced at him, and Mr. Danvers raised his eyebrows.

"Your mum is lost?" Mr. Danvers asked.

"She was taken away."

Mr. Danvers looked at James.

"She ran away when we were...dating," James said. He stared into Jon's eyes. "She asked me to take him when she became ill."

Jon caught James' meaning and held his tongue. Mr. Danvers had a quizzical look on his face.

"Wasn't there a situation involving you and the daughter of Vincent Wentworth?"

"There was."

Mr. Danver's waited for James to elaborate, but when no explanation was forthcoming, he put his hand on the paper in front of James.

"Well, then, have you decided to take the papers home to read them?"

"I will take them home, but I'd like to sign the trust papers for Jon now."

Mr. Danvers handed James a pen.

"That first page is the signature page for Jon's trust. It is exactly like the one your mother created for you." James signed the paper. Mr. Danvers took the page and added it to a new folder without gold lettering. "And the papers regarding your disbursement are in this folder." He slid a manila folder across the desk. "Take your time, James. Ordinarily, a trust is kept intact, and you can draw on the interest. We will open an account that allows you to write checks. Let me know your thoughts after you've read everything."

"Where is the money now?" James asked.

"The Bank of Moreland. Your Uncle William's bank."

"Right, but I can put it anywhere I like."

"Absolutely, though I would advise against it. The bank has a sterling reputation." Mr. Danvers folded his hands on the desk. "How is Billy?"

"He lives in Hong Kong now," James said.

"I haven't seen him in many years, not since your grandfather died." Mr. Danvers pursed his lips. "If you'll excuse me for a moment." He got up and went out the door. He returned with another file in his hand and sat behind the desk. "Your maternal grandfather bought the Moreland bank when your mother and uncle were children. I wanted to check his file because you are his only living grandchild. His file was overseen by one of the partners in our firm. As your solicitor, I want to apprise you of all business pertaining to your interests, including that of the Bank of Moreland. However, it seems as if Conrad Horton chose to leave the entirety of his fortune to his son, William."

"Cut me out, eh?" James said.

"He did, but this is what I was looking for – the distribution of William's estate." Mr. Danvers smiled. "You are his sole heir, James."

"You're kidding."

"'Should I leave this world without issue, I, therefore, endow and bequeath my estate, minus certain bequests to named individuals and organizations, to my nephew, James Huxley.' That means the Bank of Moreland, James."

"But that's only if he doesn't have any children," James said.

"He's in his fifties. Of course, there is always a chance that he might sire a child or two, but odds are you will inherit his estate."

"Shit," James whispered.

"Indeed."

James turned his head to see Jon.

"We're talking about a lot of money, James. You'd do best to learn all you can about how it's handled and invested."

"I've no interest in business," James said.

"Well, you'd better develop one if you want to hold onto your money. I'll help you in any way I can, but if I were you, I'd contact William. Let him teach you what he knows."

"I haven't seen him since I was a child."

"Well, you have money now. Take a trip to Hong Kong. Introduce him to Jon."

"Aye." James smiled. "We could go to Hong Kong."

Mr. Danvers stood. "Well, I think we are done here today. Go home. Read the papers, and look for the checks in the mail. Do we have your address in…?"

"Morseton," James said.

"Right. Make sure Miss Reade has your address."

James and Jon bid Mr. Danvers goodbye. They stopped at Miss Reade's desk and verified that she had the pub's address. As they left the office building, James recalled a small restaurant he'd gone to with Miss Nithercott when she brought him to the zoo.

"Why don't we get something to eat?" James asked.

"I'd like that."

James took out his wallet and checked his cash. He pursed his lips and sighed.

"We'll have to walk."

"I don't mind," Jon said.

The café was ten blocks away, and by the time they got there, they were both starving. The waiter took their order and brought them a basket of bread and butter. James watched Jon eat and noticed that the boy seemed preoccupied.

"What's on your mind?"

"I was wondering what your mother's name was."

"*That's* what you were thinking about?" James asked, and Jon nodded. "Her name was Celeste."

"Do you miss your mother?" Jon asked.

"I do, but not as much as when I was your age." James buttered some bread.

"I miss my mother. I miss Greyson, too."

"It's only right that you should," James said.

Jon buttered some bread. He hesitated while he ate and observed James' expression. He took a bite and put his bread on his plate.

"I want to find my mother."

James put down his knife.

"I know." He put his bread down. "We have the money now to hire someone."

"Then let's do that."

James missed that feeling of total confidence children have when they make a decision. He smiled at his son and nodded.

"Right. First thing tomorrow, we look in the directory for a private detective."

"A private detective," Jon repeated.

James picked up his glass of water and held it up. He nodded to Jon, who then picked up his, and they touched glasses.

"To finding your mum."

"To finding Mum."

Jon looked uncertain.

"Now drink it," James said.

They drank, and a feeling of peace settled on them both. It was always better when you had a plan, and even if that plan was destined to fail, at least you had something to hold on to.

Chapter Forty-Seven

MARYANNE BURST THROUGH THE FRONT DOOR AND MARCHED toward the kitchen without so much as a nod to James, who was putting the clean glasses under the bar.

"I'm done," she said. "You hear me, I've had enough."

"What's wrong?"

"You bloody well know what's wrong." She came up to James, and he backed away. "You know how I feel about him."

"Who?" James asked.

"Don't you act all innocent. You know bloody well who I mean."

James leaned against the back counter and folded his arms across his chest.

"This is my pub, you know."

"Aye, it's yours, all right. And you can have it."

"You sure that's the way you want things to go?"

Maryanne stepped back. James wasn't backing down. She eyed him up and down, and then a smile creased her lips.

"You've found your balls," she said. "Is it Jon? Has he done this to ya?"

"Don't bring Jon into this."

"You've never talked back to me before. You trying to impress him?"

"I don't have to impress my son," James said.

"But you want to, don't ya?" Maryanne tilted her head. "Now, you want to be a man."

"I've always been a man."

"No, James, you weren't. You've never spoken to me like that before, not in five years. I'm proud of ya."

She put her hands on her hips and smiled at him as if he had just scored the winning goal in the FA Cup final. James smiled, shrugged, and then braced himself when Maryanne embraced him in a bear hug around his waist.

"I'm still gonna kick the shit out of you for what you've done," she said. "But I'm still proud of ya."

"Are you talking about Tom?" James asked.

Maryanne pulled away. "Aye, and who else would I be talking about?"

"I needed someone, so I could have some time off with my son."

"Well, you still should have asked me."

"It's my pub!" James cried.

"And it's time I got things started in the kitchen."

Maryanne went to the kitchen, and James was still unsure as to whether she would allow Tom to work for him when the pensioners began to fill the stools at the bar. Every time Maryanne came out of the kitchen, James braced himself, and when she turned and winked at him, he was confused. Artie noticed it too, and when James brought him his second beer, he put his hand on James' arm.

"What's going on?" Artie asked.

"What'd you mean?" James said. Artie nodded toward the kitchen. "I have no idea. She came in itching for a fight because of Tom, and I told her it was my pub, and then she smiles and says she proud of me."

Artie lifted his head and furrowed his brow.

"And that was it?"

"Aye, that was it. She's been smiling ever since. I'm afraid to go into the kitchen."

"Well, maybe she'll respect you now," Artie said.

"Why?"

"Because you stood up to her."

"Is that all she wanted?" James asked.

"Women. Who knows what they want?"

James shook his head. "I'll drink to that, brother."

"So, is Jon reading the book I gave him?"

"He's upstairs. He was reading when I left."

"He's a good lad he is, James. He'll do fine in school. It won't take him long to catch up."

James nodded and then refilled some beers before the football game started. He ran to the shelf holding the old telly and put a chair beneath it. He stood on the chair, turned on the telly, and adjusted the antenna until the picture cleared. Maryanne came out of the kitchen with a jar of pickled eggs and eyed the pensioners at the bar.

"I'm collecting today," she said. "Get out your money before the game begins."

The grumbling started after she returned to the kitchen. The old men took out their wallets, and each laid a fiver on the bar. Maryanne brought a stack of bowls to the bar and filled them with crisps, nuts, and beef jerky.

"We're having meat pies today," she said. She walked down the bar and grabbed the five-pound notes. "I'm also inclined to make fish finger sandwiches."

The old men looked at each other and then at James, who shrugged.

"Jon, me lad," Artie said.

James turned to find his son standing at the end of the bar.

"Did you finish your reading?" James asked as he walked to the bar.

"Aye," Jon said. "I finished both of them."

"That's a lot of reading, boy," Artie said.

"I like to read." Jon looked up at the TV. "What's that?"

"It's football," James said. "Why don't you sit, and I'll get you a meat pie while you watch the game?"

Jon nodded and took a seat at the table nearest the bar. James hesitated at the kitchen door and then went inside to see if the meat pies were ready.

"Do we have any meat pies yet?" he asked.

"What am I, a bleedin' magician?" Maryanne said. "I just put them in the oven. Give 'em half an hour."

James returned to the bar and saw that Artie had moved to the table and was explaining football to Jon, who cocked his ear whenever Artie spoke. As he studied his boy's face, James looked for Mia. The boy was so like James that it was as if he'd been cloned. While he had seen her photo in the newspaper, James had trouble remembering what she was like in person, but the image of her narrow blue eyes peeking out from beneath her bangs was as sharp as the day he woke up and found her with her head on his chest.

"I think I love you."

The searing ache of her loss returned, and he fought to push it back down to a place he could control.

"James!"

He snapped out of his reverie to find Old Smythe waving his empty pint at James. Jon was still focused on the football game, and Artie was in his glory as his team had just scored a goal. Life went on.

The day passed, Jon ate a meat pie, and Artie's team won the match. When the pensioners left, the young men took their place, and James' back ached. He wished he had asked Tom to come in, but he could only afford him two days a week until James started drawing money from the trust.

You have enough to live on, he thought. *You don't need the pub.*

He leaned against the counter behind him and folded his arms. What did he want to do now that he didn't need to work for a living? He used to ask himself that question when he was in college. At the time, he wanted to travel, but now he had Jon, and he would have to go to school. James thought of what Mr. Danvers had said and pondered the idea of learning how to handle money, but his thoughts soon drifted to sunny beaches.

James watched Jon cheering as one of the men threw a dart. He was such an easy boy. Jon asked so little of James, but he was always full of questions. He loved to learn and soaked things up like a sponge. It would be fun to travel with him and show him all the places James had wanted to see when he was a boy.

Jon's eyes drooped, and he laid his head on the table. James came to him and put a hand on his back.

"You look knackered," James said. "It's time for bed. Don't forget to brush your teeth."

James heard himself reminding Jon to brush and sighed. He sounded like Miss Nithercott.

The rest of the night was a blur, and when the last man left the pub, James locked the door and leaned against it for a while. Maryanne was tallying up the receipts and putting cash in a sack for the bank. She had dark circles under her eyes, and she moved slower when she got off the stool and went into the kitchen. James followed Maryanne to the office and stood at the doorway while she finished entering sums in her ledger.

"I'll tell Tom I made a mistake," he said.

Maryanne sat back and rubbed her neck. She winced, baring her teeth for a second or two, and then relaxed her mouth.

"Why did you hire him knowin' how I feel?"

"He was just there, and I was thinking about Jon."

Maryanne got up and took the money and the ledger to the safe. James took off his apron and tossed it in a hamper with the other soiled linens. He'd have to take them to the laundromat in the morning.

"Let him stay," she said. "Just put him on when I'm off."

"You sure?"

"Aye. At least you can trust him."

She stood back and tilted her head.

"You look awful."

"Thanks a lot," James said. "Does it ever get easier?"

"What? Running your own business or being a dad?"

"Both."

"Me Da used to just get up every morning and put one foot in front of the other."

Maryanne put on her jacket and grabbed her purse.

"I'm stopping at the market on the way tomorrow. I'll be late."

"I'll see you when you get here."

After he saw her out and locked the door, James put the chairs on the tables and the glasses in the dishwasher. He climbed the stairs to the flat and lifted the door so it wouldn't creak when he opened it. Jon was asleep, and James looked at the settee. He felt a twinge in his back and sighed. It was time to go shopping for a new bed.

Chapter Forty-Eight

THE PENSIONERS HAD TAKEN A SHINE TO JON. EVEN MARYANNE would smile when she saw him and would always rush to the kitchen to fetch him something to eat. Jon had filled out a bit since his days in Havenwood, and he'd grown a few inches taller.

James now saw his life as before and after Jon. Before Jon, James had no direction in life, no care as to what happened to him, but now, every thought had to do with Jon's happiness. He was grateful to Artie for teaching the boy and thankful to Maryanne for being his surrogate mother. James didn't look forward to the day Jon would have to go to school, for it meant they'd be separated most of the day, but until then, he would keep Jon near him.

Now, at the end of the day, when James climbed the stairs to the flat, the first thing he did was check on Jon, who had finally set aside his teddy bear and was sleeping on his stomach the way James had slept as a child. Sometimes, James would stand there for ten or fifteen minutes just listening to Jon breathe, and then he would be able to go to sleep. As long as Jon was safe, then all was right with the world.

One morning a few weeks after he brought Jon home, James woke to find Jon holding a cup of coffee, which he placed on the end table. James had been dreaming about the day his father discovered that Mia had gone missing.

"You stupid boy!" Harold had shouted. "How could you let this happen?"

"I didn't know what she was going to do," James said.

"She was your responsibility. What am I to tell her father?"

"I didn't know…"

"Stop saying that! Dear God, you are a fool."

The word fool resonated in James' mind. The memory kept him mindful of his own words to his son. Harold had spent an hour berating James before he left him sitting alone at the dining table. James went to Mia's room and searched for the disk she'd gotten from Rotrude. He then looked through the attic. When he didn't find it, he fell to his knees and pounded the floor until the side of his hand was bloody.

James sat up and grabbed his coffee.

"Do you want eggs?" Jon asked.

"Just toast today."

Jon went to the kitchen and took two slices of bread from the wrapper. He put them into the toaster as James sat at the table. Jon had already set the table with butter and jam, so he got a small plate from the cabinet over the sink and set it before James. He saw that James' mug was half full and picked up the percolator.

"Do you want more coffee?"

"No, thanks. I want you to sit and relax."

Jon sat and folded his hands. He rubbed a spot on the table, and then folded them again.

"I like reading the books Artie gives me," Jon said

"Is he a good teacher?"

"He knows a lot."

James sipped his coffee and watched his son over the rim of the mug.

"I want to ask you something," he said. Jon looked into James' eyes. "I'm thinking we might go on vacation. I've never seen Italy, or Germany. I thought it might be nice if we saw them together."

Jon was thoughtful for a moment.

"Artie says travel is a good way to expand your horizons."

James suppressed a smile.

"He did, did he?"

"Aye."

"Well, I agree," James said. "We might visit my uncle, too. He lives in Hong Kong."

"Is that close to Italy?" Jon asked.

"No. It's farther east."

The toaster popped, and Jon went to fetch James' toast. He brought them back and dropped them onto James' plate.

"When can we go?" Jon asked.

"Well, I have to talk to Maryanne about leaving first. She'll need someone to help her while I'm away."

"Maybe Tom would help her," Jon said.

Tom had turned out to be a fine barman. James had received the checks, and he could draw on the trust now, so he gave Tom two more nights a week. The working lads liked to hear his stories. If Maryanne was agreeable, Tom could take James' place, and no one would miss him.

"As I said, I have to talk to her first." James glanced at the clock. "Shit. It's late." He drained his coffee and grabbed the toast before bolting to the door. "Can you clean up the kitchen, mate?"

"Aye."

"Then come down."

"I will," Jon said.

When James came down to the pub, Artie was standing outside. James unlocked the door and let him in.

"You been waiting long?" James asked.

"No."

Artie went to his stool at the bar and sat. James went to the kitchen to get the clean mugs and brought them to the bar in a plastic tub. As he set them underneath the bar, Artie eyed James.

"Jon was telling me that you are going to look for his mum." James froze. "What?"

"He said you and he were going to find his mum."

"When did he say that?"

"A few days ago, when we were going over his geography assignment." Artie tilted his head. "I thought his mum was too ill to care for him."

James finished putting the glasses under the bar. He returned the plastic tub to the kitchen and stood for a moment with his eyes closed. Could he trust Artie with the truth about Mia? The burden of keeping the secret was as hard for Jon as it was for him. Now that Jon had brought her up, it might be a good time to tell Artie in case Jon said something else about his mother that didn't fit the narrative James had created. When he left the kitchen, he found Jon sitting beside Artie talking about their impending vacation, and then Jon slid off the stool and ran up the stairs to their flat.

"Jon says you're going to Italy," Artie said.

"We're talking about it," James said.

"You should go. You need some time together before he starts school."

James leaned against the back counter and folded his arms across his chest.

"Aye. I'd like that."

"He's a smart lad, James. He doesn't miss a thing."

James came to the bar.

"I need to tell you something, but you have to promise to keep it a secret."

Artie raised his eyebrows. "I'm the soul of discretion, mate."

James exhaled sharply.

"Jon's mum isn't sick, at least not that I know of." Artie eyed James. "Do you remember that girl who went missing from Dorley about ten years ago? An American girl named Mia?"

"I was teaching then. Everyone was talking about it. Huxley." Artie shook his head. "You're that Huxley."

James put his hands on the bar.

"Aye." James took a deep breath. "She was staying with us for the summer. We fell in love. I didn't know she was pregnant when she ran away."

"So, if she's still missing, how did you get Jon?"

James heard the flat door close and saw Jon coming down the stairs.

"We'll talk later," James said.

James watched Jon come to the bar and climb onto the stool beside Artie. He'd shared their secret with someone, which meant someone else knew that Jon was Mia's child. What if her parents found out? Would they try to claim him?

The idea of Mia's parents nagged at him for the rest of the day, and by closing time, he knew he would have to find out if Mia's father still worked in London, and that meant talking to the one person he'd hoped to avoid for the rest of his life – his father.

Chapter Forty-Nine

The flight from Zurich to Hong Kong was almost twelve hours long, so James made sure Jon had plenty of exercise before they boarded the plane. Within half an hour, Jon was snoring softly beside him, and James had some time to gather his thoughts. He had managed to avoid telling Artie about Mia and Havenwood, but he knew he'd have to tell him someday. James put that day in a box, and then recalled the day he offered to sell the pub to Maryanne.

"I'm broke," she said. "All I have is my father's house."

James knew Maryanne had no money, and he had already worked out a plan that he'd hoped she would agree to. He needed a home for Jon; he would suggest they exchange what they had so each would get what they wanted.

At first, Maryanne balked at giving James her house.

"Me Da would turn over in his grave," she said.

"But what about what you want?" James asked. "Everyone knows you wanted the pub. Well, this is your chance to have it, free and clear."

A few days later, she agreed to his terms, and they each felt they had gotten the better end of the bargain. James and Jon moved into the narrow, two-story house near the ocean, and Maryanne, who agreed to leave them the furniture, moved into the flat above Bixby's Brewhouse. Shortly after, James and Jon packed their bags and hopped a plane to Paris.

James and Jon had traveled through France, Germany, and

Italy before heading to Hong Kong to visit Uncle Billy. James had questions regarding his mother and the Bank of Moreland, which he had written down during the flight. Jon woke up an hour before they landed.

A limousine picked them up at the airport and took them to a tall building with the words "The Bank of Moreland" emblazoned on the front in big, gold letters. It was one of the tallest in the city, and the staff must have been prepped for the visit, for they all took pains to address James by his title. The whole scene made James uncomfortable, and he wished they had come to Hong Kong without notice. He loved his anonymity, and seeing how they fawned over him served as a reminder of why he had left it all behind to work as a publican.

Jon, though, seemed at ease with the attention. He smiled and responded appropriately to their questions. He did, however, have one question for James when they got on the lift, something he had asked James about on more than one occasion.

"What does lord mean?"

James leaned against the wall and pursed his lips. He worried that Jon, having learned of his father's nobility, might one day expect to be Lord Huxley, too. His illegitimacy prohibited it, and James didn't want to have to explain that to Jon. But as he looked into Jon's blue eyes, he decided to take a leap of faith and tell Jon the truth.

"My father is an earl," James said. "And that makes me a lord."

"What does a lord do?"

"They work, or they become public servants, just like anyone else."

"Oh." Jon tilted his head. "Why don't the people in the pub call you lord?"

"Because I didn't want them to. I just want to be like everyone else."

"And your father is an earl. What's an earl?"

"It's a bloody stupid title that he inherited from his father." James saw how Jon bit his lip. "Sorry, mate. I just…he inherited it because centuries ago, one of his ancestors did something for the king, and the king gave him a title."

"Oh," Jon said. "Will I be a lord someday?"

James exhaled sharply.

"When we get home, we can go to the bookstore and find a book about it, okay?"

"Okay." Jon rocked from side to side. "Can I meet him?"

James imagined introducing his illegitimate son to Lord Harold Huxley, the Earl of Dorley. Harold was no fool. He would discern Jon's age and figure out that he was Mia's child. He would also accuse James of knowing where she was all these years. It would be a nightmare, one that James wasn't ready to confront.

"We'll talk about it when we get home."

The lift doors opened into Uncle Billy's office, and they saw him sitting behind a massive oak desk. Uncle Billy raised his eyes and smiled broadly before getting up to greet them.

"James, my God, but it's good to see you, lad."

They embraced, and then Uncle Billy turned his attention to Jon.

"And who's this good-looking chap?"

"This is Jon," James said.

Uncle Billy studied Jon's face and then winked at James.

"Welcome, Jon. I look forward to hearing your story."

Jon looked at James. "Do I have a story, Dad?"

"Everyone has a story, Jon," Uncle Billy said with a smile.

Uncle Billy led them into his office. James and Jon stared at the elaborate, gold inlaid ceiling, the red velvet drapes with gold tasseled tie-backs, and the carpet that reminded James of the Oriental Rug in his father's dining room.

The penthouse office had a stunning view of the city. James noted Uncle Billy's graying hair, his blue eyes, and that he walked with a slight limp. He led them to a sitting area and indicated that they should sit. He watched Jon and smiled at the boy's fascination with a gold dragon embroidered on a pillow on the sofa.

"He reminds me of you, James."

"He's smarter than I was," James said.

"And how old are you then, my fine lad?" Uncle Billy asked Jon.

"I'm nine."

"Nine, eh, well, then you must be in year four, or is it five?"

"He has to take his exams," James said. "Jon, why don't you go and look at those swords?"

James pointed to a large wood and glass case against a wall several feet away. Jon did as he was told and left James alone with Uncle Billy.

"Where did he come from?" Uncle Billy asked.

"His mother...she had some problems. She contacted me and asked if I would take him."

"And you're sure he's yours."

"Have you looked at him?" James smiled.

Uncle Billy raised his eyebrows and nodded his head.

"And what does his lordship think of all this?" Uncle Billy asked.

"He doesn't know, and I'd like to keep it that way."

"Do you really think you can?"

"I do."

Uncle Billy nodded. "Then, I shall refrain from mentioning it to him. So, what brought you to Hong Kong?"

"I wanted to see you."

"Well, I'm glad you did. We can catch up on old times."

Jon returned to James' side, and Uncle Billy smiled.

"And what would you like to see while you're here?" he asked Jon.

"I don't really know what I'd like to see yet," Jon said.

"Well, I'm sure we can find some interesting things for you to do." Uncle Billy leaned forward. "Jon, there's an aquarium in the next room just through that door. Why don't you go and take a look?"

Jon looked up at James, who nodded. After the boy was out of earshot, Uncle Billy sat back and tapped his finger on the arm of the sofa.

"I'm sure you noticed my leg."

"You're limping," James said.

"They discovered a tumor on my knee. The doctors removed it, and I underwent treatment, but they also said it might return." Uncle Billy tilted his head. "You, James, are my sole heir. I've decided that should I become incapacitated, you would be named as my successor." James' expression was not what Uncle Billy had hoped to see.

"Surely, you're not serious."

"James, you are all the family I have left. The bank must stay in the family.

307

"And when were you planning on telling me?" James got up and went to the window. "I have absolutely no interest in running the bank. I wouldn't even know how."

"I have people in place who do know, and they will continue in their present positions once I'm gone."

James shoved his hands in his pockets and shook his head.

"This is insane."

"James," Uncle Billy said. "No one expects you to take the reins until you feel comfortable."

James swung on his heel to face Uncle Billy.

"But I don't want to take the bloody reins." James lifted his hands and shook his head again. "I don't want any of this."

Uncle Billy got out of his chair and stood face to face with James.

"This business was my grandfather's dream. He bled for it, and my father built it so that we, Celeste and I, would have something real we could hold onto, but she preferred her bohemian lifestyle over her duty to this family."

"Don't do this," James said.

"She damn near broke our father's heart, but she redeemed herself when she married your father."

"You call that redemption!" James cried. He fisted his hands. "She buried herself so she could please him. Is that what you want me to do?"

"No, James, I don't want you to bury yourself to please me. I just want...I have no one else."

James saw the pained look on Uncle Billy's face and closed his eyes. Guilt would win the day. He went to his chair and eyed Uncle Billy.

"Jon is the most important thing in my life now. He's the only one I care about." He sighed. "My life has been upside down for months, and I'm only just seeing a light at the end of the tunnel."

"James, perhaps if you tried it, you might find that it's not as bad as you think."

James laid his head back, and his shoulders slumped.

"What do I have to do?"

"Well, I envisioned you running the company, but since you are so opposed to taking the reins, I might have to make some changes to my will. Perhaps you would agree to sitting on the board?"

James nodded. "I can do that." He sat up. "I'm sorry, Uncle Billy. I'm just not cut out for it."

"I know. It's my fault for assuming you would be more like me."

"Instead of my mother," James said.

"James, when I found out about the cancer, I panicked. I hadn't seen you in years. I had to make a decision, but you're right. Celeste would have withered away had she been in my place, and my father would have never understood." Uncle Billy looked at the door Jon had gone through. "Is he more suited do you think?"

James smiled.

"He just might be, but it has to be his choice."

"Then that's what I'll put in the will. You will sit on the board until he's old enough, perhaps thirty or so, and then he will take over as CEO."

"If he wants to," James said.

"If he wants to."

Uncle Billy returned to his chair behind the desk.

"It's just as well, I guess. There's a chap I've been mentoring for a long time who would love the opportunity. He can run things until Jon is ready. You'll sit on the board and keep an eye on things. I'll make sure you get notified of the meeting schedule. Well, then, I have some things to attend to, so I thought you two might want to go to my flat to rest up before dinner."

James sighed. It was as if Uncle Billy hadn't heard a word he said.

"Great," he said. "I'd like to change my clothes."

Uncle Billy pushed a button on his desk.

"Please send Li Wei to my office." He looked at James. "Li Wei is my driver. He speaks English. He can take you wherever you want to go."

"That sounds wonderful," James said. As if on cue, Jon walked in and came to James' side. "We're going to Uncle Billy's flat."

"Bi is my housekeeper," Uncle Billy said. "She's prepared two bedrooms for you. I'm afraid you must share the loo."

"I'm sure we can manage," James said.

The lift door opened, and a small, Asian man in a uniform saw them and bowed.

"Li Wei," Uncle Billy said. "This is my nephew James and his son, Jon. They want to go to the flat."

"Yes, sir," Li Wei said.

"And I'll need you here by seven."

James and Jon went to the lift and joined Li Wei, who was poised to press the button to take them down to the garage under the bank.

Chapter Fifty

When the lift doors opened, Li Wei took them to Uncle Billy's limousine and opened the passenger door in the back. Jon got in first, and he was fascinated by the bar facing them.

"Can I have a drink?" Jon asked.

"Are there any fizzy drinks?" James asked Li Wei.

"Try the refrigerator," Li Wei said.

Jon got on his knees and opened the tiny fridge under the shelf holding the liquor bottles.

"No fizzy drinks," Jon said.

"Then wait 'till we get to the flat," James said.

Jon sat and kicked up his legs. He watched the colorful crowds rushing along the sidewalks.

"Everything is so bright here," he said.

"I've noticed," James said. "It's nothing like Morseton."

The apartment was on the beach near Repulse Bay. It was an opulent, Asian dwelling with huge windows overlooking the water. The frenetic activity of the city seemed far away as they gazed out the living room window, and Jon's huge smile made James grin.

"You like it here, don't you?" James said.

"I like the water. It's closer than at home. I want to live here."

"Aye, well, perhaps you'll live here when you take over the bank."

Jon furrowed his brow. "What do you mean?"

"Nothing. Let's go find our rooms."

The apartment had a kitchen, dining area, study, three bedrooms, and the loo that James and Jon would share. The furnishings were Asian styled chairs in brightly coloured patterns, teakwood tables, and an abundance of wicker. The dining area was raised and separated from the living room by one step. There were sliding glass doors in James' room that led to a balcony, which offered a view of the city.

"You have a balcony," Jon said as he walked into James' room.

"Aye. But you have a view of the ocean."

"I'm hungry, Dad."

James ruffled Jon's hair, and then put his arm around Jon's shoulders.

"Let's see if we can find something to eat in the kitchen."

Uncle Billy's housekeeper was cutting vegetables in the kitchen when James and Jon walked in. She held up her head and eyed them carefully.

"Hi," James said. "I'm James, Mr. Horton's nephew."

"I know you," she said.

"This is Jon."

She pursed her lips.

"You want something to eat?" she asked.

"Yes, please."

"Go, sit. I will bring you food."

James and Jon went to the formal dining table. The wicker chair creaked as Jon sat, and he made a cringy face. James smiled, and then pursed his lips. There were no settings on the table, so when the housekeeper brought the food, she brought the settings as well.

"Are you Bi?" James asked.

"Yes," she said.

"Nice to meet you, Bi."

She didn't acknowledge him. She put the food and settings on the table and then left them without another word.

"I guess she doesn't like to be disturbed," James said.

Jon smiled and then looked at the food.

"Lots of vegetables," he said. "This looks like Greyson's stew." James watched his son's face for signs of grief, but Jon remained content. "Dad, remember when we talked about looking for a detective?"

"We did talk about that, didn't we? So, when we get home, the first thing we'll do is find a detective."

Jon smiled. James heard him kicking his feet under the table and put his finger to his mouth. Jon stopped.

"I read about a place called The Peak in a pamphlet," Jon said. "Maybe we can go there."

"Sure. We can do that tomorrow."

"Am I going to run the bank?"

James eyed him and smiled.

"If that's what you want to do."

"I think I'd like to run the bank."

"When you grow up, but for now, eat."

When they finished their food, James took their plates to the kitchen, and Bi glared at him.

"Sorry," he said. "Force of habit."

"You call me to get them," Bi said.

"Next time. Believe me. We will call you the next time."

In the short time he'd been with James, Jon's reading had improved, and he had already gone through the novels James had taken years to read. Jon was thrilled to see that the bookcase in his room at Uncle Billy's was full of books he hadn't read.

"Can I read for a while?" Jon asked.

"Sure. I'm probably going to kip in my room."

As Jon settled into his room, James went to his room and laid on the bed. He'd been taken aback when Jon asked about the detective. He'd planned to hire a detective, but it had slipped his mind, and then he and Jon moved into their new house before starting their holiday. It was obvious that Jon was eager to find his mum, and James wanted to please Jon. They would go through the directory as soon as they got home.

James fell asleep and woke an hour later when Jon tapped on his shoulder.

"Dad," Jon said.

James peered up at his boy and smiled.

"Aye."

"I'm hungry," Jon said. "Do you think Bi will mind if I ask for something to eat?"

"I do think Bi would mind. She didn't like us barging in when we arrived."

Jon looked toward the interior of the apartment.

"Can we go out and get something to eat?"

James looked at the alarm clock on the end table. It was a few minutes after two in the afternoon. He assumed that his uncle would eat at a fashionably late hour and he knew Jon couldn't wait that long.

"I have to find out how to call Li Wei and see if he can take us for a ride."

James and Jon looked around the living room for a button or a list that would help them summon Li Wei, and found a panel near the front door. Beside each button was a name. Li Wei was near the middle. James pushed the button and Li Wei answered.

"We'd like to take a ride around the city," James said.

"I'll meet you in front of the building in five minutes," Li Wei said.

As they left the apartment, Jon smiled broadly.

"I'll race you downstairs."

He took off before James could answer but he went after his son as fast as he could. Jon went through the fire door with James close behind, and for a time, James worried that his son would lose his footing and stumble down the stairs, but Jon was nimble. He made it down the ten flights of stairs unharmed, but James was out of breath when he reached the bottom.

"Don't do that without telling me, you hear?" James said.

"Sorry," Jon said, but he didn't look the least bit sorry.

Lie Wei pulled up to the curb in the same black limo. He got out and opened the door for them.

"Where to?" James asked.

"Food," Jon said.

"Li Wei, the lad would like some food, preferably the fast kind."

Li Wei smiled and turned onto the busy street in front of the building. Unfortunately, Li Wei's idea of fast food didn't match Jon's idea of fish and chips served in a paper wrapper. It was more like the fare he'd eaten in a Chinese take-away they frequented in Morseton. But Jon soldiered on and ordered a dish with rice, vegetables, and chicken, while James ate a spicy soup. They then asked Li Wei to take them sightseeing.

Li Wei drove them around the city and pointed out places Jon had read about and some that hadn't been highlighted in

Jon's pamphlets. As the sun began to dip in the sky, Li Wei dropped them off at the door and went to fetch Uncle Billy.

"Does Uncle Billy have a telly?" Jon asked as he pushed the lift button.

"I'm sure he has one somewhere."

"Should I ask Bi?"

"You take cover while I do it."

The flat smelled of spices, peppers, and onions when they entered, and Jon urged James to go and talk to Bi. She was wiping down the counters when she saw him at the door.

"I'm sorry to bother you," James said. "Does my uncle own a television?"

"Each bedroom has one," Bi said. "In the cabinet above the chest of drawers."

"Of course, well, thank you, Bi."

James returned to Jon and smiled broadly.

"The telly is in a cabinet above the chest of drawers in your room. There must be a clicker for it somewhere. Look in the bedside tables."

Jon ran off to his room while James went to his and took a shower. He changed into a button-down shirt and khaki slacks. As he looked at himself in the mirror, he noticed a gray hair on his head and plucked it out. The discovery led to thoughts of his mortality. Artie had told him he should choose a guardian for Jon in case something happened to James.

As he brushed back his hair with his hand, he thought about whom he would choose to take care of Jon, and realized that the only person he knew young enough to take on the task was Maryanne. This revelation made James shudder, and he understood that finding Mia was now number one on his list of priorities.

Chapter Fifty-One

Uncle Billy arrived home at twenty after seven. Bi had set the table and was at attention when he walked in. He washed up, changed his clothes, and found James in the living room when he came out of his bedroom.

"Where's Jon?" Uncle Billy asked.

"He's sleeping. He had a long day."

"Poor chap. He must be exhausted. Well, come, let's eat before Bi gives us what for."

Once they were seated, Bi brought out the food and placed it near Uncle Billy. She also brought a bottle of wine, set it at the center of the table, and Uncle Billy filled their glasses.

"Thank you, Bi," Billy said, and then he looked at James. "I've offered to hire kitchen help, but Bi seems to prefer doing everything herself. I do have a girl who comes in once a week to give Bi a day off, but she always returns with a frown on her face."

"I get the idea that she doesn't like anyone mucking about her kitchen," James said.

"And you'd be right." Billy took some food and passed the dishes to James. "I'm glad in a way that Jon isn't here right now. I thought we could resume our conversation from this morning."

"Must we?"

"Look, James, I've known you since you were born. You've always been a bit of a dreamer, but you must start thinking of Jon's future."

316

"I do think of his future. I'm going to let him do what *he* wants to do."

"Which is all well and good, but to be fair, a boy needs some guidance." Uncle Billy noted the scowl on his nephew's face. "You are so like your mother."

"Am I?"

James' earnest expression touched Uncle Billy's heart.

"You are indeed."

"What do you remember about her?"

"She had big dreams when she was a girl. When she got old enough to go off on her own, Celeste was always running off to this protest or that. She also liked to hang with artists. There is a painting of her in my study from that time."

"What was she protesting?" James asked.

"Probably the war."

"I talked to Mr. Danvers about her. He said he was surprised when she married my father, and you said she redeemed herself by marrying him. Did she marry him just to please her father?"

Billy took a deep breath, and his shoulders slumped.

"I suppose you are old enough now to know the truth. Celeste made some unfortunate choices and often ended up in the tabloids. My father was beside himself. She was such a lovely girl, and he felt she was throwing away her future. Then she met Harold Huxley, a man on the verge of losing his family estate. A titled man in desperate need of money. For some reason that I still can't fathom, Celeste agreed to marry him. I suppose he brought her dignity, and she brought him a quarter of a million pounds."

"Shit," James whispered. "So, it was her idea."

"Well, my father did encourage the relationship, but yes, it was her idea. Harold had enough money to refurbish the manor house and a seat on the board of Moreland Bank, which Harold took very seriously. I think it was the first job he ever had."

James pushed his plate away.

"I never knew any of this."

"Perhaps Harold was protecting you."

"Bollocks. If anything, he was protecting himself. I don't think he'd want me to know that he married for money."

"You really do dislike him, don't you?"

"Yes, I do." James folded his arms on the table. "I remember my mum being sick."

"Celeste had cancer, too," Uncle Billy said

"She was soft," James said. "I remember getting into her bed, and she'd put her arm around me."

"She was worried about your future," Uncle Billy said. "She loved you very much, James."

"Why was she worried about my future?"

"Because you were a dreamer."

"Mr. Danvers said she worried that my father would ask me for money."

"You know, the odd thing is that since Harold's been working for me, he's done rather well. Of course, she didn't live to see that happen."

James sat back and exhaled loudly.

"I was always a disappointment to him. He never let me forget it."

Uncle Billy tapped his fingers on the table.

"Well, Harold is about as warm as an English pond in winter. Perhaps he would warm up if you introduced him to his grandson."

"I'm not ready for that," James said.

"So, what's the real story there? How did he come to you?"

"Jon's mother…is someone we all thought had disappeared."

Uncle Billy's forehead creased, and then he raised his eyebrows.

"Not that American girl?" James nodded. "You found her?"

"No. I just found Jon."

"How?" Uncle Billy waited for his reply. "James."

"You're not going to believe me."

"Why wouldn't I believe you?"

"Because I wouldn't believe it if someone told me," James said.

Uncle Billy folded his arms and leaned on the table.

"Now, I'm intrigued."

James glanced over his shoulder and then looked at Uncle Billy.

"Do you remember the festival in Dorley?"

"Lots of medieval bullshit."

"Exactly. When Mia was staying with us, we went to the festival. There was a woman who came there every year. She sold charms and trinkets, and my old governess had warned me away from her, saying she was a witch. Her name was Rotrude. Despite my warnings, Mia was drawn to the wagon. She bought a necklace, this gold disk on a thin leather strap, and Rotrude told her to use it if she was ever in dire need."

"Use it, how?" Uncle Billy said.

"She said the disk would lead Mia to Rotrude's cottage in the woods."

"Of course it would."

James took a deep breath. "Anyway, Mia and I, well, we'd been making love ever since she arrived. The night before she disappeared, we fell asleep on the divan in the attic. When I woke up, she was gone, and I couldn't find the gold disk. I didn't know it at the time, but she ran away because she was pregnant."

"And she didn't leave a note or anything?"

"No, nothing, but I thought about that disk."

"So, where did she go?" Uncle Billy asked.

James swallowed hard.

"She went to Rotrude, and she took Mia to Havenwood."

"Havenwood. Is that a town in England?"

"It's not in England," James said.

"This sounds as if it might take some time. Why don't we go sit on the balcony."

James followed Uncle Billy to the sliding doors, and they went out onto the balcony. There were sun loungers with plush mattresses and small tables to hold large drinks. A built-in bar was fully stocked, and the only sound came from the roar of the sea. James sat as Uncle Billy poured them snifters of brandy. He handed one to James before lying on his sun lounger and lighting a cigar.

"Continue," Uncle Billy said.

"I didn't realize how ridiculous it sounded until I said it."

Uncle Billy cocked his head toward James.

"I want to hear about Havenwood."

James lay back, looked up at the stars, and then took a swig of his brandy.

"Rotrude had this thing, this coin that she used to take people to another world."

"What I wouldn't do for something like that."

319

"It's called the Silver Stag. It had the head of a deer with an eight-point rack on it, and it was cut in half. To travel to Haven-wood, you just pressed the halves together at the seam, and off you went."

Uncle Billy puffed his cigar.

"You were right to keep this to yourself, James."

"I've been there. I used the coin to go there, and that's when I found Jon."

"Dear God," Uncle Billy said. "Did you take him from his mother?"

"No. She wasn't there. She had been kidnapped by a man named Boris Black."

"The gangster?"

"Aye. It's a long story."

"Which you would rather not tell me," Uncle Billy said.

"I'm not sure I understand it myself," James said.

"So, you found Jon and brought him home."

"He was living with this old man, and they were starving. It was a miracle I found him when I did."

"I've always believed in divine intervention," Uncle Billy said.

"I don't know what I believe in anymore," James said. "Now that I have him, I worry about things that never mattered to me before, like what will happen to him if something happens to me."

Uncle Billy finished his cigar and stamped it out.

"You have a father, James."

"Lord Harold won't acknowledge an illegitimate heir."

"Possibly, but you won't know unless you talk to him."

"I don't have to talk to him to know," James said.

The pause that followed lingered while Uncle Billy finished his cigar.

"So, what happened to the girl?" Uncle Billy asked.

"I have no idea," James said. "Jon wants us to try and find her. I thought I'd try and contact her father if he's still working for the bank."

"What's his name?"

"Vincent Wentworth."

"The name is familiar," Uncle Billy said. "I can find out if he's still with us for you."

"I'd appreciate that," James said.

James lay his head back and stared at the stars overhead.

"Jon wants us to find her."

"You should hire a private detective," Uncle Billy said.

"That's what I plan to do when we get home."

"And when you find her?"

"Then, I'll probably want to see her before I tell Jon."

"Are you angry with her?" Uncle Billy said.

"Mostly, I feel bad that she didn't trust me."

"Well, try not to judge until you hear her side of the story." Uncle Billy sat up. He got to his feet and patted James' shoulder. "I'm going to bed."

James got up and put his hands on the railing. He had kept himself from thinking about Mia while he sorted his life with Jon, but if they found her…there would be things he and Mia would have to work out.

What if Mia had returned to America? Would she want Jon with her? Fear gripped James as he thought of losing Jon, and he fought back the urge to get him out of bed and take him somewhere far away where no one would find them.

And then he thought about his feelings for Mia. They had been a significant factor in his divorce, and despite what she had done, James still loved Mia. If she felt the same way, they might be able to make a life together, and that would be the best thing for Jon.

Time would tell. He had promised Jon they would hire a detective and that's what they would do. For now, though, he wouldn't make any more promises regarding their future. The last thing he wanted to do was to break Jon's heart.

Chapter Fifty-Two

Jon was up and watching the TV when James came out of his room the next morning. He stopped by Jon's bedroom before going to the breakfast table.

"Hey," James said.

"Hi, Dad."

"Have you eaten?"

"Bi made me breakfast. I ate with Uncle Billy."

"Oh, good, then when I'm done eating, we can decide what we want to do."

"Okay."

James found two scrapbooks and a note from Uncle Billy on the table next to his plate when he sat down.

"Thought you might want these. My mother kept them. I got them when she passed."

James opened one of the scrapbooks and saw a large photo of Celeste. He flipped through the pages and saw other photos and newspaper clippings about his mother. The other album contained photos of her wedding to Harold and James' childhood.

James eagerly turned to the newspaper clippings, which his grandmother had kept in plastic sheeting. Many highlighted Celeste's escapades, which took place at various locations around Europe and the United Kingdom.

In an article dated June 15, 1963, James found a photo of her on the arm of a tuxedoed boy who looked as if his ascot was strangling him. The caption read, "Ernest Campbell escorts Celeste Horton to the Debutante Ball." There were several of Celeste attending Wimbledon, the races at Ascot, Celeste modeling a Mary Quant mini skirt and white boots on Carnaby Street, attending a Halloween ball in New York City dressed as a beheaded Anne Boleyn and sunbathing nude on Aristotle Onassis' yacht. The discrete photo showed nothing but her back and that of an unnamed man.

In all the photos, Celeste smiled broadly. She looked happy, so what on Earth had made her settle for Harold Huxley?

The second book began with a photo of Celeste *"on the arm of 'Lord Harold Huxley' as they attended a concert at the Royal Albert Hall. The young socialite has been seen in the company of Lord Huxley for several weeks now, and it is rumored that a wedding is in the offing."*

James checked the date – January 17, 1969. He sat back and raised his eyebrows. James had been born on August 17, 1969. The wedding announcement appeared on March 5, 1969.

"Lord Harold Huxley and Celeste Horton were wed in a private ceremony in the small church at Winchester Cathedral. The bride wore an ivory gown designed by Oscar de la Renta."

The article went on to describe the ceremony and the reception. James recognized his mother's parents as he had spent one week a year with them during school holidays, and he also recognized a young Uncle Billy celebrating the marriage. Celeste wasn't smiling; her expression reminded him of one who had chosen to accept their fate with joyless dignity and grace.

Celeste's obituary had its own plastic sleeve and was sandwiched between two long-stemmed yellow roses, presumably from an arrangement sent to honor the deceased.

"On Friday, June 15, Lady Celeste Horton Huxley passed away following a long illness. She was born Celeste Yvette Horton, daughter of Charles and Esme Horton, and is survived by her husband, Lord Harold Huxley, a son James, her parents, and a brother, William Horton.

"Lady Huxley grew up in Yorkshire. She earned a reputation for being a "free spirit" and embraced the counterculture movement of the 1960's. As heir to a banking fortune, Celeste often balked at the restraints placed on her by society, and her antics were fodder for the tabloids.

"In 1969, she married Lord Harold Huxley, whose estate in Dorley was a crumbling reminder of a bygone era. Following the marriage, the manor house was refurbished and restored to its former glory.

"In 1969, Lady Huxley gave birth to their son James. Shortly after his birth, Lady Huxley stopped attending public functions. In 1971, Lady Huxley went public with her diagnosis of uterine cancer.

"'I wanted to share my diagnosis with other women so they would learn from my experience. Too many women delay seeing a doctor until it's too late.'"

A detailed description of the funeral arrangements followed. James sat back and reread the paragraph about his mother's "free spirit." His father had forbidden any discussion of her, and James had always wondered why.

"...her antics were fodder for the tabloids."

At the back of this scrapbook, Grandmother Horton had included articles about Lord Harold Huxley's involvement in the Bank of Moreland with a brief history of the bank itself. According to the Times, the bank had been a small, local concern for years, and then Charles Horton decided to open a branch in Hong Kong following the Second World War. So, this is why Uncle Billy went to live there. There was a photo of Uncle Billy and Harold Huxley taken in Hong Kong in 1978. Harold Huxley was identified as the COO of Horton Holdings, Inc., which owned and operated the Bank of Moreland.

James read the article again as the old, adolescent anger rose inside him. James had always been led to believe that the Huxleys' fortune had been depleted supporting the manor house and the surrounding lands. One of Harold's favorite refrains was that of their need to maintain a strict budget, especially when James asked for an increase in his allowance, which was a paltry ten quid per month. The lads he befriended in college would laugh when they found out how much he was given, and would always pay for drinks when they went to the local pub. James hated not being able to return the favor, but as he believed his father was on the brink of ruin, he'd kept this to himself.

When he married his college sweetheart, Cynthia Babcock, her father, Lloyd, had asked him when he'd be joining the family firm, and James had just smiled and shrugged for he had no idea what "firm" Lloyd was talking about. One day before they married, James found his father in the study and asked him what he did when he was in London.

"And why the sudden interest?" Harold asked.

"Cyn's father asked me if I was joining the family firm."

Harold's eyes drifted to the fireplace.

"And what did you tell him?"

"I didn't tell him anything," James said. "So, what was he talking about?"

"I've always known that you had no interest in business," Harold said. "You always had your head in a book. I just assumed you would pursue a career in education."

"What did he mean, Father?"

"I sit on the board of your uncle's bank. It's an honorary position for which I receive a monthly stipend. Lloyd Babcock probably assumes that my association with the Bank of Moreland is more substantial."

James took Harold at his word, and whenever the subject of James' future arose, he'd say he was considering a career in education. It was an honorable profession that paid little, but despite this, Lloyd was thrilled to be aligned with Lord Harold Huxley. His daughter would be Lady Huxley, and he bought them a small townhouse in London so they could be near school and Cynthia could be near her mother.

Lloyd helped with their living expenses as well. The marriage foundered after three months when Cynthia grew tired of competing with Mia's ghost, and James dropped out of college, went home, and sequestered himself in the attic where he wrestled with the black dog.

James recalled asking Harold for the money to buy the pub. The idea came after James saw an advertisement for a business opportunity in Morseton. He'd cut it out of the paper and kept it in the attic for two weeks before approaching Harold.

"That's the most ridiculous thing you've ever said to me," Harold said.

"I'd be able to support myself," James said. James showed him the advert. "It comes with a flat."

"And how do you propose to pay for such a thing?"

"Uncle Billy is going to give me half. I was hoping you would give me the rest."

Harold's cheeks reddened, and he looked as if he might explode, but then his expression softened.

"I'm willing to give you the money on one condition; you will forfeit any claim you have on this estate."

As far as James knew, the "estate" consisted of an old, drafty manor house and the land that surrounded it. He had no idea what it was worth, but his needs were few, and the idea of living miles away from Harold made him glow with excitement.

"I'll sign anything you want," James said.

Now, as James looked at the photo of Uncle Billy and his father grinning in front of a new branch of the Bank of More- land in London, he gritted his teeth. His father had hidden his wealth from his only son because he felt James wasn't fit to run the family firm. When had Harold made that decision? When James was five, six, or when he saw James wrestle with the black dog?

His mother, however, had more faith in him. She'd left him a large amount of money with no instructions. She had trusted James to do the right thing. As he closed the scrapbook, James thought of Celeste in her mini skirt and boots. That girl had loved him, and he would honor her memory by being the best father he could be, and Harold Huxley be damned.

Foolish romanticism often led James to do things he knew in his heart were wrong, and he thought of this as he thought of Jon. The boy had come into his life and changed everything. The responsibility had been thrust upon him, but despite this, James hadn't faltered. He had embraced his fatherhood, and the one thing James was sure of in his life was that he loved his son with all his heart.

Chapter Fifty-Three

It was time to leave Hong Kong and return to England. Uncle Billy took them to a restaurant for a lavish dinner, and then he took James aside.

"I just want to say thank you," Uncle Billy said. "It's been wonderful seeing you and Jon."

"It's been great seeing you, too."

"I know you aren't keen on working for the bank, but you must think of Jon's future." Uncle Billy hesitated for a moment. "That story you told me of how you found Jon, perhaps it's best if you keep it to yourself."

"You think it's just a story," James said.

"I don't know how you found him, and frankly, I don't care because he's a wonderful boy, but not everyone is as open-minded as I am."

"Right, well, I usually say she was sick and asked me to take care of him."

"And that makes sense. Tell them that."

James felt his heart fall a bit when he heard this, but Uncle Billy was right. The world would laugh at the idea of Havenwood, and Jon might be ridiculed. They would have to make peace with the lie so they could have some semblance of a normal life.

Before they parted, Uncle Billy grabbed James' arm. "Vincent Wentworth is dead. He died of a stroke a few years ago."

This news lifted James' spirit for it meant that Mia's father would not try to take Jon away from him.

Shortly after they returned home from Hong Kong, Jon awoke to the sound of a bird cawing near his window. He sat on the edge of the bed and watched a large crow sitting on a tree branch staring back at him for several seconds before taking flight. The departure left him feeling sad, for it reminded him of Havenwood. His father was a good man, but he didn't understand how deeply Jon missed Greyson.

Jon was fortunate in that he'd been given gifts that enabled him to survive when others might perish. He'd lost his mother at an early age, but he never wavered in his belief that Mia had loved him. Jon had lost his best friend, an aging wizard who taught him well, and he applied those lessons of love, honor, and fidelity every day. He had been taken to a place so foreign to everything Jon knew and had thrived, so why was he feeling so glum?

Jon went downstairs and to the kitchen. He took bangers and eggs from the fridge and grabbed a pan out of the oven. It was his routine to prepare breakfast, but no one had told him it was his responsibility. He'd merely continued on as if Greyson was about to enter the kitchen and regale him with stories of the past. But James was not Greyson, and Jon was not the boy he'd been when he left Havenwood. He looked at the pan, placed it on the stove, and then went upstairs, got dressed, and left the house.

There was a murder of crows assembled near a field dining on an unfortunate rabbit who must have wandered into the path of a car traveling at high speed. Its entrails were scattered across the road, which allowed the crows ample room where each received a hearty portion. Jon watched them for a while from his yard, and then walked across the street, into the field, and on to the woods. He felt directionless as if the compass that guided him had lost its arrow, leaving him to wander with no goal in sight.

The grass was wet, and his footsteps quiet as he approached the woods. He stopped and stared at the tangled branches intermingled with tall grass that barred him from entering the woods. Jon had heard tales of children losing their way once they walked inside, but he dismissed them. One could always find their way by looking at the stars. But what if one couldn't see the stars hidden by a veil of trees?

"A veil of trees," Jon said.

He often had such thoughts, and it worried him a bit. He wasn't like other children; he felt old in many ways. Greyson said Jon was a deep thinker, and he thought Jon should become a writer.

"You're as good as anyone I've ever read," he said. "Start writing things down."

But Jon hadn't followed his advice, and many such thoughts were left to disappear over time. Oh, how he missed his dear friend.

Jon's thoughts now turned to Mia. His mother was a great source of pain for him, for he remembered her with his senses – a soft kiss or a touch against his skin. The only aberration to these fond remembrances was the scene that took place shortly before she left Havenwood where Jon was forced to watch an evil man take her away.

Jon had woken up that night and seen the man, who he now knew was Boris Black, force his mother down the stairs. He saw the girl, too, but didn't remember her. Jon followed them out the door and down the road and then saw Boris push the girl to the ground. Jon heard another gunshot before he saw his mother disappear in a whirlwind.

He ran to the girl's side. Blood ran from the top of her down the front of her shirt. Jon watched the light go out in her eyes. He got up, backed away, and then ran to Greyson's farm, but Greyson was on his way to find Mia. Jon stayed with June until Greyson returned alone a few hours later.

It was quiet at the edge of the woods, and Jon sighed. James Huxley had saved Jon from what Greyson said was the end of the world, and Jon was grateful, but he also felt disloyal to the man who had raised him. Was he still alive?

Jon thought of the Silver Stag. Perhaps he could take one trip back to see Greyson. He would only be gone for a few minutes, and maybe he could persuade the old man to return with him so Jon could make them breakfast again.

No. Jon couldn't go back to Havenwood. He'd give Greyson his word, and a man's word was his bond. Greyson had given him a quest, and Jon had to honor that quest. He had to stay with James until he became the man he was meant to be.

Jon shoved his hands into his pockets. He felt a southerly breeze ruffle his hair and heard a car speeding on the road behind him. Gray skies warned of a storm that was due, casting a pall over the field and over Jon's heart. He wallowed in it for several minutes and then heard someone approaching him from behind.

"Are you all right?" James asked.

Jon turned and faced his father. James' wavy hair was sticking out all over. He wore the jeans he'd worn the day before with the same T-shirt. Jon saw the scene in his mind, of his father, coming downstairs and seeing that Jon was gone, panicking as he picked the clothes off the floor, put them on, and then ran out the front door. Had he seen the crows, or had they finished their meal?

"I'm fine, Dad."

"What are you doing out here?"

"I just felt like walking," Jon said.

"You should have left me a note," James said. "You scared the bejesus out of me."

"I'm sorry."

"Well, no harm done. Would you like me to walk with you?"

"I'm hungry," Jon said.

"Then we'll make breakfast."

James put his hand on Jon's shoulder, and they walked to the road.

"Dad," Jon said. "Do you think Greyson is still alive?"

"No, Jon."

"But I keep thinking about him."

James faced Jon and hugged him tightly.

"This, here, is what he wanted for you. He is happy knowing that you are with me and that you're safe. We have to honor what he wanted, Jon."

One tear rolled down Jon's face as he buried his face against James' stomach.

"Okay," he said. "Dad, I really want to find my mum."

James took a deep breath.

"Aye, right, and I said we would do that when we came home."

Jon peered up into James' eyes.

"We have to find a detective. I have another week before I have to go to school, and then it will be months before I'm off again. We have to find her now."

James exhaled loudly.

"Well, then let's go home and take a look at the directory."

There was something different about Jon that eluded James, some steely resolve that made James fear what would happen if they didn't find Mia. Would it break Jon? Would the sunny boy he'd grown accustomed to disappear forever?

"What if we can't find her?" James asked as they crossed the street.

Jon cast his eyes on the pavement.

"We have to."

"But…" James hesitated. "Right. We have to."

They went in the front door, and Jon went to the kitchen.

"Why don't you let me cook today?" James said.

"You hate cooking."

"Well, yeah, but I'll do it for you."

"It's all right, Dad. I'll do it."

Jon's dejected tone sent James into the role of fixer. He went to the kitchen, sat at the table, and pulled the directory toward him. Jon had placed a piece of paper as a bookmarker in the section for private investigators. As Jon cooked the bangers and eggs, James looked through the ads. His eyes stopped at one name that he recognized immediately – Pete Barret.

James remembered Pete Barret from a run-in they had after Arthur Wentworth offered the reward that had sent Boris Black to Havenwood. Pete was convinced that James had killed Mia, but had mysteriously backed off the case shortly before Arthur had the stroke that ended the search. Pete would have a file on Mia. It would save them time and money to hire him, but could James work with someone who had been so convinced of his guilt?

"First, we have to write down all we know about your mum."

"But we don't know anything," Jon said.

James' cheeks burned.

"Well, I might know something."

Jon turned to face James.

"What do you know?"

"I remember when she left my house before she went to Havenwood."

Jon turned the cooker off and put the food on their plates. He brought the plates to the table and sat. He saw the look on James' face as James thought of Mia.

"Are you angry?" Jon asked.

"No. Why do you ask?"

"Because you look angry."

James studied Jon's face.

"Sometimes, I get mad when I think about your mum."

"Why?" Jon asked.

"Because she ran away from me and never told me about you."

"Oh." Jon picked up his fork and moved his food around his plate. "Will you tell her that when we find her?" Jon stabbed a banger and took a bite.

"You really should cut that, mate."

"I like eating it this way," Jon said.

James smiled. "My father would have sent me to my room if I'd eaten a banger that way."

"Why?" Jon asked.

"Because it wasn't the way things were done. There are rules for everything, and he expected me to follow them."

"That must have been hard."

"Not so much. He wasn't around all the time."

Jon put his fork down.

"You didn't answer my question."

James was shoveling his eggs into his mouth with his fork. He looked at Jon as he chewed and swallowed.

"Which one?"

"Will you tell Mum that you're angry that she left without telling you about me?" Jon said.

James put down his fork.

"I'm not sure what I'll say to her."

Jon thought for a minute.

"You could tell her it's good to see her again," Jon said.

James smiled. "Aye. It will be good to see her again."

"And you could tell her that I'm going to school."

"I should write this down," James said.

"And then you could tell her you're mad because she left you."

James watched Jon eat the last bit of his banger.

"Are you mad that she left you, Jon?"

Jon put his fork next to his plate.

"No. She didn't want to leave me."

There it was – the thing that had nagged at the back of James' mind since the day she left him. Had Mia wanted to leave him? Was her condition just an excuse to get away from him?

They had spent all their time together, and it seemed as though she wanted it that way, too, but what if she had only gone along because she had no choice? She was stuck in Dorley, abandoned by her father, and forced to befriend him because he was there. What if it was all a lie?

James tried to remember her eyes as he always did to reassure himself that Mia had loved him as he loved her, but the memory had been receding to the farthest corner of his consciousness for a long time, and sometimes all James could recall was the way he felt with her in his arms.

James also worried that Mia might not have survived her ordeal with Boris Black. She had been taken to hospital, but that was all he knew. She might have died on the way, or during surgery, or from an infection. If she were alive, why hadn't she contacted James?

"Dad?" Jon said.

"What?"

"You all right?"

"I'm fine. I just was thinking is all."

They washed the dishes together. and then sat at the table with the directory. Jon saw Pete's ad, which claimed he was the "finder of lost things."

"That's the man!" Jon cried. "The finder of lost things."

"Again, your mum isn't a thing, Jon."

"But he's on the radio. And look at what it says on most of them – sur-veil-lance and debt collections. Nothing about finding anything."

"If he's the only one who finds things, he might be busy," James said.

Jon slid off the chair and went to the phone on the kitchen wall. He grabbed the receiver and brought it to James.

"I'll dial the number," Jon said.

He read the number, and then ran to the phone and dialed. James put the receiver to his ear and waited while Jon dialed the number on the old rotary phone. A man answered on the third ring.

"Barret Investigations. Pete Barret speaking."

"Um, yes, hello. I don't know if you remember me, but my name is James Huxley."

Silence followed, and a moment later, Pete sighed.

"Aye, I remember you."

"I...that is my son, and I would like to talk to you about finding his mother."

Another moment of silence.

"Are you talking about Mia Wentworth?"

James heard the edge in his voice.

"Yes."

"And you really want to hire me to find her?"

"Yes. We do."

"And you say you have a son."

"I do, but I want you to treat this in confidence," James said.

A moment of silence followed, and then Pete continued.

"What's the address?"

James looked at Jon as he gave Pete the address. He hung up the phone, and Jon was rocking back and forth.

"What did he say?" Jon asked.

"He said he'll be round in an hour. Why don't we clean up a bit before he comes?"

James' stomach was in a knot. How would he explain Jon to Pete? It had been foolish to call him. James hadn't thought it through, and now he picked up the receiver to call him back and tell him he'd be using someone else, but Jon came to him before he could dial.

"Who are you calling?"

"I think we should call someone else," James said.

"Don't, Dad, please. He's the finder of lost things."

"There are other detectives, Jon."

"But I have a good feeling about him," Jon said. "Come. We have to clean up, remember?"

Jon dusted the tables in the living room while James emptied the trash bins. He heard Jon mumbling to himself as he worked and sensed the boy's excitement. They were finally doing something to find his mum! As the hour of Pete Barret's arrival drew near, Jon ran upstairs to change his clothes.

"I want to give him a good impression," he said as he climbed the stairs.

James went to a small cabinet where he kept a few bottles of whiskey, took one out, poured himself a shot, and downed it quickly. As he put the bottle away, he saw a car slowing down on the street. He went to the window and watched Pete Barret turn into the driveway.

Chapter Fifty-Four

FALL 1996

PETE BARRET WORE A TURTLENECK UNDER A TAN RAINCOAT, plaid, bell-bottom trousers, and brown ankle-high boots. James guessed he hadn't bought new clothes in twenty years.

"Would you like some tea?" James asked.

"No, I'm fine."

Pete sat in the chair near the fireplace while James and Jon sat on the settee. Pete carried a battered old briefcase from which he took a lined pad and a pencil, but he held it for a moment as he looked James in the eye.

"Ask your son to leave," Pete said.

"He wants to be part of this," James said.

"He can come back in a minute."

James glanced at Jon.

"Go upstairs for a minute."

"Why do I have to leave?" Jon asked.

"I want to talk to your Da alone," Pete said. "Leave us."

Jon got up and went up the stairs. Pete sat back and studied James.

"So, what's this about?"

"We want to find Mia."

"You want to find Mia. That's rich."

"Look, I know you never believed my story..."

"You got that right."

"But I wasn't lying. She disappeared, and I knew nothing about it."

336

"And where did he come from?"

James had dreaded this moment. He could tell him that Mia had gotten sick and asked him to take Jon, but then James would also have to tell him where Mia was when he went to fetch Jon.

"You're wasting my time," Pete said.

"Look, what I'm going to tell you, you won't believe, but it's the truth."

"Get on with it."

"When Mia left me, she went to…the witch in the woods."

"That old fairy tale?" Pete asked.

"Her name was Rotrude. She sold charms from a wagon during the festivals in Dorley."

"I remember her. Go on."

"I didn't know that Mia was pregnant. She ran away to have Jon because she was afraid her parents would make her have an abortion."

"And you expect me to believe she never told you."

"She didn't. I don't know why. So, she went to Rotrude for help, and Rotrude took her to…shit. She took her to Havenwood."

"Never heard of it."

"It's in an alternate world," James said.

"Jesus," Pete said. "Look, Lord Huxley, I don't have time for this bullshit."

"It's not bullshit, and it doesn't matter if you believe me or not. The point is that Mia had Jon, and they lived there for at least five years before Mia was kidnapped by Boris Black."

Pete remembered the accounts of Black's death in Dorley. He was found in the woods. The police reported that a woman had crawled out of the woods around the same time and that there was a blood trail leading away from Black's body.

"Boris Black," Pete said.

"He took her, and my son was left behind. I…found him a few months ago and brought him here."

"How'd you find him?"

James closed his eyes and shook his head.

"I went to Havenwood."

"The alternate world," Pete said.

"Look, I know you don't believe me, but that doesn't matter. What matters is that Mia was brought here, and she might still be alive. Jon wants to see his mum again, and you already know what happened. You have a file on it."

"I have a file, sure, full of nothing but dead ends and false leads."

"That's because she was…"

"In an alternate world, yeah, right." Pete stood. "I don't think I can help you."

James stood. "Yes, you can. I know what hospital she was taken to and I know the name of the woman who helped her, and I know where *she* lived before she died."

"Then why don't you find her yourself?"

"Because I have Jon, and you have ways of finding things I don't."

"Can you afford to pay me?" Pete asked.

"Yes. Whatever you want."

"My fees are in line with those charged by others."

"Then, you'll do it?" James and Pete looked at the stairs and saw Jon. "You'll find me mum?"

Pete exhaled sharply.

"I'll do it, but I ain't promising nothing." Pete eyed James. "How old is the boy?"

"He's nine."

"He does favor you. So you must have been what, sixteen when he was born?"

"Seventeen."

"You were too young. You were both too young." Pete wrote something on his pad. "I'll be honest. I don't know what I can do for you that the police haven't already done."

"Look, I love Jon," James said. "And he loves his mum, and I told him we would do all we could to find her."

Pete smiled. "Right. So, give me the name of the hospital and the woman you mentioned."

"Mia was taken to Brandmore Hospital. She was found by Hettie Nithercott. Miss Nithercott lived in a house in Woollcott owned by a woman named Miss Profitt. Miss Profitt told me that Miss Nithercott had a sister in a care home in Brakenshire that she visited all the time."

Pete raised his eyes to meet James'.

"And you don't believe it was her sister staying there."

338

"She never mentioned having a sister to me. She was with us for over ten years."

Pete jotted this down, and then put his pad back into his case. He looked up at Jon on the stairs.

"Well, lad, as soon as I know anything, I'll call your dad." He glanced at James. "And I'll be needing a check for three hundred and fifty pounds to start."

James wrote the check, gave it to Pete, and followed him to the door.

"I'll tell you the truth, Huxley, I agreed to this because of the boy."

"And I appreciate it."

"I'll be in touch."

James watched him get into his car and drive away. He glanced over his shoulder and saw Jon sitting on the stairs.

"I think he's going to find her," James said.

"Thanks, Dad."

"You're welcome, Jon."

Chapter Fifty-Five

JAMES WAS STILL GETTING USED TO THEIR NEW HOUSE AND finding little nooks and crannies to store his books and other things. Maryanne's house was a two-story near the sea. It had been built at the turn of the century by her great-grandfather. There were three small bedrooms and one bath on the second floor. The first floor had a sitting room, dining area, and kitchen. It wasn't what James had envisioned for their first home, but it would suffice until Jon was a bit older. Maryanne had left the furniture, too, which was older than she, and due for replacement. James planned to swap out one piece at a time once Jon was safely tucked away in school.

The night before Jon's first day of school, James helped him sort his uniform and stayed with him until Jon fell asleep. He sat beside Jon's bed, watching the boy's chest rise and fall and then went downstairs. James hoped his decision to let Jon go to public school would be the right one.

He had received a call from Pete Barret regarding the Brakenshire care home. James was right; Hettie didn't have a sister.

"The administrator told me it was a daughter named Mary," Pete said.

"She didn't have a daughter, either."

"Well, I couldn't get her to tell me where this Mary had gotten off to, but I'll get on it and keep you informed."

After they hung up, James went to the settee and looked at the letter he'd received from Uncle Billy's law firm. Uncle Billy

340

wanted James to sign a letter stating he would be taking his place on the board. He was still reluctant to accept it, but Uncle Billy promised he wouldn't have to learn anything.

"You can be like Queen Elizabeth," Uncle Billy said. "A figurehead."

James sat back and laid his head on the back of the settee. He was at loose ends and knew that if he didn't do something soon, he might never do anything at all. A man needed a job; otherwise he would drift aimlessly through life. And James had to set an example for his son.

So, after Jon left for school, he signed Uncle Billy's letter, slipped it into an envelope, and drove to town to drop it off at the post office. When he picked up Jon from school, the boy was rosy-cheeked and grinning from ear to ear.

"I met a boy," he said. "He lives on a farm."

"What's his name?" James asked.

"His name is Jordan."

"How'd you meet him?"

"He sits next to me, and he has a cow," Jon said. "Can we have a cow?"

"There's no place for a cow in our backyard," James said. "Maybe we can get a dog."

"I'd rather have a cow."

"Aye, well, we're not farmers you and me, lad. A dog is about all I can handle."

"I guess a dog would be all right."

"So, did you get tired during your classes?" James asked.

"No. I wasn't tired at all."

James had always fallen asleep during class and woken with a start when a teacher slammed a book on his desk. He glanced at Jon and thought of how different he was from James at that age. Jon could take care of himself if he had to. James would have starved to death if Miss Nithercott hadn't called him to meals.

"The teacher had a calendar on the wall, and I wrote down everything that is due for the next year so I can get started on them." Jon gazed out the window. "I want to learn everything."

Jon was a marvel. He was on top of things at school and was up in the morning long before James opened his eyes. He'd make breakfast. He'd start the washing. And he'd do it with a smile on his lips.

James discovered that the public library had computers, and every morning after Jon left for school, James would go to the library to use the internet. The librarian taught him how to search for things, and within a month, he bought a personal computer and had signed up with a service called Demon Internet. He put a desk in the alcove under the stairs and spent most of his days "surfing" the internet.

Jon showed little interest in the "gadget" as he called the computer and would often go straight to his room to study when he came home from school. On weekends, he and Jordan would ride their bikes to the library. James felt woefully inadequate when it came to helping with Jon's studies because the boy was far ahead of him, but at least James knew how to use a computer.

In fact, James loved using the computer more than anything else he'd ever done in his life, so he signed up for a course at a nearby college that taught adults how to use different software. He proved a competent student and signed up for the more advanced course the next semester. When he had finished both courses, a professor asked if he was interested in joining a team he was assembling.

"You'll learn how to write code," Professor Reade said. "You learn fast. I think it will suit you."

James' heart beat faster as he thought of delving deeper into the code and agreed to join the team, which would meet on Monday nights.

"Can I bring my son?" he asked. "I can't leave him alone at night."

"Does he like computers?" Reade asked.

"Not particularly, but he does like to read."

"I don't see why not. Tell him to bring a book."

James brought Jon to the first meeting, and as James thought he would, Jon went to the back of the room where the light was better, sat at an empty desk, and opened his book. The meeting was to end at nine, but it ran on until ten, and by the time James went to fetch Jon, the boy was fast asleep.

"Shit," James whispered.

He gathered up Jon and with the help of another team member who gathered Jon's things, got him to the car without waking him. He drove home and left Jon's things in the car while he carried him inside. Jon never opened his eyes as James took off his shoes and trousers. He covered him with the blanket and kissed him goodnight.

As he booted up his own computer, James knew he would have to find someone to stay with Jon while he attended the meetings, but the only people he knew were from his old pub, and he didn't think any of them would want to take a night away from their beer to watch telly with Jon. Still, Artie had become close to Jon when they were studying together. He was like a grandpa to Jon, so it would be worth asking if he would do a mate a favor for the next six months.

James turned on the radio before sitting down at the computer. First, he checked his Yahoo email account. There was a message from Uncle Billy about a board meeting. James made a note of the date. Next, he read emails from the other men in his team concerning changes they would discuss during the next meeting. He also got an email from a charity called Jackson's Animal Refuge, which he labeled as spam, a term that referred to anything that was not important, but you still didn't want to delete all spam, such as a charity request that you felt remorseful for trashing.

Jon had left the radio on in the kitchen. A Madonna song came on, and once again, James' memory conjured up an image of Mia hovering over him with the moon behind her like a halo. He let the pen fall and sat back in the chair.

James had chatted up girls when he worked at the pub and had shagged a few, but he never felt that emotional connection as he had with Mia. She had his heart. He'd never gotten it back, and he didn't know if he would ever find someone who could replace her.

As he thought about going to bed, he looked at the calendar above his desk. The team didn't meet again until the following Monday. He had a week off. Once Jon was in school, he'd be free for eight hours. It was enough time to go to Morseton and talk to Artie about staying with Jon and catching up with his mates.

Chapter Fifty-Six

PETE BARRET RETURNED TO HIS OFFICE, WHICH WAS ALSO HIS home, and went to the small dining room. His dining table was full of files, scraps of paper, a telephone, a typewriter, and a Comprehensive Map of England. He took his notepad from his briefcase, sat in the swivel chair, flipped through some pages, and stared at Mia's name for a long time.

A small file cabinet sat behind his chair. Pete swiveled around and opened the bottom drawer, extracted a file, and then set it on the table. On the tab was the name, "Mia Wentworth." Pete looked at the dog-eared file and remembered what it felt like when James Huxley said her name aloud the day Pete visited his house.

Pete had been the lead investigator on her missing person case. He'd grilled James, a lovesick teenager who had told the same story over and over as Pete tried to break him. Pete was pulled off the case due to a lack of evidence, but the media had still hounded Pete for information.

Pete received steady promotions in his department. He was a good investigator until the media frenzy surrounding the Wentworth case put him under intense scrutiny. Pete began having panic attacks, and once he made his twenty, he retired, but before he left the force, he made a copy of Mia's file. Pete planned to work the case again, but had instead thrown himself into private investigations.

Then, Arthur Wentworth asked him to look into the case as a

private detective. Once again, he grilled James, but as before, the young man's story never changed, and now, Pete believed him. James didn't know where Mia went, but the investigation ended anyway when Arthur Wentworth had a stroke.

This time, James Huxley himself had called, and it was as if the universe was telling him he couldn't hide, that it truly was his duty to find her. Pete had given up too soon. But what if he failed again? What if Mia was not meant to be found?

And then there was the boy. His earnest expression was heartbreaking. He wanted his mum back, and he'd called upon Pete Barret to find her.

"I'm no bloody miracle worker," Pete said aloud.

The details listed in the file had been gone over many times, but the ones James Huxley had given him were new. He believed Mia was the girl found with Boris Black. If she'd been on drugs or prostituting herself, she could have easily come into contact with Boris.

Or perhaps Boris recognized her photo in the paper, the one accompanying the advertisement offering a reward for her return. Pete had put a copy of it in Mia's file.

Pete recalled the media coverage of Boris Black's death. Black had been on the Met's radar for over ten years. He'd done time for aggravated assault and had a nasty temper. He'd been living in Liverpool at the time of his death, so why had Black come to Dorley?

Pete still had relationships with his colleagues at the Met. The lead James gave him involving a woman named Hettie Nithercott had led him to a Mary Nithercott, supposedly her sister in Brakenshire Care Home, but when he asked about Mary at the care home, one of the aides told him that Mary was a young woman near twenty years, not sixty. It would be easy for his colleagues to run a check on her name if he told them he might have a lead in Mia's case. Any one of them would be happy to claim that they had solved the Mia Wentworth case. He would let them take the credit in exchange for some information.

Pete had several small cases to finish up and set Huxley's case aside for a couple of weeks. James called once and Pete gave him an excuse that was only half-true, but it kept Huxley from bothering him for a while. The truth was that Pete had been having nightmares again, and the harder he worked on Mia's case, the worse they became. He promised himself that as soon as he finished up his caseload, he would get in touch with the Met.

Another two weeks passed and James called again. This time, Pete told him the truth, that the case was a bugger and was taking more time than he'd expected.

"But I'm on it."

That bought him more time with Huxley, but now he had to get on with it. He'd already cashed the three hundred and fifty pound check.

Pete punched a number into the phone and waited for someone to pick up. He was happy to hear Joe Keizer's voice come on the line.

"So, how's retirement, you old sod?"

"I'm hardly retired. I do private investigations now."

"Private investigations. Catching cheating husbands and chasing after your money."

"Actually, I'm doing very well, thank you."

"So, I know you didn't call just to tell me how well you were doing," Joe said.

"No, I called because I need a check on a driving license."

"You know I can't use our computers for your private investigations, Pete."

"Aye, I know, but this one is special. I might have found Mia Wentworth."

Silence. "You're joking."

"No, mate, I'm not. I have a name. I got it from someone who knew her well."

"Shite." Pete heard Joe tapping on his keyboard. "What's the name?"

"Mary Nithercott."

* * *

PETE DROVE UP THE DIRT ROAD LEADING TO JACKSON ANIMAL Refuge and parked behind the gate barring the driveway. Pete looked for a way through the gate, and then walked to the other end of the ticket booth to see if there was some way to bypass the gate. A hedge was all that stood between him and the stables, so he got on his knees, crawled between two shrubs, and then took a look inside the stables. He walked past an old, golden horse who was more interested in his oats than in Pete, and another sad-looking beast who whinnied when Pete went by. He came out onto a pigsty where a fat sow suckled her piglets, and a three-legged goat eyed him suspiciously.

"No harm, son," he said to the goat. "Just taking a look around."

It had rained, and the ground was damp. The mossy smell reminded Pete of his childhood in Devon. He walked past the sty and found a path leading away from the center of the refuge. He saw the manor house on the hill behind it and went around the barn. He stopped to admire the old well that had long since been dry and leaned against it as he pondered what he would do next. The driving license had this address, but it didn't specify whether "Mary" lived in the manor house or the hermit's cottage across from the stables. He decided to check out the hermitage first.

The hermitage was nestled in the remains of the Victorian garden that had once been the talk of Plankton. The branches of a massive oak sheltered the cottage, and morning glories reached for the sky while clinging to walls. There was no sign to indicate the resident of the cottage, but a dog, an odd-looking fellow with ears like a basset hound, barked at him from the window.

Pete looked for a car that might belong to Mary but found none. He went around the cottage to the back, but the over-growth of flora and fauna was too unkempt to provide a place to park, but he did see tracks that went to the side of the stables. If Mary had a car, it was in use, which meant she might not be here. Since he loathed the idea of making a second trip to Plankton, Pete decided that if no one answered at the cottage, he would hike up the hill to the manor house.

Pete knocked as the dog barked frantically. A bigger dog might have broken the window, but this strange creature merely wet the panes with his nose. Pete waited a bit longer before leaving the cottage and heading for the manor house.

The place had seen better days, though it still retained a sort of Edwardian charm. The brick building was set back as the centerpiece of a garden. The shutters were newly painted, as was the front door. He walked past the neatly trimmed hedges and recently swept stone walkway to the front door, rang the bell, and stood back on his heels.

A woman flung open the door.

"How did you get past the gate?" she asked in anger.

"My name is Pete Barret. I'm a private investigator. I'd like to speak to Mary Nithercott."

The woman narrowed her eyes and stared at Pete.

"There's no one here by that name."

She tried to shut the door, but Pete pushed back on it and held it open.

"This is a nice place you've got here." The woman remained silent as she tried to push the door shut. "Can I ask who lives in the hermit's cottage?"

"A young man who helps us tend the animals."

"A young man, you say?" Pete took the printout Joe had faxed to him from his pocket. It was a photocopy of Mary's driving license. "This is the address on Mary Nithercott's driving license." He held it up. "I'm not looking to hurt her. I've been hired by her son to find her, and I'd hate to disappoint the lad."

The woman took the printout from his hand and studied the license.

"Her son?" she said.

"Sweet chap, just nine years old. Eyes as blue as the sky."

The woman's jaw twitched as she clenched her teeth. She handed him the printout.

"I'm sorry, but you are mistaken. There is no Mary here. Now, please leave my property, or I shall call the police."

Pete waved his hand in front of her.

"No need. I'll go." He took his card from his pocket and handed it to her. "But just in case you remember something, here's my card."

The woman took the card and then shut the door. Pete walked away from the house as she watched from a window.

Pete went to his car and got inside. The woman hadn't fooled him. He knew Mia lived in the hermit's cottage. He had a choice – either wait for her to return home, or come back another day. It was four o'clock. He'd passed a restaurant in the small town center that advertised a daily special.

Pete started the car and got back on the road. After a good meal and a pint, he would come back and see if Mia was in residence.

Chapter Fifty-Seven

When Mia opened the door to the hermitage, Ralphie, a combination basset hound and cocker spaniel, came to her wriggling from head to toe. She knelt down and rubbed his ears, kissed his head, and then got up and shut the door.

"I guess you missed me," she said.

She hung her purse on a hook by the door and went to the fridge. As she surveyed its contents, she wished she'd stopped at the Chinese takeaway before coming home. The freezer yielded even fewer temptations, but as she contemplated taking Ralphie for a ride and getting dinner, there was a knock on the door.

"I'll bet Gloria wants to ask me about that new piglet," she said to Ralphie. He barked, and she gently pushed him aside with her foot as she opened the door. A small man with squinty eyes took her by surprise. "Oh."

"Mary Nithercott?"

Mia felt the hairs on her neck rise.

"Yes."

The man smiled.

"My name is Pete Barret. I'm a private investigator. If we could talk for a moment?"

Mia felt her throat tighten as her cheeks burned, and her hand began to shake.

"Um, why?"

Pete pursed his lips.

"I was hired to find you."

"Who hired you?" Mia asked as the image of James came to her mind.

Pete exhaled sharply.

"Jon Huxley," he said. Mia swayed, and she gripped the door. It was the reaction he'd hoped for. "Perhaps we should sit down?"

Pete took Mia's elbow and led her to the dining table. He left the front door open and waited until she sat before taking a seat there himself. Ralphie growled at Pete, who glared at the dog, which stiffened Ralphie's resolve. He positioned himself between Pete and Mia.

"Are you all right?" Pete asked.

"I'm fine," Mia whispered.

"Would you like a glass of water?"

Mia shook her head.

"You said Jon Huxley hired you," she said.

"He did."

"How?" Her eyes rose to meet his. "How is that possible?"

Pete cocked his head.

"I'm not sure I understand."

"How is it possible that Jon…is he here?"

"Jon lives in Morseton with his father."

Mia's eyes widened.

"But how is that possible!" she cried.

Pete thought about James' fantastic story as he moved to sit in the other chair. Ralphie growled, and he hesitated.

"Ralphie," Mia said, "bed."

Ralphie obeyed, and Pete sat in the other chair.

"So, why is it impossible?" Pete asked.

Mia stared at the table for a moment, and then her eyes met Pete's

"I guess you know I ran away."

"I was a detective at the Met when you were reported missing."

Mia sat up. She held her hands out in front of her and pressed them together.

"I was sixteen. I was staying with James. We… and then I found out I was pregnant." Mia slumped in the chair. "My mother had made it clear she didn't want any grandchildren. I panicked when I thought of going home. I didn't want...I wanted the baby."

"So, where did you go?"

Mia rolled her eyes, smiled, and shook her head.

"I'll tell you, but you won't believe me." She stood up and went to the stove. "Do you want some tea?"

"If you don't mind."

Mia turned on the light under the kettle and then got two cups out of the cabinet. She put a teabag in each, went to the table, and sat.

"Have you ever been to the festival in Dorley?" she asked.

"Once or twice."

"James and I went there together with his governess, Miss Nithercott." Mia smiled. "She was more like a chaperone by then. Anyway, one of the vendors was a woman named Rotrude. She dressed like a gypsy and sold charms and jewelry."

"So I've heard."

Mia eyed him for a moment, and then continued her story.

"I bought a necklace – a gold disk on a leather strap. The disk had a cottage etched on it, and Rotrude told me that if I was ever in dire need, I should use the disk to find her."

"And you bought that story?" Pete asked.

"I was desparate. I wanted to believe her. And it worked."

"The disk led you to her," Pete said.

Mia nodded. "She lived in a small cottage in the woods."

"Like the one on the disk."

"Exactly like the one on the disk."

"Is this Rotrude the one who helped you run away?" Pete asked.

"This is the part you won't believe," Mia said.

"She took you to an alternate world called Havenwood."

Mia's eyes widened. "How…?"

"Shite," Pete said. "That's the same bloody story Huxley told me."

The kettle went off, and Mia rose to make their tea. Her hands shook as she brought the cups to the table.

"Milk and sugar?" she asked.

"Neither," Pete said.

Mia returned to her seat and again slumped in her chair.

"Rotrude took me there. I gave birth to Jon and lived there until…"

"Until Boris Black came looking for you. But how would someone like Boris Black get to this place, this Havenwood?"

"This girl who had lived there for a while brought him. I don't know how they got the Silver Stag."

"The Silver Stag?" Pete asked.

"It's a coin we used to travel back and forth between here and Havenwood."

Pete laughed. "I'm sorry, luv, but this story is just bollocks." He leaned toward her. "Where were you, really?"

Mia clasped her hands on the table and tears shimmered in her eyes. Pete saw her hand shake as she gripped it tightly.

"Did you really see Jon?" she asked.

"I saw him."

"How is he?"

"He's a good lad. He takes after his father."

"And how is…his father?" Mia asked.

"He's doing all right for himself. He's good with the lad if that's what you're asking."

"Where are they?"

Pete studied her for a minute. He hadn't gotten permission to share this information.

"I'll have to ask him if he wants me to share that with you."

"Oh," she said softly.

"We didn't get into the particulars," Pete said. Mia looked sad. "Look, luv, I don't have a horse in this race, so I can just tell you what I think. That boy deserves a chance to see his mother. He was clear about wanting me to find you and his dad was willing to pay me to find you. Now, what you need to decide is if you want to see him."

"Of course, I want to see him!" Mia cried.

"Then this is what's going to happen next. I have a duty to tell my client that I found you, and that's what I intend to do, but I won't tell him where you are unless you say it's all right."

Mia gripped her hand tightly. She pressed it against the table, but it continued to tap against its surface. She put her other hand on it, but now her shoulders shook. The tightness in her chest forced her to press on the table with both hands as she struggled to breathe. Pete stood, went to Mia, and put his hands on her shoulders.

"Some of the lads at the Met would shake like that after being shot," he said. "Took early retirement. They said it was something called PTSD."

Mia nodded. She willed herself to breathe, and Pete saw that she was calming down.

Mia nodded. "I…it started when I was in the care home. My therapist thought it might be because of the way Boris took me. I was shot…."

Pete believed he was a good judge of character. Mia wasn't faking the symptoms of PTSD. She couldn't control what was happening. He returned to his chair and exhaled loudly.

"How often does this happen?" Pete asked.

"Not as much as it used to," Mia said.

Mia's shoulders trembled.

"I have to tell him I found you," Pete said.

"I know."

"Can I ask why you never contacted Huxley?"

Mia was calming down and looked Pete in the eye.

"I thought I'd never get back to Havenwood, that I'd never see Jon again, and I dreaded telling James that I had lost our son."

"You didn't lose him. You were taken from him. There's a difference…"

"I should have told him!" Mia cried. "I thought he'd hate me."

Mia folded her arms across her chest and kept her hands under her arms.

"Well, if it helps at all, Huxley seems like a reasonable man." He stood. "I'll stop by there tomorrow. Do you have a phone number?"

Mia's eyes met his. "Tell Jon that I can't wait to see him."

"And his father?" Pete asked. Mia closed her eyes and bit her lip. "I don't think he hates you, luv."

"I don't know what to do."

"If you ask me, you should see Huxley first. That way, you two can work things out before bringing the boy into it."

Mia nodded. "Right. You're right. He should call me."

Pete took out his notepad and pen and slid it over to her. Mia found a blank page and wrote her number on it.

"I guess that's it then," Pete said. "He's a good lad your boy."

Mia nodded. Pete turned to go to the door and saw the netting hanging off a hook screwed into the door frame. Mia noticed it and got up.

"I used to sleepwalk. Sid put that up to stop me from leaving the house."

"Did it work?" Pete asked.

"It did. I would wake up on the floor with my hands gripping it, but it stayed in place."

Ralphie followed Pete to the door, and then Mia stood in the doorway and watched Pete get inside his car.

She waited until he had driven away before she sat at the table with her face in her hands, and cried until her eyes hurt.

Chapter Fifty-Eight

AFTER MUCH CONTEMPLATION, JAMES DECIDED IT WAS TIME FOR Jon to meet his grandfather. He chose a Saturday in October when the crisp air was turning the leaves a brilliant red and orange. They parked in the car park at Peterson's farm, and then James took Jon to the bakery. The last time they were there, James had just found Jon, and the boy had just left the only home he'd ever known. As they ate their raspberry tarts, James noticed that Jon was quiet.

"Does being here bother you?" James asked.

"No."

James almost asked about Greyson but decided not to bring him up.

"Do you want anything else?" James asked.

"Can I have a scone?"

James ordered one and handed it to Jon, who ate it before they left the bakery. When they walked outside, Jon looked toward the park.

"Is that where Grandfather lives?" he asked.

"Aye, down that road."

They returned to the car and drove down Huxley Road to the manor house. James turned onto the drive and remembered riding his bike down this road with Mia beside him. The memory wasn't fraught with angst this time. It was sweet, and now it included this wonderful boy they'd created.

James' heart had been broken, but now all he wanted was to

give Jon the best life possible, and if by some miracle that life included Mia, James would embrace that as well.

"Your mum and I rode our bikes to Dorley from here," James said.

"Where are the bikes now?"

"Probably still in the garage."

"Can we take them home?" Jon asked.

"I don't think we've room in the boot for them," James said.

"Oh."

"Besides, you have a bike. What would you do with two?"

"I'd use one on Monday, and the other on Tuesday. Then I'd do it again."

James smiled. "Those bikes are ancient. I doubt the tires hold air anymore."

"We could buy new tires," Jon said.

"Aye, we could, but I think one bike is more than enough for now."

The manor house loomed ahead, and James' stomach was in a knot. He kept smiling, hoping that Jon wouldn't notice how anxious he felt. James and his father hadn't spoken for a long while. All the conversations he'd had in his head ended badly, so he had no reason to believe they would be better in person, but Jon was eager to meet his grandfather, and James wanted to please Jon.

"Does it really have a castle?" Jon asked.

"The ruins of a castle," James said.

"Do people visit it?"

"They try to visit it, especially during the festival, but my father hires guards to keep them away."

Jon tilted his head and stared at James for a moment.

"Is that why you don't like your dad?" Jon asked.

"What makes you say that?" James said.

"Whenever you talk about him, you sound different, like you're angry."

"I do?"

"And you clench your teeth."

"I never." James looked into Jon's eyes.

"You're doing it now," Jon said.

James looked in the rearview mirror and saw his furrowed brow. He raised his eyebrows and smiled.

"See, I'm not angry. My dad and I don't always see eye to eye is all."

"Do you think he will see eye to eye with me?" Jon asked.

Now, James clenched his teeth. If Harold said one word against his son...

"You're not worried about that, are you?"

Jon tapped his finger on the armrest.

"No. I just don't want you to be upset if he doesn't."

James took his son's hand.

"I'll be on my best behavior."

Jon examined the house.

"It's not as big as I thought it would be."

"It's big enough."

James parked the car at the entrance. When they got out, Jon looked up at the attic window.

"Is that the attic? Jon asked.

James looked up.

"It is."

"Can I see it?"

"Let's see how things go first."

James rang the bell, and they waited a moment before Bruce opened the door. He offered them a perfunctory smile.

"Lord Huxley," he said.

"Bruce. Is my father at home?"

Bruce looked at Jon and saw his blue eyes.

"He is home, sir."

Bruce stepped aside so they could enter the foyer.

"This is Jon," James said. "He's my son. I'd rather talk to my father first before introducing them."

"Very well. Wait here, please."

James and Jon exchanged glances.

"He seems nice," Jon said.

"He's paid to be nice."

"Do you think Grandfather will tell us to bugger off?"

James' eyes widened.

"Where did you hear that? That's a terrible thing to say."

"Jordan says it," Jon said.

"Well, I doubt his mum hears him say it. It's not polite."

Bruce returned and indicated they were to follow him. While

James expected him to take them to his father's study, Bruce stopped at the sitting room door.

"Lord Huxley, your father is gravely ill."

"Since when?" James asked.

"It's only been a few months. The doctor has advised us to avoid agitating him."

"Just seeing me will probably agitate him."

Bruce hesitated for a moment.

"He has cancer. It's advancing rapidly." James leaned against the wall and stared at Bruce. "I shall take the boy to the kitchen where Caroline is making shortbread cookies."

"Can I go, too?" James said with a smile that faded when he saw Bruce's grim expression. "Right." He turned to Jon, "You go with Bruce now."

As Bruce opened the door, a medicinal smell assailed James. Lord Harold Huxley was lying in a hospital bed with an intravenous bottle hung above his left shoulder. He saw James and forced a smile. James' emotions betrayed him, and he felt a lump in his throat.

"James," Harold said. "It's good to see you."

"It's good to see you, too." James walked over to Harold's bed. "I hear you're not feeling well."

"Ah," Harold said and waved his hand. "It's nothing. I'll be right as rain in no time."

Harold was very thin, and his hair unkempt.

"Are you eating?" James asked.

"Oh, yes, every day." Harold looked toward a chair beside the bed. "Sit."

James sat and looked around. The furniture had been pushed to one side of the room, and the TV was on a table at the foot of Harold's bed. An end table next to it held several bottles of medicine.

"Why didn't you tell me you were sick?"

"Didn't think you'd care," Harold said. "We haven't been the best of friends you and I."

"You're my father," James said.

James heard his voice and saw the look on Harold's face. The old man had never looked at James that way before. His eyes were soft.

"I have something to tell you," James said.

"Bruce told me you brought someone with you," Harold said.

"I asked him not to."

Harold waved his hand, and even that small gesture seemed to cause him pain.

"He's worse than a sister at hospital." Harold eyed James. "Bring him in."

"I'll have to fetch him from the kitchen."

Harold tried to point to the door, but his hand dropped.

"We have buttons…"

James saw the panel by the door and got up. He pushed the one for the kitchen, and he heard Caroline's voice.

"It's James. Please ask Bruce to bring Jon to meet my father."

James opened the door and waited for Bruce and Jon until he saw them coming toward him. James put his hand on Jon's shoulder and brought him into the room. Jon's eyes were wide when he saw Harold and stayed that way as James brought him to Harold's bed.

"He has your mother's eyes," Harold said. "Your eyes."

James fetched another chair from the other side of the room, and Harold held out his hand to Jon.

"You look just like your father when he was your age."

"Do I really have his eyes?" Jon asked.

"You do."

"Shall I call you Granddad?"

Harold smiled. "It would make me happy if you would."

James brought a chair and placed it next to the bed. He saw Jon's happy expression and smiled.

"What did I miss?" James asked.

"He said I could call him Granddad."

"He did, did he?"

James glanced at Harold before sitting.

"So, where have you been hiding all these years?" Harold asked Jon.

"I've been in Bristol," Jon said.

James looked at Jon. Where had the boy gotten that idea?

"I was raised by my other grandfather. His name was Greyson."

"And what about his mother?" Harold asked as he looked at James. "When did you meet her?"

James wanted to lie. He wanted to tell Harold that he had met someone when he was in school, that it was right after Mia ran away, but James saw Harold's hollowed-out cheeks and his pallor and knew that it was time to tell the truth.

"It's was Mia," James said.

Harold looked puzzled.

"You found her?"

"Mum asked Dad to take me," Jon said.

Since when had his son become such an accomplished liar?

"She did," James said. "She contacted me and asked me to take him while she sorted herself."

"Poor Vincent. He was beside himself when she went missing. Always said you had something to do with it, poor chap, but I knew you had nothing to do with it."

James felt his spirit lighten a bit.

"Are you being serious?"

"Oh, James, I knew you could never kill anyone. You just didn't have it in you. You were too much of a dreamer, too soft for that sort of thing."

The lift he'd gotten just moments ago left James.

"Right," James said.

"Oh, I see that look," Harold said. "You know as well as I that you were never meant to be anyone's hero. If you had been, you would have married the girl instead of letting her run away."

Red patches appeared on James' cheeks, and he felt Jon's hand on his leg.

"Dad, can we see the castle now?"

"Yes," Harold said. "Show the boy the castle why don't you? I'm very tired."

Harold closed his eyes. Jon stood and put out his hand as his eyes beseeched James. James got up, let Jon take his hand, and they left without a backward glance.

"How do we get there?" Jon asked.

"We can go out the kitchen door," James said.

When James and Jon entered the kitchen, Caroline grinned.

"He's a charmer that one," she said. "He reminds me of you at that age. So handsome."

James smiled.

"He's a good eater, too."

"And why do you think you were always at my table?" Caroline came to James and hugged him. "He's a good lad, he is. You should be proud of him."

"I am proud of him."

Caroline tweaked James' chin.

"So, is this why you disappeared that day?"

"What day?" James asked.

"The day you came to visit. You were going to spend the night and…"

"Yes, I remember now. I got a call and had to go straight away. I'm sorry I didn't let you know."

"It's all right, luv." Caroline put her hand on James' cheek. "Don't you listen to his lordship. He's not himself."

"If anything, he's more like himself than ever," James said.

Caroline pursed her lips and shook her head.

"Well, never you mind what he said. I know you, and I know you'll be a wonderful father."

"Thank you. I was just going to take Jon to see the ruins."

"Well, don't let me hold things up," Caroline said. "And when you're done looking at that old pile of rocks, you come in and have some shortbread."

James and Jon walked across the lawn in silence. When they reached the mud where once the moat had stood as a barrier against the Scandinavian hooligans, Jon jumped across, barely reaching the other side, but managed to avoid getting mud on his trainers. James was able to bridge the "moat" by taking a giant step.

The ruins had deteriorated since James and Mia had wandered its perimeter eleven years before, and James felt a twinge of sadness for he knew in his heart it would never be restored.

"Granddad is wrong," Jon said. James was lost in his reverie and didn't hear Jon. "Dad!"

"What?"

"I said Granddad is wrong."

"What are you talking about?" James asked.

"He said you were never meant to be a hero."

"Oh. He was just talking."

Jon took James' hand and peered up at him.

"You came to Havenwood and saved me. You are my hero."

James' lip trembled, his eyes filled with tears, and he praised whatever god or universe or fate had brought this boy to him. He embraced Jon and held him tightly as his tears wet the boy's hair. Jon returned the hug and patted his dad on the back.

"It's all right, Dad."

James pulled away and looked into Jon's eyes.

"I love you so much."

"I love you, too, Dad. Let's go inside. I want to see the attic."

They went in through the kitchen door and up the back stairs to the second floor. James stopped at the entrance of his old bedroom, and Jon's eyes grew wide.

"You had a big room, Dad."

"Aye. I did."

James looked at the bed and remembered how it felt to wake up beside Mia. He put his hand on Jon's shoulder and squeezed.

"Let's go to the attic."

They climbed the attic stairs, and Jon went straight to the bookcases.

"You had so many books," he said.

"And I read them all right there."

James pointed to the legless chair, and Jon's eyes followed.

"It must have been hard to read there. It's dark."

"I had a lamp. I kept it lit while I was up here."

"And you read all these books?"

"Every one," James said. "We can take some if you like."

While Jon looked at the titles, James looked for something to carry the books to the car. He found a basket filled with old kitchen utensils, dumped them on the floor, and let Jon fill the basket with his choices. When he was done, they went down to the foyer, and James went to find Bruce. He saw him coming out of the sitting room.

"How long does the doctor give him?"

"In truth, he has gone on longer than they expected."

"So, he could go at any time," James said.

"Yes, sir."

James took a business card from his pocket. He'd been given them when he joined the board of the Moreland Bank.

"That's my mobile number. Call me when it's…"

"Yes, sir."

Before they left the house, Jon saw Celeste's portrait in the drawing room.

"Who is she?" he asked.

"That's my mother," James said.

"She has blue eyes."

"Aye, she did."

Jon stared at James for a moment.

"She's very beautiful."

"That she was." James stared at the portrait and contemplated taking it off the wall, but Bruce was standing behind them. "Well, we'd better be off."

They went to the car without stopping by the sickbed, and Jon put the basket on the backseat. He was quiet, and James saw that he had something on his mind.

"He's very sick, isn't he?" Jon asked.

"He is," James said.

"Can we come here again?" Jon asked.

"I'm not sure how long..."

"Oh. Okay."

As they drove down the long drive, Jon stared at the woods. He was quiet all the way back to Morseton, and was delighted when he saw Pete Barret parked on the street outside his house.

Chapter Fifty-Nine

When Pete saw them turn into the drive, he got out of his car and met them at the front door. James acknowledged Pete and then turned to Jon.

"Jon, would you go in and put the kettle on?"

Jon's eyes went from Pete to James, and then he went inside.

"I guess we're staying out here," Pete said.

"If you have something to tell me, yes."

Pete had some papers in his hand, and he gave them to James.

"She's living in a place called Jackson's Animal Refuge. They know her as Mary Nithercott. She helps with the animals and lives in the hermitage."

James was stunned. He had found her. She was real. James would see her again.

He looked at the papers and read the first paragraph of Pete's report. He had to read it three times to comprehend what it said as his mind reeled over the idea of seeing her again. The third time he saw the words *Post Traumatic Stress Disorder*.

"Post Traumatic Stress Disorder?" James said. "What is that?"

"They used to call it shell shock. My grandfather had it when he came home after World War I."

"I've heard of shell shock, but how did she…"

"She was kidnapped and shot. She was taken from her son. This is how her mind deals with it."

James read the rest of Pete's short report and then looked Pete in the eye.

"Did you tell her about Jon?"

"It came up in the conversation," Pete said. He leaned against the wall. "She wants to see him."

James leaned against the door

"Did she ask about me?"

"She wondered if you wanted to see her."

"What did you say?"

"That you hadn't shared your feelings with me," Pete said.

"But she didn't say she *didn't* want to see me," James said.

Pete shoved his hands into his pockets.

"I told her you two should talk and work it out before bringing the boy into it. Look, James, she's...fragile. You should meet her on her turf. The animal refuge is familiar to her. If you asked me, you should go up there. Call her. Let her know you're coming, and after you see her, tell Jon."

James looked at the report again.

"How was she? Really?"

"Her hands shake, but her mind was sharp. Sometimes, she walks in her sleep."

Pete thought of the netting on the hook but kept it to himself while James thought about Mia dancing in the moonlight. Her confidence had always impressed him. He couldn't imagine her being fragile.

Jon came to the door and saw the papers in James' hand.

"The water is hot," he said.

"Aye," James said. "So, Mr. Pete, would you like some tea?"

"Thanks, but I have to be going," Pete said.

"Did you find my mum?" Jon asked.

Pete looked to James.

"I have a lead I'm following," Pete said. "I should know something soon."

"You have a lead?" Jon was glowing with excitement.

"Aye. As soon as I know, you'll know." Pete looked at James. "I'll be in touch."

"Thanks for your help," James said.

Pete gave Jon a small salute and then went to his car. Jon stared at the papers in James' hand.

"What kind of lead does he have?"

"A good one."

Jon had set three cups on the dining table, and now he took one off and put it in the cabinet while James sat. He filled the two cups with water and then added a teabag to each. He'd already set the milk and sugar on the table, along with a plate of biscuits. Jon brought the cups to the table and then settled in his chair.

"How will you feel when we find her?" James asked.

"I'll feel wonderful," Jon said.

"But what if she's…changed?"

"What do you mean?"

"What if she's not the way she was?" James leaned his head toward Jon. "When bad things happen to people, their minds do things to help them cope. She was kidnapped. It probably upset her, and she's still upset."

Jon thought for a long time.

"I could take care of her."

"The way you take care of me," James said. Jon nodded. "But we're supposed to take care of you."

"You take care of me. We take care of each other." Jon's eyes lit up. "We'll both take care of Mum."

"You're right, mate. We can both take care of her."

After they had their tea, Jon retrieved the basket of books from the car and set them up in his bookcase. He took one out and began to read it while James watched TV. James kept thinking of Mia and knew he should call her, but wanted to wait until Jon was asleep. There were things that might come up, old wounds that had yet to heal, and James didn't want Jon to hear their conversation.

Jon came downstairs and stood by the settee.

"What?" James asked.

"I'm hungry, but I don't feel like cooking."

"Me neither, mate. What'd you say we get some takeaway?"

"I'd say yes."

They drove to town, got their food, brought it home, and by the time they'd finished eating, Jon was knackered. He fell asleep beside James on the settee, and James got him up and guided him up the stairs. When Jon was done with his teeth, James tucked him into bed.

James booted up his computer and searched for information

about PTSD. Soldiers who'd seen horrific things during war would often come home suffering from anxiety, depression, and other symptoms caused by their mind's need to protect them. Some suffered more than others, and some learned to cope with their symptoms, but there was no cure.

James sat back and thought of how Jon would react to Mia's symptoms. Sometimes, he was so mature that it was hard to remember he was just a kid, and other times, James would find him clinging to his old teddy bear. Jon hadn't seen Mia in years, and his memory of her had dimmed since Jon came to live with James.

"I don't remember me mum's voice," Jon said one day after they hired Pete.

"I don't remember my mum's voice either, Jon. It's nothing to be ashamed of."

James' words had placated his son, but Jon's nature was to care for others. He was always asking James how he was, and if James complained about anything, Jon would try to "fix" whatever it was. In this way, he took after his father, but Jon could never fix Mia, so what would that do to him? Could Jon accept that his mother would never get over what had happened to her?

And what about James? If Mia was not the same person she had been, James wasn't, either. Raising a child changed you, brought out the best and worst in you. It shone a light on who you really were, and that portrait didn't always reflect the person you wanted to be.

As he shut down the computer, James picked up his mobile phone. He took Pete's report out of the top drawer and saw Mia's number written on the top. He held his finger over the keypad on his phone and imagined what her voice would sound like. James looked up at the ceiling and listened to his son snoring. Once he dialed the number, their lives would never be the same. For better or worse, Jon wanted to see his mother, so James steeled himself and pressed that first number.

Chapter Sixty

JAMES PULLED INTO THE CAR PARK OF THE ANIMAL REFUGE. THE
sun was shining, and the breeze was coming off the pigsty. It
reminded James of Peterson's farm in Dorley and the jousting
contests he'd watched during the festivals.

Horses whinnied, and a dog barked as he walked toward
the gate barring the entrance to the animal refuge. The
hermitage was in view, and James felt his throat tighten. In a
few minutes, all his questions regarding Mia would be
answered.

"We're closed." James jerked his head and saw a middle-aged
man leading a horse toward him. "We're open on the weekends."

"I'm here to see…Mary Nithercott," James said.

"Aye. She said someone was coming to visit. She might be in
the field with Galahad." The man unlocked the gate, let James
pass through, and then James followed the man to the stables.

"Mary!" the man cried. "She might be hiding in a stable."

When no one appeared, the man pointed toward the open
field behind the stables.

"She would have gone that way. There's a path leading to the
woods."

"Thank you," James said.

The cloudless sky was a brilliant blue, but the grass was dry
and turning brown as the temperatures grew colder. James
passed the pigsty and smiled at the litter, many of whom sought
to follow him, grunting at his feet as he walked away. He

wondered what happened to pigs at an animal refuge. Were they sold for Christmas dinner?

James was halfway down the path when he spotted a small figure walking between a horse and a strange-looking dog as they came out of the woods. His heart started pounding, and he slowed his pace. As the figure grew bigger, his courage grew smaller until he stopped and waited for her to come to him.

Mia saw him, too, and she stopped as her heart beat faster, and her hands tingled. Her lip quivered, and her mouth was dry. Madonna's "Papa Don't Preach" began in her head, and she recalled how his face looked in the moonlight.

"I love you," he said.

That night, her heart was breaking because she knew she'd have to leave him, and every part of her soul begged her not to. The years between hadn't changed anything. She still loved James Huxley. She dropped Galahad's reins and ran to James with Ralphie at her heels. When she reached him, she jumped into his arms and wrapped her arms around him.

"Oh, James," she said, and then she pressed her lips against his with an urgency that matched James' own. They kissed and held each other for a long time, and then he pulled himself away and put his hands on her cheeks.

"You're real," he said.

"I'm sorry, I'm sorry, I'm sorry," she said through her tears.

James kissed her sweetly.

"It's all right," he said. "We're all right."

"I didn't know what to do. I was so scared."

"It doesn't matter now. You did the right thing." He put his hands on her shoulders. "Jon is the best thing that ever happened to me."

Tears rolled down Mia's cheeks.

"Oh, Jon. How is he? Is he okay?"

"He's good, Mia. He's smart and kind and bloody wonderful." He looked down at Ralphie, who was trying to get between them. "He's an odd fellow, isn't he?"

Mia knelt down and rubbed Ralphie behind the ears.

"This is Ralphie. He was the runt of the litter, and no one wanted him." She smiled up at James. "He takes care of me."

James looked at Galahad.

"And who's that poor old thing?"

"That's Galahad. He was neglected by his owner. When I first came here, we sort of learned from each other."

She went to Galahad and took his reins in her hand.

"It's time for your nap," Mia said. She glanced at James. "And I want to show you where I live."

They walked back quietly, observing the change of seasons and sharing bits and pieces of their lives. It was as if no time had passed and they were sixteen again with their whole lives before them. James' heart was so full that he wondered why he had ever worried about seeing her again, and Mia felt as if she had finally come home.

Mia put Galahad in his stable and promised to come and brush him down after she showed James the hermitage.

"Did you look through the window?" she asked.

"No. I met this man, and he told me where to find you."

"That was Sid. He and his wife own this place. They've been very good to me."

Mia unlocked the door, and they went inside. James looked around the room as Mia went to put the kettle on.

"It's like the flat I had over the pub," he said.

James took a seat at the table. When the kettle whistled, he watched as Mia took two mugs from a shelf before joining him at the table.

"When that man told me you had found Jon, I couldn't believe it." She looked into his eyes. "How did you go to Havenwood?"

"When Miss Nithercott died, her landlady sent me her things. The Silver Stag was in the box."

Mia's mouth gaped.

"She did have it." Mis shook her head and her hand shook. "I should have talked to her. I could have gotten Jon…"

James reached for her hand.

"He's okay, Mia."

"But I could have brought him here years ago."

"It wasn't your fault." James clasped his hands. "How did you and Miss Nithercott find each other?"

"You met Greyson?" she asked. James nodded.

"He told me you were taken away."

"By Boris Black. A girl who used to live in Havenwood brought him to my house. I didn't know my father had offered a reward for my return. I think that's why Boris came looking for me."

"Greyson told me that that girl and Black had murdered Rotrude," James said.

"Oh, no," Mia said. "That's why her cottage was gone."

"Aye. I went looking for her, hoping she could help me find you," James said.

"I went to the woods hoping I would find the Stag."

"So, you and Miss Nithercott…"

"I don't remember much. I was told that I crawled out of the woods near the park and people came to help me. That's when Hettie found me." Mia smiled. "She told them I was her daughter."

"Miss Nithercott? You called her Hettie?" James smiled broadly. "I could never imagine doing that."

"She became my friend. She was there when they took me to the hospital and when I went to the care home. She got me this job."

The kettle whistled and Mia got up to make their tea. She brought the cups to the table and sat.

"I thought Rotrude was immortal," Mia said. "And she should have sensed they were coming for her."

"Greyson didn't tell me how it happened," James said. "He said that after she died, Havenwood began to die, too, and Greyson thought of bringing Jon to me, but he was afraid you would come back looking for Jon, so he stayed and waited." James shook his head. "I didn't even know what the Silver Stag was. I had taken it with me when I went to see Miss Nithercott's landlady, hoping she could tell me, but she said she hadn't seen it until she cleaned out Miss Nitercott's chest of drawers. I had it in my pocket and put it on. Next thing I knew, I was in Havenwood." Mia reached for his hand. "Greyson was dying, but I believe he would have taken Jon to England if I hadn't come."

"Oh, God," Mia said. "My poor baby." Her eyes met James'. "I want to see him."

"I have to tell him we found you," James said.

"I don't know if I can wait."

Fear rose in James' heart. What if Jon saw Mia and wanted to come here to live with her? Thoughts ran through his mind at a frenetic pace as he tried to imagine his life without Jon's constant companionship. Jealousy made him look at Mia differently as he saw the look of yearning on her face. He understood that yearning, and it worked on him as she squeezed his hand.

"Can we go to him now?" she asked.

"He's in school," James said.

Mia noticed the edge in his voice.

"Are you all right?"

"I'm fine."

"You're not fine. I hear it in your voice."

James closed his eyes so he wouldn't see her face.

"I haven't even told him yet."

Mia sat back and folded her hands in her lap.

"You're afraid."

James opened his eyes and looked into hers.

"Wouldn't you be? I've had him with me all these months, hearing him talk, seeing the look on his face when he learns something new. I can't give him up, Mia."

"Do you still love me, James?"

"Yes. I never stopped."

He said it without hesitation.

"Do you love me?" he asked.

"Yes. I never stopped either." Mia leaned toward him. "Why do you think I'd want to take him away from you?"

James' lip trembled.

"Because I woke up and you were gone."

Mia closed her eyes as tears rolled down her face. She got up, went behind James, and put her arms around his neck.

"I will never take him away from you, James."

He put his hand on her arm and held it tightly.

"Can we…do this?" he asked.

Mia knelt beside him and gazed into his eyes.

"There are things you should know. I have problems. I can cope with them, but I'll never be cured."

"I know. I looked up PTSD. I know there's no cure."

She exhaled sharply.

"That man told you." Mia stood and put her hand on his shoulder. "Do you think you can handle living with me?"

"I still wrestle with the black dog," James said. "Do you think you can handle him?"

Mia scoffed, and James smiled.

"Oh, poor Jon," Mia said.

"He's the best of us. He said we could take care of each other."

"Jon said that?"

"He's amazing, Mia."

Mia returned to her seat and clasped her hands on the table.

"So, what are we gonna do?"

James slumped in his chair and looked into her eyes.

"I guess you're coming home with me," James said.

Chapter Sixty-One

Mia was quiet as they drove to Morseton. James glanced at her from time to time, but it was hard to read her face. Sid and Gloria had seemed cool as Mia tried to explain who James was, where she was going, and why she'd be gone overnight, and James understood why — they had treated her like a daughter, and Mia hadn't even told them she had a son. James hoped that in time, they would understand why she had done what she did.

"You're not alone anymore," James said. "You have us."

Mia smiled wanly.

"They were hurt," she said softly. "I feel awful about keeping it from them."

"Look, what would you have told them? They never would have understood."

"But I could have told them about Jon. I could have made up some story about where he was."

"Mia, you did the best you could."

"It wasn't good enough."

James put his hand on hers and squeezed.

"Just think of Jon's face when he sees you." James looked at his watch. "We should be arriving just as he gets out of school. I'll drop you off at the house, and then I'll go and pick him up. We'll stop for takeaway on the way home."

"I want to go with you when you pick him up," Mia said.

James kept his eyes on the road as he pictured Jon running into Mia's arms.

"Are you sure?"

"I want to see him. I don't want to wait anymore."

James took his hand away and put it on the steering wheel. Mia glanced at him and saw his jaw twitch.

"James," she said. Mia kept an eye on him for a few minutes and then put her hand on his. "He loves you."

"I know."

Mia took her hand away and sighed.

"I'm gonna tell the Jacksons I'm leaving."

"I saw you with that horse," James said. "You love what you're doing."

"I also love you, and I want you and Jon to be happy."

James hunched up his shoulders and then let them fall.

"I don't think you would be happy if you couldn't work there."

"There are other places I can work with animals," Mia said.

"But those animals…they're different. They're hurting, and you understand how they feel."

"James, if I have to make a choice, I choose my family."

James' heart leapt when she said the word "family."

"I'm you're family?" he asked.

"You and Jon."

James took her hand, brought it to his lips, and kissed it. He looked at Mia, and she put her head on his shoulder.

They were quiet until James took the exit off the motorway.

"We're almost there."

Jon was waiting at the curb when they arrived at his school. He saw that someone was sitting in the passenger seat. He watched James park across the road and stared at the pretty, blond woman. A vague memory of a photograph he'd seen when his father showed him photos of his mum emerged. Jon's heart began to beat wildly, and then he dropped his rucksack and ran across the road.

"MUM!" he cried.

Mia got out of the car and went to him with open arms, and when they met, they embraced.

"I missed you so much," Jon said.

"Oh, Jon, Jon, I've missed you."

"Oh, Mum, I'm so happy you're here."

James watched the reunion as his own emotions ran the

gamut of extreme happiness to paralyzing fear. This was all new to him, seeing Jon enthralled by the presence of another, and it forced him to back away when all he wanted was to run to them and pull them apart. It was all so confusing, this strange family of his, and he would have to adjust sooner rather than later. James would have to share his son's love with someone else.

As he watched Jon clinging to his mother, James' mobile phone rang. He saw the number and the image of Harold Huxley lying in his deathbed came into James' mind.

"Hello," he said.

"Hello," Bruce said. "You asked me to call."

"Right. I'm on my way. Thanks, Bruce."

Mia and Jon were walking toward the car, and she saw the look on James' face.

"What's wrong?" she asked.

"It's Harold. I have to go to Dorley."

"Grandad is sick," Jon said.

"How sick?" Mia asked.

"I have to get there fast," James said.

Mia stood behind Jon with her hands on his shoulders.

"We'll come with you."

"I'm not sure it's…"

"We can walk around town and get something to eat while we catch up."

Jon was beaming.

"Mum can drive," Jon said.

"Oh, she can, can she?" James asked.

"I got my license," Mia said.

"Well, then we'd better be off."

* * *

AN AIR OF GLOOM SURROUNDED THE MANOR HOUSE, AND JAMES felt the black dog's whiskers brushing his cheek as they rode up the drive. The sun had already set and there were no lights on in the drawing room or the floors above. One window in the sitting room was illuminated, and a large, black car sat in front of the entrance door. James parked behind it and left the engine on.

"I'd forgotten how big it is," Mia said.

"Do you have any money?" James asked.

"Not really."

He couldn't see her blush in the dark car. He pulled out his wallet and took out some pound notes.

"This is for your supper," James said. "Come back when you're ready."

He handed Mia the notes and got out of the car. She got out and went to the driver's side. James went to Jon's door and leaned on it with his hands as Jon opened the window.

"I have to go see your granddad now," James said.

"Will you tell him I said hello?" Jon asked.

"Aye, mate. I'll tell him."

James backed away from the car, and they drove off while he walked to the door. Bruce answered the bell, and then James followed him to the sitting room. James went to Harold's side without noticing that someone was sitting near the fireplace. Harold looked peaceful, and James wondered if he had taken his last breath before James arrived.

"He's been given morphine," the doctor said. James whirled around with wide eyes. "I didn't mean to startle you. I'm Dr. Hughes."

"I remember you," James said. "You came here when I had fallen, and you set my leg."

"Oh, my God, is that you, James?" Dr. Hughes got up and came to James. "Ah, yes, I see Celeste in you." Dr. Hughes glanced down at Harold. "He's been declining and he slipped into a coma late last night. I fear the end will come soon."

"I'd like to stay with him," James said.

"Oh, by all means. I'll be in the drawing room if you need me."

The peaceful atmosphere in the room belied James' tumultuous emotions as he sat in the chair beside Harold's bed. His father had always been so big in James' mind, and now, as he looked at Harold's emaciated frame beneath the blanket, James' feelings coalesced into one emotion – pity. This was the ignoble end of Harold Huxley's daunting reign.

"Did you ever love me?" James asked.

Bruce entered the room with a tea cart. He parked it beside James and looked at Harold. The array of machines that measured Lord Huxley's breathing, heartbeat, and oxygen would soon be silenced, and the butler took care when he saw James's expression.

"Would you like some tea, sir?"

"No, thank you, Bruce."

"Would you rather I take the cart away?"

James glanced at the cart. His mother's china teapot sat at the center. A plate of Caroline's shortbread cookies were on one of Celeste's rose-patterned dinner plates, and the teacups and saucers were from another tea set. The incongruous setting was the product of a household thrown into disarray by the master's impending death, and James smiled as he thought of Caroline placing the cookies on the plate.

"Leave it," James said.

"Very well, sir."

James took a cookie from the plate, bit it, and the magical essence of shortbread made him close his eyes in ecstasy. He was five again, watching Caroline roll out the dough, and holding onto the round cookie cutter so he could cut the first cookie himself. It was his first Christmas without Celeste, and Harold chose to stay in London for the holidays.

"You selfish bastard," James said. "I was wrong to come here. I should be with my family right now; my wife and my son, but I'm here playing the dutiful son."

James stared at Harold's face as he willed him to open his eyes. He wanted that last conversation, the last words spoken between a father and son, the dramatic conclusion to a tempestuous relationship that James had longed for all his life. He wanted Harold's apology, his admission that he was wrong about James, and that James was, in fact, a great source of pride.

"Bollocks," James said.

James recalled the day he brought Jon to see his father and remembered what Harold had said when he still had the breath to speak.

"You know as well as I that you were never meant to be anyone's hero. If you had been, you would have married the girl instead of letting her run away."

Pain had washed over him at the time, but anger washed over him now. Death took away all opportunities to get it right or to make amends. Harold could have said something kind, but Harold didn't even know it mattered. As James understood this, he sat back and exhaled loudly. He'd been such a fool. He'd lost so much time brooding over his father's words. He vowed that as far as Harold was concerned, their battle was over.

"I forgive you, Father," James said.

Harold's steady breathing continued, but his eyes remained closed, and he had no idea of the peace that had befallen his son.

* * *

Lord Harold James Rupert Huxley, the Earl of Dorley, expired at six-fifteen a.m. just as the sun rose over the windowsill. James had fallen asleep, and when Dr. Hughes put his hand on James' shoulder to tell him his father was gone, James started.

"I'm sorry, James," Dr. Hughes said.

James stared at Harold's stony face. He saw the sun rising and thought of Mia and Jon.

"My family…" James said.

"I think they're in the drawing room. I've signed the death certificate. You should contact his lawyer about the arrangements."

"I will," James said softly.

James stood and stretched.

"I've left all the paperwork on the coffee table in the drawing room." Dr. Hughes put his hand on James' shoulder. "Again, I'm very sorry for your loss."

"Thank you."

James walked the doctor to the front door and then went to the drawing room. He saw Mia lying on the settee, and Jon curled up in a wingchair. He saw the papers on the table and went to grab them before going back to the study.

"I see you," Mia said as she opened her eyes.

"He's gone."

"Oh, James, I'm so sorry."

Mia sat and then stood. She went to him and put her arms around him.

"Are you okay?"

"I'm fine."

Mia looked up at him.

"I'm gonna get you some tea."

"Coffee if they have it."

"Coffee it is."

When he knew they would be in the office, James called his father's lawyer. After offering his condolences, he said he would come to the house to go over Lord Harold's will. The funeral arrangements had been made, and his lawyer would handle things. All James had to do was don his navy blue suit.

Chapter Sixty-Two

Mourners shook James' hand as he stood near the entrance of the manor house. They had been there for hours, and James was knackered. He hitched up his shoulders and then let them fall a few times, but the ache between his shoulder blades remained. Jon was asleep on the settee in the sitting room, and as James watched him from the door, he smiled. Mia came up behind him and put her arms around him.

"He looks so much like you," she said.

"So I've been told."

"How are you?"

"I'm fine. I just want this day to be over."

Artie and Old Smythe had come to pay their respects, and James had fallen into Artie's arms.

"I've missed you, mate," James said.

"You never come 'round anymore."

"I know. The time just gets away from me."

"Well, you know where to find me."

Uncle Billy greeted Jon with a hearty hello, and then took James' hand and nodded his head.

"So, sorry, James. How are you doing?"

"I'm fine."

They chatted about the board of the Bank of Moreland for a few minutes, and then Uncle Billy excused himself so he could chase down a man holding a tray of cocktails.

Artie spent the rest of the day by Jon's side, which left Mia free to stay close to James. She had a bout of nerves before the guests arrived, and her hand shook violently. Mia was able to talk herself down, but a tremor remained. She was also the subject of conversation amongst those who remembered the girl who stayed at the manor house and went missing. Many guessed at her identity, but James always introduced her as Mary Nithercott.

Lord Harold Huxley had been laid to rest with little pomp and circumstance. Close friends and relatives James had never met came to see Harold off to his great reward, amongst them a woman named Clair Dubois, who claimed she had been a close friend of his mother, Celeste.

"We were school chums," Clair said. She peered at James through a lorgnette and smiled. "You favor her."

Clair mingled with the crowd, but James noticed her watching him from across the room on several occasions. She hung back when the others left, and now he saw her coming toward him. He smiled and thrust out his right hand, but Clair didn't shake it; she held it and cupped it with her left hand as well.

"James," she said. "There is something you should know, something Celeste told me in confidence before she died." James narrowed his eyes. "Do you know the circumstances of your parents' marriage?"

Her hands were cold, and James wished he could take his away. "No."

Clair squeezed his hand tightly.

"Your grandfather arranged the marriage. He was eager to have them wed." She looked over her shoulder. "Celeste was pregnant when they married."

"Oh," James said. "That's not unheard of, is it?"

"Not if you're marrying the father of your child."

James cocked his head.

"What?"

"Harold Huxley was not your father. He agreed to marry Celeste in exchange for a rather large dowry." Clair held onto his hand. "I tell you this now, for I fear what your father might have written in his will." James thought of the conversations he'd had with Uncle Billy. He never mentioned that Celeste was pregnant before she married Harold. "Celeste fell in love with a man she met on the Riviera. He was married. When her father found out, he threatened to cut her off, but then he met Lord Harold. William Horton gave her a choice – marry the impoverished nobleman or live on a small allowance she'd inherited from her mother."

James felt strange, as if a giant hand was squeezing him. He swallowed hard, as Clair held onto his hand.

"What…was his name?" James asked.

"Hugh Ridley." James pulled his hand from Clair's and stared at her. "Yes. That Hugh Ridley."

Hugh Ridley was a well-known motion picture producer who had recently won a BAFTA award. His name had been all over the tabloids because he and his wife were going through a contentious divorce.

"Does he know about me?"

Clair shook her head.

"I doubt Celeste ever told him. What purpose would it have served?" Clair put her hand on his arm. "James, she truly loved you. Whatever Harold did or did not do with his estate, you should know that." She glanced at the front door. "Walk me to the door, will you, love?"

James watched Clair walk to a limousine, and then he closed the door. He pressed his forehead against the door and closed his eyes. So much of his life made sense now – his father's stern looks, the way Harold dismissed him when he was done berating James for some small infraction, and the fact that Harold had accepted James' desire not to use his title without reminding James of his duty, and duty was all to Harold Huxley.

James turned around and leaned against the door. He looked up the palatial staircase that he and Mia had trod on their way to their attic rendezvous, and all of a sudden, he longed to hold her. He knew Harold's lawyer was waiting in the study so he could inform James of the contents of Harold's will, and that Uncle Billy would be there, too, but he couldn't bring himself to move.

James glanced at the drawing room where a portrait of his mother hung over the massive fireplace. It was a full-length study of Celeste Huxley in a gauzy white gown. She peered at him with the confidence of a woman who had given up her freedom to marry a man she didn't love. She, like Mia, had chosen to have her child, and she, too, had done something courageous to ensure that child had a future.

James' emotions were as jumbled as on the day he brought Jon home. He was angry and grateful at the same time. He had been worried about his responsibilities now that he would own the manor house, but perhaps this new information would release him from those duties. He wasn't a true Huxley. Though Harold had allowed him to use the title, the truth was that James wasn't authorized to use it, and Harold was under no obligation to leave him a bloody thing. He had accepted James to save face while he was alive, but there were no Huxleys left on Harold's side of the family, and therefore, no reason to hide James' illegitimacy any longer.

A sliver of joy rose inside him. James had made a break for freedom when he bought the pub, but that was nothing compared to what he felt now. He'd consult a solicitor regarding the name Huxley. Perhaps James would adopt something that suited him, such as Jones or Smith, something that had no connection with Harold or this Hugh Ridley fellow. Yes, he and Jon would have a name of their own choosing.

His steps were lighter as James walked to the study. He stopped at the door before entering to compose himself. This was a funeral after all, and he would have to suppress his smile. James shook his arms and stood straight, and when he opened the door, he saw Harold's lawyer, Angus Morgan, seated behind the desk, and Uncle Billy in a chair by the fireplace. No one else had been called to hear the reading of the will.

"Sit, James, so we can get started," Uncle Billy said. "I have a plane to catch."

James sat in front of the desk and crossed his legs. The lawyer had a document on the desk before him.

"Since it's just the two of you, I'm going straight to the bequests, if that suits you?"

"It suits me," Uncle Billy said.

"It's fine," James said.

"Yes," Angus said. "Harold's first bequest is to William Horton, Jr. He wanted you to have his sword collection."

Uncle Billy raised his eyebrows.

"Harold knew I coveted those swords. God bless the man."

"Well, now to the estate. As you might know, Lord Harold always felt that this estate was a bit of an albatross around his neck. He thought it was time to release his family from the burden. It was his wish that the estate go to the National Trust. Of course, you can take any personal items away before the transfer of ownership. They have agreed to a period of three months to vacate the property."

"He's...given it away," James said.

"He has," Angus said. His expression softened. "James, I want to preface this next bequest with an explanation. Your father felt that since your mother had so generously provided for you, it would be unnecessary for him to leave you a financial bequest. He did, however, leave you this."

Angus pushed a small box toward James. James picked it up and lifted the lid. Inside were his mother's engagement and wedding rings.

"As for Jon, Harold has placed a sum of one hundred thousand pounds in a trust that will be in place until Jon's twenty-fifth birthday."

"When did he have time to do that?" James asked.

"He called me the day after he met Jon and asked me to prepare the trust."

"Well, wasn't that a nice gesture?" Uncle Billy said. "Harold had a heart after all."

"I can't believe he did that," James said.

"He was quite taken with the lad," Angus said.

"He's quite a lad," James said with a smile.

"Well, that concludes our business," Angus said. "If you have any questions, James, I'm always available to take your call."

"Can I ask who he left the rest of his money to?" James said.

"Your father liquidated his assets when he became ill. His private care was expensive, and whatever is left will go to pay off his debts."

"So, there's nothing left."

"I doubt there will be, but I can send you an accounting if you'd like."

"That won't be necessary," James said.

Uncle Billy got up, and James stood.

"I need to talk to you before you leave."

Uncle Billy waited while James escorted Angus to the front door. When James came back to the study, Uncle Billy was examining the sword display.

"I didn't expect him to give me these," Uncle Billy said. He glanced at James as he tapped his watch. "So, what is it you'd like to talk about?"

James looked Uncle Billy in the eye.

"Did you know that Hugh Ridley was my father?"

Uncle Billy cocked his head.

"I did. Celeste told me before she agreed to marry your… Harold. She wanted to give you a good name."

"Why didn't you tell me when I was in Hong Kong?"

"What would that have achieved? Your relationship with Harold was captious, to say the least. Why make it worse?"

"It would have made things easier between us. I wouldn't have felt the need to please him."

"Is that what you were doing, James? All the times you hid up in that tower when your father would come home from London for the weekend you were trying to please him?"

"If I'd understood *why* he treated me the way he did, I wouldn't have felt like such a failure."

"Perhaps you're right, but I never felt it was my place to tell you. I'm sorry if you disagree." Uncle Billy leaned forward. "Who told you about this?"

"Clair Dubois."

"Oh, dear God, that gossipy old bitch. If I'd been there… well, it's spilt milk now. Let's hope she hasn't shared it with anyone else."

"Shit," James said. "Jon. He doesn't need to know about this."

"Yes, well, I guess if she was going to tell anyone, she would have done it long ago. Anyway, we mustn't dwell on the past."

"I can't believe my father left him that money," James said.

"Are you upset about the estate?"

James shook his head.

"No, in fact I'm glad it's not my problem anymore."

"Take all the time they've given you to vacate this place. Make sure you get everything you want."

"All I want are my books and the pictures of my mother."

Billy tilted his head and peered at James through half-closed eyes.

"Do you mind if I look around before I leave?" Uncle Billy asked.

"No, take whatever you want."

Uncle Billy put his hand on James' shoulder.

"Listen, James, if you need anything, anything at all, please let me know."

James nodded. "It was good seeing you."

"Bring that boy to Hong Kong next summer. I'll take some time off."

James got up and went to the drawing room while Uncle Billy took a short tour of the manor house. Jon was still asleep on the settee, and Mia was reading a magazine. He went to her, took her hand, pulled her out of the chair, and led her to the patio outside the French doors. They sat on the sun loungers listening to the sounds of the countryside, and for a moment, they were sixteen again with their whole lives ahead of them.

Chapter Sixty-Three

THE BATHROOM WINDOW IN JAMES' HOUSE DIDN'T AFFORD MUCH light, so Mia went back to James' bedroom to brush her hair and apply her makeup. He was snoring when she returned, but she heard Jon in the kitchen. The funeral had dampened the high they had all been on since their reunion, and the news she received when they got back to Morseton made it worse. Galahad was dying.

Mia dressed hurriedly, and then went to James and woke him.

"We have to go," she said. "Galahad isn't good."

"Right. I'll be down in a few."

Mia went downstairs and smelled coffee brewing. She marveled at her son, who had been so small when she was taken from him, and the way he had taken responsibility for James. Jon was always on the lookout for the black dog, which made Mia worry that he might be putting too much stress on himself.

"Morning," she said when she went into the kitchen. "I just woke your dad."

"I took Ralphie for a walk," Jon said. "He's a good walker."

"I'm surprised he took to the lead. He's used to just running around the farm."

"He's a smart dog. I told him that he had to wear the lead here, and he let me put it on without any fuss."

Mia saw the table set for three and smiled.

"Do you always make breakfast?" she asked.

"Dad is a heavy sleeper. If he wakes up too soon, he gets moody."

Mia looked through the cabinets for a mug and found them above the sink.

"I'm still getting used to this place," she said.

"Are you going to come and live with us?" Jon asked.

Mia turned and leaned against the sink while Jon scrambled eggs.

"Dad and I talked about it." She watched his face, but Jon was consumed with his task. "How do you feel about it?"

Jon shrugged.

"I would like it," he said.

"Even though I have this problem?"

Jon took the frypan off the cooker and went to the table. He filled each plate with eggs and then took the frypan to the sink.

"You said you walk in your sleep," Jon said.

"I used to, but now not so much."

"And your hand shakes."

"When I get stressed."

"Well, that doesn't seem like so much. I think I can handle it."

Mia embraced her son and kissed the top of his head, which meant standing on her tiptoes.

"You've grown so tall," she said.

"I'm the shortest boy in my class," Jon said.

"Do the other boys pick on you?"

"No. Jordan won't let them."

Jon took a plate of toast to the table and sat.

"We should eat," he said. "Dad will be a while."

Mia sat and watched Jon butter his toast. Everything he did fascinated her, and she wished she had brought her camera when she left the hermitage. Jon raised his eyes when he heard James' footsteps on the stairs and got up from the table to fetch James' coffee.

"Can't he get that himself?" Mia asked.

"I do it for him because he forgets when he sits down. Then he has to get up, pour his coffee, and if I didn't do it for him, I'd be late for school."

Mia watched Jon pour the coffee and bring it to the table. He didn't seem upset or out of sorts, but he might be good at hiding his true feelings.

"If I come to live here, I can help out in the morning," she said.

"I don't mind making breakfast," Jon said.

"But I could help you."

"I don't need any help, Mum. I've been doing it for ages."

James came in, saw them at the table, and he was taken aback by the emotions that the scene evoked. His son and the love of his life were finally home at last. He kissed Mia's cheek before sitting, and Jon returned to his seat.

"So, we have to go to the refuge today," James said.

"Galahad is down," Mia said. "They don't think he'll recover."

"Is he a very old horse?" Jon asked.

"We're not sure how old he is, but he had a hard time of it before he came to stay with us." Mia sipped her coffee. "He helped me through some bad times."

"I'd like to meet him." Jon tapped his finger on the table. "Dad, are you going to eat?"

James was sipping his coffee and rubbing his eyes.

"Yes, I'm going to eat."

"Well, please hurry. Mum has to get to Galahad."

James smiled and picked up his fork. He shoveled the food into his mouth and managed to clean his plate in a matter of minutes. Mia had eaten some, but her appetite was impeded by thoughts of Galahad. Jon watched her for a moment and then peered at James.

"We have to go, Dad."

"I'm almost done."

"It's okay, Jon," Mia said.

"But he always takes too long." Jon got up and took his plate and Mia's to the sink. She went to the sink and washed the dishes. James pushed his plate away and drained his coffee as Jon stood beside him.

"Take it," James said. "I'll go start the car."

When James left, Mia leaned toward Jon.

"I don't want to come between you and your father."

"I'm not sure what that means," Jon said.

"It means I don't want you to fight with your dad because of me."

Jon dried the dishes.

"It's not because of you. He just takes too long getting ready, and I have to push him."

"Does he get mad when you push him?" Mia asked.

"He used to, but now he just makes a face at me."

Mia smiled as she rinsed the last plate.

"I guess that's progress," she said. She handed Jon the plate. "I guess I should get ready to go. Can you take Ralphie to the car?"

Jon nodded, and she went upstairs to use the loo and get her handbag. When she got outside, she saw Jon and Ralphie in the backseat of the car, and James fiddling with the radio. It was a sweet, domestic scene, and it warmed her heart. It was right; it was what was meant to be.

The uneventful ride to Plankton took two hours, and the car park of the refuge was full when they got there. James had to park near the end, and they all ran to the stables where Mia saw the veterinarian near Galahad's stall. Sid stood beside him and saw Mia enter the stables. She wasn't sure how he would react considering the way they left things before she went to Morseton, but he had seemed fine when they spoke on the phone, and now he waved and urged her to come.

"Go and look around," she told James. "Show Jon the piglets. Oh, and let Ralphie off the lead."

Jon unleashed the dog, and Ralphie followed Mia to Galahad's stable. James put his hand on Jon's shoulder and guided him into the yard where the piglets were grunting in unison. A goose ran across their path, and ducks added their quacks to the cacophony of barnyard sounds. Jon was fascinated by them and examined each species, mentally cataloging their colors, sounds, and gaits.

"I like this place," Jon said.

Back in the stables, Mia was sitting beside Galahad's head and stroking his forelock. His eyes were closed, and he was comfortable.

"Ray doesn't want to perform surgery on him because he's old," Sid said. "He would suffer needlessly and most likely not survive."

Mia nodded. She understood that Galahad's time had come, but the pain of losing him was overwhelming. Ray joined them and saw the tears rolling down Mia's cheeks.

"Have you decided?" he asked Sid.

"How long will it take?" Mia asked.

"Once I give him the shot, it shouldn't take more than a minute or two."

Mia stroked Galahad's cheek. He opened one, glassy eye, and then closed it. He was so still that for a moment, Mia thought he had slipped away, but his ear moved when she touched it. The vet came beside her holding a large syringe. He knelt down and stroked Galahad's neck, and Mia kept her eyes on Galahad's face.

"Are you ready?" the vet asked.

"I love you, Galahad," Mia said. "You saved me, but I can't…." Mia sobbed, and the vet put his hand on her shoulder. She nodded, and in a moment, Galahad was gone.

Chapter Sixty-Four

RALPHIE CAME ALONGSIDE MIA AND PUT HIS HEAD ON HER LEG. She was sitting beside Galahad, and the dog pushed his nose under her hand. She stroked his head and then picked him up and cradled him.

"He's gone, sweetie," she said. "He's not in pain anymore."

Ralphie snuggled against her. He let her hold him for a long time and then saw Jon standing near the stable door.

"What happened to him?" Jon asked.

"He was old and in pain," Mia said. "The doctor said it was time for him to go to heaven."

"He looks like a nice horse."

"He was my best friend for a long time."

"You'll miss him," Jon said.

Mia put Ralphie down and got up.

"I want you to meet my friend," she said.

They walked out of the stables, and Mia saw Sid talking to Ray. She and Jon came up to them, and Ray nodded at her before walking away. Sid looked at Jon and smiled.

"You must be Jon."

"I am."

"Have you had a chance to visit the animals?"

"My dad took me around. It's a very nice refuge." James was walking toward them from the barn. "That's my dad."

When James came alongside Mia, he put his arm around her shoulders.

"This is some place you have," James said.

"It's a lot of work, but it's worth it." Sid looked at Mia. "And we missed having you here these past few days."

Mia blushed, and James took his arm away.

"Jon, let's go for a walk."

"We went for a walk," Jon said.

"Then we'll go for another walk."

James took Jon's hand and led him away while Sid and Mia avoided each other's eyes. After a minute, Sid folded his arms across his chest.

"You could have told us about him," Sid said.

"I wanted to, but I didn't know where he was or if I'd ever see him again."

"We would have understood, Mia."

"I know, and I'm so sorry."

"Gloria is very upset."

Mia closed her eyes.

"I never meant to hurt you, either of you. I'm so grateful for everything you've done for me…"

"She is less forgiving than I," Sid said. "She told me to ask you to take your things out of the hermitage."

Mia bit her lip.

"Will she see me?"

"No. Just leave it alone." Sid put his hands on his hips. "I put some boxes aside for you. They're in that empty stable near the end." He cast his eyes to the ground. "I'm sorry it had to end this way."

"So am I."

"But you're not alone now."

"No, I'm not alone," Mia said.

"If you leave me the address, I'll send you what I owe you for the month."

"Forget it. You're going to need someone to take my place."

"No, no, I insist. You did your job. You should get paid."

A visitor came up to Sid, and he left Mia standing alone. Mia looked up at the manor house and thought of Gloria. She had always been a bit standoffish but had always treated Mia with respect. She was tempted to go to the house and apologize, but Mia heeded Sid's admonition and went to the stable instead.

Mia found the boxes and took two to the hermitage. She'd

lived there five years, but had accumulated little. It wouldn't take long to pack up her things, which included Ralphie's bed and bowls, and by the time James and Jon came to the door, she already had four boxes packed.

"Will they fit in the car?" she asked.

"In the boot, and maybe on the backseat."

"I can hold Ralphie," Jon said. He grinned. "Does this mean you're going to live with us?"

Mia looked into James' eyes.

"Does it?"

"Of course. Absolutely." He grinned, too. "Are you okay with that?"

Mia looked around the room.

"Yeah, I'm good."

James and Jon each picked up a box and carried it to the car. James managed to get them into the small boot but worried that the other two might not fit in the backseat.

"I'll hold one," Jon said.

"You said you'd hold Ralphie," James said.

"Maybe Mum can hold Ralphie."

"Aye, she might have to."

Mia met them at the car with a box in her arms. James put it on the backseat, and then they stood back and looked at the car.

"We might need a bigger car," Mia said. "You know, like for a family."

James took her hands.

"Are you sure you want to do this? I can help you get a place of your own until you decide."

"James," she said. "I want to be with you. I was always going to be with you." She glanced toward the refuge. "This place was my refuge when I needed it." She looked into his eyes. "But you are my home."

James' lip trembled as he embraced her tightly. She held him, burying her face in his chest, and then pulled away so she could put her arm around Jon. They stayed that way for a while, and then Mia went to get the last box from the hermitage. James and Jon watched her walking away.

"Are you happy, Dad?" Jon asked.

"Yes, Jon, I'm happy. Are you happy?"

"Yes, Dad, I'm happy."

James put his arm around Jon's shoulders. He thought about the last few days and all the things he'd learned that helped him make sense out of his life. His father's death, the revelation of his own paternity, and finding Mia. He had waited for the black dog to take over for a while, but Alfie never arrived.

James looked down at Jon. He was sure his son loved him. He was sure Mia loved him, too. While James knew the black dog was only hiding, he also knew that his family, this family, would never abandon him. They wanted him and needed him.

As they watched Mia walking toward them with the last box, James and Jon smiled. She saw their glowing faces and smiled too. She was home at last.

Thank You For Reading

If you enjoyed The Silver Stag, please tell your friends or book club. And share your thoughts by leaving a review. A few words is all it takes to bring a smile to someone's face.

About the Author

For over twenty years, Jersey girl A.L. Jambor has lived in sunny Florida with her husband, Hans. Amy began writing at the tender age of fifty-eight when she was inspired by a photo of her granddaughter. The result was But the Children Survived, an apocalyptic story about how a pharmaceutical company's greed led to the destruction of North America. From there, Amy began writing fantasy mysteries that incorporated both her love of puzzles and her humor. Nick Dandino and Lord Percival Plep are two of her protagonists – the first a private investigator in heaven, the second an English lord reincarnated as a pudgy terrier named Libby. She has also written an historical time travel series and a dark crime thriller. You can find all her books on Amazon.com.

For information and updates visit
aljambor.weebly.com
ALJambor on Facebook

Also by A. L. Jambor